# Praise for Best Friends

"Berger's . . . style [is] at once elegant and casual, with his usual mix of sweetness and cynicism."

—*Los Angeles Times*

"[Berger's] precise and exquisite dialogue [are] entertaining, even when the plot is ridiculous. And his deeply ironic view of the world we live in is refreshing, especially these days when irony is in short supply."

—*Milwaukee Journal Sentinel*

"Incorrigibly subversive."

—*The Hollywood Reporter*

"[*Best Friends*] is, in fact, a compact accomplished novel of ideas. That Berger's take on adultery, loyalty, friendship and myriad other intangibles is both deeply satirical and deeply felt is perhaps the book's real wonder."

—*LA Weekly*

"No other writer can build a symphony of seriocomic confusion with such a sure touch. Berger's terrific plot takes several unforeseen and unsettling turns en route to its savage denouement. And it's capped by an absolute killer of a final sentence. Nobody writes them like Thomas Berger. Not to be missed."

—*Kirkus Reviews* (starred)

# PRAISE FOR MEETING EVIL

"Nicely complicated . . . the entire contraption claps together in a great unpredictable, satisfying calamity."
—*The New York Times Book Review*

"Berger's new novel is a clever, stylishly written black comedy."
—*San Francisco Chronicle*

"Spare, meticulous prose . . . sharply evocative of human weakness and rage."
—*The Washington Post*

"A brilliant and troubling book. . . . Thomas Berger is the laureate of the ludicrous tragedy."
—*Chicago Tribune*

# PRAISE FOR THE HOUSEGUEST

"*The Houseguest* is Spooky-land, where the twists of reality are more frightening than any gothic horror tale and domestic confessions as expressed by the accomplished satiric wit of Mr. Berger are certainly not to be trusted. . . . *The Houseguest* is wonderfully bizarre."
—*The New York Times Book Review*

"[*The Houseguest*] . . . is a rare example of buoyantly irresponsible comedy, a piling up of non sequiturs for the pure pleasure of creating progressive confusion. At his best, as he is here, Thomas Berger can command attention solely as a lonely, insidious voice insisting that fiction can be stranger than truth."
—*Time*

# Praise for Thomas Berger

"One of America's most important comic artists."

—*The Boston Globe*

"Thomas Berger is a writer of enormous wit and incisive wisdom."

—*San Francisco Review of Books*

"One of the century's most important writers of the English-speaking world."

—*The Times Literary Supplement* (London)

"Thomas Berger is a magnificent novelist."

—*National Review*

"Berger properly belongs up there with the living greats, with Burgess, Nabokov, and three or four others."

—*The Cincinnati Enquirer*

"A cutting, ironic wit and a precision of detail so deadly it hurts when you laugh."

—*Ms.*

"Humbling, eye-opening, and enormously funny."

—*Newsweek*

"Thomas Berger is a magician . . . he never hits a false note. The effect is as if a snapshot has suddenly come to life, as we experience the sights and sounds and smells of that time and that place."

—*Detroit Free Press*

"An exquisitely subtle artist who can conjure character and emotion from the slightest verbal means."

—*The New Republic*

# BEST FRIENDS

## A NOVEL

## THOMAS BERGER

SIMON & SCHUSTER

NEW YORK   LONDON   TORONTO   SYDNEY

SIMON & SCHUSTER
Rockefeller Center
1230 Avenue of the Americas
New York, NY 10020

First Simon & Schuster trade paperback edition 2004

SIMON & SCHUSTER and colophon are registered trademarks
of Simon & Schuster, Inc.

For information about special discounts for bulk purchases,
please contact Simon & Schuster Special Sales:
1-800-456-6798 or business@simonandschuster.com

Book design by Ellen R. Sasahara

Manufactured in the United States of America

1  3  5  7  9  10  8  6  4  2

The Library of Congress has cataloged the hardcover edition as follows:
Berger, Thomas, date.
Best friends : a novel / Thomas Berger.
p.  cm.
1. Male friendship—Fiction. 2. Psychological fiction. I. Title.
PS3552.E719 B47 2003
813'.54—dc21          2002042617
ISBN 0-7432-4183-5
0-7432-5584-4 (Pbk)

To Dan and Justine Hager

# 1

As of September 2000, his best friend's ways with women were still a wonder to Sam Grandy, not because there could be any question of Roy Courtright's physical or personal charms, but rather because Sam's own temperament was such that he could not have pretended, let alone sustained, an intimate interest in more than one woman at a time.

"It wouldn't have anything to do with whether they believed me or not. I just can't handle distractions in emotional matters. Do you tell 'em all the same things? Or if things are different in each case, how do you remember who's who or what's what?"

"I don't have any trouble distinguishing one woman from the next," Roy assured him. "Think of your male friends: Do you forget their names, where they live, what their tastes and opinions are?"

"You're not telling me there's no difference? You don't change men friends once a month. You don't take them out, flatter them on their looks and clothes—"

"Or go to bed with them," said Roy.

"You know what I mean."

"You can't get away from the idea that it's a sport for me to pursue females. Lust, not genuine emotion. If I go to bed with her, it's a conquest by your theory, another scalp on the belt." Roy quaffed some beer from a stein, a vessel he disliked using because of the lid that had to be thumb-blocked from falling against your cheek. "I just don't think that way. I've never raped anyone, and I'm not attracted to the underaged. I assume everybody else is an adult in full possession of her faculties."

"Since when," asked Sam, "is lust not a genuine emotion?"

Roy sloshed the remaining beer in the stein, on the ceramic exterior of which appeared a pair of elks in glossy high relief. "Furthermore, I don't have carnal knowledge of every woman I eat dinner with, or want to, for that matter."

"Want to have dinner with, or want to boff?"

Such terms made Roy uncomfortable, and he himself never used them. "I'm trying to tell you there's no boffer or boffee. There's just your humble servant and another self-commanded person. Sometimes we're lovers and sometimes not."

"Lovers?" Sam gestured with his own stein, which he had long since emptied and was politely waiting to refill at Roy's convenience. "See, that's what I don't get. The sex I can understand better than what you call love. How can one-night stands, even with the same partner for a week or two, be love?"

Sam would never understand that for Roy, making love could be a three-second meeting of the eyes with a woman in the window of a passing bus. At the same time, Roy still loved all the women with whom he had ever had intimate relations, a sizable company if not as multitudinous as Sam imagined, though no account was actually kept. Roy liked to think a great many of his former partners shared the feeling, though he knew not all did. There were of course those who felt rejected, even betrayed, when it was he who brought it to an end, and not even all of those who took the initiative in terminating the affair could forgive him for sincerely agreeing with their decision.

Roy tried to recognize his own inadequacies, though more than one of the women he had frequented disparaged his sort of self-criticism as being actually an insidious form of conceit. But there were those who found it attractive in a man forthrightly to admit his flaws without using such an admission as a pretext for an array of attention-demanding excuses. Roy would readily apologize, but he rarely explained. There were those who saw that as a kind of honesty all too uncommon in the male sex. Not all women want to be lied to, as Roy would tell the ones he thought might agree, and he was right often enough.

The friends, who had had such discussions forever, were drinking the amber product of the latest microbrewery of which Sam, the beer connoisseur of the pair, was enthusiastic. They sat in oversize chairs covered in an unctuous leather that conformed to the body as if custom-molded to each behind lowered into it. The entertainment center in the room in which they drank beer from Sam's collection of hinged-top Old Country steins must have cost an outlandish sum of money, with its six-speaker surround, giant-screen television, DVD system, digital satellite receiver, every band of radio, and even all forms of outmoded sound reproduction, from a three-speed turntable for antique discs (Sam was a purist who preferred to have the originals on hand for comparison, however faded and scratched) to tape and CD players.

Roy might be the womanizer, but Sam was promiscuous with money. He had always lived beyond his means. As a boy he overspent his allowance, which happened to be larger than Roy's. When Sam grew up, he reversed the predictable change and became even more profligate. He was the kind of prey dreamed of by those who actively sought investors for business opportunities. Though a personal god had thus far sheltered him from outright swindlers, and others apparently profited from the same franchises, video rentals, pet care investments, etc. that went bad for him, Sam made little from such ventures while diminishing his inheritance, none of which he ever used to pay his debts except under threat of legal action.

He had been borrowing money from Roy for two decades and never yet had offered to pay back a cent. Roy was aware of this situation only if he forced himself to think about it, and when he did, it was with a certain satisfaction. He had more money than he, never a big consumer, needed; it was something he could do for his friend.

They had been best friends since adolescence. As a child Roy was undersized, but as an adult he grew to stand five feet ten, whereas Sam had always been larger than average in all dimensions, rising when fully grown to six-four. Tall as he was, he could support extra weight, but at three hundred pounds he carried too much. Roy was the one who kept in condition. One-eighty was heavy for his height, but owing to the weight training he had practiced since boyhood, it was mostly muscle.

Sam's only consistent strenuous exercise was lifting a loaded fork from plate to mouth. In this he had been abetted by the females in his life, beginning with the mother whom he had lost at an early age and continuing through a series of housekeepers and his father's lady friends to his own wife of three years, a bank officer whose enthusiasm for cookery was so avid that after a day's work she could go to the kitchen and prepare gastronomic marvels, though it was the Grandys' frequent guest Roy Courtright who appreciated these meals with more discrimination than his best friend, for whom the concern with food was more a matter of quantity than quality.

Kristin Grandy seemed nevertheless not to care much for Roy, and, her cuisine aside, he had little in common with her. Had she not been the wife of his best friend, she was not a woman he would likely have known. Her tall, slender, blonde person was probably attractive enough, though he loyally avoided making physical assessments of a friend's spouse, but her manner made him uncomfortable, unable as he was to decide whether it was disdain or indifference. She stared at him from time to time through gray-blue eyes that seemed to become glassy for that function alone, returning to normal when they focused elsewhere, especially on her big bear of a husband, of whom she was obviously very fond, which was admittedly another point in her favor. Roy too had always been partial to old Sam, whose spirit was as generous as his appetite.

Roy and Sam had had similar boyhoods as partial orphans, with the untimely death of Sam's mother and the abrupt departure of Roy's in a love affair and subsequent remarriage, after which he and his twin sister never saw her again. Both boys lived in the same prosperous community and each disliked his father. Each was the brother the other never had, and in that role Sam was the far more enterprising. Though unlike Roy he was never an athlete, Sam could talk spectator sports for hours. He also collected neat stuff: horror-movie posters, even some predating the pictures they had seen together; antique baseball caps, many signed by their original wearers, though he suspected some were forgeries and didn't care; and souvenirs of war: a defused German grenade from World War II, shaped like a potato masher, brought back by one grandfather, and rusty North Korean memorabilia from the other.

They went to the same prep school and later entered the same humble branch of the state university because neither was a good enough student to be accepted by a more demanding institution nor wanted to be. Roy dropped out as soon as he got his inheritance, while Sam stayed on and actually got a B.S. in Business Administration, an accomplishment still capable of giving them a laugh.

It was now twenty years since their friendship had begun, and both their fathers were dead, though by quite different means, and the friends' respective inheritances were markedly dissimilar in sum. An only child, Sam certainly got more than a pittance from his stockbroker parent, combined with what his mother had left in trust; had he used it wisely he would never have wanted for another dollar. But Roy and his twin sister, heirs of a manufacturer of shipping containers with an international market, split major money, a state of affairs that had long been a preoccupation of Sam's.

Roy now finally swallowed the dregs of the beer and, to Sam's audible relief, surrendered the empty vessel. "You get started on this subject every time you have to wait for me to empty a glass. If you'd just simply go get a refill when you want one, you'd never have to kill time in that way."

"If—" Sam said, grunting in the effort needed to lift his poundage from a soft chair while he clutched the two beer steins, his forearms doing much of this work, "if I did that . . ." He resumed when his legs were firmly under him, "I'd be an alcoholic."

"Don't talk that way!" Roy despised his best friend for admitting to such a weakness. "If you would exercise a little—"

"I would be so bored I'd end up drinking more." Sam's big face showed an affectionate smirk. "I can get more of a reaction from you by mentioning beer than by sticking my nose into your love life."

"My own appetites don't give me any problems," said Roy. "When I find the right woman, I'll know. I won't go on this way for the rest of my life. Meanwhile, I can handle it."

"I'm glad to hear that," said Sam. "And you don't have to worry about me. My blood pressure is normal, and my cholesterol count last time was, if anything, on the low side. Being a bit heavy is all to the good for drinking, you know: You can soak up a lot of booze without damage."

*If you consider that an accomplishment*, Roy did not say. He might needle Sam, but would take pains not to wound him. This was only self-interest. Where could he ever find another such best friend? Not to mention that he was, as so often, under Sam's roof. A single man, he seldom entertained at home, unless you could classify as true guests the women he brought to his apartment when their own residences were off-limits for one reason or another (lack of privacy, owing to room-mates or the presence of a husband). He endeavored to repay Kristin and Sam with gifts of white truffles, real balsamic vinegar, and château-bottled vintages, and he took them to the restaurants of auteur chefs. But he was aware that no such measures could supply the equivalent of their hospitality.

He and Sam concluded their colloquy with an exchange of shrugs. With Sam it was necessarily a gesture of substance. He had a larger bosom than that of his wife. He lumbered to the bar at the end of the room and found two more bottles of beer in the half-size fridge underneath. By the time he brought them back, Kristin's cheery "Hi-hi" sounded from the doorway.

Roy turned to wave at her, not an easy movement in the clasping chair, but, soon swathed in Sam's embrace, she did not see him. He glanced at his drugstore digital watch, which he would have been derided for wearing had Sam's back not been turned. Six-twenty, a little early for Kristin's return from work, though her bank was only five miles away. She expected to be appointed branch manager one of these months, replacing the only male employee in the building (the men in the nighttime cleaning crew worked for an outside service). Sam took satisfaction in this state of affairs. "Hell," he said on occasion, "women are always better with money than men." Roy was not sure that the theory was always valid, his mother having been a notorious squanderer, but given his friend's situation, brought no questions to bear upon its particular application in the Grandy household.

Staying turned was giving him a crick in the neck, so he looked away, apparently just as Kristin emerged from the bear hug and addressed him. His relations with her were often so mistimed, for nobody's fault.

But she was in a positive mood at the moment, speaking in exclamation as she walked into his line of sight. "What a great-looking car!"

"We just acquired it," Roy said, genuinely pleased. "It's an Alvis."

"British? Steering wheel's on the wrong side."

"You have a sharp eye," said he, then regretted making what she might well hear as a patronizing observation, because he had, after all, left the top down on this dry, clear September day. "In giving it a price, we have to calculate whether the snob appeal will outweigh a certain inconvenience." Roy was sole owner of a vintage-car business; the "we" included only his part-time assistant, a middle-aged woman who played no role in pricing the cars, having no interest in them. But he was sensitive with regard to the use of the perpendicular pronoun when speaking with female persons he did not know well. "It's mint. After more than forty years, the mileage is under eighty thousand."

"You used-car dealers all talk alike," Sam said in joking abuse, choosing the most offensive name for his friend's business. He opened the wire-and-porcelain plug on the brown beer bottle.

Roy, who loved his profession, responded to the serious implication in the gibe. "The odometer hasn't been touched. You can always tell. Well, I can't, but Diego and Paul can." For Kristin he identified the names as those of the mechanics whose garage was on the basement level of his hillside showroom. They were specialists in high-performance machinery and in exchange for free rent worked on the cars he sold.

"I've heard you mention them before," said she. "I remember. Masters of their craft. I wish I could say the same for the people who work for me. It must be a satisfying feeling."

"Brew?" Sam asked his wife, extending to her his own replenished stein. He cared nothing for cars as works of art, preferring routine Detroit iron so long as it was lengthy and wide. He was jealous now and anxious to display the expertise he had in another area. "Brown ale, from a little operation run by a guy named Bob Dolby, out back of his pub in Weirton. Only produces a few cases a day, and not every day at that. I taste a hint of hazelnut, maybe, with an overtone of sorghum."

Kristin put up her hands to fend off the stein, though he had not moved physically toward her. "Are those china plugs necessary?" she asked, staring at the bottle. "Would metal really change the taste?"

"Absolutely!" Sam affirmed. "Not to mention the ecological factor. Metal caps are thrown away. I bet you wouldn't even mind cans." All this was good-humored. Kristin did not care much for any kind of beer, except for the Berliner Weisse that Sam brought home once, but that was a sourish product customarily sweetened in the glass with raspberry syrup, and not finally real beer.

Kristin pointed at Roy. "Refill our guest."

"I already did so while you two were talking cars."

Roy lifted his stein and, with an idea of maintaining his new rapport with Kristin, smacked his lips and said, "I'm picking up the hint of hazelnut."

But she turned coolly away.

"Oh, screw you," said Sam. "You and your Alvis. Are you making up that name? Remember, I've known you when. I can still recall some of those fake models you invented when we were young punks: the Crapmobile, the Pussycafé."

Kristin returned with a smile.

"I was young," Roy told her with upturned palms. To Sam he said, "They used to race Alvises in England in the twenties. This one's a three-liter drophead coupé, made in the Coventry works in fifty-four. Only two owners. We've got the provenance."

"Both little old ladies," Sam said. "Drove it only to church teas, hot scones in baskets on the back seat, clotted double-Devonshire cream, gooseberry jam." He kissed the air.

"I'm going to the kitchen," said Kristin.

It was after she left the room that Roy decided her clothes were the product of more than good taste. She wore them well, in bearing and stride. Today the colors were a perfectly coordinated lime green and olive. But he could not believe her apparently better opinion of him was permanent. It was probably not natural for a wife really to like a husband's best friend, or vice versa. There was a normal rivalry that had no homosexual reference. However, speaking for the man, or at least himself, the reverse resentment, if it existed at all, was much weaker. He had no problem with Kristin.

The meal she made, in little more than an hour, was superb as usual: salmon fillets on a bed of potatoes sliced paper-thin, under julienned fennel, carrots, and kalamata olives, inside little hobo bags of parchment paper, tied with scallion strands. Of the selections of wines Roy had brought, the Sonoma-Cutrer Russian River Ranches Chardonnay was righteous, though Sam stubbornly, maybe even perversely, stuck to the same boutique ale despite its treacly-sweetness, not at all suited to the fish at hand. Today he seemed to be the one defiant of Roy.

The cognac he produced later on, however, had been an earlier gift of his best friend, and it was Kristin who declined that, as well as any help with the cleanup. She became even somewhat irritated when Roy's offer seemed too insistent, so he lost the advantage gained by the Alvis, the subject of which had occupied some of the dinner conversation, along with other of his exotic wares such as the Aston Martin DB-1 that won at Le Mans in 1959 and a customized 1940 Packard that had supposedly been owned by the bygone movie star Errol Flynn, a claim made by the previous owner, which Roy frankly doubted because it could not be confirmed by any paper trail.

"We certainly wouldn't pay what he was asking."

Kristin sympathetically nodded her sleek blonde head, money being her profession.

But Sam, no doubt grateful for a possible diversion from motor vehicles, asked, "Wasn't Flynn supposed to be quite the lech? Raping young girls, and so on? Still, *Casablanca* is a great picture."

"Errol Flynn wasn't in it," said Kristin.

Sam groaned. "Now, why did I say that? I *know* he wasn't. I owned the cassette for years, and it was one of the first films I got on DVD."

Roy came to his friend's aid, if lamely. Maybe that was what annoyed Kristin. "Flynn was a lecher, though, I believe, and involved in a lot of scandals in his time. My father mentioned him."

"That's right," Sam chimed in. "That's where I first heard his name." Sam spent a lot of time at Roy's house when they were teenagers, and Roy's father was always partial to him. "Hey, you want to look at *They Died With Their Boots On* later? I've always had a crush on Olivia de Havilland."

"I know," said Roy, and as to the movie, "Sure."

"Not me," said Kristin. "I'm sleepy." Though you could not have told it from her alert eyes.

Dessert had been sliced peaches in a stemmed glass filled with sparkling Vouvray, accompanied by *langues-de-chat* that she had baked over the weekend, but when thawed were as if new from the oven. It was after this course was finished that the brief argument about the washing-up ensued. Of course, not much was needed for the job but the dishwasher, a lately updated model no doubt selected by Sam, given its multitudinous touchpad offerings, more elaborate than the dashboard on any of Roy's vintage cars.

When he discerned that Kristin would be genuinely offended if he insisted further, Roy smiled to bring her back and said, "I just wanted to run that fantastic dishwasher."

Sam asked loudly, "Hey, remember that old joke about a guy who got his dick caught in the dishwasher? How'd that go, exactly?"

Roy was embarrassed in front of Kristin. He answered truthfully, "I don't remember it."

Sam stood ponderously against the counter, a hand on it for security, though he could hardly be drunk on a few beers. "It hinged on the sex of the dishwasher, I think. The dishwasher was human, you see, in a restau-rant."

The hesitation between syllables caused Roy to look more carefully at the man he had known for so long. Sam *was* drunk, probably had poured down a bit before Roy arrived, or more than that. It took quite a lot of extra alcohol with a body of his size.

Roy was least fond of any situation in which he himself was sober and his companion was inebriated to any degree. This was worst when the latter was a woman, for it meant she was preoccupied by some personal problem that had no reference to oneself, but for which one would be blamed if present when the emotion reached critical mass. Any kind of sexual relations in this context would be disastrous, but neither was it a simple matter to escape with grace.

No such special problem came into play with Sam, but Roy was reluctant to leave his friend alone to drink through the old movie. He wondered whether Kristin was really sleepy or just politely determined to avoid a film in which she had no interest. In the almost three years of their marriage, Roy had never seen them quarrel. Sam was too good-natured for that, and Kristin seemed too smart. Or such was Roy's interpretation. He had never thus far come close to marriage, not having yet found that woman for whom he could forsake all others. He suspected that for a man of his temperament, being formally attached to one woman was to lose the possibility of being a friend to any, and in most cases he began and ended a romantic connection on an amicable basis and remained on good terms with former intimates for years.

The exceptions, and of course there had been some, were unrepresentative: Usually these were errant wives, risking more than those who did not have to deal with injured or possibly vengeful husbands. It was true that Jane Waggoner threw a glass of Gewürztraminer in his face when he wondered whether they should begin to ease off, and this was in public, though fortunately in an inn fifty miles away in an untrendy corner of the county, ignored by the kind of people who would recognize them. As ill luck would have it, Jane had just that morning asked her spouse for a divorce, else she might not have been so bitter, and Roy's gently but justly disclaiming personal responsibility had not helped.

Showing how drunk he all at once was, Sam suddenly relieved Roy of the current dilemma, asking, "Gimme a rain check on the movie, willya? Don't feel up to it, if you don't mind."

As if it had been Roy's idea! He nevertheless went along with the game, as he usually did. "We'll do it another night." He was eager to get away. He praised Kristin's meal again and said that week after next it was *his* turn, the Auberge if that would be okay, Gérard promised a saddle of venison, and she responded graciously. He never called her "Kris," as did Sam and, apparently, her other friends, nor had he ever exchanged even air-kisses with his best friend's wife. For her part, she had never offered him a handshake.

"Talk to you, kid," he said to Sam.

"Hey," said Sam, winking blearily. "There you go."

There was a touch of coolness in the evening breeze and the sports jacket Roy wore would be a bit light in the open car, but raising the Alvis's canvas top was too much work, especially in the darkened driveway. Sam if sober would have switched on the outside lights and even might have come along to help with the top.

Roy worried that the Alvis would not start immediately, as he had not driven it much, but the engine came throatily to life with one touch of what one who sold vintage British cars should be careful to call the self-starter (as in fact the canvas top was the "hood," and the hood, the "bonnet") and echoed loudly throughout the neighborhood of broad lawns and designer landscaping.

At home there were five calls on his answering machine, one from a usually overwrought woman named Francine Holbrook, the other four, one per hour, were from his sister. He elected to call his twin first, who was always exasperated with him—but he had known her since birth.

"Goddammit!" she cried. "Why can't I get you when I need you? The IRS is after Ross. He might go to jail."

Robin's husband was almost twenty years her senior and, perhaps for that reason, in a hurry to sire another string of kids to replace the three from his first marriage who had been commandeered by his ex-wife. Therefore Robin was usually pregnant and more self-concerned than ever.

"Come on," said Roy. "You're overreacting." Over*acting* was more like it. Born second, Robin got all the emotion left over after Roy had been furnished with the reasonable amount, or so he saw it. She spent much of her childhood in a tantrum. When their mother decamped, Robin made the most of being the only female under the family roof. "This is America. You can't be sent to jail without a trial. He's probably just being audited at this point."

"Easy for you to say. You don't have two children with another on the way, and I'm alone tonight. Ross is being bicoastal." Alone to Robin meant with at least one au pair, if not a team.

"I've been working my head off," Roy said, answering the, to him, deafening though silent accusation. "I'll drop in tomorrow evening."

"Late enough to miss the kids."

"I was trying not to stick you with dinner. How about I come earlier and bring Chinese?"

"You do what you want, Roy. You always do."

This of course was a blatant misrepresentation, and she knew it. He had never done what he wanted, but rather what he had to do according to standards that few others noticed, let alone respected. For example, he was careful never to mention Sam's name to Robin, who had had an affair with his best friend years earlier, before either was married. It had ended so unpleasantly, at least for Robin, that she could never bring herself to disclose what went wrong. Sam himself had not brought up the matter, no doubt finding it too delicate by reason of the complex loyalties involved.

Roy's final duty on this Sunday evening was to return the call from Francine Holbrook. Because Robin was only his sister, at her most waspish she was easier to deal with than Francine, a divorcée with whom he had been having an attachment that for several weeks had been either phasing out or being reawakened. Francine could not make up her mind on this matter and Roy was shrewd enough not to fix a position of his own, having learned by painful experience that in such a situation he could not but lose unless he remained undefinable.

It was also true that Francine was extremely ardent in bed, or in any other venue in which they found themselves momentarily alone.

"Francine."

"I don't care where you've been or who you've been doing," said she in a voice made throatier by the phone than it was face to face. "I want you to come over."

"Now?"

"Roy, if you had anything better to do right now, you would not be returning my call." Having said which, she began to talk dirty. As usual, he was both appalled and aroused.

He began to rebutton his shirt.

# 2

Sam suffered sharp chest pains the next morning, not long after
Kristin had left for the bank. Luckily it was one of the cleaning
woman's days, for he was inept when a situation demanded a prompt
response.

By the time Roy was notified, late in the afternoon, his friend was
resting comfortably in a hospital room, having undergone an angio-
plasty and the insertion of a stent to keep the artery open. He should be
out in two days.

Roy interpreted Kristin's staccato report as evidence of an intensity of
emotion not apparent in her tone, which was mint-cool as always; much
the same, he could assume, as that in which she conducted business.

"I'm relieved to get the good news as soon as I got the bad." Though
in reality he was somewhat hurt that he had been informed only now.

"You could see it as a warning," said she. "He's a good fifty pounds
overweight."

What a time to criticize the man. Nevertheless, Roy found himself
vocally agreeing. "I've been after him on that matter for years. Maybe he
will have learned his lesson now." He was appalled at how vapid that
sounded in his internal echo. "When can I visit him?"

She gave him the hospital's schedule, then asked, "Know the first thing he said when he saw me? He wanted to know about the Stecchino."

"Is that a medical term?"

"It's a fancy espresso machine from Italy. It came yesterday afternoon, too late for him to fire it up and give it a maiden run before you were due."

"That's what he was doing this morning when he felt the chest pains?" Typical of Sam, who was competitive in such matters; he had to establish mastery over a new gadget before displaying it to his friend. Machinery, however powered, being as temperamental as it was, his insistence on putting his pride on the line this way was silly. It happened all too frequently that some new device he believed he dominated would wait until there was a witness on hand to see its sudden failure. At such times Sam might become violent toward the offending object. Roy once saw him fling a twenty-eight-hundred-dollar laptop into a blazing fireplace. At Roy's bon mot, "Now, there's a Grandyose gesture," Sam had exploded in laughter. There was some reason to believe that he had been in an up mood throughout the incident. It was ominous news that an inanimate adversary could now seriously threaten his health.

"It's polished brass," Kristin said. "All dials and little spigots and stands almost three feet high. Seven hundred something. For three cups a day."

"*You* don't drink coffee, do you?" This was hardly news, and sounding the emphasis might be offensive—he was always worried about that possibility—but in fact it was apparently not so here, for she laughed almost carelessly. "I'm usually the joy-killer."

Maybe it was his imagination, but he heard some poignancy in this statement, the first he had ever identified in her. But also, on general principles, his heart went out to self-critics. "Don't say that! It's not true. You've brightened that guy's life in every way. Take it from me."

"But you're his friend."

Roy found this seemingly straightforward assertion to be cryptic. It could mean anything from he was flattering her because her husband was ill to he was Sam's lifelong comrade whereas she was only the wife of a few years. "I sure am," he said. "That's how I know."

He was reassured to hear her say, simply, "Thank you."


Sam was probably a little paler than usual and, if assessed by the eyes alone, older than when last seen, but there had certainly not been time as yet for him to diminish in bulk by reason of the starvation diet of which he had complained instead of saying hi.

He made the hospital bed, for all its attendant white and stainless-steel accessories, look smaller than it was. There was an incongruous white identification band on his thick hairy wrist.

"Next time smuggle me some rations. I'll *really* have a heart attack if I have to live long on the cat piss and bird poop they call food."

"Yeah, a cheeseburger and a hot-fudge sundae," said Roy, standing at the foot of the bed.

"Also a bottle of any decent double-malt Scotch."

"If I know you, you mean it." Roy shook his head. "Pathetic." He located an enameled steel chair, drew it closer to the bed, and sat down. Sam was now considerably higher than he, a big dark head on the glaringly white pillow. "You're worried about your coffee machine?"

"I wondered if it got turned off before it exploded. I guess it did. . . . Maybe that thing's bad luck. Kris really hates it. Want to take it off my hands?"

"The Stickerino?"

Sam humorlessly corrected him. "The Stecchino. You won't find a superior—"

"Sure," Roy told him quickly, finding a lecture on specialty-coffeemaking at odds in this setting, that peculiar hospital-stench in his nostrils. "I'll get it tonight. I'll leave a check with Kristin."

"No! I don't want her attention called to it. Just get it out of there before she comes home. . . . I'll give you the code. You won't have to write it down. It's—"

"What code?"

"The front door. Didn't you ever notice? Well, I guess you aren't supposed to. The keyhole's for show, but it's dead. The lock is controlled by the touchpad under the house-number plate, to the left of the door."

"I'll be damned."

"You won't even have to write it down," Sam repeated. "It's my birth date, backward. Get it? Okay, you begin with *five sixteen sixty-seven*. You don't just switch it to *sixty-seven sixteen five*. That'd be too easy for somebody to figure out. What you do is reverse the entire thing to *seventy-six sixty-one five*." He narrowed his eyes. "Got it?"

Roy sighed. "I guess so." Their birthdays were only ten days apart. For most of their lives they had celebrated in common, on a chosen day between May 5th and 15th. "But I hope you're not telling me to go to your house and swipe the espresso machine while Kristin is at work."

"That's exactly what I'm asking you to do. She'll get the idea immediately, and neither of us will ever mention it again."

Was this an example of the kind of delicacy that characterized their marriage and was perhaps essential to its success? Roy was impressed. "All right."

"Bring a blanket to wrap it in," said Sam. "So the brass won't get scratched. Kris will already have tossed the bubblewrap."

"Good idea." Roy intended to take the machine straight from the Grandy house to Robin's. Not only did he not drink enough coffee to give the Stecchino the work it deserved, but his brother-in-law swallowed gallons of the Starbucks product daily and would surely be comforted by the limitless availability of latte at home, especially with the audit threat looming. Ross also remained a prodigious smoker of cigarettes. How he had lived to the age of fifty-one was a miracle. Roy sometimes reflected that he himself was the only man he knew whose habits were healthy, and yet he was one of the few without familial responsibilities.

He had intended to visit awhile longer with his friend, but Sam was anxious for him to get going, so as to reach the Grandy house while there was no chance of encountering Kristin, who would soon be leaving the bank and driving to the hospital before visiting hours expired.

"I'll make it up to you, kid," said Sam, rolling his eyes as he thought of a suitable reward. "Next time I'll set you up with my day nurse. She couldn't be cuter: natural red hair, turned-up nose . . ."

Sam's idea of what attracted Roy was seldom Roy's own. Cuteness, for example, seemed a kind of infantilism to Roy, who had never been drawn to those who demonstrated it, even when he was quite young. In school and college, Sam had dated some cheerleaders, more than one of whom returned his interest though he was not, despite his size, a football player or in fact any other kind of athlete. He was even engaged for a short time, early on, to a girl named Honey Fitzgibbon, whose retroussé nose (always a winner with Sam) was covered with freckles and who walked with a bounce even when barefoot on sand. Kristin was nothing like her predecessors.

"You do what they tell you here," Roy scolded. "Remember, you came to them for help, not vice versa." The sermonizing was not like him. If he did more of it, Sam would likely jeer. "Okay, I'm on my way. Consider your problem solved."

Having accepted the mission, he carried it out with more care than Sam had asked. He took the stairs instead of the elevator on the way out, should Kristin understandably have left work early. Driving the car, he used the rear exit from the parking lot, which debouched on to a back street used mostly for deliveries. He was again driving the Alvis.

The Grandys had bought an existing house with an agreeable stone façade that Sam considered not pulse-quickening enough by his standards; but as yet, so far as Roy knew, the idea of renovating the exterior had not come into play. Kristin might put up with her mate's extravagances of everyday living, but there were limits. Perhaps with this espresso-machine incident, a general pullback might be instituted, which Sam hoped to forestall by getting rid of the device.

The driveway was surfaced with gravel, more chic than blacktop but threatening to the paint on an automobile, vintage or otherwise. Sam saw this as a desirable check on those who might otherwise speed up it. So as not to offend Roy, who for *his* taste always drove too fast, he explained he meant the drunken or stoned teenagers who theoretically menaced prosperous neighborhoods, at least in old television movies. Despite what seemed a general naïveté, Sam regarded everything with a certain irony. Roy saw Sam as more complex than himself.

Roy considered himself pretty much an open book, though women seldom failed to be amazed when they heard that. What he meant was he liked the understandable things: comfort, convenience, good manners, affection; they were easy to name.

He continued along the stretch of driveway that led behind the house and, so as not to throw up a spatter of scarring pebbles, braked gently when he got there. The rear of the building was more glass than stone, with its big sunroom giving onto a tiled terrace, from which the pool, screened by a stand of poplars, was inconspicuous, though it was sizable when you swam there. Roy had occasionally done so, always alone, for Kristin apparently did not care for the sport, and though Sam did nothing to improve his figure, he was averse to revealing it.

At the door to the kitchen Roy remembered that Sam's directions had applied specifically to the coded buttons under the house-number panel near the front door. Naturally, no number was posted in back. Could that mean, for all the security out front, access to the rear was gained by a simple key? Unlikely with anyone else, but to be called possible if not probable in Sam's case.

Well, he could not find a key, either, though he suspected one was secreted someplace in the proximity of the door, perhaps in a fake plastic rock or another disguise. He ended up hiking around front and, using the prescribed method, which surprised him by functioning without a hitch, he entered the Grandy abode. From a blinking red light he became aware of another and more elaborate touchpad that flanked the front entrance on the inside. It was reasonable to assume that punching the code outdoors had disarmed the alarm system throughout the interior, but these gadgets were tyrannical by nature and usually required further pacification measures lest they exact raucous punishment.

Sam, of course, had neglected to instruct him to do more than spring the lock, but Roy punched in the same reversed birth date, with evident success, for the red light stayed on but stopping winking.

The house, unlike most others of his acquaintance, had no smell at all when entered. A restaurant-strength exhaust system disposed of culinary odors, which Roy thought was too bad, for Kristin's were aromas. The greatest contrast would be offered by Robin's residence when he delivered the coffee machine. Children, even though they personally did not stink except with loaded diapers, could cause a place to smell, sometimes by ricochet, so to speak: A grape-juice spill might be treated with a stain remover that left a chemical stench for hours.

In the kitchen the Stecchino was not as prominent as he anticipated. Kristin, or perhaps the Dominican cleaning woman, had moved it into the farthest corner of the polished granite counter at the perimeter of the room, as opposed to where Sam surely had installed it on the center island overhung by the glistening copper hood that housed the exhaust fan. Tall and heavy, bristling with dials, spouts, buttons, and levers, it was even gaudier than promised. Knowing what gadgetry could cost, more from Sam's experience than his own, he who preferred vintage stuff, he saw immediately that the "seven hundred something" of Kristin's estimate would not even be in the same ballpark with the true price.

He had forgotten the matter of padding. Sam was right that this machine should be handled with care—for the sake of the Alvis's upholstery; it was much too big to fit in the boot, which was to say, trunk.

His quest for the linen closet would probably take a while. Living only a few miles away, Roy had never stayed the night under this roof and had not visited the second floor since his initial tour of the place a week before the Grandys moved in. He felt uncomfortable as he mounted the central stairway and had to check an impulse to tiptoe through the upstairs hall as though he were an intruder. He hoped the search would not take him as far as their bedroom or bath.

He was in luck. Having turned right at the top of the stair, he had gone along what turned out to look like the wing of guest bedrooms, on a closet shelf in the first of which he found a folded blanket of moss-green wool, trimmed in dark-green satin. The bedspread and curtains contained or represented complementary shades of the same color, which he now thought of as being Kristin's though she had surely worn many others on the multitudinous occasions he had been in her company.

Down in the kitchen, relieved to be on the last leg of the first phase of his mission, Roy swathed the coffee machine in the blanket and clasped the burden to his chest. Not heavy for someone whose lightest workout featured fifty-pound dumbbells, it was, however, extremely bulky and tall enough to obscure his line of sight, both ahead and down, and in exiting the house he was treading blindly on unfamiliar terrain, his cheek against the blanket, redolent of the natural fragrance of virgin wool.

He had reached the open Alvis and deposited the wrapped machine onto the pilot's pristine leather seat—the upholstery, desiccated by the years, was the only item of original equipment that had had to be replaced—when behind him he heard a demanding yet thin and uncertain voice. He turned and saw a policeman who displayed a drawn pistol. For an instant he thought the very young cop, smooth below the eyes and without sideburns below the blue cap, was merely demonstrating the use of the weapon in a hypothetical situation.

"I said freeze, scumbag."

Roy elevated his tremulous hands. "I'm no burglar. I'm—"

With his left hand the policeman switched on the little radio that clung to his right epaulet, but Roy's abortive comment unnerved him further. He brought the hand back to join the other in a double Hollywood grip on the pistol, and in his tenor, very near a scream, cried, "MOTHERFUCKER, *I said freeze!*"

It was Roy who brought himself under control. "Go ahead," he said firmly, even though he was now in more danger. "Call your dispatcher. I'm not resisting."

The officer did as suggested, spitting into the perforated black box in rapid code, of which all Roy could understand was "holding him at gunpoint."

Roy asked respectfully whether he could say something, but he was first obliged to turn and spread 'em, endure a frisk, and then submit to a small-of-the-back handcuffing. "Okay," he said when this was done, "my best friend owns this house. He's in the hospital, and he asked—"

The young cop had holstered his gun, but left the strap loose so as to be able to draw at the first hint of funny business. He interrupted, sneering, "Sure he did. You just sit there on that fender."

"No," Roy told him. "Nobody sits on the coachwork of a vintage car. This is the original paint."

The policeman was so new in authority as to be hypersensitive to what he identified as insubordination and might well have done something at this point that would have jeopardized his career at its outset, had not another patrol car roared around the corner of the house and skidded to a stop, spraying gravel—a fragment or two of which flew close enough to the Alvis as almost to give Roy the seizure he had not quite suffered at the point of a gun.

Two more cops left the vehicle, one brandishing a shotgun. "Have you got 'em all?" he asked the officer with Roy.

"Mr. Courtright!" cried the taller policeman.

"Hi, Hal," Roy said drily. "Tell your associate who I am."

Hal addressed the young officer. "What's going on here, Howie?"

The thickset man clutching the shotgun asked, "Any more inside the house, Howie?"

Howie frowned at Hal. "You know him?"

"He's Mr. Roy Courtright. He owns Incomparable Cars, you know, on Peregrine?" Hal prognathously smiled from one to the other, then noticed the Alvis. "Hey, what's this one, Mr. Courtright? A Doozy?"

"Can you get me out of these things, Hal?" Roy asked impatiently. "Mr. Grandy owns this house. He's my closest friend, as you may know." He explained about the coffee machine, even as Hal stepped forward and opened the cuffs with his own key.

"Mr. Courtright," Hal told the other two officers, "is also a friend of the chief's. Isn't that so, Mr. Courtright?"

It was not much of a question. In a town this size most local business owners were on good terms with the police, who were of course dependent on them and homeowning taxpayers for their modest salaries. Not only was Roy, though a habitual exceeder of the speed limits, innocent of that dislike or even dread of the cops which some people found normal, he if anything felt sorry for them. This was another area in which he and Sam were not at one. Sam had a distaste for policemen that seemed more instinctive than generated by experience. But then he was also by nature an inattentive driver, failing to notice stop signs and posted limits for school zones, where going a few miles faster than permitted might be considered worse, near children, than driving 120 on a deserted late-night highway.

Roy held no grudge against Howie, to whom he said, "You can verify it by giving Mrs. Grandy a call at First United Bank." He rubbed his wrists. It was uncomfortable to wear manacles if your forearms were thickly muscled.

Howie tried to look proud. "That won't be necessary, sir. We got the call from that security service. I had to do my job."

It was Sam's fault for not providing the inside disarm code. To the cops Roy made light of the matter, and they all soon turned with relief to the subject of the Alvis, the chunky officer, whose nametag read VELIKOVSKY, showing some technical interest.

"What's the horsepower on this baby, Mr. Courtright?" And when he got the answer, 115, asked further, "Would you happen to know the compression ratio?"

"Eight point five to one." Roy had to be prepared for such questions from clients.

"Nice," said Velikovsky.

Howie nodded his capped head. "Damn nice."

"What's something like that go for, Mr. Courtright?" asked Hal.

Roy never answered such a question unless it was put by a potential buyer. So what he said now was, "I hope enough to pay for the reupholstery and the detailing."

The officers all had a knowing chuckle, and after a walk-around, they drove away in their respective Ford Crown Victorias.

Roy prepared to leave the Grandy property at last, but got only as far as behind the steering wheel of the Alvis when a dirty beige Corolla rolled into view in his rear-view mirror. Who should get out of it but Kristin.

Roy scrambled forth onto the crunching gravel. "You caught me red-handed."

Kristin's car did not do her justice. He assumed it was an example of what Sam called her parsimoniousness. She wore an elegant pin-striped suit in banker's gray.

"Doing what?" She extended her hand, perhaps being still in the business mode, and he shook it for the first time ever, letting it go as quickly.

Sam's confidence had already been betrayed by events, so Roy did not hesitate to reveal all. He loyally concluded with, "I'm afraid I botched it. By his original plan, I would have been long gone by now."

Kristin frowned for a moment and then glowed with a smile. "Let's not tell him you were caught! That would solve everybody's problem. That is, yours and his. *I* don't really have a role in this situation. I didn't hate that machine, as he seems to think. I just thought seven hundred dollars was an awful lot to pay for the use we'd get out of it." Her fine nostrils flared and then contracted. "You know how he is, once the novelty has worn off? . . . But you've been burdened enough and shouldn't have to hear about our budgetary squabbles."

He could not have explained why he impulsively sold Sam out at this point. "I seriously doubt the Stecchino costs as little as seven hundred bucks."

Kristin closed her eyes and shook her lowered head. She was within an inch or so of his own height, and he had never before seen her fair crown, which for an instant seemed exquisitely vulnerable.

"Don't tell me."

"I shouldn't have said that." His regret was sincere.

"How much more?"

He chewed his lower lip. "I don't know for sure."

She recovered her aplomb with an attack on him. "Then you *shouldn't* have said it."

In a way he was flattered that she had turned personal, but he was also annoyed with what could be taken as an invidious response to his confession of error. "All right," he said defiantly, "I'll find out and get back to you."

She took a cell phone from her purse and, telling Roy, "I know the number by heart," she punched it in. She had the consideration to walk to and lean on her own car and not the Alvis while the call was in progress.

Roy sulkily strolled in the opposite direction. At the far end of the curving driveway could be found a garage that, like the pool house, was screened by trees. In this case it was a longish walk, but the man who had built the house liked to get automobiles out of the way when they were not in active use. Sam never garaged his Town Car, but the reason why Roy had not noticed Kristin's Corolla before must have been because she routinely put it away. On the other hand, she apparently was not quick to have it washed. The weather had been dry for a week. Noticing peculiarities about her made him uncomfortable, however. She was no business of his.

As he turned and trudged back, she was folding the telephone. When he was near enough, she said, in a dispassionate tone, "Fourteen hundred sixty-five dollars. Part of that is tax, of course."

It was probably odd that Roy did not feel vindicated. "I'm sorry I brought it up. I hope he wasn't too upset."

She winced at him. "I didn't call Sam. I called American Express."

Roy brought out his checkbook and probed himself further for a pen. Anticipating an objection from her, he hastened to explain. "It's a present for my brother-in-law. He's having tax trouble and could use some cheering up."

"That's, uh, Robin's husband?"

"Yeah, Ross Gilpin."

Kristin remained silent as he put a handkerchief on the Alvis's bonnet, then the checkbook on the handkerchief, and scribbled the check.

She thanked him, folded it without examination, and tucked it into her purse. "I wanted to ask," in his opinion smiling too warmly to be derisive, "why you drive that car everywhere if you have to be so careful with it?"

"Good question. A car is kept in better condition with a little use than always sitting cold. I don't drive it much. In the last twenty-four hours I've been here twice and once to the hospital—"

Kristin gasped. "I have to get going! I dropped by to get some stuff Sam wanted and run it over there." Without another word she trotted to the back door, opened it with a key, and vanished within.

Reasonable as the explanation of her behavior was, Roy still felt hurt by the abruptness of her leave-taking—unless she expected to see him again on her reappearance with the things for Sam. But she would be in no less a hurry then than now. He decided to make the prompt departure he had been denied twenty minutes earlier.

He had had an unsatisfactory experience in every way, courtesy of his best friend, and not for the first time in his life. When they were teenagers, Sam delighted in doing such mischief as squeezing a girl's behind in a movie lobby. When she angrily whirled around, she would blame Roy, who looked her in the face while Sam stared in another direction. Sam was also then a head taller than his best friend.

# 3

Roy was telling Sam that he had not been in love with Francine Holbrook for some weeks and had been trying to find a way to bring their intimacy to a close without destroying their friendship. Why this was so difficult to manage had to do with his conviction that Francine had never, at any time, been in love with him.

Sam looked none the worse for his ordeal in complexion or mood, but naturally he looked forward to leaving the hospital, where the doctors wanted to keep him one more day for observation. He said now, "You're going to have to explain that."

Roy had remained standing by preference—putting his weight on hospital furniture made him uneasy. "Nobody likes to be told they can't have something even when they don't want it."

Sam's head looked larger on the pillow than when he was standing. "You're saying that suppose I didn't like something—" his eyes abstractedly surveyed the ceiling. "What? I don't know, a striped shirt or whatever, but was told I wasn't allowed to buy it, your contention is it would drive me wild until I got hold of it?"

"I was thinking in terms of personalities. I was really keen on her for a while."

"Oh, come on," Sam said. "You've seldom mentioned her name."

"I don't take you into my confidence on every matter that concerns me." They had argued in this fashion, if it could be called that, all their lives.

Sam winked at him. "Thank the Lord for small favors. You depress me enough as it is. But I ain't ever—incidentally, Kris hates me to say 'ain't' and 'he don't' and all—I haven't ever been able to picture you telling a woman you love her."

"I didn't say I *told* her." As to the bad grammar that Sam had wilfully used since their teen days when speaking with Roy, it was presumably intended as a he-man sort of idiom. Whether he noticed it or not, Roy had not joined him in the practice after they reached their twenties. "Is it the word that matters?"

At this moment a nurse entered on fast-moving rubber-soled white shoes. She smirked at each of them in turn, after which she scanned the chart that hung at the foot of the bed, to give her free access to which Roy had moved aside.

"Suzanne Akins, meet the guy I was telling you about," said Sam.

Undoubtedly she was the redhead he had mentioned to Roy, judging from the orange hair under the white cap and, when she glanced Roy's way, the turned-up nose and freckles. He would not have been attracted to her in street clothes; in a hospital uniform, with the power to administer injections and enemas, she impersonally repelled him.

"Hi," said she, returning to the chart. Then she told Sam, "Be a good boy," and with a nod to his friend, made a brisk exit.

Sam sounded his cackling laugh once the door was shut. "She came only to give you the once-over, kid. She didn't have no other business here."

Again he had forgotten his wife's injunction against barbarisms, and Roy had been bored by sophomoric sexual raillery for twenty years, but as usual he humored his best friend. "I think it's *you* she's got the hots for. Flat on your back, you're at her mercy."

"I'm not kidding. I told her all about you."

"Thanks, pal." Roy finally drew up the metal chair and sat down at the angle at which Sam could see him best. "But as I'm trying to tell you, I have enough trouble with the women at hand."

"There's more than Francine? I mean, I know there's always more, but I mean more causing trouble?"

"Figure of speech," Roy said. "You know I'm more or less a one-woman guy at any given time."

"Which might mean as little as three dates." Sam referred to Roy's practice of making no sexual advances whatever before the third time he took a woman out—not even when he had good reason to believe she would welcome them. He knew he sometimes risked being thought gay, but it was more important to his sense of propriety, call it old-fashioned, not to be taken for a superficial lecher.

Roy changed the subject. "I decided against my original idea of giving Ross and Robin the coffee machine and instead took it over to my place. I can offer clients a cup."

Sam chuckled. "Nothing like a free cappuccino to get some nut to part with half a mil for an old Bugatti."

"Bugattis only turn up at auctions, and there'd never be a bid that low."

"My plan worked," said Sam. "I knew if I got the Stecchino out of there, Kris would never mention the subject. That's the way she is. Above all, she hates confrontations."

Roy looked carefully for signals of disingenuousness and was not amazed to find none. Sam himself abhorred serious wrangling with others. This had nothing to do with the goodnatured needling he and Roy might exchange. "Never noticed it was gone?"

"Not a word. There won't be one, I tell you." Today he was wearing silk pajamas in baby blue, as opposed to the hospital gown of the day before. Obviously Kristin had been there since. "That's how it goes with us."

Roy did not begrudge his smugness about having the perfect marriage, especially in Sam's current condition, yet he could not refrain from asking, "What happens when the credit-card bill arrives?"

Sam's eyebrows rose. "It will be paid without comment."

"Who writes the check?"

Sam reached toward the bedstand. "Kris is the banker in our family."

Roy jumped up. "What do you want?"

"Glass of water. I'm not disabled."

"I doubt you're supposed to twist that way." Roy filled the tumbler from the carafe atop which it had been upended.

On receiving the glass, Sam tested the water with the most meager sip, made a face, and returned it to Roy. "It's brackish and warm as piss."

Roy lifted a wrist and touched the watch on it. "I've got an appointment."

"You still wearing that supermarket Casio?" Sam asked derisively. "Would it bankrupt you to buy a grownup's watch? At least let me lend you one of my PPs." He owned at least two Patek Philippe's, as well as a five-figure Rolex he called an investment. "Kris is bringing some decent water, in case I don't get out of here tomorrow as early as I'd like. I would love something stronger, but I guess I ought to take a diet seriously. . . . She's bringing my portable DVD player as well. You might try to find any recent releases I don't have, but better check with me on the titles. I'm pretty well up to speed on the films I want to see. There's always shit I *don't* want to look at."

Roy clicked his heels, like a Nazi in an old black and white movie. "*Jawohl, mein General.*" He was about to say goodbye when the telephone rang on the little table at the other side of the bed, easily reached by Sam's long right arm.

"Sure. . . . Well, you know I drink gallons. . . . Wait a minute. Roy's here. Lemme tell him." He lowered the phone to his thick neck. "She's got a case of Apollinaris. Imagine what it weighs—"

Roy took the phone. "Kristin."

"Hi, Roy."

"If you could bring a bottle or two for him to drink tonight, I'll haul the case over tomorrow, if he still wants it. I've got an appointment right now."

"Thanks, Roy, and good luck. I hope you make a nice profit on the Alvis."

She hung up before he could go into the ticklish matter of how he would collect the case of water: Let himself into the house again? It was of minor importance that she had wrongly assumed his current business concerned the Alvis.

He returned the phone to its base. "You better give me the inside disarm code for that security system."

Sam displayed the bland expression by which he suggested a query was simpleminded. "Inside you punch in my birthdate in the right order."

"Why didn't you tell me last time?"

"It never occurred to me."


Francine Holbrook had been divorced for a year, but suspecting her ex-husband of stalking her, she insisted on meeting Roy at the bar of a country inn, an hour's drive upstate, so that by using a stretch of back road she could determine whether she was being shadowed.

What had caused Roy to lose his ardor for Francine was her solipsism. She seldom took account of what other people believed or felt, even or perhaps especially when they were her intimates. Either she or everybody else lived in a dream. However, it might have been just this approach to life that had attracted Roy to her in the first place, he who thought of himself as someone restrained by a concern as to how he was regarded by others. Francine habitually parked next to fireplugs and in bus stops, and did not get as many tickets as you might think. She threw any she got into the glove compartment, never paid them, and got away with it while she was married, leaving such matters for her husband to settle, which he uxoriously seemed to do. This was the same man who now supposedly stalked her.

Francine was wont to light cigarettes in no-smoking venues, to take cell-phone calls during movies, and to voice clarion and provocative comments in crowded restaurants ("I don't dare tell her how hot-looking I think she is since the makeover or she'll shove her tongue down my throat!"). She was also sexually rude. On her own volition in the absence of any stimulus of which he was aware, Francine might open Roy's fly and fiddle around with his genitals while speaking of unrelated matters, such as the current feud between her sisters, though he was driving or trying to watch the weather report on television. He had enjoyed this stunt when their connection was new and made the mistake of admitting it. For quite some time now, however, it had seemed an invasion of privacy, but, as with the whole affair of which this was only a minor feature, he had not been able to conceive of a means by which to terminate it kindly.

He had decided to leave the Alvis in the showroom from now on, before the law of averages ordained that its finish got scratched or chipped, and for transportation this evening had chosen the rare example of a fixed-head MGA coupé, oyster-white, which he had recently purchased from an elderly widow whose husband had bought it new in 1958 and maintained it reasonably well over the years, though it had acquired a new exhaust system and a replacement set of tires. Most MGAs had been roadsters, with a folding canvas roof and plastic side-curtains, but this was a hardtop, one of the relatively few exported to America. He had bought it cheap, while still, ethically, paying the woman more than she expected. It was still on his hands only because his client who specialized in the marque did not want another with wire wheels, so at the moment it was listed with the other offerings in his ads in the car magazines and at the Website *Incomparable.com*.

As he turned the nimble little car into the parking lot of The Hedges after a pleasant drive at an easy cruising speed of eighty-five when the coast was clear—which was within 10 mph of the MGA's maximum—he found himself wishing he was meeting Kristin, at the moment the only person of his social acquaintance, of either sex, who might have been interested in seeing this handsome vehicle. Francine had a total disregard for all machinery. Also, her ego was such that she refused to acknowledge any departure from the mean on the part of any-one but herself. He could have driven a handyman's Chevy pickup or a king's Hispano-Suiza without attracting her notice.

He walked up the lane from the parking lot to the inn, looking for the nearby willow-bordered duck pond, which was too dark to see except as a glimmering reflection in the wan light from the carpark. The Hedges was a fetching place outside and within, warm in winter, refreshing in summertime, with alert but unobtrusive servitors and short but well-conceived menus and wine list. It would have been an excellent destination with any woman, or least any Roy was likely to court, but it was perfect for clandestine dates—and a discreet glance around the room most evenings would suggest many of one's fellow diners could qualify for the latter.

Roy had been introduced to the place by its owner, to whom he had sold a classic 507 BMW Sports-Tourisme, exported from Munich by a NATO general. Francine was the only woman with whom Roy had yet visited The Hedges. On the threshold now, between the wrought-iron lighting fixtures that bracketed the entrance, he found himself yearning poignantly to do so with someone other than she.

Hand on the thick doorknob, he heard his name hissed from the darkness behind him. He turned, stepped back, and peered at the thicket near the pond, but could discern nothing through the foliage.

"Is that you?" He received that most annoying answer, palpable silence. "Francine?"

Suddenly there she was, not where he looked but just behind his right shoulder, having stolen out noiselessly from some nearer cover, probably the large shrub to the left of the entrance. But playing such games was not like her. Francine was never kittenish.

"*We have to get out of here.*" Her voice was intense but scarcely louder than a whisper.

"Huh?"

"*Get going.*"

Disinclined to take such direction, Roy did not move. "I want a drink," he said. "And I'm hungry."

She seized his arm at the elbow and tugged with unusual strength in someone so small, who however in any posture other than standing at full height seemed much larger than she was. "*Will you get out of here?*"

"Jesus, Francine." As so often, it was less fuss to comply with her wishes than to resist, even though he was well aware it was because of just this sort of gutlessness that he had come to the point at which he found her unbearable. And it was more self-respecting to walk as if of one's own volition than to be pulled. His decision was further influenced by the exit of some people from the building behind them and the simultaneous appearance of a party of three at the bottom of the path from the carpark, making for a potential jam in human traffic.

His fear that Francine would want to display her anguish to these strangers proved groundless. She freed him from her grasp and walked decorously beside him. Roy scanned the faces of those in the oncoming group, so as not to cut anyone with whom he had done or might do business, but recognizing nobody, he smiled faintly toward all while stepping off the narrow path in deference to the other claimant to the same space, an adolescent girl who surprised him with her murmured thanks. He quickly discerned that she was not the date but the daughter of the portly middle-aged gentleman in attendance, and her slender and still handsome mother brought up the rear, proving that the clientele of The Hedges was comprised of more than furtive adulterers. He must congratulate his friend Jack Judd, innkeeper and car collector.

In the parking lot Roy stopped, though Francine continued to walk, even now picking up the pace, and he asked, raising his voice, "Wait a minute, will you? My car is over there. Where do you want to go?" Then, because she was still in motion, "Will you stop!"

She did so, her back toward him, and lowered her dark head. Roy had come this far to avoid social embarrassment, but he would go no farther without good reason. However, she looked very small in the light of the nearest ornamental lamppost, and against his better judgment he was moved by what might prove a genuine distress.

She turned toward him as he approached. She had as youthful a figure as the teenager to whom he had surrendered the footpath, though she had borne two children. This little girl and boy, seven and eight, played no part for Roy in his affair with their mother. He had seen them only once, at a distance, and he rarely thought about them, for to do so might lead to a reflection on whether he, after all, shared some moral responsibility for the breakup of their family. Francine claimed he was her one and only lover as wife, parent, and divorcée, even though the court had awarded her husband custody of the children.

Roy suspected that she had always been promiscuous, though he had never caught her at it and never tried to. By the current phase of their association, he wished ardently that she did have other guys on the string and preferred them all to him.

"*He's* inside," she said now.

Roy made an instant translation. "Your ex? Okay, we'll go . . . let me think where." He did not mind another trip so soon—he would have had to make the return later on anyway, and driving the little coupé was a treat—but he really was hungry at the end of a long day. But he could understand her wish to leave, and was himself not eager to be seen for the first time by Martin Holbrook though not being at legal or moral odds with the man.

Francine immediately cast victimhood aside, which was her style. Throwing her head back, her eyes in shadow even larger than nature and cosmetic enhancement maintained them, she cried, "Race you back!"

He had no taste for such a foolish contest. He would have to let her win it, in a Lincoln Navigator that was dangerously top-heavy on the twisting secondary roads, in the corners of which the MGA, at speed, was as if in the clutch of God.

"Bad idea. I saw cops everywhere on the way up," he lied, then truthfully pointed out that with one more ticket her license would be suspended. "Where'll we meet? La Boite?"

Francine grasped him at the crotch and groaned savagely. "All I want to eat is this."

In the next moment a figure came hurtling into view, seized her shoulders, and ripped her away. It was a man whose approach had, though apparently at the run, been unnoticed by Roy, though, as he came to believe later on, it could hardly have been so to Francine, who faced the inn from which her assailant had come.

"You're a piece of garbage," the man shouted and, clutching

Francine at the throat, forehanded her face with sufficient force to produce more thud than slap.

He lost the opportunity for a backhand return. Roy spun him away
from her and with a reverse punch hit him in the solar plexus with such
force that, had it been applied over the heart, might well have stopped
it: this according to his old karate master's warning. He had never used
the punch before on any target but the human-size swinging sandbag at
the dojo.

Holbrook (it was either he or an unknown madman), clutching his
thorax, buckled to his knees on the asphalt. He seemed to be trying to
cough but could not gather enough breath for it.

To Roy, Francine screeched, "You've killed him!" But she stepped
well away from her fallen ex-husband.

Roy bent to Holbrook and told him to breathe as deeply as he could
through the nose, expelling his breath by mouth. This was the best
means by which to bring much-needed oxygen into the system after
physical exertion. But the other man could not get further than a series
of discordant gasps.

Francine molded herself against Roy's right side. "Is he dying?"

"He'll be perfectly all right in a minute or so." Roy spoke really for
his victim's benefit. "It's not lethal. I've been hit in the solar plexus.
There's no permanent damage." He had nothing against the man. In
fact he pitied him and not because of the punch. Anyone to whom
Francine meant so much was in trouble.

She thrust away from Roy, crying, "I have to get out of here. Right
now!" She even stamped her foot, which caused him incongruously to
remember she had exceptionally small feet and could not always find
her size in the shoe she set her heart on. That was the kind of stuff he
knew about her, but next to nothing about her children and very little
about poor Holbrook except that he was dull, which might not even be
true in a universal sense. He might be the kind of guy with whom Roy
would hit it off, discussing the business situation or playing golf. Roy was
not a very good golfer; Holbrook might enjoy beating him.

Roy extended a hand to the fallen, which Holbrook however could not yet see, head toward the ground. "Come on, Martin. It'll help if you try to walk it off."

Holbrook groaned. He raised his head far enough to squint up and say hoarsely, "I'm suing you," then hung it low again.

"Okay," Roy said amiably, "but you ought to come up where you can get more air. It'll make all the difference. You'll see."

His attempt to be decent to her ex was seen as treachery by Francine, who shrieked in fury, "Stop talking like a fag. He could have killed me! Call the police. I'm going to charge him with attempted murder."

Roy stepped behind Holbrook, bent, and, grasping him under the armpits, lifted the man as if pressing a barbell of equivalent weight, one fifty-five, sixty pounds.

Holbrook did not resist. He was so passive that Roy feared he might collapse again and therefore warned him, "I'm going to let you go now. Try to walk some. It won't take long till you're back to normal."

He did as promised and Holbrook sagged but did not fall, though neither did he try to walk.

"He's all right," Francine said. She was quieter now, not so angry as bitter. "He'll survive. He always does. *I'm* the one the shit sticks to."

"Let me see your face. Come over here under the light." Roy drew her to the nearest lamppost, the wrought-iron standard of which was wrapped with wrought-iron ivy. "Some reddening on your cheek, it looks like." Francine's skin was naturally on the wan side. She was much concerned about makeup and would now want to effect repairs. "Better go inside to the powder room, under good lighting."

She raised her eyes to his and produced a soulful expression that he could not remember as being in her repertoire. "This hasn't worked out," she said, a statement that seemed to reflect a state of mind that was also unique. "I'm sorry." He assumed the regret was for herself as always.

Behind them a car's engine came to roaring life, and in the next instant a vehicle gunned past them and shot out of the exit onto the dark road. Its taillights did not come on until it had traveled at least a hundred yards at a speed that was probably not all that high but seemed desperate.

"I guess he'll live," Roy said when the red lenses had dwindled to the vanishing point.

"You don't really care, do you?"

"Sure I do. I didn't want to hurt him."

"I don't think you care about anything that breathes." Francine's latest mood sounded stoical, but there may have been irony in her faint smile.

Roy had had enough of her for this night, or, in truth, for the far side of never. "Better go into the ladies' room and tend to that bruise. It's getting darker."

"Goodbye, Roy." She abruptly turned away and, at a measured pace, walked to her Navigator, its big black bulk standing by itself in a corner of the lot, well away from the other parked cars.

Roy kept watch lest any further harm was offered to her, until she had driven away in the direction her ex-husband had taken, but at a much more deliberate speed. Roy had lied to Sam about once having loved her, because lying to one's best friend was the next best thing to lying to oneself. How could it ever have been love? It was nothing but lust. Lust could be defended as having merits of its own, but he or she who mistook it for love was pitiful. Francine, to give her her due, had never made that mistake.

# 4

Roy lived in a duplex apartment fashioned from the north wing of a mansion built by a rich eccentric of the early twentieth century. The imposing pillared façade and the great semicircular sweep of the front driveway made a superb backdrop for photographs of Rolls-Royces and Bentleys. It would have been perfect for a Model J Duesenberg, but he considered such great classics as out of his reach now that they fetched millions at auction.

After the daily workout in his home gym, he breakfasted on the usual high-protein, multivitamin cocktail of which the base liquid was skim milk. He had awoken with a clear head and a positive prospect. The incident in the parking lot of The Hedges had not been pleasant, but maybe it would prove therapeutic for all concerned, including the unfortunate Martin Holbrook.

As to Francine, Roy assumed his previous problem in getting free of her had now been solved in the cleanest way; that is, by her being able to believe *she* dumped *him*. At least so he interpreted her final, curt goodbye, a style of leave-taking she had never used before. For Francine, one moment was but the prelude to the next. Whenever they parted company she responded to his farewell with a fluid turn on the ball of the foot and quick, almost dancing steps away, all in utter silence. Then, soon as he reached home, if that was where he went—and if he had not, he had better explain why—she would check on him by telephone. She would not admit this was policing. "I'm always worried, driving the way you do, and more about you getting arrested than having an accident."

She had never loved him, but neither did she want him to have any alternative existence. Being himself largely immune to jealousy of a sexual kind, which could never be anything but negative and grow more destructive in the degree to which more energy was applied, he had little patience with hers.

He had just stepped out the front door when a police car entered the driveway, probably in response to a call from the aged widow who lived, with a female companion almost as old as she, in the remainder of the cavernous house. Her late husband, C. Edgar Swanson, had been a good customer of Roy's, and when Swanson died he bought back, at favorable prices, some of the vintage cars he had once sold to the man. Not to mention that the rent Roy paid for the high-ceilinged apartment, from which the river was visible through the upstairs windows in all seasons, was set by old Doris at scarcely above the level she remembered from her bachelor-girl days many decades earlier when she had worked as secretary to Swanson, who had made a fortune manufacturing plumbing fixtures.

Doris frequently called the cops to come check the premises after a night in which she and Myra believed they had heard unusual noises in the wee hours but did not want to bother the officers with it then; and because she was rich, and generous to the charities they endorsed, they always showed up and performed a cursory inspection that found no cause for alarm.

As a courtesy to the policemen, Roy waited now until the two of them left their car. Usually only one came on these calls. Doris was getting royal treatment today.

The officer who emerged from the driver's side was Howie, whom Roy had met in the contretemps at Sam's house the day before. The man leaving the navigator's seat proved to be the chief of police, Jim Albrecht, who except on ceremonial occasions usually wore mufti.

Today it was an open nylon golf jacket over a navy-blue T-shirt bearing the logo of the television program *America's Most Wanted*.

"Hi, Jim," Roy said, nodding at Howie. "I hope Doris doesn't have a serious problem."

"No, sir, Mr. Courtright." Albrecht was almost as big as Sam, but a dozen years older and hard of body, and had served as a marine in both Grenada and the Gulf actions. As usual he was diffident when speaking with Roy. "I was wondering if we might have a word with you?"

The chief looked especially uncomfortable, so Roy spoke with levity to lessen the man's strain. "It's not that coffee machine Howie caught me stealing from Sam Grandy's house, is it?"

Albrecht frowned briefly but otherwise disregarded the question. "Would you mind coming down to Central?"

Roy had no clue as to what this was about, but he liked the chief and thought the department did a fine job of keeping civic order. "I've got a better idea. Why don't you fellows drop in at my place and have a cup of cappu—uh, fresh-made coffee—any way you like it."

"That would be nice, Mr. Courtright, but I'd rather you come down to Central, if you don't mind."

Roy suddenly understood the invitation bore more weight than a polite request and was extended by an officer of the law. "Why sure, Chief, any time."

Albrecht had yet to show the broad smile that he displayed so liberally on other occasions. "We'd like you to come right now."

Suspense was now in play, one of Roy's least favorite emotions. "Jim," he asked, "mind telling me what's going on?"

"I'd rather wait till we get to Central, Mr. Courtright. It makes more sense."

Which of course is what it definitely did not do, at least for Roy, nor did riding as a passenger in the police car, which the chief preferred him to do rather than follow in his own vehicle.

Nobody said another word until he and Albrecht, joined by three other men in civilian clothes, sat in the chief's office in the overcrowded municipal building, only a block and a half from Roy's place of business.

"Mr. Courtright," said Chief Albrecht, behind the littered desk in front of which was Roy's straight, armless, hard wooden chair. "Will you tell us how you spent last evening and night?"

Roy spoke levelly. "I want to know what this is all about."

Albrecht nodded with his jutting jaw. "Make a deal with you, Mr. Courtright. Soon as you tell us what you did last night, I'll tell you exactly what's going on. Now, you can't say that's not fair."

Another questionable theory, along with the one about making sense, but Roy proceeded to comply to the letter, even unto the little dust-up in the parking lot, which, as he was summarizing the incident, he recognized as surely the pretext for the matter at hand: Holbrook was charging him with assault and battery!

"He *hit* her, and then he was *choking* her. So I slugged him to get him to stop. I'd do it again. Any of you would have done the same."

Albrecht had listened without expression. The putative detectives stood somewhere behind Roy, where he could not see them.

One now spoke up. "What did you do after the fight?"

"It wasn't a fight. It was what I just described. . . . I drove back to town."

"With Francine Holbrook?" The voice was of yet another man.

"No. She left in her own car, SUV. I was driving a vintage model from my inventory. I took it back to our showroom and switched it with the Jeep Grand Cherokee we use, because I don't have a garage where I live and I don't like to leave a valuable automobile outside all night."

"Where'd you go then?" Albrecht asked. "And what did you do?"

"Drove home, drank a beer, put on the TV, and fell asleep immediately. I woke up in the middle of the night and went to bed. . . . Now, keep your part of the bargain."

"What time did you get home?"

"Tennish, ten-thirty?"

"And you didn't leave again?"

"Not till this morning." Roy snorted. "Don't tell me Holbrook claims I followed him and beat him up further. I hit him exactly once, in the solar plexus."

"It's not Martin Holbrook who was found dead," Albrecht said in an official-sounding drone, "but Mrs. Francine Wilkie Holbrook. It's a homicide. Nobody beats themself to death, alone in an apartment."

"My God, how terrible!" said Kristin, whom Roy had phoned at the bank.

"I couldn't upset Sam with this." He found his voice hard to control. "We were just talking about her yesterday."

"Where are you calling from?"

"The lobby of the Municipal Building."

"You're free to leave?"

"Yes, I am," said Roy. "I can't believe they ever thought I did it, and they never charged me with anything, which is why I didn't call my lawyer till the whole thing was almost over, and then of course he's in court and hasn't gotten back to me. . . . I'm running off at the mouth. This thing has really shaken me up."

"You wouldn't be much of a person if it didn't," Kristin said. "Stay where you are. I'll be right over to get you."

When the report came in that Martin Holbrook's dead body had been found with an accompanying suicide note, the police were abruptly and unapologetically finished with Roy. He learned later that Holbrook had deposited the children at school, then returned home to a self-inflicted death by an unlicensed .32-caliber pistol, leaving behind the note confessing, or perhaps bragging, that he had furnished his ex-wife with the punishment the slut had long deserved. But nobody at headquarters gave a full account to Roy. He now felt abandoned by all, alone with the awful conviction that had he not humiliated Holbrook in Francine's presence, both of them would be alive today.

That Holbrook had been at The Hedges at the same time as they was no coincidence: Obviously Francine had set up the encounter. But try as he would to blame the victims, rage against himself was Roy's predominant emotion. By the use of poor judgment he had killed two persons. That a loser like Holbrook would have murdered Francine at another time was no mitigation, nor was the near certainty that she

would have provided her ex with ample pretexts for rage. But would Roy
have felt better if he had let Holbrook strangle her in the parking lot?
There are times when all choices must, as if by divine law, be disastrous,
but heretofore he had only heard of this as happening to others and
more typically in works of the imagination than in the structurelessness
of real life.

It had been, to say the least, presumptive of him to call Kristin, but
he had no one else to turn to at the moment. Sam was in the hospital in
a delicate condition that might well be adversely affected by hearing his
best friend's awful news. All their lives, Robin had been the worst person with whom to seek solace. He did not dare approach her with anything to announce but a success, and of course she would endeavor to
disparage that. A failure of any kind would make her crow. In the case at
hand she would say, "Sleep with dogs, get up with fleas. What do you
expect when a trollop is your idea of a suitable girlfriend?" Her idea of a
woman for him was someone from her own circle of embittered divor-
cées with child-support problems: Ironically, people much like Francine
in situation but presumably less bawdy or anyway more circumspect.
Francine in fact had been a neighbor of Celeste Brownson, a pal of
Robin's whom his sister had urged him to date. "I call her Celezzy to her
face," Francine told him, "and she doesn't mind at all! Her trouble is,
she can't ever admit to herself that she basically hates men. Poor Evan!
It must have been like sticking it into a bowl of cold risotto."

When Sam was well, Roy did not have to search for a confidant. If he
thought about the matter, he would have to confess to himself that
Kristin was a surrogate, so he must try to avoid an impulse to overapolo-
gize for intruding on her workday, which he would not have had to do
with Sam, who usually had no work as such and when he did, its demands
could never have been as important as the needs of his best friend.

While Roy waited for Kristin at the curb outside the Municipal
Building, the cell phone vibrated in his pocket.

"Roy, returning your call."

It was Seymour Alt, his lawyer, during a recess in some trial in a
courtroom in the very building from which Roy had just emerged.

Roy told him what had happened. "I guess I'm lucky that Holbrook left the note. Poor Francine. It would have been even worse if I was suspected of killing her. Well, I'm legally in the clear now, so I won't need your services."

"You let me be the judge of that," said Alt, switching off.

Roy regretted having called the counselor, with the man's vested uninterest, if not disdain, for morality. Sy was a nice person when with his family or playing golf but changed into another order of being when he practiced his profession. Unfortunately it was not possible to operate a business for more than an hour nowadays without consulting an attorney. To your lawyer you were always right in every phase of every matter, as everyone else was wrong and even if badly hurt deserved no sympathy when their interests were not your own. "Of course," Alt said when Roy once privately made that point to him. "Else you'd sue me for taking money under false pretenses."

Kristin was as good as her word, arriving in the Corolla soon after he had put the phone away. Her promptness was all the more impressive in the traffic of what he realized, looking at his watch for the first time all day, was already noontime.

"This really helps," he said. "At the moment I can't stand being in my own company. . . . I'm sorry. That sounds like anyone would do. Obviously I don't mean that."

She was an attentive driver, keeping her eyes, after a quick glance at Roy, on the car ahead. "And I was about to say I'm only doing what Sam would be doing if he could." She smiled at the windshield. "Obviously, I don't mean exactly that. You're my friend, too."

Roy was moved by the sentiment while being aware that any humanitarian acquaintance might say the same under the conditions at hand. The need for caution in his associations with women—even those with whom his relations were only polite, as with Kristin—had been more than confirmed by the tragedy of the Holbrooks, which he found more unbelievable each time he reviewed the sequence of its events . . . yet he felt compelled to keep doing so.

She drove, and he talked. He paid no attention to where she drove and did not really care whether she was listening to what he said, which could hardly have been fascinating to her. He sensed he might even feel a retroactive humiliation later on, looking back on what was the moral equivalent of vomiting or diarrhea.

It was pride that finally brought him back to self-control. This was not good old Sam, before whom in all these years he probably could not be embarrassed, but rather Sam's wife. Despite her formalistic profession of friendship, she owed him nothing beyond routine courtesy, certainly not approval, perhaps not even sympathy.

"I really appreciate this, Kristin," he said, not to her but looking out his window. "You've got better things to do with your lunch hour than hearing me bare my soul. Is that Clear Brook Park? Let me out at the corner there, if you will. It's only a mile or two from home, and I could use the walk."

Her tone had an edge he had never heard before. "But that's just what you *haven't* done, Roy. You haven't bared your soul."

He felt an infusion of blood in his cheeks, as if, absurdly, he was blushing. He turned to her immaculate profile. "I thought I was going on too much about myself. I guess it was just gibberish. I can't stop thinking about the what-ifs, useless as that is. I should have followed her home, should have known if the guy would attack her right in front of me, he'd do it when she was alone, do it all the worse after I stopped him the first time."

"Were you really in love with her?"

"Sam's been talking to you."

"Well," Kristin said, "we're married, and we have normal conversations." She pulled up at the designated corner and braked.

"I didn't love her," said Roy. "As for the 'in love,' I guess I thought I was early on . . . actually, I probably wasn't even then. It was just exciting. I know women never understand what men are attracted to in other women. Even when they say they do, they don't. But I do believe they know what attracts men to themselves. Francine certainly did. Not all men, of course." He smiled at Kristin. "Sam has much better taste than I— in human beings, not just the female sort. He has a bigger heart."

She accepted the statement with a little shrug, perhaps not of indifference but modesty. She had gotten no easier to read. She asked, "Is that what it takes?"

It was just the right thing for her to say, whether she realized it or not. "I don't know," said he. "I don't usually know what I'm talking about unless the subject is vintage cars. That should be obvious."

She looked at him with her cool blue eyes. "I don't think that's true at all. I don't doubt your knowledge of your profession, but I don't think that's all you know by any means."

"You haven't ever approved of me, have you?" He surprised himself with the question; asking it would have been unthinkable had he been in command of himself. He did not, however, regret asking it. It gave him some substance in this time of confusion.

Kristin continued to stare at him. "It's not a matter of approval," she said at last. "I simply didn't like you."

Once again he was actually relieved by what she said, to the degree that he could, awful as he felt, produce a kind of grin. "That's what I thought."

She did not join him in wryness. "What I didn't begin to distinguish between, until lately, was you, the living individual, and Sam's idea of you, which is really different—maybe more different than you suspect."

Not sure quite how to take her interpretation of his best friend's opinion of him—which could be designed more to provoke than inform—Roy said seriously, "He might know me better than I know myself. We've been pals since we were kids, and his memory is sometimes better than mine." Then, jokingly, "And he's bigger than me."

"I'll bet you're really scared of him."

Roy refused to join in any implied derision of Sam, if such this was. "He was not only always a lot taller, but in my early teens I was underweight and scrawny. I wouldn't eat. I couldn't. Food was like medicine to me. I never developed an appetite till I started weight training." In fact he had started to build himself up in conscious response to Sam's advantage in size. What Roy had done, however, was not to be mistaken as competitive, and as for his friend, Sam cheered him on. It was inconvenient to be undersized, taking an array of compensatory measures: walking faster than the longer-legged, being assigned to the inside seat in diner booths. When they both learned to drive in a car owned by Roy's father, who was six-one, the seat had to be moved forward to the limits of its forward travel with Roy behind the wheel, then run all the way back for Sam.

"Speaking of food," Kristin said now, changing the subject to his relief. "I'm on my lunch break." She squinted at him. "Would you want to go someplace and eat? Or just watch me? I'm hungry." The girlish grin briefly deformed her lips, which Roy noted, for the first time, had been so perfect in repose, but it made him feel more comfortable.

"I don't really want to walk home by myself," he said. Then, remembering, "I've got to get that case of Apollinaris over to Sam."

"We'll deal with that after lunch," Kristin said decisively. She quickly put the car in motion, as if he might change his mind.

Having turned one corner, they were back in urgent traffic. Kristin drove with an easy confidence that was a contrast to Sam's demeanor behind the wheel. Driving a car evoked from Sam a display of emotions of which he was otherwise publicly innocent. When afoot it was he who apologized to those who collided with him or stepped on his foot, though such things were almost never his fault—despite being oversized he maneuvered gracefully through crowds. But at the controls of an automobile he trembled with resentment toward any other vehicle that shared the road. However circumspectly its driver performed at one moment, the situation could change for the worse in the next. If the car ahead of him obeyed an established stop sign, the habitually tailgating Sam was obliged to panic-brake. But when he was leader, any driver who followed him too closely (in his opinion they all did) was sure to be tormented with many pseudobrakings, quick touches of the pedal to flash the red lights. He usually drove too slowly, which practice showed more uncertainty than genuine prudence and might be downright dangerous in certain applications, such as penetrating a high-volumed thruway.

To Sam, though, Roy, who never met a speed limit he could respect, was a reckless character, and he avoided riding with his friend; for many years now each drove his own car when they were to be companions at a restaurant or entertainment event.

Roy remembered that he should get in touch with his office. Excusing himself, he brought out the cell phone and called his assistant. He found he had no taste to produce more than a superficial lie to the effect that he was staying home ill and letting the machine take all messages. He predicted a full recovery by the next day.

"You call her Mrs. Forsythe?" Kristin asked as he lowered the phone.

"She's old enough—well, almost—to be my mother," said Roy. "Damned if I want to call her Margaret."

"What does she call you?"

He smirked. "Well, Roy." He quickly went on. "She only works half a day but does more in that time than anybody I've ever hired."

"Minimum wage? No benefits?" Kristin glanced at him, smiling slyly. "That's right, I'm prying."

"I'm flattered," said Roy. "I do a little better for her than that, but she's still a bargain." He did not mention that of Mrs. Forsythe's merits, perhaps the greatest for him was that she provided no sexual distraction. He would never have made an advance toward a female employee, but would have been uncomfortable with one he desired.

Kristin's cell phone, mounted in a dashboard holster, rang as Roy was putting his own in his pocket. Its signal was repeated as, excusing herself, she brushed his knee with her elbow, opened the glove compartment, and brought out a headset.

"Guess who that is?" she asked Roy, putting the device in place over her fair crown and making the necessary connections and adjustments. An insistent telephone always made Roy nervous, but this one had no discernible effect on Kristin. She fiddled with the mouthpiece, impervious to the sound. Finally she was ready.

"Yeah," she said to the caller. "It always takes a while with this gadget of yours, and I'm in traffic. . . . Going to lunch with some people—no, I'm sure he won't forget the water. Told me it will be late afternoon. All right. I can remember. Loois, The Hot Fives, volume one.

Okay, Mingus Moves . . . I'll find them more easily without the directions. . . . You're kidding. Seeya."

She returned the headpiece to the glove compartment. "I assume he
was joking when he asked me to smuggle in a thermosful of martinis, but
you never know. He wants those jazz CDs. Bet you could find them
quicker than me. You guys listen to them all the time. Do you recognize
the titles?"

"The Charles Mingus will be easy to locate," Roy said. "Sam doesn't
have that many. But he's got shelf after shelf of Louis Armstrong, in no
particular order."

"Is that correct: Loois, not Looey?"

"The man himself always pronounces the name that way on the TV
interviews Sam's got on video and on the audio tapes."

Kristin sighed. "I thought Sam was just being pretentious."

"That's the kind of thing he usually knows." Roy suppressed an urge
to reprove her except by implication. "Much more than I am likely to
do. Most of the hobbies we share were begun by him, and I've gone
along because he was my pal. I'm not complaining. As I probably don't
have to tell you, you can have a lot of fun with Sam. It's that enthusiasm
of his." He hesitated. "But it has to go his way. I'm not talking behind his
back; I've told him to his face—he hasn't returned the favor with cars."

"Of course it's not equivalent," Kristin said immediately. "Cars are
your profession, maybe even a vocation."

In an instant she had recognized a truth that had never occurred to
Roy. For as short a time, he disliked her for showing him up on a subject
of which he should have been a master. But his was a reflex action,
expiring as quickly as it had come. He was pleased by her loyal defense
of Sam, which was as it should be.

"You're right," he said. "I never looked at it that way."

And then she proceeded to nullify her moral position. "That's his
problem. He's never had a profession, let alone a vocation."

Roy winced. He really should not listen to serious criticism of his
friend, but he was not sure how to discourage it without insulting Sam's

wife and thus, in effect, Sam. "I know he's tried a lot of things on for size. I think he's eventually going to find one that fits." It was lame. Worse, it was false. He had no faith in Sam except as a friend, which was saying a great deal, but it was not to the point here.

Kristin kept her eyes on the road. "He doesn't have the capital now to try much more. He's pissed it all away."

The gross expression was not like her, at least insofar as Roy's limited experience of her company went, but sometimes people changed or revealed more of themselves when you knew them better. Francine had begun more foulmouthed than she ended. . . . God almighty, what an end. The desolation from which he had been temporarily distracted came flooding back. Sam's problems seemed surmountable. "He's survived this heart thing. He's still young."

"I'm going to run a risk in even bringing this up," Kristin said, braking to a stop under a traffic light. "I've never interfered before in the friendship between you two. I doubt I would be doing it now if Sam wasn't in the hospital. This *is* behind his back: There's no other way to do it." She looked at Roy. "I'm going to ask you not to lend him any more money."

For the second time Roy felt as though he blushed, and on this occasion he had no clear sense of why. What could be embarrassing about lending money to a friend when you had it and in so doing were not taking food from someone else's mouth? He and Robin had each inherited considerably more than Sam had been left by his own father, on whose estate the creditors made many claims.

The driver behind them sounded his horn on the green light. Kristin looked back at the road and put the Corolla in motion. "This is the time if there ever was one for him to make a basic change."

"It hasn't been all that much," Roy said, "and Sam—"

She interrupted, and in an offensive style. "Oh, come on, Roy. I'm married to him, remember? Not to mention that I'm a banker. I have a damn good idea of what he's taken from you."

"That's more than I do. Look, he's got it coming. My father thought a lot of Sam. He told me he would have left him something if my sister would have put up with it, but he was sure Robin wouldn't. He didn't even want the subject brought up with her."

"Well, that's your business," Kristin said, peering through the windshield more intensely than the now lightly trafficked road demanded. "Mine is to see he acquires more financial responsibility, and I'm asking you to help. As his friend." She glanced quickly his way, frowning. "As *my* friend."

Roy nervously slapped himself on the kneecap. "That's more easily said than done. We've been sharing stuff for years. If it was something one had, the other could always make a claim on it. He's usually the one who's had more possessions than I. He's the collector, not me, except for cars."

"And you sell them. That's completely different. How often have you *asked* to borrow Sam's movie cassettes? Doesn't he always suggest some title, even press it on you? Same thing with CDs, boutique beers, or whatever, at least since I've known the two of you."

Roy was made resentful by what was indeed the truth, but who was she to have recognized it so arrogantly and, worse, to announce it in this style?

"He's the one with the ideas. He's better at having fun than I've ever been. He gets so much pleasure from sharing his interests. Sometimes I've gone along just to please him, watched a movie I knew I wouldn't like; and you know Sam, you have to do your homework, he's not going to let you give a simple pro or con reaction to anything he's suggested you do or watch or taste. So you're forced to pay attention to detail, and more often than not I've ended up liking whatever it was." He cleared his throat. "Or sort of liking it, which is different from liking something in the natural way without being influenced."

"Oh?" asked Kristin, without irony and as if to herself. "You've noticed that, too."

Subliminally he also noticed that they had entered a familiar neighborhood. She now turned into the driveway of the Grandy residence.

"I'll pick up that water," he said as they pulled up behind the house. "You handle the security system." He turned to open the door.

Kristin asked, "Do you mind, Roy?"

He looked over his shoulder. "I'm not trying to evade the matter. I'm trying to figure out how not just to turn him down next time he asks, but also explain that I'm doing so because his wife wants me to." He stared at her. "Because that's the only way I'll do it."

"That's the only way I would want it done."

He left the car. He was too proud to admit immediately that both her cause and her means were just.

"Your kitchen always smells good," he said when they were inside the house. In Sam's absence the high-tech exhaust system was not overused. "Mine often stinks of the fluids used by the cleaning woman. Soon as the odor's gone, she's back with more."

Kristin deposited her purse on the polished-granite counter. "You ought to do more cooking there. Or just boil water with cinnamon in it. That's what real-estate agents advise home sellers to do before they bring around a prospect."

"Someone buys a house because it smells good?"

"Probably helps establish a positive mood. You don't deal with what could be called the general public, do you?"

"Over the years a few people have come in off the street and three or four have ended up buying a car, usually one of the less expensive marques, an MG Midget or Triumph Spitfire. But once a guy in work clothes walked in and bought a Ferrari Two-Fifty GTE right off the floor. For cash: seventy-five grand. The car was a sixty-three."

Kristin wrinkled her nose. "He carried that kind of money on him."

"A check," said Roy. "Of course he didn't drive the car away until we cleared it. He's a local contractor."

She pointed to one of the stools at the middle island. "Take a seat. What do you want to drink? I got these chores to do."

"Want me to locate the CDs?"

"That would be nice of you."

The wall phone rang, startling him. Kristin punched the button that put it on speaker.

"HI," boomed Sam's voice. It was disquieting for Roy to hear his friend so amplified.

"Hold on," Kristin said. "I've got to turn the volume down. Maria's been up to her old tricks."

"There are a couple more things I want you to bring over," said Sam.

Kristin grimaced at Roy. Then she surprised him by saying, "If it's more CDs, tell your best friend."

"Hi, Sam," said Roy.

"Roy, you're there?"

"I came to pick up the Apollinaris."

"Oh, sure . . . well, listen, then." He proceeded to name what he needed: Monk at the Five Spot in '58 and specific performances by Bird and Coltrane. Sam's jazz collection was enormous and included tapes and LPs as well as vintage shellac 78s. He had paid too much for the last and not for the quality of the music, all of which had been digitally remastered and was available on CD, whereas much on the deteriorated soundtracks of the originals was audibly compromised.

Roy felt obliged to explain. "I'll find them and give them to Kristin. I'll bring you the water around six."

"Kris," asked Sam, "you meeting the others at the restaurant?"

"That's right. And I won't tell you where so you can't phone me. You'll swear you won't, and then you'll break your promise."

"I'm a real bastard that way."

Roy thought he heard bitterness in the reply, but perhaps that was only an electronic effect of the speaker phone, which he felt introduced a false, public-relations element into, and so warped, any personal conversation.

Sam's voice brightened. "Hey, Roy. Help yourself to anything you want. Look through the tapes and LPs: There's still stuff that's never been put on CD."

This was a standing offer, and at any given time Roy had at home a stack of recordings pressed on him by Sam, but listening to them alone, without his best friend's occasional commentary and frequent groans of bliss at John Coltrane's soprano sax or Mingus's bass riffs, did not do for him what it should. After a few weeks he would bring them back, mostly unplayed, and face Sam's grilling.

"Catch you later, kid," Roy said now. When he heard Sam hang up, he asked Kristin, "*Are* you meeting some office people for lunch? If so, I'll take a raincheck." He had heard her say as much when speaking with Sam on the phone in the car, but reacted only to this second reference.

"I was lying," she said flatly, while consulting a little notebook taken from her purse. She raised her golden head. "Oh, excuse me. I prefer to jot notes on paper instead of one of those gadgets, but then I can't read my own writing." She sighed. "He's not jealous. He's just curious and lonely. He would have to hear what we ate and drank, and where we went, of course. If it was one of the places where he knows the proprietor or the maître d' and thinks they like him aside from the money he spends—well, it isn't news to you."

Roy tried to conceal how deeply he disapproved of this tactic. He had never had reason to lie to Sam and resented being forced to now. "I just have to remember what *not* to say to him."

"It isn't complicated. We just told him you're here to pick up the water and find the CDs. You're free to tell him anything we said to each other."

She had a way of being right, or pretty nearly so, after seeming to have been wrong. "Okay," said Roy. "You're married to the guy. He and I have always been perfectly straight with one another. It hasn't always been easy. I lost a couple of his most valuable baseball cards when we were kids and had to confess to it. Another time I was supposed to look after his golden retriever when he went on vacation. I wasn't too careful and it got out and ran away. The dog was inclined to do that anyhow, and Sam probably wouldn't have blamed me, but it was my fault and I owned up to it because I knew he would have done the same."

"Was the dog ever found?"

"My father had to offer a sizable reward. Sam gave him away not long after getting him back."

Kristin returned to her notes, but she had not abandoned the conversation. "And what has he done when *he's* been at fault?"

"I can't recall anything he's done."

Her head was still lowered. "Wasn't there something about a vintage car he borrowed?"

"Oh, yeah! Did he tell you about that? It was an Aston Martin DB-Five, the only car I ever had that he was interested in, because that was the James Bond model and he loves those movies to this day. It was my idea he borrow it for a few days and drive real high-performance machinery for a change, instead of that lifeless Detroit iron. It was my fault. I talked him into it. He had a lot of trouble using the stick shift, and then when he left it parked for five minutes at a curb in town, somebody sideswiped the car. He offered to pay for the body work, but it wasn't his fault. It must have bothered him a lot more than it did me, if he told you about it."

"Yes, he remembers," said Kristin. She returned the notebook to her purse. "Could I offer you some lunch right here? Omelette or *croque monsieur*, something simple." She opened one of the brushed-steel doors of the refrigerator and bent like a dancer to look inside. "There's also cold lamb. You're welcome to it, but I only like it with something garlicky, like hummus or *baba ghanoush*, and I can't get away with that at midday."

"Anything will be fine," said Roy from his stool. "I don't have much of an appetite." He was grateful to her. "I would have found a restaurant hard to take today."

He had previously seen Kristin only in the company of Sam, by comparison with whom she looked shorter than she actually was. The same thing could be said of Roy himself. She had now exchanged the jacket of her suit for a full-size, vertically striped butcher's apron, which emphasized her height. She was only a few inches shorter than he. It was remarkable to him that someone so keen on cooking could remain so slender.

# 5

After Roy put the crate of bottled water on the floor of the closet, pushing a space for it beside an outsize pair of custom-made lizard half-boots, he went to Sam's bedside. His friend was dangling a delicate-looking set of earphones from one thick finger. "These things weigh only a couple ounces. The sound is concert-hall quality."

"How are you feeling?"

"Perfect," said Sam. "There's no reason to keep me here another day. The doctors love to terrorize the layman. You know that."

He laid the earphones on top of the little Sony player to which they were attached. It was unusual for him not to have insisted that Roy verify the claims he had made as to their performance. The table on Sam's right was all but overflowing with heaped gadgetry: PalmPilot, cell phone, portable DVD player, miniature voice-operated recording device, remote for the television mounted high on the far wall.

Roy asked quietly, "Have you watched or listened to the news today?"

"Hell with it," said Sam. "If I have to stay in here, I don't care what happens in East Timor."

All the television and most of the radio stations were in the city where there had been a scary near-disaster on an airport runway, a big bank robbery, and the death by auto accident of a popular anchorman of the evening news. Francine's murder and the suicide of her ex-husband were so low on the gauge of public importance that Roy had as yet encountered no media reference, at least as long as he could bear to wait. There would not be a local newspaper until the following morning.

On the way to the hospital he had debated with himself whether to shock Sam with the whole story now or wait till his friend finally heard it from some impersonal source and was justifiably hurt, given the premium he put on loyalty.

Roy had made the painful decision. He began to pace about at the foot of the bed. "I've got to talk about this. Something terrible happened after I left here yesterday. I still can't believe it. I forget about it for a moment or two, then it comes back again. I'm sorry to burden you at this time, but——"

"That woman you were running around with got killed," said Sam without audible emotion. "I guess it was only a matter of time."

"What?"

"It's stupid to blame yourself. For what? *You* didn't kill her. You defended her. Your conscience should be clean."

"That's it? I should just shrug it off?" He reminded himself that Sam was still supposed to be a sick man. "I shouldn't be troubling you with this."

"It's no trouble," Sam said, but not in his familiar expansive way. "That's what friends are for. Kris and I are glad to help, but I can't see much is gained from going over and over the incident. Nothing can be changed now. What's done is done."

"Kristin told you."

"Well, we're married."

"I didn't mean she shouldn't have," Roy said quickly. But he lied. He had taken her into his confidence. He might not have used those terms, but he had expected her to understand them by implication. . . . But he was now lying to himself. She had had every reason to assume she was

serving as a substitute for Sam. She had even said as much, had she not?
"I was grateful to her for listening to my troubles."

"That's one of her specialties," said Sam, who seemed to be watching him for a reaction.

"Yes," said Roy. "I can understand that." The subject made him
uneasy. Though Kristin had given Sam the secondhand account of what
happened at The Hedges, she had apparently not told him the truth
about lunch, though there was nothing incriminating to conceal. She
had prepared an omelette *aux fines herbes* for each of them and a salad.
Roy ate very little of either. They both drank only mineral water. The
entire incident lasted half an hour, give or take.

"She can talk too," said Sam.

"I'm afraid all she got a chance to do today was listen to me whine.
You're right, I should try to get past it. I've decided to do something for
Francine's poor kids. They're orphans now. God knows what they've
been left by their parents, if anything. Holbrook was a loser at everything he tried, according to her." It took a moment of silence for him to
realize what he had told his best friend, of whom the same characteriza-
tion could well be made.

Sam moued. "Well, that's your business. I'll be glad to tell you what
Kris would have said if she *had* done the talking." His smile suggested an
undercurrent of anger. "She would have asked you not to lend me any
money." It was typical of Sam to have omitted the, to Roy, essential
word "more."

Had his friend not been bedridden, Roy might well have made that
point, because they had always been honest with each other. As it was,
he could say only, lamely, "Is that right?"

"That's a laugh, ain't it? I'm married to a banker, and I'm strapped."

"This whole thing must cost a fortune," Roy said guiltily, meaning
the complex of charges incurred by a hospital patient.

Sam dismissed that consideration. "Kris's insurance covers most of
it, I guess. That's not what I'm worried about."

It was obvious Sam was about to put the bite on him in the interests
of another bad business idea. Had it not been for Kristin's plea, Roy

probably could not have rejected an entreaty by his best friend, or rather, lacking in valor, have evaded it at least at this moment. Still, it was to his credit that he did not carry out his threat to put the blame on her.

He consulted his watch. For once Sam did not comment on the cheap timepiece. "I've got to go, kid. Catch you tomorrow. I'll call first to hear what you need, but I hope you're getting out."

When Sam saw his friend was serious about leaving, he sneered at him. "Shit, she *did* talk to you."

"What do you mean?" Though he knew full well.

"Kris told you not to lend me any money."

"You're out of your skull," said Roy. "You've got too much time on your hands here. Better try to get well soon." He winked, then headed for the door but had not quite reached the knob when he was halted by an anguished appeal in a contorted voice he had never heard before in all the years they had been best friends.

"Give me your word," Sam cried. "Are you fucking her?"

Reflecting later on this vile question, Roy could only assume that Sam's medication had mind-altering side effects. At the moment it was asked, however, he knew only an almost ungovernable rage, followed by so violent a fear of what he might do in such a state that he felt as though set afire. Incapable of speech, he stepped into the hallway and walked rapidly among white-coated people and stainless-steel con-veyances until he reached the parking lot, where distracted momentar-ily by a loss of memory as to which car he was using, he had to recover a sense of himself in space and time.

"Excuse me, but are you feeling okay?"

It was a woman, a pale-complexioned, redhaired young woman wearing a tan raincoat.

Roy was leaning against a blue Taurus of recent date. "I'm sorry," he said, straightening up. "Is this yours? I just felt a little shaky for a minute."

She pointed. "Maybe you ought to go over to the outpatient and have yourself checked out."

"I'll be all right. I've just lost a close friend, and it hits me from time to time." Lowering his head, he noticed white shoes and stockings below the raincoat.

"That's awful. I didn't know we lost anyone today. I'm very sorry."

"No, it was last night, and not in the hospital. . . . You work here, don't you?"

"In fact, I think I met you the other day. You're Mr. Grandy's friend?"

"Oh, sure," Roy said, his memory reviving to the degree that he could not only spot, in a rank of cars thirty yards away, the Jaguar E-Type he had parked there, but almost recall the nurse's name. "You're Miss Atkins."

He had never been attracted to redheads, but her smile was endearing. "It's Akins. But I'm impressed that you came so close on such slight acquaintance. You're living up to your reputation."

Roy was more incredulous than flattered. "How in the world do you know anything about me?"

"Your friend."

He had instantly forgotten about Sam. "Of course."

"He gives you the big buildup," Miss Akins said, twitching the retroussé nose Sam thought cute. "He has a high opinion of you."

"He'll say anything, Miss Akins. He's notorious for that. I wouldn't listen to him if I were you."

"It's Suzanne."

He felt considerably better than he had only a few moments earlier. "I hope you're not offended if I ask how is it that you are so much friendlier now than you were in Sam's room?" He was on safe ground, having never met a woman who did not enjoy most those questions which the typical man would think rude.

She produced an enumerated explanation. "I was on duty, one. Two, just now you looked like you were in trouble. Three, I didn't want to make your friend jealous. I'm serious. Patients are sensitive about the attention paid to them by nurses and, it goes without saying, doctors. Have you ever been a hospital patient, Mr., uh—"

"You don't know my name, do you?" Roy asked triumphantly.

"You own the fancy car store in town."

"I haven't been in a hospital bed since my mother delivered me. My name is Roy Courtright."

"Tell me, Roy, what do those cars cost? I can't see any posted prices through the show window, and that sign on the door says 'by appointment only.'" Her twinkling eyes reminded him of some star of the old movie musicals he had watched with Sam, but right now any association with his best friend had negative connotations for him.

"The phone number appears there as well." Roy spoke with a certain impatience, having heard this frivolous complaint more than once. "The prices vary greatly, according to the car, based on its rarity, condition, and so on."

"What's the 'so on'?"

He could not yet determine whether he was being baited. "Demand. There have to be people who want to buy it." He lifted his index finger. "See that XKE Jaguar over there? It's considered one of the most beautiful automobiles ever built. You don't see a lot of those on the streets nowadays, but quite a few were made during the years they were in production, and many were imported into the U.S.A. Because they aren't terribly rare, the demand for them is not great enough to bring really high figures. You could buy that one for about what your Ford Taurus cost you."

"That's not mine. *There's* my car. I bought it new last month."

"The BMW?" It was a black 530i, surely an extravagance on a nurse's income.

She laughed at him. "'Howinhell can she afford *that*?' You're right, I can't. I haven't got any clothes and I've stopped eating. I'll have it paid off in ten or fifteen years, if I live that long, but I broke up with somebody and needed to lift my spirits."

"A doctor who drove an S-class Mercedes?"

"Hey!" said she. "Close enough. You've been reading my diary."

Her vivacity seemed genuine enough, and Roy was reluctant to part with her and be alone with his troubles, which had continued to multiply. Now he could no longer even be friendly with Kristin.

"Suzanne, would you want to have some dinner with me? I'm aware we are hardly acquainted, but we do know each other's place of business."

"If I don't like the food I can throw a rock through your show window?"

"If you like."

"I'm not going to go in my uniform," she told him. "And I wasn't kidding about not owning any clothes. My one dress is at the cleaner's and I lately ripped my skirt and haven't fixed it. If jeans are okay, I'm your date. Could you pick me up at—"

Roy impulsively threw himself on her mercy. "Obviously you owe me nothing, but at the moment I don't want to be by myself." He took a breath; he had never made such an appeal before. "Could we get some take-out—not junk but decent stuff—and eat it at your house?" He closed his eyes and shook his head. "Please forgive me for being so pushy. This is awful." But he did not withdraw the request.

"I share a small apartment with two other women," Suzanne said. "All of them are home most evenings. You could come and eat with us if you just want company. Though I warn you, the others will be all over you. You're safe with me. I go out with men all the time, at least twice in the past seven months, both times with my dad. So I'm not desperate like the others. If you want to invite me to *your* house, you can trust me not to try to overpower you."

She was a remarkably good sport, but no woman not a blood relative would care to hear as much from a man.

He gave Suzanne the address, and she followed him in her car. He drove with moderation and did not play the childish tricks he pulled when Sam followed, no four-wheel drifts at the corners, no sudden flooring of the accelerator, nor downshiftings to slow the car, without applying the brakes, as he approached a stop sign or traffic signal. The last was most unnerving to Sam, who took his cue from the car ahead, braking only when its red lights came on.

"God," Suzanne exclaimed as she stepped from the BMW to the driveway and surveyed the façade of the building in which he lived. "Is this Courtright Palace?"

"I just have an apartment. I think it was probably originally the servants' quarters." He led the way, through the side door and up the staircase.

"Yeah, sure looks like where maids would live," said Suzanne on seeing the high ceilings and grand proportions of the sitting room.

"I hardly ever use it," Roy said truthfully. "Let's go to the kitchen—unless you'd rather stay here."

"If I did I'd be nervous that at any moment the cops would crash in and arrest me for trespassing."

This was an unpleasant reminder of the earlier part of his day. It was not easy to keep anguish at a distance.

"Is this furniture yours? And that tapestry?"

"Some of it is inherited stuff. The rest is on loan from Mrs. Swanson." Whom he identified for Suzanne.

"She lives in the rest of this castle?"

"In the sense that I'm her only tenant," Roy said. "I think she actually occupies fewer rooms than I've got. She's almost ninety, with a female companion in her late seventies."

"Bet you've got a rent-free deal for mowing the lawn and carrying out the garbage," said Suzanne, lightly punching him in his right biceps. She winced. "What have you got up your sleeve? A wooden arm? I think I busted a knuckle."

They were entering what might have served as a dining room had not Roy furnished it as a gymnasium instead, with floor mats, loose weights, a lifting bench, and a tall, elaborately branched contraption of black steel that in another context might pass as a work of kinetic art.

"Your chamber of horrors," Suzanne noted. "And that's your torture machine. What kind of hell have I gotten myself into?" She went to the Bowflex and touched one of its many extremities. "This is that exercise gadget I've seen advertised on TV. I didn't know anybody actually owned one." She turned back to him. "The mystery of your arm is solved. In my line you seldom encounter anyone so healthy."

"I've been working out since I was a kid. It just got to be a habit. I probably couldn't stop now if I wanted to." With women he often felt as if he should apologize for weight training. With men it was the other fellow who was put on the defensive, unless he too performed heavy lifting—but if he had a job in which it was a requirement, he felt superior to the recreational athlete.

She smiled. "I can find it in my heart to forgive you, but only if you give me a real drink and not some cat piss from the Juiceman."

"I'm not too much of a nutrition crank," said Roy, conducting her along the hallway and into the kitchen, "and no teetotaller."

"Now this," said Suzanne, who was still wearing her raincoat, "is the first room that makes sense. It's big enough without being outlandish. It's also the first that looks as if it could have been used by servants. I like that long table."

The kitchen was smaller than the Grandys', but had ample space for a big central table of oil-finished wood under a hanging lamp. Roy took away Suzanne's coat and returned to list for her the available libations. She chose Maker's Mark, neat. She had meant it when asking for a real drink. Roy had heard that the hard stuff was coming back into fashion, but had not till now met any female who displayed that taste. Perhaps he was on his way to fogeyhood. When he looked at Suzanne with age in mind, he estimated she was probably still in her twenties, younger than he by five or six years; Francine had been almost three years older. He was not attracted to youth as such. There was something about Suzanne, despite her wisecracking insolence, that seemed basically old-fashioned. Perhaps it was her white uniform; nursing was not a fashionable profession for the young women of today.

"What did you do with your hat?" he asked when they were seated at the table with their whiskey.

"I had already put it in the car when I spotted you looking like you were going to faint." She swallowed the remaining third of the liquid in her glass and narrowed her pale-lashed eyes. "You're not one of those who likes to be paddled by someone dressed as a nurse?"

"Sorry to disappoint you." His drink was diluted with water and ice. The cubes clinked unpleasantly against his teeth, so he rose and ditched them in the sink, then reinforced his glass from the bottle, which he afterward brought to the table. "I don't want to be accused of plying you with strong drink, so please help yourself."

"I trust you," said she. "Mostly because you do not call me Suzie."

He swirled the whiskey in his glass. "He who avoids diminutives, in a minimizing world, can be relied on absolutely." He could not remember whether that was a quotation.

She became solemn for a moment. "This is a professional question. You're not drunk, are you? That wasn't why you looked like that in the parking lot?"

"This is the first alcohol I've had all day. I'm feeling it already, on an empty stomach." He lowered the empty glass. "What would you like to eat? There are some places I can call for edible take-out. Say, the veal chop and wild mushrooms from the Maison or white truffle pasta from San Pietro."

"I've never eaten that kind of stuff," Suzanne said. "It would be lost on me. I probably couldn't hold it down." She poured herself a stiff portion of Maker's Mark. "I'm not playing poor little poor girl, believe me, but I can't afford expensive food, and while my friend of recent memory could, he spent it all on his wife and kids." She swallowed some bourbon. "As he should have, let it be said! I'm no enemy of society." She drank some more. "I'd settle for some crackers and cheese, though I guess what you would have is Brie."

He went to the fridge and peered within. "How about Gorgonzola?"

"Is that full of blue veins? I see enough of those when I take a shower."

"Cashew butter?"

"Is that like peanut butter only with cashews? Where in the hell would you get something like that?"

"My brother-in-law," said Roy. "Somebody gave it to him, and he thought I might eat it. I haven't. That was months ago. It might be rancid by now. I'm going to toss it one of these days."

She was at his side, looking into the almost vacant refrigerator, holding her glass. "You eat every meal out? That must run into money."

He pointed to the condiment-laden shelves in the door. "I live on whole-grain mustard, cornichons, and pepperoncini."

"You're rich, aren't you?" asked Suzanne. "According to your friend." She appeared to be more curious than resentful.

Of course this question had been directed to him before, in one way or another, usually unspoken. It always seemed rude, but he was aware that many of those to whom it was of interest, if sober, intended no insult.

"I've had a small business for seven years," he said after another sip from the glass he had returned to. "It's consistently been in the red, even when I pay myself no salary."

"That's what I mean," Suzanne said. "That's *all* I mean. If that's the case, then you've got other income. *I* couldn't go without a salary for seven days."

Sam's gratuitous contribution was festering under Roy's skin, but he would not reflect aloud on his friend, except to say, "He shouldn't go around giving people the wrong impression."

She shrugged. "I'm not criticizing you." She refreshed her glass from the bottle and sat down again. "Mr. Grandy himself seems to do well. He's got some wife."

Roy was prepared to take offense. Fortunately he did not, for before he could ask aggressively, "What do you mean?" Suzanne said, "What a classy lady. I guess I should hate somebody like her, but I have too much awe for real quality."

Roy was now drunk enough so that he had to be careful of his speech, especially the pronunciation of names with sibilants. "I'm glad to hear you say that, because Kristin's father started out as a driver for a trucking company, and her mother was a waitress at the lunch counter across the street."

"You've just stripped me of every excuse for being a clod," Suzanne said with mock chagrin. "Except I did get moved around a lot as a kid. My dad's a career army officer, and my mother got a B.A. and once published a children's book."

"Positively lace-curtain," said Roy. "I should go on to say that by the time Kristin grew up, though, her father had his own trucking business. He and her mother drove twin white Cadillacs."

"Oh." She inspected his face, eye by eye. "You're making that up."

"Of course not."

She displayed a triumphant if slightly blurry grin. "My mother never published a book. She used to talk about writing one about army kids, the way they see the world." She emptied what was left in the glass, then swallowed some air, making a deliberate process of it, raising her eyebrows when it was over. Roy realized they were cosmetically darkened, else they would probably have been pale as the lashes she forgot to color. The freckles were subdued on her cheeks, perhaps by makeup, but more prominent across her small nose. He liked her more and more, but if anything, desired her less.

"If I don't get out of here now, I'll be in no condition to drive." Yet she made no move to go, sitting there at his table in her white nylon outfit.

"It's already too late for that," said Roy. "What you need is food."

"I have to go to the toilet." She stood up, more staunchly than he had expected.

"First door on the right." He curved his finger to suggest the turn. As soon as she was gone he felt worse than he would have if he had faced the evening alone. He wished he had never imposed himself upon her.

When Suzanne returned, he apologized.

"For what? I'm having a great time."

"You're being ironic."

"Really, I'm not. I might be exaggerating a little. . . . But I wouldn't want to be anyplace else." She took his hand. "I just wish I could help."

He related the salient events of the last twenty-four hours, omitting only Sam's unprecedented turning on him, which, though not involving loss of life, had left a disabling wound.

When he had finished, Suzanne took his hand again. "Come on, Roy. At least I can hold you." She led him along the hall to the right bedroom, though she had never been here before and there was a choice.

The answering machine was blinking redly. He disconnected it and the telephone before taking off his clothes. She was already in bed when he turned. Of her body he saw only her very white shoulders, and that was just as well, because he did not want her. Her flesh was warmer than expected when he lay down and she rolled against him. Now that he was here, he wanted to hold and not be held.

. . . He understood that he had fallen asleep only when he awoke at three-thirty. The bedside lamps were still burning and Suzanne was asleep in his arms. Had they done anything? It was unlikely. He had never been so drunk as to lose that sort of memory. He visited and returned from the bathroom without waking her. He turned off the lamps and slept till the digital clock on the dresser registered, in big red numerals, seven-thirty A.M.

The place beside him was empty and not even warm. He could not find her anywhere throughout the apartment. Finally he penetrated far enough into the kitchen to see the note, held down and obscured by its saucepan anchor:

Roy—

Had to get to work. Thanks for the drinks. I'm sorry I disappointed you by not wanting anything to eat. We live in different worlds. I do hope your fortunes take a turn for the better. You are a good guy.

S.

PS: Unless you tell me it's okay, I won't say anything to your friend.

Roy discovered he was naked except for slip-on sandals and repaired to the bathroom lest it be one of the days the cleaning woman was due; he could never remember which. But she had standing orders, when arriving early, not to open any door firmly closed.

After dressing, he reconnected the answering machine, which

resumed its frenetic blinking, and the telephone, which immediately rang. He answered and heard the voice of his lawyer, Seymour Alt.

"I'm due in court and can't enjoy a leisurely conversation. I won't ask where you've been, but I have been trying to reach you for twelve hours. Just as I advised when you came up with the idea, Francine Holbrook's survivors, as well as those of her late husband, not only rejected your offer to give financial assistance to her children, but are about to sue you for provoking the incident which led to the deaths of the parents. Also, the police are looking for you."

Roy found the first matter so outrageous that he postponed facing it until he had disposed of the lesser problem. "The cops know where I live. I've been here all night. What do they want? To arrest me for murder?"

Alt, however, preferred the former. "I don't know yet if there'll be two suits. Either way, it could be for big money."

"What does that mean?"

"We should probably begin to think about dealing. We don't have to let on to them—as if they wouldn't know! Francine's brother and sister-in-law are represented by Ashford, Fine & Corrigan. There's nobody better."

While being cockily aggressive with adversaries and obsequious with anyone addressed as Your Honor, Alt habitually employed a professional pessimism with clients, but Roy had never heard him this defeatist.

"It stinks, Sy."

"I got to go, Roy. We can talk divine injustice on Sunday morning. I hope you're still on."

"I don't want to look at a golf club at the moment."

"Make your mind up by tomorrow. I need to fill out the foursome."

Roy listened to the messages on his machine. The first was from Chief of Police Albrecht, asking him to get in touch. The next had been left by a Midwestern scout of his who had located in an Indiana barn a rusted but restorable example of the classic Cord 810 of 1937.

The final message was registered as of 7:22 the evening before, which signified that it had long been there when he went to bed with Suzanne. He felt an odd initial thrill when he heard the voice, but that was gone as soon as it had come.

"Roy, Kristin. Sam has had another scare. I'm in the car now, en route to the hospital. I'll try your cell phone again. The time is"—she paused to check and then came back to report it. She ended the call. Her voice was cool as ever and did not waste a word.

It was now half a day later, and his best friend could well be dead. They had last parted with jealous rage on Sam's side and bitter disgust on his own. That might have been enough to kill one of them.

# 6

Roy immediately tried to reach Kristin at the bank, but whomever it was he spoke to, perhaps for reasons of security, had no information on Sam's condition and declined to say where Kristin might be found. Calling the Grandy house, he was obliged to speak with the Central American cleaning woman, whose distraught replies were incomprehensible to him. Maria was partial to Sam, the most generous of employers.

Roy had no confidence that the urgent requests he left at both places for Kristin to contact him would ever reach her, but he did not know what else to do at the moment. Showing up at the hospital without first clearing the way might only damage Sam further, if indeed his friend had survived the night.

He forgetfully phoned Mrs. Forsythe, who was not due till noon, and was greeted by his own recorded voice. He punched in the code by which he could listen to the incoming calls that had accumulated on the office machine. Most favored clients had his unlisted home number. All others used either the business line or e-mail. Roy usually let Mrs. Forsythe deal with the latter; she was the one whose fingers operated the keyboard. The texts, responses to his ads on Websites and in classic-car magazines, were supplied by him, but he disliked submitting himself in person to the Internet, which had not existed at the time his youngest cars had been made.

He heard nothing of interest, and two messages had negative connotations. He was insulted by an offer of $10,000 on the '63 E-Type Jag, fully restored but needing new paint, for which he was asking a modest twenty-five large; and an overly intimate-sounding vocal note from a woman he scarcely knew would have embarrassed him had it been collected by Mrs. F.

Though not a true man of action, as he had discovered in amateur sports-car racing a decade earlier, unwilling as he was to go quite as far as it took to finish before those who would put their life on the line for a minor trophy, Roy found motion a more useful state in which to deal with his feelings than any pursued through a static means. Meditation, contemplation of his navel or the wall, made him only more anxious.

The reference to the Jaguar XKE reminded him that unless it had been stolen it was parked outside, where uncharacteristically he had left it the evening before. The odd experience with Suzanne Akins now seemed like one of those inconclusive dreams that can barely be remembered a moment after awakening. He went down to the car, which was unharmed by a dry night though somewhat dusty from the driveway, started the throaty engine, and accelerated, recklessly scattering gravel, out onto the road, heading away from town. He had not really driven at speed, 100 mph or better, time out of mind. The thruway, with its long level straightaways, ideal for fast driving to the automotively naïve, was boring; also it was heavily policed, radared and lasered. The twisting back roads could be hazardous, not so much for the skilled driver as for the cyclists and runners who frequented them in strength; but once behind the wheel, with the powerful engine under his control, Roy converted his initial depression into defiance, though against whom he could not have said. Against *what* was a better question, the answer to which would have been: a sequence of negation, bad to worse. Sam, Francine, Sam again and still, the only affirmative having been the newly established friendship with Kristin, which soon enough was denied him.

He drove deep into a corner, braking, then downshifting at the precise point that enabled the car to accelerate out, overcoming centrifugal force, without loss of rpms. He still had the touch. At appropriate points he glanced at the tach and not the speedometer. How fast he drove was irrelevant to the joy of driving well.

The police car announced its presence too soon, sounding its siren when still far behind him. On a road like this, in an E-Type, he could put a second turn between himself and even a souped-up Crown Victoria before the cop could maintain adhesion through the first. And so he did, then just before a sweeping right-hand bend saw a blacktop lane on the left, probably a long private driveway to a house concealed from the main road by the grove of thick evergreens an eighth of a mile away.

Roy braked hard and executed a four-wheel drift, penetrating the driveway a good seventy yards, and stopped before the police vehicle wailed past on the road, probably without seeing him, though he could not be sure and therefore reversed, drove back to the road, and turned in the direction from which he had come. As soon as an intersecting route was available, he took it, lest the cop too soon suspect what had happened and return flat-out.

Circuitously, and at a moderate speed, Roy reached town and his place of business, the hillside building at the rear of which, on the lower level, was a garage. The doors were open now, and he drove the car inside.

Diego and Paul, the mechanics who enjoyed a free lease from him in exchange for which they gave precedence to the servicing of the cars in his inventory, were never seen except at the garage, where they were at work before he ever arrived and often stayed after he left. The guys were masters of their craft. As he had boasted to Sam, he could have brought these wizards a box full of assorted bolts, gaskets, and cotter pins and come back in the afternoon to find an assembled engine that when started would run like the pouring of cream from a pitcher.

To which Sam's usual response had to do with their being gay. He could not have known that for sure, as Roy himself did not. There could be no doubt they were exotic of origin. Diego was not simply Hispanic but a genuine native of Barcelona, whose English had British overtones due to his having served an apprenticeship in the United Kingdom; Paul spoke with an accent acquired during his boyhood in central Europe as the son of a German woman married to a black sergeant in the U.S. Army.

The guys were, of course, at work when he pulled the Jaguar in. Not only were they extraordinarily skilled with internal-combustion engines, they were fanatics about cleanliness and order, or anyway, Paul was and Diego followed his lead. Never could a drop of oil, a smear of grease, or even the stains of earlier drops and smears be found on the concrete floor. All elements of their equipment, from the big hydraulic lift to the smallest gauge of hexagonal wrench, glistened as if new. The men themselves wore powder-blue coveralls, always as pristine as the floor, and at the neck a navy-and-white kerchief, which Roy had once called an ascot but was corrected by Diego, a stickler for precise nomenclature.

"Cravat," said he. "Ascot is the racecourse. For hosses."

Paul was nearer at hand this morning. "I don't like what I hear," said he, as Roy emerged from the E-Type. "Ve'll do a tune-up."

"No need for that," said Roy. "It drives beautifully. But the cops may be on my trail, so if they show up, make it look like you've been working on it for some time."

Paul winked. He was a strikingly handsome man, the color of milked coffee. "Ach, you been a bad boy."

Diego lowered the hand tool he had been using at a workbench and walked over to them, a stocky man in contrast to his tall and slender partner. The Jag's engine was still running. Diego put one ear as low to the bonnet as he could without making contact. He straightened up to say, "I don't like what I hyeah."

"Have it your own way," said Roy. "All I want is for the cops to think it's been here all morning—if they show up at all."

He left the guys and got the Jeep, the only vehicle he normally would leave all night in the parking lot and, without visiting his street-level office, drove to the Municipal Building. Eluding the police car had rehabilitated his morale. For a short but effective time he had not been the passive recipient of assaults on his moral essence. For a change *he* had chosen the rhythm of events.

Chief Albrecht's manner was different from what it had been the day before. He begged Roy's pardon for asking him to repeat the account of the incident at The Hedges and dictate it this time as a formal statement. Albrecht also scoffingly disclosed that he had heard both bereaved families intended to sue. "In my position I can't take sides, Mr. Courtright, but as I'm sure your attorney already informed you, the whole bunch are scumbags."

After he had finished giving the statement, Roy phoned Sy Alt and was surprised to be put directly through to the lawyer.

"That's right," Alt told him. "Harrison Wilkie—that's Francine's brother in case you don't know—he's a registered sex offender. He likes to flash his little wilkie at Catholic schoolgirls, and I tell you it's little. The cops took reenactment photos; you can hardly see it in his hand." Alt cleared his throat. "The late Martin Holbrook was charged with embezzlement eight or nine years back. It was settled out of court when he agreed never to work again as an investment counselor. I guess you know Francine had a shoplifting record."

"I did not," said Roy. "But then I never knew her well."

"You ought to get acquainted with the women you *shtup*," Alt said over his raspy chuckle. "Second thought, better you don't. Francine was also arrested for A 'n' B in ninety-four. She threw chilled soup on another woman in a restaurant."

"She didn't deserve to get beaten to death."

"Well, *I* never touched her," said Alt, rasping again. "I can't wait for those self-satisfied shits at Ashford, Fine & Corrigan to return my call. They didn't do their homework, accepting clients like these. You can pretty much forget about the suit, Roy. Are you on for Sunday?"

"No," Roy told him. "I'm not much of a golfer."

"Which is why I always welcome you in a foursome," said Alt. "You're a lousy player on the course but the best-looking at brunch. You do have a way of attracting the ladies. Wish that wife of mine wasn't too old for you. I'll be in touch."

"Yeah, with a big bill." But Alt had already hung up. Roy was depressed again after speaking with the lawyer. He got no satisfaction from knowing about the delinquencies of Francine and her clan. He sincerely hoped he would be allowed to do something for her orphaned children before they joined adult humanity with the failings for which it is notorious.

He was en route to the office he had not visited for two days when his cell phone rang. Recognizing Kristin's voice, he pulled into an empty parking space in front of one of the Main Street antique shops that did little weekday business.

Her tone was demanding. "Is this really you? I've been trying all your numbers for hours."

Roy asked docilely about Sam.

Her voice softened. "This second episode turned out not to be that dire."

"Do the doctors know what they're doing?"

"I'm not qualified to judge," Kristin said with her usual coolness. "But if *they* don't know, who would?"

According to Sam, his cardiologist was, like his electronic gear, top of the line, which might only mean expensive, but neither did Roy have medical credentials. "I tried to reach you at the bank this morning and also talked to Maria. I hadn't gotten your message till then." He felt she might despise him for supplying too much excuse. Anyway, what he had been doing was his own business. He had had no reason to suspect Sam would have a setback; besides, it had not turned out to be that serious. He wasn't married to Sam or to Sam's wife.

"I'm not checking up on you," Kristin said, as if she had heard and been chastened by his internal reflections. "I was worried you'd be offended by not hearing from me sooner."

"Oh."

"Well, I know you'll want to see Sam. Our trails will probably cross over there." She was obviously about to hang up. "I'll see—"

Roy spoke quickly. "I'd like to talk with you first, if you could spare a minute."

"Of course."

"I don't mean on the phone."

"Gee . . ." Her reluctance disappointed him. "As you can understand, I haven't put in a full day at the bank for some time now, and I've got a staggering backlog."

"All right," Roy said. "I will say it here and now, because the air has to be cleared. Last time I saw Sam he accused me of having an affair with you. I just walked out. That was too much for me."

He had never heard her laugh in this fashion, if in fact he had ever heard her properly laugh at all. Over the phone it sounded like splashing water. Finally she said, "That was his joke. You know how he is, you of all people."

"I never heard him joke about something like that, even when he was well."

"Then it's the medication. But I assure you he was joking. He told me about it—and thinks you leaving in a huff was part of the joke. You and he have been kidding each other like that since you were boys, haven't you? Trading fake insults?"

No, not that kind, never anything that was really personal, and Roy could not remember a girl or woman for whom they had ever competed. To begin with, their respective tastes in females were so different. Sam of course derided Roy's so-called lechery, but that was another matter altogether from accusing his best friend of an illicit connection with his wife. Such a charge had to do not with sex but with betrayal, with dishonor, with a shame that Roy would have found unbearable. . . . For all that, he could admit, and in fact was eager to do so, that any wife, and especially one as sensitive as Kristin, would know her husband better, certainly in this area, than any male friend of however many years.

"You may be right."

"I know I am, Roy," Kristin said. "And after all, it reflected on me, too."

For a moment he did not understand this comment, but to maintain his pride he murmured an assent.

Kristin was proving she also knew *him*. "I mean, he would also have been accusing me."

"Oh, sure," Roy said hastily. "He wouldn't have given you a passive role. I should have recognized the joke from that. I'm not myself these days. Self-pity may not be a good excuse, but it's the only one I can find."

Her voice suddenly became very tender, even in this means of transmission. "It's good enough for me."

He was moved by the statement, though it might represent no more than common courtesy. It was just as well they were speaking by telephone, so that she could not see the flush he felt heat his face.

"Sam can still have visitors?"

"Of course. He's expecting you."

"What should I bring?"

"Nothing. He's got too much stuff there already. The staff is complaining."

"Something I noticed but never got around to mentioning: There aren't any flowers in the room. Men don't usually send them to other men, but I was wondering—"

"He's allergic to flowers," said Sam's wife. "Didn't you know that? All of those at home are silk or paper or something."

Roy sighed. "Well, there you are. After twenty years I seem to be barely acquainted with the guy."

"He sneezes if he sees a picture of a rose," said Kristin. "Any kind of flower makes him tear up as if his heart is breaking."

Roy remembered Sam's copious tears at Roy's father's funeral. Fond as he had been of the man, Sam had perhaps wept overmuch, more even than Robin. Given the affection between them, Sam would have been a more appropriate son for Victor Courtright than Roy, who preferred the mother who had deserted him at a tender age. He always believed her more foolish than wicked. She was also beautiful.

"I've seen him cry at funerals," Roy told Kristin. "It never occurred to me it might be the flowers."

"I've got to go do some work, Roy."

"Oh, sure." He was about to make some polite closing comment when she briskly hung up. And why not? It was the rational thing to do. In these few short days he had begun to see, beyond the superficial attributes, what made her so attractive to Sam, though in fact that had never been in question. He still could not understand the reverse, though he might be getting closer. Sam needed taking care of. Could it be as simple as that? Many people had such a need. Lately he could include himself in their company, but that had not always been true. Normally he was self-reliant. Now that he was temporarily otherwise, Kristin seemed to like him as earlier she had apparently not. Did she simply have a preference for losers? . . . He shocked himself with this reflection. He had never before thought of his best friend with such stark candor . . . though now that he did, it was, if unfortunate, no surprise. Perhaps it had always existed as an assumption, too established to require conscious legitimizing.

"Hi there!" The window on the passenger's side was open, and a winsome young woman's smiling face was framed in it. She looked vaguely familiar to him, but he had no clue as to her name.

"Hi," said he. "It's *good* to see you." The emphasis was instinctive in such a situation, when he cautiously withheld any more enthusiastic greeting. She might after all be poised to ask of him something he could not gracefully provide, in this period that had suddenly become so disorderly.

He was relieved by her producing a slotted can into which he could stuff a bill for whatever cause. Apparently they had not previously met, and she was asking nothing else of him. But he had not folded the money carefully, and it went only halfway in before clogging the narrow aperture.

The young woman took over, leaning in, her unbrassiered breasts plumped and defined by the lower edge of the window frame. She plucked the money out and, in refolding it, saw the denomination.

"Fifty bucks? My God. *Thank* you. You must love animals." She had short glossy black hair, and her eyes looked somewhat Asiatic.

"I do, in fact. I also like you."

She quickly pushed the bill into the can, as if he might change his mind. But her smile was wider. "You don't know me."

"If I knew you better, I might find you obnoxious."

This statement made her laugh. "That's a new one."

Roy opened the glove compartment and took out a business card. He presented it to her.

She straightened up and read, "Incomparable Cars. You're Roy Courtright?"

He put the Jeep in drive. "Give me a call if you want to buy a pre-owned Rolls-Royce." He turned the steering wheel and took his foot from the brake. "Or just want to take a free test drive in one. Check me out with the Better Business Bureau."

In the rearview mirror he could see her staring at him as he drove away. This whole thing had been involuntary, a kind of reflex triggered by the appearance of a woman who was attractive to him. He felt somewhat foolish now, only a moment later. She was young enough to be a college student. As a rule he could not endure college girls, who made him feel old and who had no history, no current or ex-husbands by contrast to whom he seemed glamorous.

While he waited for the green light at the last traffic signal on Main, a police car going the other way crossed the intersection and abruptly stopped parallel with him.

The officer in its open window was Howie. "Mr. Courtright," he called over, "are you missing a sports car from your place this morning?"

"Nope. I just came from there."

"I was chasing one out Meadowbrook a while ago," Howie said. "I lost him. He was driving like he stole it." Traffic was backed up behind the cruiser, blocking the intersection in all directions. The cars in the rear, not able to identify the police vehicle, were leaning on their horns. "I thought it might be one of yours."

"Maybe it was one I sold somebody in the past." Had this been a real possibility, Roy would never have made a suggestion so disloyal to a client. "But not all sports cars are vintage models. Check with

Porsche-Audi, or maybe it was a Miata from Logan Mazda, in Crawford."

"Whatever." Apparently Howie had not even recognized the marque. There were now probably two dozen cars in the bottleneck he was creating with the easy arrogance of a policeman. But at last he acknowledged the horns, winking at Roy. "Got to calm down these irate citizens," he said. "Seeya, Mr. Courtright." He put the car in motion, but as slowly as possible, freeing the blocked vehicles only to begin a crawl.

Roy's earlier pleasure in eluding the pursuit was compromised now that he put a face on the cop who chased him. Howie might not drive that well at speed and could have been killed taking one of those corners on Meadowbrook. Outrunning the police was adolescent behavior. Nevertheless, had he not been aware that it would be reported immediately to Kristin, he might have boasted of the escapade to Sam, whose disapproval of Roy's driving enhanced the pleasure his best friend derived from it, as did similar moralizing about his sex life: a wimp sitting in judgment on virility. For an instant it occurred to him, awfully, that he despised Sam. He thrust the thought away as quickly as it had come. If he had contempt for his friend, then why want to impress him?

They had never been competitors. When they were teenagers Sam would gorge on candy bars and potato chips while watching Roy work out for an hour with a barbell. For his own part, Roy had never been envious of the gadgets Sam was addicted to even as a lad, the vest-pocket voice-activated tape recorders, the pen-sized Mace canister, the radio-sunglasses, or for that matter the girls for whom in those days Sam seemed the greater attraction. Nowadays both of them found common amusement in remembering Roy's early lack of success with females. Sam's first score was at least a year and a half before his own, not to mention that when Roy's opportunity arrived at last, he failed to give an adequate performance. He was so embarrassed he never dated the girl again, and it was another year before he even tried to have intercourse, except with prostitutes, who are professionally indifferent to a client's humiliation, unless of course they have been paid to provide it.

Sam heard from a girlfriend that Roy was thought to be gay. "I told her you went to that Korean massage parlor all the time. But you know how women are." But Roy had not so known, in that era. Nor, though in fact he did frequent them, did he know anything nonphysical about Asian masseuses, for they either did not speak English or were averse to speaking with him and communicated exclusively by hand signals.

Sam feared that paying for it was an aphrodisiac to Roy, but such proved not to be the case. "I know sex is supposed to be largely mental, but with me the physical can control the mind."

Sam asked, "They say a stiff prick doesn't have a conscience. Is that what you mean?"

Roy would not go so far, but he went on to reverse his initially poor reputation among the ladies, whose next complaint was of his promiscuity. "You really can't take seriously what women say to one another," he told Sam. "What matters is what they do."

"With men."

"With anybody. I don't mean just sexually."

"You can say that about everyone."

Impulsively Roy asked, "But does what *men* do really matter that much?"

"Now you *are* talking about sex, I hope. Otherwise it doesn't make any sense."

"You're right," Roy had said. "I guess I wasn't thinking." With your best friend you could say stuff that with anyone else, especially girls, would only earn you scorn. Old Sam had been listening good-humoredly to a lot of crap from him in twenty years. He had to love the guy.

# 7

Roy returned the Grand Cherokee to the lot behind the garage and went inside to reclaim the E-Type from the guys, but they had already elevated it on the lift and taken away the entire exhaust system: mufflers, tailpipe, and chrome-plated resonators. The late model Bentley that had previously occupied the lift had been lowered and temporarily abandoned, demonstrating the impracticality of the guys, for this car belonged to an independent client of theirs who paid them a king's ransom for routine servicing, whereas they would get no fee from Roy for labor. He might, however, be saddled with the cost of parts, which for marques long out of production could be hefty. This was annoying, for, as he had assured them, the car's performance on his run from Officer Howie had been faultless.

But he knew better than to protest while a project was underway, for Diego could turn sullen and Paul waspish, and how often in contemporary life did one get the opportunity to complain about anyone's taking too many pains with anything?

He went up via the interior stairway to the showroom, which was level with the sidewalk and street beyond the big front windows—a pair of which were hinged and could be swung open for the passage of classic automobiles to and from the floor. The office occupied a shallow space at the rear, separated from the glistening wares by a thin partition that offered little privacy of conversation, but then Roy's was not a used-auto business in which salesmen connived with a manager to fleece the customers. Roy had nobody at the office with whom to conspire against a client—after working for him for several years, Mrs. Forsythe was still unable to distinguish one car from another.

It was his idea to address her as Mrs. Forsythe and hers to call him Roy, and in both cases the reason was, presumably, the difference in their ages, which took precedence over the orthodox employer–employee protocol. On the other hand, she herself preferred the old-fashioned, perhaps patronizing "secretary" to the "assistant" standard in contemporary use.

A plump-cheeked, purse-lipped woman in her early fifties, Mrs. F. was either a widow or a divorcée. She had never specified which, and Roy did not ask. She had herself filled out all the forms required by the various governmental agencies that oppressed the small-businessman, to do which was why Roy had hired her. He signed everything without carefully reading the details; he swore by Mrs. Forsythe. Of her personal life he knew only her home phone number and that she had a teenaged daughter who looked reasonably pretty in the desktop photograph. The girl had never appeared at the office during the years her mother worked for Roy, no doubt because of his reputation for lechery, of which Mrs. F. would have been aware, (owing to the phone calls from women who obviously had no interest in classic cars), but to which she never alluded, denying him an opportunity to aver that he offered no threat to Juliette for a good five years, by which time he hoped to have settled down at last.

As he reminded himself occasionally, Roy really did want to find a good woman with whom he would fall in love, get married, and even have children. That these impeccable intentions had remained thus far in the abstract, as opposed to a promiscuity all too concrete, was an obsession of his sister's, to which Roy's answer was to ask whether Robin would prefer him not even to dream of an alternative to his stupid, irresponsible dead-end existence? That would stop her for a while. It was thoroughly hypocritical. Roy enjoyed his life. He loved the company of women even when they were being unpleasant to him. He had never had a close male friend other than Sam.

Before going to his desk, where he anyhow rarely stayed long, he tarried among the array of cars now on the floor. They were his babies, though of course he would not have used the term even with collectors, for whom it was not passionate enough for such works of art, such expressions of virtue in the original sense of strength, courage, virility; such spiritualizing of the material, poetry in metal, or, in the case of the canary-yellow Lotus Elite, fiberglass.

There was the handsome Alvis, admired by Kristin, and the oyster-white MGA fixed-head coupé that he had driven to the fateful episode at The Hedges, which already seemed remote though, if anything, more terrible. Nearer the show windows was a red Porsche Speedster; a '52 Rolls-Royce Silver Wraith; a green Mercedes roadster, in mint condition but with an automatic transmission, power brakes, and removable hardtop, vulgarities to the cognoscenti of high-performance cars; and the current leader of his inventory, a silver Lamborghini Espada, twelve cylinders, six Weber carburetors, a 200-mph performer, with blue leather interior and fewer than 40,000 miles on its odometer, for which he was asking about a dollar per mile. The others were priced at even less. Selling vintage cars, at least in his fashion, was not a route to riches. Manufacturing shipping containers, in his father's way, had produced extraordinary profits without which Roy would not have been able to indulge himself in a business his father had considered a joke.

For the first few weeks he had been open on Peregrine Street, a block off Main, the showroom was as accessible to the public as a Chevy dealership; and especially on weekends, when the village was thronged with antiquers, the collection had attracted many visitors. Roy had no objection to being included in the list of suggested Things to Do that accompanied the map for tourists distributed by the local chamber of commerce, offering, as in effect he did, a little free museum. But the policy proved unfortunate. Children pawed the coachwork, and adults climbed into the leather interiors and tried the horns and headlamps. After Roy posted PLEASE DO NOT TOUCH signs, not only at the entrance but also on a standard beside each automobile, a mother bitched at him for shooing away an offspring of hers who dripped corrosive cola on the finish of a recently detailed Maserati 3500GT, and an elephantine man lowered his enormous lardass onto the wing, i.e., fender, of a perfectly restored little MG-TC, imperiling its suspension. Politely asking him to rise provoked the threat of a lawsuit.

Subsequently he locked the door against the general public, but could do nothing to expunge his listing from the tourist brochure unless he wanted to pay for a new edition thereof, and visibly irritated persons occasionally slapped the glass of the show windows in indignant response to the posted notice, BY APPOINTMENT ONLY.

Roy gathered the mail that had been pushed through the front-door slot to scatter and slide across a floor as highly polished as the cars. Not many potential buyers nowadays submitted bids by this means, so the postman usually delivered only bills. Those today included a statement from a company that insured vintage cars; the rates having gone up again, it was a whopper.

He deposited all the envelopes on Mrs. Forsythe's desktop, which was clean except for the computer and telephone, and took the periodicals to his own, which was littered, though with nothing current. In the big newspaper, he turned first to the classified advertisements for imported and sports cars, where now and again you might find something of interest, though not today. Then he took up the local paper. The report of Francine's murder and her ex-husband's suicide was featured prominently. Sy Alt, though seemingly distracted by more demanding cases, had done a good job in keeping Roy's name out of the story.

When he was finished with the papers and magazines, Roy took them to the corner table, where Mrs. Forsythe still managed to keep the periodicals on hand neatly shingled, despite the now-limited room because of the espresso machine. The moss-green blanket in which he had wrapped the Stecchino for transport was in a neat fold atop a filing cabinet. He had better return it before Mrs. F. complained.

He returned to his desk and, biting his lip, dialed Sam Grandy's cell phone number.

"It's not too early?"

"I wake up at dawn in this place."

"Sorry the way I left there yesterday."

"*I'm* the one who should apologize. It hit me only after you left that something was really wrong, but I didn't actually get it till Kris kicked my ass. I thought you knew I was kidding, I swear."

There was still something wrong here, but Roy had no stomach for pursuing the matter. "How in hell are you today?"

"I guess this is hard to believe, but I feel fine. I still think these greedy doctor bastards exaggerate the hell out of the slightest gas pains—how else would they stay rich? . . . So where'd you go last night with Suzie Akins?"

Roy had not asked her to keep it from Sam; she had volunteered to do so. Why do women lie about their intentions? "You know about that?"

"I can see the parking lot from my window if I get up to use the toilet. I wouldn't piss in a bedpan if I was dying. It was still light enough to see you two talking down there. The rest is just an informed guess."

"We had a drink," Roy told him, relieved to find that Suzanne had kept her word. "That was all." But now he worried that Sam might, in some japery with her, suggest that Roy had gone into detail about their "date."

Sam proceeded to justify the fear. "I'll wait till I hear her version."

"I'll be over later." Roy hung up and immediately called the hospital number.

It was not easy to reach Nurse Akins when she was on duty. He had to do some lying.

"Who's this?" she asked when found. "I don't have a brother, so he can't have gotten hurt." She was scarcely mollified when she heard Roy's explanation. "You bothered me for *that?*"

"I just didn't want you to be embarrassed."

"You mean *you*, Roy. I think you always mean yourself."

Francine said something of the sort the last time he ever heard her speak, but she had been going to bed with him for months.

In the big bottom drawer of Mrs. Forsythe's desk he found a copy of the telephone directory and turned to the yellow-page list of florists. He dialed the number of a shop two villages away and asked the woman who answered to send flowers in memory of Francine Holbrook to the appropriate funeral home—and quickly, for according to the newspaper, the services were to be held before noon this very morning.

"Signed—?" asked the woman on the phone.

"Oh . . . I guess, 'A Friend.'" He gave her his real name, phone, and credit-card number.

Mrs. Forsythe appeared on the stroke of noon, as always. She carried a black purse large enough to hold the made-at-home sandwich she would eat at her desk and the plastic mug in which a teabag would be steeped.

"How do you feel today, Roy?" Below her curly brown-rinsed hair was the kind of sensible face that he had implicitly trusted on first seeing it. He had never since had reason to believe otherwise. Therefore he tended to humor her.

"I'm feeling better, Mrs. F., thank you. Touch of food poisoning, probably."

She unloaded her bag and took the mug into the little lavatory at the far end of the office, where she kept an electric hotpot in which to heat water for her tea.

When she emerged Roy said, "When I remember to bring coffee for it, I'll make you some espresso." He pointed toward the Stecchino.

Mrs. Forsythe's smile sometimes seemed tinged with mockery, though that could have been his imagination. "Thank you," said she, "but plain old Lipton's good enough for me." After quickly opening and scanning the bills that had come by envelope and assembling the faxes that had arrived overnight, she returned to the washroom and brought back the steaming mug with its little hanging tag. She sat down before the monitor, her now unwrapped sandwich to the left of the keyboard and the steeping tea to the right.

She looked over at Roy, who had retained and was now studying the latest issue of *Thoroughbred and Classic Cars*, a glossy British monthly that provided a wealth of useful information in his area of professional interest, including prices being asked in the U.K. for the marques in which he traded. Such research was part of his job, but he suspected Mrs. F. believed he did no work at all.

"Did you want to ask me something?"

"I went to see poor Mrs. Holbrook last night. She looked beautiful."

He was not prepared for this. "Did you know her?"

"Unfortunately, I never saw her when she was alive." Mrs. Forsythe moued as if holding back tears. "I heard her on the phone a lot." She squinted and said, with the hint of a sob, "She had such a sweet voice."

Roy produced the kind of lie that is informed by sincerity of intention. "She was a sweet person."

"What time is the funeral?"

This was pushing it. "I'm not going," he said, with a putting-the-foot-down edge of voice. "I've sent flowers." He nodded, signifying the messages that had accumulated. "See if a decent offer has come in for the E-Type Jaguar. Remember, that's also called XKE."

"You've told me that many times," Mrs. F. said reprovingly and turned back to her sandwich, mug, and keyboard.

But she could forget it as often. Ignorance, and perhaps even dislike, of cars was the source of the only weakness in her work. Mrs. Forsythe could have strolled past a 300SL without noticing that its gullwing doors were raised.

Roy found the special hand mop for the purpose, took it into the showroom, and whisked the dust off the cars, the high-sheen finishes of which were magnets for it, even on such a lightly traveled side street as this. He would do the same several times before the day was over.

When he returned to the office, Mrs. F. smiled at him. "You keep those things cleaner than I do my house."

"That's because I'm trying to sell them." He should not have had to point that out.

Beaming, she waggled a stubby forefinger. "Bet you'd do it anyhow."

Which no doubt was true, but her manifest satisfaction was due to something else. "You've got something?"

"Fort Lauderdale." She peered at the monitor. "He'll meet your price, but what about delivery? He doesn't want anybody driving it that far."

"Tell him about Exotic Car Transport," said Roy. "You know the drill." In fact, better than he.

Though without bearing on matters of life and death, this was the rare positive occurrence of the past several days, and a quarter hour later Mrs. Forsythe introduced another.

"Here's a person in Vermont looking for an old Ford," said she. She had finished her sandwich but still sipped at the tea as if it were not stone cold by now. "Thirty-seven. I think my grandpa had one of those when he was young. Didn't they call them Model Tees?"

"I believe the Model T was even further back," said Roy. "Any other details?"

She snickered, "Well, he has mistyped 'Cord' for 'Ford.'"

"I think he *means* Cord, Mrs. F.! Tell him I can put my hands on an Eight-Ten, but it's rough. Make us an offer as-is, and/or if we handle the restoration."

"You've got my head spinning," said Mrs. Forsythe. "If I didn't know you, I would think you were joking about Cord versus Ford." She first patted her hair just above her nape and then made her fingers dance over the keyboard.

Roy's afternoon went by in such a fashion. He had made no appointments for today. He passed up lunch, being still devoid of an appetite. At four o'clock Mrs. Forsythe went around the corner to a deli and brought herself back a piece of yellow layer cake and a plastic cup of heavily milked coffee.

As it happened they never heard back from the guy in Vermont, who perhaps after all *had* meant a 1937 Ford. But the deal for the Jag XKE seemed to be holding. There were more e-mails and messages by fax, as well as a number of telephone calls on business matters.

And then, while Mrs. F. was en route to the delicatessen, having switched on the machine—Roy's practice at the office was never to answer the phone directly—he heard a juicy young female voice ask, "Then there really *is* an Incomparable Cars?"

He lifted his extension. "Who is this?"

"Michelle."

"Oh."

"You don't have any idea who I am, do you?"

"I'm waiting for you to incriminate yourself."

"You always seem to have a ready answer," she said with a lilt that elevated the final words as if they posed a question.

"That's supposed to create the illusion that I'm clever," said Roy. "But I doubt you are fooled." Without making a conscious effort to identify her, he suddenly, for no good reason, could do so. "You collect money for animals."

"Now you really have impressed me." Michelle chortled in a deeper tone than that of her speech. "I thought your business card was fake! Gee. Were you serious about letting me test-drive a Rolls?"

"No, I just said it to make fun of you." She produced more contralto laughter. "Of course I meant it. When can you come over?"

"God, any time you say."

"How about," asked Roy, "I pick you up in the Rolls-Royce at seven. *You* can drive it to the restaurant where we'll have dinner."

"You're not kidding, are you?"

"Where do you live? I'll come in so your parents or roommate can check me out."

"I'm twenty-one," said she. "I don't need anybody's okay."

"You need mine," said Roy. "Before you go out with somebody you don't know, you should at least identify him for someone else close to you."

"Now you sound like my father, not a guy with a Rolls. Are we going someplace fancy? I'm asking because I want to know how to dress."

Being ignorant of her tastes, personal or generational, Roy was tempted to ask what kind of place she would like, but when you do that with a woman you deny her the opportunity to blame you if it proves unsatisfactory. Francine was not the only one who had taught him that. From Michelle's question he divined that she probably wanted to go to an expensive restaurant, or else she would not have asked it. But who could tell what her idea of a "fancy" place might be? Perhaps Baghdad, where the waiters, local lads, wore turbans and carried flaming shish kebabs through the dining room.

He would reserve his decision until he saw what she wore, always the most prudent course.

"Wear what you would want to be seen in by the people you admire most," he said now.

"You say the most original things I ever heard anyone say. I don't mind telling you that."

"That will probably end now that I'm aware of it. Do you have a last name?"

"It's Llewellyn."

"Michelle Llewellyn," said Roy. "Anyone with a name like that should always travel by Rolls-Royce. Now I'd better have your address and phone."


Sam seemed to make a special effort to be amiable this evening, perhaps in atonement for his obnoxious performance last time.

"So, what are you driving tonight?" The patient showed no visible effects of the brief detour in his recovery; in answer to Roy's questions he had again disparaged his doctors as mercenary alarmists.

"A fifty-two Silver Wraith Rolls-Royce."

Sam made a face. "You park it in the lot out there?"

"Nobody's going to steal it. What they steal are Honda Accords or Toyotas," said Roy, "which can be chopped for parts."

"How about scratching or denting?"

"I'm trying to impress a young girl." Roy could not have explained why he volunteered this information, which would only confirm Sam's opinion of him. He hastened to add, "But I'm not trying to seduce her."

"Then why impress her?"

"I guess I'm feeling old at the moment." He had craved girls in their twenties only when he was himself a teenager. He had always been attracted by a maturity relative to himself. His school-day crushes had been on teachers, not students. Of course he was now aware that everything he told Sam reached Kristin soon afterward. "I think I feel paternal."

Sam chuckled, though not derisively. He was still on his good behavior. "Well, that's a new one."

"Maybe I'm finally growing up."

Sam raised his big soft hands. "I don't want to hear that. Please, I'm a sick man."

Roy turned toward the door, as if by instinct, an instant before Kristin opened it and entered the room. He was not consciously expecting her, nor had he heard an annunciatory sound. It was strange as anything could be, perhaps disquieting.

She wore a sleek beige suit he had never seen before. He could not remember whether he had ever noticed that her eyes were on a level with his own when they stood near each other. Sam of course, if not flat on his back, would have dwarfed them both.

She gave Roy a quick, silent smile and went to Sam and kissed him. Only then did she say, "Oh, hi, Roy," as if he had been overlooked.

"Kristin." He brought a chair for her to the bedside.

She sat primly down and addressed her husband. "Maria wanted me to explain why she hasn't visited you. She's scared of hospitals. She wants you to come home soon so she can nurse you." Kristin smiled at Roy. "Maria's in love with Sam."

Was this some kind of mockery? Sam didn't seem to think so. He was grinning.

"Know about old Roy's latest conquest? My nurse Suzie."

Kristin looked up at Roy. "She's very attractive."

He shrugged. "Any connection between us is only a fantasy of Sam's. I just gave her a lift last night when her car wouldn't start." He waited for Sam to refute this invention, but it did not happen. Perhaps Sam had not stayed on watch long enough to see them leave the lot in separate cars.

"She was setting you up, kid." Sam snorted. "When did you ever hear of a new BMW not starting on demand? And you're the car guy."

Roy thought his best friend was a shit for persisting in this vein, embarrassing him before Kristin. The best way to dispose of the matter, however, was jocular. "And the upshot is that now she is bearing my child."

Kristin at last lost her smile and turned back to Sam, not offended but rather bored, her habitual response to their sophomoric banter. He feared he might fall back in her estimation to where he had begun.

It was a relief when Sam changed the subject. "How much are you asking for the Rolls?" To Kristin, "That's what he drove over here and left in the parking lot."

Kristin turned her golden head to Roy. He said, "Nobody's going to bother it. If they did, they might do me a favor. I could collect the insurance."

Sam showed incredulity. "Why haven't you been able to sell it? What are you asking?"

Kristin said, "Sam."

Roy should have picked up on it at this point, but he was oblivious. "Well, starting at twenty-five, probably, but I'd probably go significantly lower if the offer was serious."

"How about twenty?" Sam asked brightly.

"Sam," said Kristin.

It would not be the first time Sam had found a supposed customer for one of Roy's automobiles. None of the several persons for whom he had Roy make appointments bought a car or even made a respectable bid. One did not even show up. But, with the probability that his friend's intentions had been kind—the delicate matter of whether he had expected a finder's fee never came to the moment of truth—Roy had not chided him till now.

"You're not going to send around another of those stiffs, I hope."

Sam pouted briefly. "Thank you too, pal." He lifted multiple chins; to see a prep-school picture of him nowadays would be a shocker. "I'm calling you on it: *I'll* pay you twenty."

Roy horselaughed for Kristin's benefit as much as Sam's. To her he said, "Can you believe this?" He reminded Sam, "You hate foreign cars, especially vintage models."

"Kris just became branch manager at First United. She ought to drive something that befits her position. I can't afford a new Rolls, but they look more or less the same whatever the year, don't they? Nobody but you could tell the difference."

This statement evoked a number of emotions in Roy. Before the could find a voice for any of them, Kristin spoke up gently, asking her husband, "Can't we let this go till you come home?"

Sam pouted again. "I thought you'd be pleased. Take a test drive. Roy doesn't sell these things unless they are in tip-top condition, as he always tells me. Tell her, Roy."

Roy was under the complex pressure of conflicting importunities. Such dilemmas were necessarily resolved by satisfying nobody, if not damaging everybody. *God damn you Grandys*, he could say only in fantasy.

In reality he caved in favor of Sam, who after all lay in a hospital bed with a faulty heart. Sam's wife had just become manager of a bank.

"Drive it on loan for a while, Kristin. See how you like it. No"—he was going to say "strings," but the word was incongruous in this context—"no obligation. I mean, it's among friends. Oh, and congratulations!"

"Thank you. The present manager is retiring, and—"

"They offered it to me," was Sam's jest, "but I got stuck here." He then made amends for the interruption. "Ain't she something? Fact is, she had to fight like hell for the job. She's a tough customer. Don't fall for the modest act."

"Please shut up, Sam," said Kristin. "Roy shouldn't have to listen to the hustle, close as he is to us."

Roy was moved by the statement, but he addressed Sam. "So get out of here soon, will you? We've got some celebrating to do: Kristin's promotion and of course your recovery. My own sole accomplishment is keeping your friendship." For the last few words he turned to include Kristin.

"We'll go in the Rolls," said Sam. "I'll serve as chauffeur. I'll get me a black cap. You quality folk can drink in back, from the built-in bar."

Kristin rose in one fluid movement, without pushing the chair away.

"You just got here." Sam's triumphant tone had turned instantly to the plaintive.

"I'm only going to the bathroom."

When she had closed the door, Sam told Roy, in a lowered voice, "Talk her into taking the Rolls. She'll resist, but I know she'll like it. And thanks for offering to lend it to us. I really couldn't do it otherwise."

He wasn't "doing" it now, but of course Roy would not make that point, though he knew Sam would never pay him a dollar, no matter what. He walked to the window and looked down on the parking lot.

Sam asked, "Is it still there?"

Roy turned. "When are they going to let you out of here?"

Sam's smile soured. "If this place bores you, think of what it does to me."

Now his best friend was chastened. "I didn't mean that, kid. I just hope you can come home soon."

Kristin emerged from the lavatory. Sam waited until she reached his bedside, before announcing to them both, head swiveling, "Now for my surprise. They're letting me out tomorrow—pending another episode, of course."

Kristin was standing, hands clamped to the back of the steel chair. "*Now* you tell us. How long have you known it?"

"Your excitement is overwhelming."

"Of course it's great news." She showed a bright face to Roy, as if asking for confirmation.

Roy played along. "That's terrific, kid. What time should I pick you up?"

"I'll do it," said Kristin.

"Let Roy," said Sam. "You're manager of the First United Bank. He just waits for phone calls from wealthy car-nuts."

That was normal needling, and Roy was relieved to hear it. "There haven't been many of them lately."

Kristin noted drily that tomorrow was Saturday. "Meanwhile, can I remove some of this stuff tonight?" She indicated the bedside table overloaded with electronic gear.

Sam said no, anything she took away would inevitably be needed as soon as it was gone: one of those truths of nature.

"I'll check at the nurses' station to see what time you'll be released tomorrow," Kristin said.

Sam asked Roy, "You're not leaving, too?"

"No. I'll hang out for a while."

"Bye," Kristin said to Sam. She did not come to kiss him this time. "Goodbye, Roy." She had hardly glanced his way.

# 8

R oy took the chair last used by Kristin.

"I wanted to talk to you in confidence," said Sam. "In case you haven't noticed, Kris has no sense of humor. That's no criticism. It's praise. She doesn't have a dark side. You have to have a decadent streak to look at things our way—I mean, you and me."

"Speak for yourself," said Roy. It was not that he disagreed, but rather that he disliked being included in someone else's self-characterization, even that of his best friend.

Sam elevated his head with an elbow hooked behind the pillows. It looked uncomfortable. "I've been on the phone with Ray and Sy." Ray Walser was his accountant; he shared Seymour Alt with Roy. "I'm thinking about Chapter Thirteen."

"Christ sake."

"How about that?" Sam snorted and rolled back, staring at the ceiling. "My wife's a bank official, and I'm about to go into bankruptcy."

"That might affect her career, wouldn't it?"

"Ha! What would it do to mine?"

*Did you ever have one, you selfish asshole?* was not said aloud by Roy, and not even, exactly, thought; it was as if muttered by a passing stranger. "You must be in deep."

"The failure of eToys was the last straw. I was still buying it when it was at the peak price, in the low eighties."

"The stock went to zero, didn't it?" This event had been of only academic interest to Roy, who never played the market.

"They were really fucked when Toys 'R' Us linked up with Amazon. I don't know how it could have been foreseen. Shit."

"What does Kristin think of this?"

"She doesn't," said Sam, still talking to the ceiling. "She doesn't know everything about me. Some guys have girlfriends on the side. I got *this*."

"You won't be able to hide Chapter Thirteen from her."

"Don't I know it." He rolled over ponderously to look at Roy from a horizontal position.

"How much do you need?"

Sam produced a laugh from the massive cavern of his belly. "I wouldn't want to scare you off by answering that literally. But I could take the edge off, avoid bankruptcy for the moment anyhow, with, say, fifty."

Roy stood up and one-handedly carried the chair to the corner.

"Mind giving me an answer?" Sam asked. "I'd kinda like to know where we stand."

Roy resented the "we." He fussed with the chair, as if its precise placement were a matter of substance.

"Okay," Sam said behind him. "How much *could* you let me have?"

Roy moved to the foot of the bed. "There hasn't yet been any year I've made a profit."

Sam grimaced. "You mean selling old cars."

"That's what I do."

His best friend produced a rhetorical groan. "That's never been what you've lived on."

"If you could call it living."

Sam was not amused by the self-disparagement. "You don't live the crummy way you do because you can't afford otherwise."

"Look," said Roy, "I couldn't just *give* you that kind of money."

"It would be a *loan*, for God's sake. Sy can set that up."

Roy deplored seeing the hope in Sam's eyes. He disliked the idea of making him happy by monetary means, which experience had proven to be the shortest-lived of states. By the time the funds reached him, Sam felt more deprived than ever.

"I've got to think about this. You can't expect to spring this on me and get an immediate answer."

Sam scrooched up until his head was higher on the pillow. "You won't even feel it. You and I both know what your dad left you."

"You've always been more of an authority on that than me."

"What's that supposed to mean?"

Roy did not want to get into an argument. "You had a father of your own."

"That fucking loser."

Because Sam had usually been at Roy's house, Roy had never seen much of Samson Grandy, Sr., a stockbroker who had not done as well as his only child thought he should have, leaving him, on a coronary failure in middle age, with only slightly more than a million in securities along with half that in real property, which Sam soon impatiently sold at lower-than-market prices. Sam's mother had died, after a lingering illness, when he was twelve, and his father, like Roy's, never remarried; unlike Victor Courtright, he had a series of lady friends, not one of whom young Sam could abide. It was fortunate for him, then, that he could enjoy the friendship of Roy's father, who preferred Robin and Sam to his own son. Roy had resented this, but blamed neither his sister nor his best friend.

"Would Sy Alt be the right guy?"

"To handle this? Why not?"

"He can't represent us both."

Sam sighed. "This ain't a divorce, kid. We're not adversaries. I trust you." He assumed a huge grin.

Roy had always been irritated by Sam's premature optimism. "It would have to be set up as a legitimate loan, with a believable rate of interest, you know. The IRS is watching." None of his other "loans" to Sam over the years had exceeded the ten-thousand-dollar annual limit for untaxable gifts. "And what could you list as collateral? Didn't you tell me your house is in Kristin's name? . . . Don't keep smiling. I'm not saying yes."

Sam turned his head away, but the visible side of his face, large as a ham, looked smug. Roy felt an impulse to hurt him in a unique way, neither physical nor emotional. But what was left? Torment him mentally with some unsolvable brain-twister? The fact was that Sam had always had his number. Perhaps that was true of Kristin as well—Sam had hers, not that she had Roy's, with whom she was still hardly more than an acquaintance. Giving Sam fifty thousand dollars because of her would be grotesque.

"I won't tell your pal Kris," said Sam, as if he had read Roy's mind, "if that's what's worrying you."

"It never occurred to me. It's beside the point."

"Didn't you give her your word you wouldn't lend me any more money?" Assuming that he had his friend morally on the run, Sam was gloating.

"I told you I have to think it over. And it wouldn't be lending in any case. You'd never return any part of it." On that note he left the room.

In the parking lot he was wary lest he encounter Suzanne Akens, with whom he had been too unguarded, justifiably earning her scorn. But it was not she who awaited him beside the Rolls-Royce. It was Kristin Grandy.

"Easy car to find in a crowd," said she, and then, perhaps as a courtesy to him, looked at the coachwork and added, "It really is lovely."

"I meant what I said," Roy told her. "Drive it on loan for a while. See how it fits."

"Please. Let's take that as one of Sam's jokes. What *isn't*, unfortunately, is his wanting to borrow more money from you." She elevated her impeccable chin. "That's obviously what he wanted to talk to you privately about."

Roy had not sworn an oath of silence on the matter, nor had he been asked to. Basic principle, however, restrained him from saying more than, "The subject came up."

"Well, it's your affair, Roy. It's your money and your friend, but Sam *cannot handle money*."

"To say the least."

Kristin and the Rolls-Royce were a natural pair. They seemed self-illuminated in the beginning twilight. Her beige suit looked golden; the white car showed suggestions of pearl.

"I'm willing to be the villain," said she, and it struck him that this exquisite woman was pleading with him. "Feel free to put all the blame on me."

"I told you the other day that the only way I would turn him down was by doing just that, blaming you. That wasn't very courageous of me. Taking the hit should be my job. As you rightly say, the money's mine and he's my friend." What Roy would not tell Kristin was that he had decided to furnish Sam with the fifty grand, thus protecting her career from the consequences of her husband's bankruptcy, while hiding the transaction from her, and Sam's silence on the deal would be a non-negotiable condition of it.

Kristin spoke in a straightforward manner. "You're an awful lot more than I once thought you were." Her smile was rueful. "I hope that doesn't sound as patronizing to you as it does to me. What I want to say is you're going above and beyond the call of duty."

Roy understood that *You're doing this for me?* was asked only in classic romantic movies. She anyway was not supposed to learn all that he was doing for her. Nevertheless, it was with a certain disappointment that he accepted her simple thanks.

She had said goodbye and was walking toward her Corolla when Roy asked, "Do you have any plans for dinner?"


It was only when he was following Kristin to the Grandy house, where she would leave her car and join him in the Silver Wraith, that Roy remembered Michelle Llewellyn.

Directory Assistance provided him with the numbers of three local Llewellyns, none of them named Michelle, but he heard her voice when he dialed the second of them. He had expected to be vigorously abused when he identified himself, but she expressed more grief than wrath.

"I bought a nice *dress*. It was *expensive*." She was sobbing. "I told my *friends*." She took a quavering breath. "Is this the way you get off? Making fun of people?"

"Michelle," said Roy, "my best friend had a heart attack. I've been with him at the hospital until just now. Please forgive me for not getting in touch sooner."

"Oh, shit. I'm really sorry. I didn't know."

"You couldn't have. Can I get a raincheck on dinner? The dress won't go to waste. I can't wait to see it."

"Great. I hope your friend gets better soon."

"Thanks a lot. I'll be calling you soon as I can."

That had been easier than he thought and employed only existing truths. She sounded like a very nice girl, though he regretted having established a personal connection with her in the first place. If now he never again got in touch, she might reach the wrong conclusion.

He was relieved when the two cars arrived at Kristin's house and she simply parked hers and joined him without going inside for any reason. Had she done so, he might have been expected to come along and wait. It would have made him uncomfortable to be alone under the same roof as she now that darkness was settling in, whereas when they had eaten lunch there, on a sunny day, he had been almost at ease.

"It seems to me we have two choices," said he. "Either eat someplace where we, or particularly you, might be recognized, or go to one where that would be unlikely."

"Huh?"

The car was still sitting in the driveway; they were lighted by the dashboard illumination.

"I'm thinking of how it might look if the new bank manager is seen dining out with someone else while her old man's in the hospital."

"Oh, yes. I see. You're right."

"You didn't think of that?"

She smiled. "I probably would have. I should have."

She seemed to suffer little from self-doubt. He admired that, being of the opposite sort, and therefore he was not sure now whether he should express his admiration and have it misinterpreted. He decided instead to register his own vote on the choice of restaurant. "I think a conspicuous place would be better. If somebody did see us at a hideaway, it would look suspicious."

"I'm sure you're right."

It appeared to Roy that she really was uninterested in the matter. "Okay then. Let's go to A Quarter to Nine, where they know us well."

He was an habitué of this place, which was named for its number on Pine Street, 845, and had entertained the Grandys there repeatedly, though he suspected Sam would have liked larger portions than those served by owner/chef Jonathan Marchbanks, whose dishes were artistic compositions for the eye as much as the palate.

Marchbanks did much of the cooking himself, and yet usually managed to come out and greet each diner at some point in the meal, wearing a chef's high-buttoned jacket, but in blue denim and with a golfer's white linen cap rather than a toque blanche.

He was just inside the door tonight. His eyes made special acknowledgment of Roy's companion.

"Kris! I should begin to serve breakfast," was his cryptic greeting to her. "Hi, Roy. I got my eye on that Lotus Elite in your window."

"I'll quote you a price after I've eaten dinner," said Roy.

"Try the lamb shank and you'll make me a gift of the car."

When they were seated at a generous-size, fresh-flowered table for two, designed for comfortable eating and not intimacy, Roy asked Kristin, "What did he mean about breakfast?"

"I had lunch here today."

"Why didn't you tell me?"

"This is my favorite place; I lunch here a lot." Then, leaning forward—on the opposite side of the table he was at some remove—"It was your discovery. I hope you don't mind."

Roy was flattered, but concealed it in his response. "Jonathan sold *me* a classic. I think he's regretted it ever since, but he hasn't yet bought anything to replace it. He gave me the first meal on the house. He had just opened the restaurant."

"We granted the loan," said Kristin.

"Your bank." He sighed. "And you never mentioned that before."

"The occasion didn't come up. . . . Are we being observed?"

He laughed. "You won't look, and because you won't, I haven't. But the place is full, as usual." Even a regular customer like himself could not have walked in the door at prime time on a Friday night without a reservation. The fact was, he had phoned one in after Michelle Llewellyn had called him.

A svelte waitress left menus. She wore a tight red vest and black silk jeans. Her shiny tight-pulled black hair was parted in the middle like that of an old-time movie gangster.

Roy said to Kristin, "You didn't mention it because, as usual, Sam and I did all the talking."

"I was probably interested in what you guys were talking about. I don't remember being forcibly gagged. Banking is fascinating to me, but it's not the sort of topic that lends itself to general conversation at dinner—well, except maybe for those few subjects the media made familiar to the rest of the world: Fed Reserve meetings, the prime rate, ATM fees, and certificates of deposit."

Roy took a risk and said, "I wonder if you enjoy the reversal: You, the professional, are quiet about your working day, while it's the men who chatter about the ways they amuse themselves."

She frowned. "*You* have a profession."

"It's not like actually working. I did that for a year or so. I tried being a salesman at a Cadillac agency."

She blinked. "Elkhart Cadillac?"

"Sam told me once that your parents bought a pair of new Caddies when your dad had his first success." He and she compared dates, but those purchases had taken place long before he joined the firm.

"Yes," said Kristin. "I was only fourteen or fifteen at the time."

If so, Roy would have taken little note of her, whatever his own age. He suspected that her appearance as a girl had not been promising, especially if she had grown to much of her adult height early on. She would have been gawky, with projecting angles that had not yet been resolved into their later elegance of line.

Their fino sherries were delivered. He paid so little notice to the waitress that he could not have distinguished her from another, which was not like him.

"What kind of car did you buy from Jonathan?"

"A sixty-six Shelby Cobra." As with so many celebrated marques, saying or hearing the very name could produce a thrill, but only to someone who recognized it. "A combination of a small, handsome British sports-car body with a huge Ford engine. The acceleration could give you whiplash: under four seconds, zero to sixty." He smiled at her lack of reaction. "Childish, no? Why would anybody want to do that? I haven't any idea, but it's fun if you're a certain type of guy. . . . But there are some female car-fanciers and even a few race drivers who are women."

"There are lady body-builders and prize fighters," said Kristin.

"What did you have for lunch?" Roy was slightly jealous of her for having already been here once today, but spotting Jonathan across the room, chatting with a party of newcomers, he realized that what really disturbed him was the chef's greeting Kristin as a familiar.

"*Soupe de poissons,*" she answered slowly, distractedly, as she perused the menu, which was physically sizable in flexible cardboard but not extensive in content, offering one dish each in beef, veal, and lamb; two of fowl; and three of main-course seafood. "A tiny bit too heavy on the saffron, for my taste anyway."

This was the only criticism she had ever made of Jonathan's cuisine, but it occurred to Roy that whenever the subject had been discussed before now, he had always been her host. Sam of course, by right of friendship, said anything he felt, and usually spoke disparagingly about any restaurant but a steakhouse, and even there never quite approved of the aging, marbling, and doneness of the meat at one chosen by Roy. His wife had better manners as well as better taste.

"You must tell me your honest opinion of what you eat tonight," Roy told her. "You're the authority."

In this light her eyes seemed green. "I'm an amateur cook. If you think about it, everybody living is a professional eater and speaks with the same authority." Then, as if she feared he would take it as a rebuke, added, "You flatter me too much, sir. But you've said nothing about my most notable attribute: modesty!"

Taken by surprise, he hoped his laugh came soon enough. He was usually, without undue effort, pretty glib with women, but he had difficulty in adjusting to Kristin's idiom. Or perhaps it was rather a matter of rhythm, phrasing, and pace, but then he had never been conscious of technique, if that's what dealing with the other sex could be termed. He always did what came naturally, but nothing was doing so at the moment, surely because he was not, in any sense of the word, on a date. He had to remind himself that he was with his best friend's better half, that it was solely because Sam had married Kristin that Roy was breaking bread with her now. Though she was nothing like her husband, in this situation she was again necessarily a surrogate.

She lowered and closed her menu. "The duck-breast paillard, I think. Is that the same as a *magret?*" This was rhetorical. "I'm suspicious of Jonathan's designations. . . . Nothing to start. I ate too much at lunch."

"Despite the saffron?"

"I didn't say the soup was inedible."

The waitress returned, and Kristin gave her order.

"The lamb shank for me," said Roy. "Nothing to begin."

"I hope you're not just being polite," said Kristin. "I'm not going to eat dessert, either. I'm trying to lose a few pounds."

"*You?*" He had actually never observed her body with the care he would have given such an assessment had she been someone else, but that as slender a human being as she could be overweight was hard to take seriously. "I've never even seen you eat much of the marvelous meals you prepare."

"You taste a lot when you cook. that takes the edge off an appetite. Anyway, what's most fun for me is somebody else eating what I make." She displayed a schoolgirl sort of grin, which nullified any threat that might be detected in her next statement. "They're in my power."

"I've never looked at it that way."

"That's because you're not noticeably competitive."

"Is that good or bad?"

"Depends on the situation, wouldn't you agree?"

Roy decided it was time to assert himself. "No, I wouldn't." He had gotten her attention; perhaps she liked dissent. "I think I simply lack ambition. Can that ever be good?"

"It can certainly be a relief for those around you."

A busboy took away the bowl of flowers—so that their fragrance would not compromise a diner's olfactory sense—and Jonathan himself arrived, bearing two small plates.

"Do me a favor, please," said the chef. "Kindly give me an opinion of this smoked-trout mousse. It won't spoil your palates, I promise, and it's a comp." He briskly served them both and left.

On the little square plates, which were glazed in onyx-black, a swirl of pale mousse had been placed slightly off center; issuing from it was a swooshing comet-tail made of tiny dots of sauce, green interspersed with those of pink and some white. Three crisply toasted discs of bread occupied the space afforded by the off-centering of the mousse.

Kristin grimaced at her plate. "This is over the top."

Roy lifted an eyebrow at her. "It's always been Jonathan's theory that going right to the main course is gastronomic heresy. The palate must be awakened first. I guess he's exerting his power."

"What irritates me is the decoration, which you are obliged to destroy by eating it. Isn't that a conflict of interest?" She applied a dollop of mousse to a crouton and anointed it delicately with a little sample of each color of sauce. She extended the finished product to Roy.

"How nice of you." He accepted it from her delicate fingers.

"Nice of you to say so," said Kristin, "when what I'm doing is using you to defy Jonathan. I have no intention of letting him bully me."

"So you stick me with it?" asked Roy in mock indignation. "That's not so nice." He realized that what she was doing, consciously or not, was providing for the kind of irreverent give-or-take in which he and Sam so often engaged in her presence but never with her participation or even probable understanding. "And I was counting on you to identify these sauces so I can pretend to be knowledgeable when he comes back."

Kristin squinted at the dots on her plate. "The green is dill and the pink, pink peppercorn. The white is sour cream and horseradish."

Roy had finished his own small serving by the time the chef returned. Kristin's was missing only the sample she had given Roy.

"So," Jonathan asked Roy, "what do you think?" But before he got an answer he stared at Kristin's plate and brought his thin eyebrows together in a frown. "What's wrong?"

"I didn't want a first course."

The chef snapped his head toward Roy, who quickly said, "Delicious."

"We smoke our own trout," Jonathan told him, as he always did.

"I like the combination of the dill and pink peppercorn sauces along with the horseradish."

Jonathan lifted his golf cap in salute, affording a brief glimpse of his shiny shaved head. "You got one out of three. Very good! The 'dill' is parsley; the pink, tomato."

"Well," Roy said genially, "what do I know?"

"Jonathan," Kristin said, "those were my guesses, not Roy's. He's being gallant."

The chef showed a faint smirk as he removed the little black plates, and went away without another word.

"I thought he might crow over my confession," said Kristin. "But no."

"You would have gotten them all right if you had taken a taste."

She lowered her empty sherry glass. "You don't have to protect me, Roy." They exchanged remote glances for a moment, and then she reached across and lightly touched the back of his hand with three fingertips. "I shouldn't have said that. I apologize." She looked away and withdrew her fingers. "Let's have a glass of red."

Jonathan Marchbanks owned a piece of a Napa Valley vineyard and therefore could offer a cabernet labeled with the name A Quarter to

Nine, but it was also a reliably good bottle whatever the vintage. Roy was relieved when Kristin made no objection to the choice.

"Really?"

"I hope I haven't given you the impression I'm a troublemaker," said she, apparently in earnest.

"I don't have any negative impressions of you at all. I never have had any. When I'm in your company, I just try to measure up. If Sam's choice of investments were comparable to his choice of wife, he'd be in the Fortune Five Hundred."

Her expression was an odd mixture of affection and distress. "Oh, please . . ."

The waitress appeared at that point and took the order for wine. Jonathan, who often performed as his own sommelier, was back in the kitchen at the moment, to Roy's approval. Whereas he usually enjoyed conversing with the chef, he had had enough of the man tonight. This was due to Kristin. He was not drunk, the fino having been his first alcohol of the day, but apparently he had gone too far and embarrassed her. They spoke no more while they waited for the cabernet.

When it came, the waitress opened the bottle and without ceremony poured them a third of a glass each and departed. Jonathan's practice dispensed with cork-smelling, glass-sniffing, color-gauging, swirling, preliminary sipping, the lot. If after a healthy swallow or two you didn't like the wine, you could send it back for an unchallenged replacement.

Roy lifted his glass. "To Sam's good health!"

"Yes," said Kristin, raising hers. "By all means." She lowered the glass to the tablecloth. "You're not going to tell me how much you're lending him, are you?"

"I haven't said whether I'm going to lend him anything. I'm trying not to think of that subject at the moment. I'm uncomfortable in the role of middleman. I've played it on occasion between my sister and her husband, and I always end up being resented by both sides. Robin and I have never gotten along since we became teenagers, but she's my sister; in fact, she is my twin. It would be unnatural to oppose her as much as I'm naturally inclined to do. So, though I invariably think my brother-in-law is right, I don't feel it's proper for me to join his cause. What I try to do is compromise."

Kristin was listening with apparent interest, which was certainly not what Sam usually did. No doubt because of his own experience with Robin, he was made impatient by any mention of her name.

"But I don't want to knock my sister. She's a good mother."

"Are you a good uncle?"

"Her kids are pretty young to do much with or for, except bring toys. Robin seldom approves of my choices, which aren't really mine but suggestions of the toy-store people or Mrs. Forsythe. My niece is just past two; my nephew, one. Robin is pregnant again."

Roy was aware that there were other diners in the restaurant, but he had not looked toward anyone else for purposes of identification. Now he was startled to hear his name spoken by a figure that had been moving past the table but had paused near his right elbow, a shadow in his peripheral vision.

He reluctantly looked up and saw his attorney. "Oh, Sy." He feinted rising from his chair and gestured toward Kristin, whom Alt was ignoring for some reason though, being Sam's lawyer too, he surely knew her.

But it appeared he did not. "I realize it's no thrill to see me. But you might at least introduce your lovely companion." Alt was a thickset man tightly swathed in a three-piece gray suit. He was less bald than he once had been, owing to a lengthy hairweaving process he had undergone the year before.

"Kristin Grandy, Seymour Alt."

The name obviously meant nothing to Kristin, who offered the lawyer a gracious smile and a slender hand, as she might have done with a new depositor at the bank.

Roy immediately understood that Sam, for whatever reason, had concealed from her his association with Alt, using another attorney for their joint concerns. He moved quickly to divert Sy, underestimating Alt's talent, as demonstrated in a practice of many years, to assess situations and act according to his clients', and of course his own, interests.

"Congratulations, Mrs. Grandy. I'm sorry your husband had to post-pone his part in the celebration, but at least his best friend can pinch-hit." Alt displayed a seldom seen broad smile, which revealed a crooked lower tooth that struck a boyish note. He nodded at Roy and walked away.

Kristin asked, "Who was that?"

"He's been my lawyer for years," said Roy. "So he knows Sam. But I haven't spoken with him since your promotion. No doubt all the local lawyers know about it."

"It doesn't take effect till November first."

"You and Sam can have your own celebration then. This wasn't planned as one, but it's not a bad idea."

As if on cue, the waitress appeared. Rapidly glancing from one of them to the other, she asked, "Mr. Alt has ordered a bottle of cham-pagne for you, with his compliments. At what point would you like me to bring it? With dessert?"

Before Kristin could object, Roy told the young woman that it would be fine. To Kristin he said, "Do you mind? Sy is a sensitive sort, like most people who can be ruthless on demand. I don't want to offend him. You don't have to drink it."

She made a face of mock outrage. "You want it all for yourself."

"Great," said Roy, taking it to mean she would cooperate; he could never tell. "Then we *will* make it a celebration."

Jonathan was quite right about the lamb shank, the tender flesh of which became almost molten in its sauce, and had he appeared again, Roy might have urged him to come tomorrow and collect the Lotus. But the sensitive chef had apparently been so miffed by Kristin's rejection of the mousse of smoked trout that he was not seen again throughout the meal.

It was Kristin who made note of his absence. She said, smirking sweetly, "That's a pity, because the duck breast is heavenly. Do I see arti-choke hearts with your lamb?"

"I would give you a taste, but I've always seen you turn down Sam when he makes such offers."

"One of the many things you can do with a husband, or anyway one like Sam, which might be misinterpreted by someone else." She rolled her eyes. "I wonder if even a wife could do that with Jonathan."

"He's married?"

"You thought he was gay, didn't you? Sam does."

Roy swirled the cabernet in the long-stemmed, big-bowled glass. "I suppose so."

Kristin was laughing silently. "I think he's probably not married, not that it would mean—"

"That he's homosexual," Roy said quickly to prevent her possible embarrassment, though she had not indicated the onset of any.

"It isn't so much that I don't like to eat off anyone else's plate," said Kristin. "I just don't want to have to pay them back from mine."

Roy was amused by this confession, maybe even more so when he decided it was a lie. It occurred to him that he had never seen her drink from a glass or cup of Sam's. Not that he was on watch for that sort of thing or any other particular of Kristin's existence. He had always been at pains to ignore her as a woman, in the physical sense. That had been easier to manage with her than with someone of more ample proportions, assertive hair, vivid coloring, darker eyes; someone fuller and smaller. For example, long as he had known Francine, often as he had had her, tiresome as she could be, he had ever been keenly aware of her flesh, the swell of her breasts, which changed with the kind of fabric that covered them; the curve of her hip, different with each sort of turn she made, in fury, in mirth or depression or triumph.

The waitress mounted a filled ice bucket on a chromium stand next to the table and twistingly embedded the bottle within the ice, then from a pocket produced a little card and gave it to Kristin.

Kristin read the card and silently transferred it to Roy. Printed in the middle of the white rectangle was SEYMOUR ALT, ATTORNEY AT LAW, below which was handwritten: *Complimenti!* S.A.

"Sy isn't all bad." Roy returned the card to Kristin's side of the table.

She was scowling. "What does Jonathan charge for Cristal? Two hundred?"

Roy's smile became more generous. "Cristal for Kristin would seem appropriate."

"I trust Alt won't think I'm beholden to him."

"He'll write it off as a promotional expense," Roy said seriously, "and won't have any expectation whatever, unless at some point he has a client whose interests are opposed to yours; then he'll expect to defeat you. If on the other hand he represents *you*, he will expect to destroy your adversary. In the practice of his profession Sy is not hampered by a conscience. Yet at home he's a family man, devoted to and even bullied by his wife and children. If you know him only in the one role, seeing the other would amaze you. You'd assume either one or the other was a hoax, but neither is."

"Maybe both are."

"That might be too deep for me." Roy reached to give the champagne a twist in its frigid bath.

"No, it isn't," Kristin said. "It's just a new way to look at something familiar to you but not to me; therefore I'm free to do it. How well does he know Sam?"

"I couldn't say." This was a true statement. He had a feeling that her fundamental concern was always for Sam, and the rest of what she said was treading water. The fact was she really loved Sam. Roy could not understand why that recognition tended to offend him. Sam was his best friend. How awful it would have been if she did not love the man. But the old question remained: What did she see in him?

Kristin said without warning, "Tell you what, Roy. Before the bottle is opened. I've had all the wine I can drink tonight, and I don't want the burden of having to butter up an attorney I don't know and do justice to an extravagant champagne I didn't order. I've already hurt Jonathan, whom I *do* know. Why not go for still another self-important personage?"

Could this be some kind of old-fashioned bitterness against men when she had done so well in a realm they once dominated? You never saw a male bank officer nowadays.

Wincing, Roy asked, "You want to send it back?"

Kristin showed her first weakness: She tried to explain. "I should have turned it down earlier. I wasn't going to until he sent his *business card.*"

For the life of him, Roy could not see the unique bad taste in that: Alt was congratulating her on her success in what was certainly a business.

He pushed his chair back. "I have to go say a word to Sy."

She weakened her position further. "I'm sorry if I put you in an awkward situation."

Roy stood up. "After all, he works for me, not vice versa. This is just a courtesy."

He went looking for the lawyer's table and found it semicircled by one of the corner banquettes. Alt was with his wife, a handsome brunette of indeterminate age, with a high bosom and, had she been afoot, a regal carriage. In her presence Sy seemed more her lawyer than her husband.

"Hi, Dorothea."

She gave him a radiant grin and continued to be the only person in his entire life who called him by his given first name, with which some years earlier he had supplied her, in answer to an idle question, at one of the Alts' New Year's Eve parties.

"Royalton!"

It took an awkward and uncomfortable lean to reach her for the double-cheek kiss, but she would expect no less. Alt meanwhile kept crunching on a seafood salad as if he were alone at an otherwise unoccupied table.

"Who's tonight's beauty?" Dorothea asked, nodding vigorously in the appropriate direction.

"The new branch manager at First United."

"Excuse me?"

"The bank," said Roy. "She's Sam Grandy's wife."

"Well," Dorothea said, smiling naughtily, "you might be more discreet about it."

Sy Alt looked up from his mollusks. "For a change Roy's not being illicit, Dodie. Sam's his close friend. Sam's in the hospital."

Alt's wife winked at Roy with a heavy-lidded eye. "I hope the change is not permanent. I want a whirl with you first. Sy's only your lawyer." She was one of those respectable women who enjoy such badinage.

"Dorothea, I don't think I'm man enough for you." He spoke earnestly to Alt. "We're taking a raincheck on the champagne, Sy. Kristin doesn't feel good. I'll tell Jonathan to hold the bottle for her and Sam to drink when he gets home."

"You don't need my permission."

Roy saw that he was nevertheless offended; on the other hand, in Alt's professional scheme of things—surely closer to Kristin's than the mystique of a dilettante dealer in vintage cars—this might redound to her advantage.

Kristin said nothing voluntarily on the way home, and after a few lame attempts to make conversation, Roy fell silent. She seemed weary, surely for good reason after the kind of business day he had never experienced, in fact would never have imagined now had he not yearned to be in sympathy with her. His own state was dispiritment. He felt he had failed utterly to connect with this remarkable woman, while having no sense of what such a connection should be. He did not desire her sexually, unless such hunger was unconscious. He had no longer any reason to seek her simple approval, which she had already explicitly given him.

It was possible that what he yearned for had nothing personally to do with Kristin, and therefore she would not be able, with all the good will in the world, to provide it. The fact remained that she was his only hope.

The Rolls-Royce glided up the driveway, as if it were under its own control, and around to the back door that the Grandys preferred as entrance. Roy got out and stood sentry as Kristin let herself into the lighted but presumably empty house.

"Want me to check for intruders?" he asked only semiseriously.

"The security system's working. Sam's got it programmed so that every bulb in the house is burning."

"He'll be home tomorrow," Roy stated as a matter of fact.

Kristin firmly shook hands with him across the threshold. He remained outside. "I had a very nice time tonight," she said. "Thank you, Roy."

This could not have been true. Perhaps it was due to his fury at the polite lie that Roy lost all command of himself. He dropped her hand with force, as if throwing it from him.

"I'm sorry, Kristin. I'm in love with you." Having said which he turned quickly so as not to witness her reaction, and leaped into the Silver Wraith and drove home, for once staying within the speed limit.

# 9

The telephone rang just as Roy returned from the shower in his gold terry-cloth robe.

It was Sam's jovial tenor. "Sorry to wake you up, kid, but I thought you'd want to know I'm home."

Roy glanced across at the chest of drawers, atop which the big red numerals of the digital clock displayed 10:21. "I ran for an hour, then worked out for another. I'll bet the doctors told *you* to exercise. You're home now, right?"

"It's asking enough of me to follow a diet," said his best friend. "Listen, I don't want to put the pressure on, but that deal we talked about? I'm ready to get going with it now this thing's behind us."

He thereby demonstrated how many fallacies could be crammed into one short speech. Everything after the complaint about having to eat wisely was a blatant untruth or an asinine misstatement: He *did* of course want to apply maximum pressure; borrowing money from a friend was not a "deal"; that this "thing" was over, meaning a heart problem when you were grossly overweight and altogether sedentary, was a foolish and possibly lethal assumption. There was more justification, for once, for Sam's habitual "us," but it reminded Roy not of the brotherly

connotation Sam intended but rather his marriage. . . . Roy had an aversion, this morning, to thinking of *her* except as an abstraction. It was the
only means by which he could avoid remembering his demented performance of the evening before and not concluding he would today be
less humiliated had he thrown up on her doorstep.

"Roy? You still there?"

"Let me put you on speaker. I've got to get dressed."

On the speakerphone Sam cavernously asked the whole room, "I
guess you've cleared it with Sy by now?"

Roy felt it necessary to raise his voice even though the built-in mike
was sensitive. "I told you I didn't think Sy would be the right lawyer for
this."

"He's already said he would handle it."

"When did you talk to him?"

"Just now."

Roy was in a quandary. Had Alt mentioned seeing him and Kristin at
the restaurant? And if not, why not? For that matter, what about Kristin
herself? Had she not confessed where and with whom she had had dinner last night? But what could be taken as illicit, in the simple truth?
Nothing untoward had occurred, unless his momentary foolishness at
the end of the evening, really a slip of the lip, could be so classified.

"Well, if he says it's okay . . ." This was the best Roy could do. He
had dropped the towel and was naked at the moment, looking in the
underwear drawer.

"He's a closemouthed son of a bitch," said Sam. "I guess that's what
you want in a lawyer. He didn't say a word about running into you and
Kris at A Quarter to Nine."

Roy felt his face become warm and, probably, red. The only mirror
in the room was affixed to the inside of the closed closet door.

"He sent her a bottle of Kristal to celebrate her promotion."

"She didn't mention it," said Sam. "I guess she thought, with the
Rolls, it would be too much. I didn't let on to Sy that I knew about you
guys having dinner. I guess he might now have the wrong impression of
that."

"What do you mean?" Wearing only blue boxers, Roy opened the closet to find a pair of jeans. At a better time he might have had the will to ignore his image in the mirror. He never found his body a satisfactory sight, a common case with body builders though never suspected by others, who often wrongly believe them narcissists. One of the reasons he stopped going to communal gyms some years earlier was having to witness the self-criticism, a form of self-pity, of those who felt their physiques were below par, though this might well be superficially masked by a competitive bravado.

Sam did not answer the question. "Did she drink much? Kris can't hold her liquor."

"She sent the bottle back unopened," said Roy, looking skeptically at his body, distending the deltoids. "Jonathan's holding it till you and she come back."

"Still, it's funny she never mentioned it. I don't know why anybody should feel guilty."

Roy ignored the tendentious statement except to ask, "I gather she's not there at the moment."

"Went to the drugstore for me," said Sam. "So when are you coming over? It's Saturday."

"I guess you don't remember: I'm open on Saturday. I've got a client coming in from Maryland."

"She swears she doesn't want the Rolls," said Sam in his solipsist way, "but don't unload it just yet, please."

"Be talking to you." Roy was now close enough to hit the button that broke the connection.

The Maryland car collector, whom Mrs. Forsythe had called "Leander" when making the appointment, was probably one of the many persons to whom Roy had given a business card at some vintage-automobile show, but he had no memory of the face that he saw in the window of the remarkable vehicle at the curb outside his showroom. Not that he inspected the man that carefully; he was distracted by the car.

Too thrilled to drive the Silver Wraith down to the parking area, he pulled that suddenly modest, even humble conveyance to a stop behind a grandeur for which the world "royal" was far too small.

He walked to the window of the right-hand-drive car, but after a quick glance therein, stared only at the coachwork. "My God, a *Bugatti Royale?* You *drove* it here?"

"I did indeed, Mr. Courtright."

Roy remembered his manners. "Please forgive me. You must be Mr. Leander." He shook hands through the window but still hardly looked at the man, immediately stepping back, swiveling his head, to survey the vast length of one of the largest automobiles ever built, almost fifteen feet, seven of which were taken by the hood. Yet its height, from running board to roof, seemed not much more than five feet. For all its size, the Type 41 was low and lean, a dark-blue silver-wheeled driving machine, whose straight-eight cylinders, equivalent to two Cadillac engines, would move its tonnage at 125 miles per hour—in 1928!

Leander meanwhile had come out to join Roy. He was not offended by being upstaged by the Bugatti. This was precisely the experience collectors craved most . . . well, most after the sometimes near orgasmic experience of gloating over a masterpiece of steel and horsepower when one was all alone with it.

"I've never before seen a Royale in the flesh," said Roy. He repeated the rhetorical question, "You *drove* it here? Am I right, there are only a handful of them in the world?"

Leander proved to be a stocky, large-chested man of about Roy's own height but considerably older than he, perhaps late fiftyish. Roy was not good at estimating male ages, which inability was no doubt related to his distaste for getting older. Leander's voice was unusually rich and resonant, even standing in the street. He wore a thick gray woolly toupee. "I made a vow many years ago when I first began collecting," said he. "I wouldn't buy a car that could not be driven, and I would drive any car I bought." He clapped Roy's shoulder with a bluff blow. He wore a double-breasted navy blue blazer with bone, not brass, buttons.

"Even so . . . well, it belongs to you, Mr. Leander. I'll bet it gets lots of attention on the road."

"But not informed attention," said Leander. "It is usually believed to be a car from a TV show or movie. I *have* had many offers from the world of entertainment, but certainly haven't accepted any."

"Yet you drive it on the public roads."

"I'm sure you can see the difference, Mr. Courtright." Leander gave him a proud smile. Within his pouchy face could be seen the ghostly lineaments of the handsome young man he had once been, and while he did not exactly look familiar as an individual, he did suggest a type.

"Excuse me, Mr. Leander, but were, are you, uh, someone in the performing arts?"

"'Were' is more appropriate than 'are,'" said Leander. "There was a time when I could call myself a tenor."

Roy remembered that only in opera were singers classified by range. "Aha," he lied, "I *thought* so. You're *that* Leander."

"Your parents owned some old records. You're far too young to have heard me in person." Leander made a stagey shrug, using his whole upper body, but he was obviously gratified. He gestured at the majestic car, which Roy had not forgotten for an instant. "I first sang Rodolfo at La Scala in forty-eight. That's when, believe it or not, in the countryside outside Milano, I found it in a peasant's barnyard, being used as a chicken house. It took me twenty years and more than a hundred thousand dollars for the restoration."

The estimate of Leander's age had to be adjusted to at least the mid-seventies, for which he was well preserved, with a proud bearing and vigorous stride.

The two men circled the automobile, from the huge round headlamps to the boxlike trunk and the rear-mounted spare tire, its tread incongruously narrow, thinner than that on a family car of today.

"Here's something you will enjoy, Mr. Courtright. Get around back and give it a push. Just wait till I hop in and let out the brake."

Roy did as asked and was amazed that one good though not excessively forceful shove easily caused the behemoth to roll forward until its owner brought it to a halt.

Leander's use of the word "hop" was justified; he deboarded in that style, saying, "It is put together with such fine tolerances."

"In my opinion," said Roy, "car design has never quite recovered from the loss of the running board. Not only is it a graceful means of entrance, particularly for ladies, but it provides the continuity of a straight line between the different curves of the back and front fenders."

"Sir," Leander cried, rearing back, hands on hips, "you are a poet." He looked briefly as if he might break into song but emitted a jolly laugh instead.

"Hey, what show is that on?" The questioner was a teenage boy in fashionably baggy pants that covered all but the tips of his red sneakers. He was one of the few onlookers who tarried along the near sidewalk.

Leander chuckled at Roy and said, "Q.E.D."

"I can't get over you driving it here," said Roy, "with what it's worth. A J-model Duesenberg recently sold for a million and a half. A Bugatti Royale would fetch what, six or seven times that? I hope you haven't come here to sell it to me, Mr. Leander, because I can't put my hands on that kind of money, and it would break my heart."

"No danger of that, my friend. I never sell. I only buy. I saw your Website and decided a visit would provide good exercise for the two of us." Meaning the Bugatti and himself.

Roy took him inside, where they spent a happy hour examining the current inventory; drinking espresso from the Stecchino, which Roy had finally loaded and fired up—Leander, old Italian hand that he was, pronouncing it *assolutamente autentico*; and exchanging accounts of fabulous automobiles acquired or narrowly missed.

Too shy to ask the old tenor whether *he* might simply sit behind the wheel of the Royale, Roy did prevail upon him to drive the car down to the parking area outside the garage. Roy went downstairs and distracted Paul and Diego until the massive vehicle was in place, then led them outside to revel in their wonder. Their equivalent to Roy's wistful desire to sit in the driver's seat would have been to be allowed to change the oil, but Leander did not produce such an invitation either.

He did, however, urge them all to come to his private car museum near Baltimore, where a collection of more than a hundred classics, including a 1912 Mercer Raceabout, a vintage Marmon, a '33 Pierce Silver Arrow, and other comparable gems, was open by special invitation only.

"My lust for cars ruined three of my marriages," Leander said in his ringing voice. "For years I wouldn't let anyone else see my treasures, except of course my mechanics." He grinned lavishly at Diego and Paul, who could not tear their eyes from the Royale. "And I would regularly *kill* them!" His laughter was loud enough to have reached the family circle without amplification. "Seriously, it took me years before I could bear to share my pleasure with fellow enthusiasts. Ha! But I was a happy monster."

Leander had thereby explained why Roy had never heard of his collection. There were many car museums around the country—including the most remarkable, that of Harold LeMay in Tacoma, Washington, with twenty-five hundred vehicles—most of them privately owned but open at least occasionally to the public.

"I'll repeat the invitation to the guys when they come out of their fantasies," Roy said. "I of course will take you up on it as soon as I can. What a treat!"

He was about to ask Leander if the dumbstruck mechanics could just take a peek at the mighty engine of the Type 41 when the former opera singer, prancing briskly, said, "Mr. Courtright, I am obliged to you for a delightful morning. I had better leave at once if I expect to get home in any kind of time. I am pleased to have met you, and do let me know if you get hold of something that might interest me. At the moment you have nothing I need. The Elite is a lovely design, but the car has proved notoriously unreliable, and as you know I drive anything I own. As to Lamborghinis, they are all far too vulgar for my taste, far too gaudy."

He shook Roy's hand and leaped into the car. Diego and Paul, on the opposite side, were taken by surprise by the awe-inspiring voice of the straight-eight as Leander started it up.

"Oh, noooo!" cried Paul. And Diego ran a few steps in pursuit of the huge, graceful vehicle as it glided out of the lot and, sounding a deeper note, effortlessly mounted the hill.

"He's invited us to come see his collection in Baltimore," Roy said by way of consolation, for the guys looked woebegone. He himself had enjoyed the first stress-free experience in a week and was actually relieved that Leander had not found anything of his to buy and thus disrupt a delightful and relaxing morning, free of corrosive emotion; just an innocent good time talking of and looking at cars, not even driving them at speed, supposedly a dangerous practice for oneself and others and therefore at odds with the common weal. A car at rest is one of the most harmless objects on earth, but an entity of great potential. Leander owned a racing Mercedes from the 1930s; parked at the curb, a Type W125 could be started up and within a mile catch the car that had passed it at 100 mph. This power was at the command of human beings, and to use it did not require a runway or a body of water or tracks of steel, nor if it fractured an appendage did you have to shoot it.

Sam had somehow managed to remain a boy even after he was married. Roy envied his friend while at the same time despising him for an incapacity he recognized as his own. Kristin was their common opponent. He had neither lied nor exaggerated when he admitted that he was in love with her, but he should never have done so. Hypocrisy requires more moral courage than candor, for truth is a destructive element, more dangerous to retain than release, whereas confession is a rude display of bad taste. He might not have distinguished himself by achievement, but he had always before been at pains to avoid gracelessness.

Mrs. Forsythe arrived a moment after Roy sat down behind his desk. After all this time she was still not entirely easy about working on Saturday, but was even more uncomfortable with replacing it with Monday as a day off.

"When you get settled," said he, "please look up my schedule for next month and see when I'm due to go to the Evansville car show."

She rested her bag. "I just saw a crazy-looking old automobile rolling down Main, big as a freight train. A real gas-guzzler, I bet. Some old coot, even older than the car by the looks of him, he was behind the wheel. Thought he ought to be coming here, but he was heading out of town."

The phone rang while Mrs. F. was in the lavatory heating water for her tea, and she shouted out, "Better get it, Roy. I got my hands full."

It was Kristin. He was shaken by an emotion he could not identify, but of the available choices it was most like fear.

"Oh, good," she said. "You're there. I hope you don't have a scheduled lunch. I know it's late . . ."

"That's okay," said Roy. He still had difficulty in breathing.

"Could we meet someplace?"

"Right now?"

"Could you, can you?"

"Of course. Where?"

"There's a place on Milburn Road, called The Corral."

"I know where it is." He was less apprehensive now that he was being given an assignment. He heard the sound of a horn at her end and realized she was already in a car. "I'll be there quick as I can. Better wait for me in the parking lot. Always a lot of jerks inside, if it's still the way it used to be."

"Dear Roy," said she, taking him completely by surprise. Was this affection, derision, irony, or, after all, mere indifference? He hesitated for a moment before realizing that she had hung up.

Mrs. F. mincingly returned to her desk with a steaming, tag-trailing mug that she had as usual overfilled. "Don't tell me you're leaving? I just got here."

"I don't know how long I'll be," Roy told her, with as much authority as he could ever assert. "I'll phone you if it's too long."


He drove the Grand Cherokee. A distinctive car would be out of place parked at The Corral, which could hardly be a regular hangout of Kristin's. It had been around since he and Sam were teenagers. In those days it was the kind of joint they found interesting to visit. Among its semitough clientele, Sam's size usually kept them out of trouble. If challenges did come about Roy could handle them, though maybe not without consequences, as when a drunken lout pulled a knife, obliging him to knock out the asshole's front teeth with a reverse punch that had been practiced against a makiwara board until his knuckles developed calluses hard as stone. Fortunately there were witnesses willing to testify against the knife-wielder, whose attorney of course intended to base a lawsuit on Roy's instruction in karate.

This was the first time that Roy's interests were represented by Seymour Alt, who had done work for his father. Ignoring Roy's protests, Alt arranged an out-of-court settlement for twenty-five thousand dollars. "We'd get slaughtered going to trial. This bum is an out-of-work laborer. Twenty-five large is like a sneeze to your dad."

Roy had never since been back to The Corral. In the succeeding years drug busts became routine there, until the place was finally closed. Since the reopening in the late nineties, it had not been mentioned in the local crime news, though why the latest owner had not changed that notorious name gave reason for doubt. Why Kristin had chosen such a venue for their meeting now was clear enough: encountering anyone they knew was most unlikely. But was stealth necessary at lunch, the most innocuous of public meals, when they had conspicuously dined together at a luxury restaurant the evening before?

Not only had Roy not revisited The Corral in two decades, he had not glanced at its new signboard on the relatively rare occasions he had driven out that way in recent years.

The former bar-and-grill had sometime since become Corral Family Steakhouse, and its building seemed to have been expanded, unless that was merely an illusion given by the bright white paint on the walls, with the front door and window frames in cherry red. The parking lot displayed no muscle cars and no battered pickups, though there was a very clean one or two of the latter, the kind some white-collar people own. The rest of the vans, SUVs, and sedans suggested no reason for Kristin to wait outside, and indeed she had not so done. He saw a parked Corolla that bore the plate number he had committed to memory.

The interior of the new Corral was so radiant in bright colors that having, despite the outside evidence, expected to step into the gloom of old, Roy was temporarily blinded. Fending off a beaming hostess, he saw Kristin in a pink booth against the far wall. To reach her he had to slip past or defer to other people among the crowded tables, many of whom were clamorous, self-oriented children.

"Roy. Thanks for coming." Kristin gave him her firm hand, as might a business acquaintance. Though it was Saturday she was dressed as if for work: pantsuit in banker's gray, white blouse, pearls. Her expression seemed routinely polite.

Roy sat down and shrugged. "Turns out my worries about this place were needless. Sam and I used to come here years ago when it was a dump."

She nodded. "Jim Smithson really does a super job in attracting the public. There would have been a long line an hour ago, and on Sundays he turns people away. He's already thinking of another addition. Plenty of room to expand in the parking lot."

"Let me guess. He does business with First United." She had made what at the time had seemed an emergency summons—and then he rushed here for talk about the restaurant trade, downscale at that: Most of the tables he had passed displayed pizza wedges and burgers 'n' fries.

"He could buy and sell Jonathan," said Kristin.

"It's the volume. It's why General Motors makes more money than Ferrari." Roy had played along with the banality and by so doing had inadvertently created the basis for a new intimacy between them. Kristin studied him with a kind of genial leer, her lips slightly parted.

She asked, "Are you making fun of me?"

"Probably." But she suddenly looked so melancholy that he hastened to say, "I'm just kidding." He wanted to grasp her hand but could not forget they were in a public place, and if it had been her bank that granted the loan to the owner, she was likely not to be unknown at the new Corral.

A vivacious waitress pranced up to take their order. "I think we could use a drink."

Roy had addressed Kristin, but the waitress told him, "I'm sorry, we don't have a liquor license."

He asked Kristin, "Should we get out of here?"

"I'll have a Diet Coke. And a plain burger."

"Sir?"

"Cup of coffee, black, and, okay, another hamburger." The waitress whirled away. Roy solemnly asked Kristin, "You want to tell me about it?"

"I've never before been accused, not seriously anyway, of something I haven't done, and I can't cope with it."

He was discreetly thrilled that she had turned to him for help. "Sam's started up again about our supposed affair."

"When you told me that, I thought he was joking. He *said* he was. I had no reason to believe otherwise, it was so preposterous."

Roy brought his unfisted hands together. "Christ. This is really tiresome."

"I think it's a lot worse than that."

He differed with her. "It's not worse, because there's no truth in it."

"You have more faith in the truth than I do."

It seemed they were arguing, as old couples were said to do. He was not unhappy to submit. "Have it your way."

She softened her tone. "What I mean is, daydreams always have more force with Sam than reality. You must know that better than I."

Roy turned his head. "Lately I've realized that maybe I don't know much about Sam at all. We have had a lot of fun together. I'm familiar with *some* of his tastes and habits and opinions. But I probably don't understand much about his feelings—and that may be because I'm not interested in that side of him." He had not found the confession amusing, but grinned nevertheless. "Isn't that an awful thing to say when speaking of a friend?"

"Not when you are speaking with another friend."

"I'll go so far as to say I never understood why my father's death hurt him more than it did me. Sam always claimed to hate his own father. I didn't hate mine, just never had anything in common with him. And he never seemed to think much of me. I should probably have been jealous of Sam, but I never was. . . . So I guess when I say I don't know why he was more broken up than I was when my father died, I'm lying. I do know: It's because I didn't care. And that may be lousy, but it's the truth." He grimaced. "Maybe he and I are friends just out of habit, though maybe the same can be said of everything else. Living may be just a habit."

"I don't believe that," Kristin said with force. "And I don't want you to believe it, either."

For pride's sake he made a burlesqued response. "Yes, ma'am." But he was pleased by her proprietary assertion.

"I'm not joking, Roy. I won't put up with it. I care too much for you."

"You do?"

"That's why this accusation is so rotten." She seemed to be glaring angrily at him. "Else it wouldn't matter."

Overwhelmed as he was, he perversely contested the point. "Sure it would! How could he—" He caught himself. It would not be proper for him to comment on Sam's performance as her husband, let alone when she was at such a disadvantage. "I only want to do what's helpful to you. I don't want to cause any more trouble. But since we haven't ever done anything wrong, how can we do even less?"

The question sounded so absurd when asked aloud that Roy laughed in spite of himself. But Kristin said soberly, "I care too much for Sam to let him believe in a lie."

Roy now resented Sam's getting any consideration at all. "He's not a child."

"But he *is*," cried Kristin. "That's exactly what he is. That's what attracted me to him. His delight in gadgets without ever really learning how they work. That damn coffee machine—he would never have made a decent cup with it. He's never taken as good a photograph with his digital camera as anyone could get with one of those disposables sold at the drugstore." Tears blurred her blue eyes.

Roy was not sure what, or whom, he felt sorriest for, but Kristin just now had forbidden him to be hopeless in a general way, and he understood why: It was not manly. It was not honorable to pile on his absent best friend, but as a man in love he did so anyway.

"He was the one who most wanted to learn to drive when we were kids. He became the rare bad driver whose smashups occurred at three miles per hour."

"Everything okay?" It was the spritely waitress, presumably asking about their orders, which had meanwhile been served unnoticed and had lain there untouched.

Waving her off, Kristin picked up the hamburger, broke it in two, and returned both pieces to the plate. She wiped her fingers on the flimsy paper napkin.

"It's getting late." Only after making this statement did she lift and twist her slender forearm to consult the small gold watch. "I ought to get back with his prescriptions."

"Wait a minute." Roy was desperate. "Where does this leave us?"

"Sam assures me you agreed to lend him fifty thousand dollars."

"I didn't want to mention this," Roy said. "Doing so now is a defeat for my principles. But then what hasn't been, lately?" By accident he noticed his own hamburger. He had a violent urge to gulp it down in all its greasy-sweet-saltiness, simply to remove it from offending his sight. As an adolescent Sam could eat three Double Whammyburgers in succession, with attendant fries, shakes, whatever, at any hour of the day or night. Roy stared at Kristin. "You and he, in your different ways, have pushed me into a corner. I wouldn't give him another cent for himself. I'm sick of him and his troubles. I don't even like him." If he had hoped to shock her, she showed no reaction. "He claims he's going to file for bankruptcy unless I lend him this money. What would that mean for your career?"

"He's lying," she said levelly.

Roy would not affront her by asking the conventional, "Are you sure?" In all the world his faith was only in her. It had come to that.

"I'm sorry, Roy. She put her fine hand on his fingers. "I didn't have any idea, though I guess I should have figured it out if you didn't turn him down when I kept asking you to."

"I hope you know I would do anything for you."

She lowered her golden head. "I suppose I could if I let myself think about it, but I don't want to." Looking up, she said in a voice angry in pitch but paradoxically soft of tone, "You're too damned gullible about him. *He doesn't wish you well.*"

Roy was embarrassed, not being used to this sort of candor, if such it was. Maybe he had misheard. "I don't understand."

"Because you don't want to."

"If you mean the money thing—well, he wasn't left penniless by any means, but people have strong feelings in that area. I overlook that kind of resentment, because it's not about anything essential, only money. I know Sam wouldn't cry his eyes out if I lost everything—I mean everything material. Maybe he'd even be pleased—okay, he probably *would* be pleased. I can accept that and not hate him for it. I can only hate somebody who betrayed me, and I'm sure Sam himself is the same."

Kristin's smile was thin and unamused. "The question is what you'd see as betrayal."

"It would have to be something personal, a violation of trust, something dishonorable."

"And you don't think *money* could figure in it?" She was incredulous.

"You're right. It could concern anything elevated to importance. But money isn't that important to *me*—maybe because I haven't had to work as hard for it as many, uh, most people. But neither has Sam, after all." He raised his eyebrows. "What you said was only that he doesn't wish me well. That's not so malevolent. He might feel like that even if he could score sometime with his business ideas."

She leaned forward, as if to soften the impact of what she was about to reveal. "As unlikely as that would be, it wouldn't be enough, I assure you. You would have to fail as well."

He wondered whether he should be suspicious of Kristin's motives. After all, he was only in love with her; he did not know her that well. But everything about being in love was new to him, as opposed to having a crush on, being attracted to, having the hots for, or loving friendship, at all of which he was a veteran hand. For a forgetful moment he found himself wishing he could talk it over with Sam. But to what avail would she unjustly defame her husband, or for that matter, with justice? So Sam resented him for his money. Was that not rather pathetic than hateful? The same judgment could be made about *him*, who envied Sam for having her.

"I only wish I had met you before he did."

"But you did," said Kristin. "You were wearing blue jeans and a navy T-shirt. You got out of a blood-red car of an exotic make I had never seen before. That was in front of the Main Street Pharmacy. I was a college freshman, home for the holidays. I stopped and asked you what kind of car it was, and you said, I've never forgotten, 'Ferrari Testarossa.' You hardly looked at me."

Roy was relieved to hear his delinquency had been so minor. For an instant he feared he had been introduced to her at some crowded party in years past, perhaps even chatted for a while, and did not remember the encounter because he had not then found her that attractive. "So much the worse for me," he said now. "But you were just a kid."

"I was only a couple years younger than you. I was also overweight with a mess of dirty-looking brown hair." Kristin showed her perfect teeth in a happy ruthlessness toward a self that no longer was.

"What did I know?"

"Tell you the truth," said she, "I scarcely looked at the car. You were the most handsome man I had ever seen."

"Now I'm embarrassed," Roy said in truth. "But you can't call that really meeting. The first time we actually met was that time at dinner with you and Sam, at Estelle's."

Kristin became almost cheery. "I certainly wasn't going to remind you then of the Main Street incident! I recognized your date from the magazine covers."

"Oh, yeah. The model. She was living around here that summer. Julie, uh . . ."

"Wethering," said Kristin.

"She bought a mint Alfa Superleggera from me, a fifty-eight. I dated her only a few times. She was engaged. In fact, the car was a gift from her fiancé, Charlie Venuta, the movie director. He's got a well-known car collection on the Coast. He and Julie went separate ways before long, and he bought the Alfa from her! I still hear from Charlie on occasion, when he's looking for a special marque."

"I've already said that I didn't much like you, but I still thought you were handsome, which made me dislike you more. All those stupid, weak women at your disposal. *You* seemed to be the sex object."

He displayed a temporizing smile. "I'm trying to find a way to defend those poor women without too much self-serving."

"You don't have to," Kristin said in her tenderest tone. "I know they were neither stupid nor weak—if they were in any other way, it wasn't because of you."

The waitress hovered briefly and left. Roy glanced toward the front of the restaurant, where a cluster of new arrivals had gathered. "I guess they want this booth. You're right about how popular this place is." He turned back to her. "You say Sam isn't telling the truth about the supposed bankruptcy. Without question I believe anything I hear from you, of course. I will definitely turn him down."

The waitress placed the check before him with one hand and, balancing a platter of food on the other, rushed on. Kristin looked as if she were about to speak, but decided against so doing and began to slide from the booth. Without examining the bill, Roy put a fifty-dollar note on top of it.

Outside, he walked Kristin to the Corolla, which still had not been washed. It was not unprecedented that a neglected car would have a perfectly groomed driver. The reverse was also true: there were slobs who maintained their everyday transportation as if for a concours d'elegance.

She unlocked and opened the door, releasing a wondrous fragrance from an interior warmed by the sun of early autumn. For the first time Roy suddenly felt physical desire for her. He had been liberated by the decision just made.

When seated inside, she lowered the window. "I'll take full responsibility. Don't feel you owe him an explanation."

"Of course I do," said Roy. "He's my friend. I can't hide behind a woman. It may be your wish, but it's my doing. I'm my own man. I guess I should welcome the chance to prove it."

His hand was on the lower frame of the window. Kristin inserted her fingers between his, one by one, worming each into place, including that which wore the gold band, the only ring on either of her hands. This was as sensual an experience as he had ever known, but if he had admitted as much to himself, it would have broken his heart.

"Thanks, Roy." She slowly withdrew her hand from his. "I'm so sorry."

"For what?"

"I could say for everybody, and it might be true in a way, but it would mostly be a lie." She stared through the windshield. "I'm sorry for myself, as most people are when they say they're sorry. I'm sorry I wasn't more attractive that time you got out of the Ferrari."

He had to deal with the sense of him she had been given by Sam. "Contrary to what you might think, I don't put the moves on every female I meet, and some of those I do want to know further turn me down, not to mention that I don't always end up in bed with those who do go out with me." It was the same account he had made more than once to Sam and his sister.

"Oh, I know that. But it doesn't matter." After a quick intake of breath, Kristin asked, "When can we see each other again?"

The surprising question made it even more difficult to say what he had to. He bent to speak through the window. "I know Sam, at least in this way. He won't forgive me for turning him down when he learns that I'm aware he's lying. His pride couldn't take it." He looked down at the hairline cracks in the asphalt between his feet. "As mine can't accept you being married to a guy like that when I want you so much. He's still my best friend, but I hate him at the moment. I don't have a strong enough character to choose one of those opposites over the other, and they can't be reconciled. . . . So the only way to handle it is by my life-long technique of avoiding the issue. The only thing is, for once it really hurts."

As if in wonderment, Kristin said, "I no longer think you're that handsome. I look at you in a completely different way. You're no longer *someone else*."

For his part, he had never even touched her in fantasy. He finally gave a direct answer to her question. "I can't see you again."

"No!" she said fiercely. "That can't be right." There were quick tears in her eyes. "I won't let you go!"

Had the situation been otherwise, how ecstatic he would have been made by that assertion. But then she would not have been Sam's wife, and therefore he would not even have known her.

"Don't put your faith in me," he said. "I can't visit the house on the old basis, and seeing you alone is out of the question."

"*Why?*"

"After being with *me* you would go home to *him*."

Someone nearby was shouting, someone with a persistent female voice that was sufficiently annoying to distract him, as he had not been distracted by the coming and going of cars in the parking lot.

He turned and scowled.

"Sir?" It was their waitress, running toward him, waving paper. "You didn't get your change."

"That's for you."

On reaching him she gasped for air. "A tip? . . . But that's like over a hundred percent." She lowered her hand with its sheaf of bills.

"I want you to have it," said Roy. Curbing his impatience, he added, "You work hard."

He quickly turned back to Kristin, but in those few moments the car was gone. She had been parked just inside the lot, nearest the exit, and there was little traffic at the moment on Milburn Road, his view of which was restricted by shrubbery, but even so she must have driven as if pursued.

# 10

Seymour Alt, who rarely ate lunch, was in the office but on another line. Roy left his cell phone number and stayed in the still-parked Jeep, in the Corral lot. He was suffering from the aftereffects of an affair he never had, which were much more confusing than those founded in the ineluctable facts of reality.

When Alt returned the call, the lawyer took the initiative. "The Holbrook business doesn't look good, Roy. *His* attorneys are staying hardnosed. They've come up with a shitsack of witnesses who say you beat him up bad and, believe it or not, they tracked down the Korean who was your karate teacher years ago."

"Right now I want to know something about Sam. Did he talk to you this morning?"

"Kindly don't involve me in your romantic entanglements—unless of course you want to start one with my wife and get her off my back. I would cheer you on."

"I'm not involved with Kristin Grandy!"

"Then you shouldn't look at her the way you do," said Alt. "And vice versa. And if so, you fooled Jonathan, who called you two 'lovebirds' when I ordered the champagne."

"She's my best friend's wife," Roy said icily. "I won't stand for the slandering of her character, which is flawless. Now answer my question: Did Sam call you this morning?"

"If he did, he didn't talk to me. I'll have Celia check the log." Alt clucked. "You're getting mighty touchy for a fellow with your reputation. Relax. I told Jonathan that Kristin's too career-driven to waste her time on romance. She's not very popular at the bank; she's stepped on too many people on her way up. She's got her eye on upper management."

"Has Sam ever mentioned asking me for a loan?"

"If that were a serious question, you know I couldn't ethically answer it. As it is, I'll just give a horselaugh at the idea of any sane person lending him fifty cents."

The ethics of friendship should be at least as stringent as those of the attorney–client relationship, but having made the major renunciation in the name of principle, Roy got some satisfaction from saying, "I've lent him a lot of money over the years, in relatively small amounts, but what he asked for lately is sizable."

"If you need my advice on the matter, you can infer it free of charge."

"I don't need it."

"Now, as for this Holbrook thing—"

"We'll talk about that later. I'm occupied at the moment." For once Roy hung up first, and scarcely had he done so when the phone rang.

"Where in the world," Mrs. Forsythe began, "have you been? I've been trying to find you for hours. Charlie Luger called from Indiana. He says that . . . uh, I've got it right here . . . Cord Eight-ten that he located, someone else is interested, and he has to know right away what kind of offer you will make if any."

Roy was bored with everything. "I have to look at it first. I'm supposed to be out there in a couple weeks at the Evansville show. If the owner can't wait till then, let him sell it to the other person."

"And then there's—"

"I'm not feeling well, Mrs. F. Kindly hold all calls until further notice. Take the rest of the day off if you like, and switch on the machine."

"That's happened all too often lately, Roy. You really ought to get a doctor to look at you, because this isn't any way to run a business."

Perhaps he should have pointed out that it obviously was not a business, but his psychic weariness was such that he could hardly hang up.

"You're *still* here?"

It was the waitress, who had come outside to smoke a cigarette. She had quite a pretty face, under soft brown bangs. Now that he actually looked at them, her eyes suggested she was somewhat older than her vivacity and lithe figure suggested.

"Yes."

"I thought she was your wife, but if you drove separate cars, she's probably someone else's. . . . So am I." She drew in and expelled some smoke.

"Good luck to you," said Roy. He was so exhausted he could have gone to sleep with his face on the steering wheel.

She displayed a wry, crooked smile. "What was the idea in leaving that big tip? Because you felt guilty about not touching your orders?"

Roy bestirred himself, being, so to speak, a professional at kidding around with any woman who was even halfway attractive. "I was just trying to get your attention, Daisy." He had just noticed the green nametag on the left bosom of her pink uniform.

"In case it didn't work out with your date?"

"You've nailed me."

"No, I haven't," said Daisy. "I'm not in your league, and you know it." She held up her left hand. "Anyway, I'm married, and I'm almost forty."

"That's a pity."

"Don't be sarcastic. I'm married to a cop."

"Some of my best friends are policemen. What's your last name?"

"Velikovsky."

"Well, there you are! I've known your husband for some time. My name is Roy Courtright. Please give him my regards."

"Believe me, Mr. Courtright, he'd be flattered if he thought you tried to pick me up. I really hate to tell him you didn't, but he wouldn't believe it if you had. We've been married fourteen years and have got three children."

"You tell him I said he is a lucky man, Mrs. Velikovsky. I thought you were twenty-five. By the way, you should know that the lady I was with is Mrs. Grandy, the wife of my best friend, who's in the hospital."

"Oh, I didn't think anything was inappropriate." She took another puff, threw down her cigarette, and ground it beneath her shoe. "Break's over, got to get back. I hope you come here again, Mr. Courtright, and thanks a million."

Roy wistfully watched her return to the restaurant. What a nice wife for a man to have. She had kept her looks, was fond of her husband, was surely a good mother. He had never doubted such women existed—in fact, if he could move beyond his natural brotherly disdain, the same could be said of Robin, who had left a successful career in public relations to devote herself to her small children and doted on Ross, a fine fellow . . . which reflection in turn reminded him he was delinquent in his familial duties. He had not been face to face with his sister in months though she lived just five miles away.

Impulsively he now dialed Robin's number.

"Hi, Robin."

"Who *is* this?"

It wasn't starting well. "You don't recognize my voice?"

"Barely."

"I just wanted, first, to say I was thinking about you."

"And?"

"Well, I wish I had been a better brother."

"Exactly what does that mean?"

He was stung. "You're not helping."

"What am I supposed to be helping *with?* Are you drunk? You must have just finished lunch and are full of wine and Armagnac."

"Oh, to hell with it."

"*Now* you're the brother I know."

"Wait a minute! Don't hang up, please. I don't want to bicker." He cleared his throat. "How about a family get-together tomorrow? On me, of course. There's this nice place for kids out on Milburn Road, called The Corral."

"I got rid of that slutty au pair," said Robin. "She wanted to spend her night off with some biker thug in *my* house. And you have no idea of quite how sick you can get hearing a Polish accent day after day, no matter how cute it was in the beginning."

"How about tomorrow?"

"Ross is flying to the Coast on Monday. I'd like to have a day with him around here."

"Well, maybe some other time soon, then."

"Roy," Robin said with an edge to her voice, "you were seen last night having dinner alone with Sam Grandy's wife."

"*Who* told you that?" Roy was furious.

"Mitzi Copeland saw you there," said she, citing a shrewish pal.

It went against the grain to go through the explanation once again, especially to his sister, but Roy did so.

"Look." Robin's tone, routinely petulant, turned nasty. "I wouldn't blame you, and I certainly wouldn't blame *her*."

"Okay, you don't like him. Let's let it go at that."

"That's what I've always done, Roy, but it might not last forever."

"In fairness I should point out that though *you* dumped *him*, he's not the bitter one."

She snorted savagely. "He's got no complaint against me."

"Just do me a favor, if you will, Rob. It's not right to besmirch the character of his wife. Please set Mitzi straight if she mentions the matter again. Tell her you got the truth right from the horse's mouth—or horse's ass, if you prefer."

"I can't remember you ever being that concerned with anyone else's reputation."

"Maybe because I'm not a liar. . . . I'm serious about having a family Sunday. Maybe next weekend?"

"I'm getting a new au pair and she has to be broken in."

"Check with you next week then," said Roy. Then, doggedly return-ing to the motive that had caused him to call her in the first place, he added, "I love you, Rob." Though the sentiment was sincere enough, he expected to get a barb in return. But he was only partially right.

"What brought that on?"

"Self-pity, if you like. You're really all I've got."

"I like to think you might eventually get your act together, Roy. I really do." This was probably as much warmth as he could expect from his sister unless he underwent a total transformation, i.e., discarded his cars, preferably at a considerable loss, and went into a real business; acquired a wife who would dominate him but be dominated by Robin and produce fewer children, worse-behaved and less talented than hers; and buy a comfortable home devoid of chic.

Nevertheless he said, "Thanks, Rob. Your good wishes mean a lot to me."

"Mind not calling me Rob?"

"I thought you liked that."

"I used to, but now I wonder if it doesn't sound like a guy's name."

He had driven only about a mile on Milburn Road, heading back to town though without a conscious destination, when he saw, parked on the shoulder not far ahead, a car by now so familiar that the very sight of its dirty-beige drabness quickened his heartbeat. It was Kristin's Corolla, resting, though on a level surface, at a slight imbalance. From his high perch in the Grand Cherokee, the Toyota's right tire was not visible, but he knew it was deflated.

He brought the Jeep to a stop behind the other car and dashed to its window. Kristin's fair head was in her hands.

"Are you okay? You had a blowout?"

She lowered her hands from her distressed face. She showed no sur-prise in seeing him. "I did everything right," she said with anger. "Didn't panic-brake, kept steering, and let the car slow itself. Came to a stop without damage—then, for no reason whatever, went into hysterics." Her cheeks were flushed.

"That's normal enough," said Roy.

"Damn. I just wish I could stop shaking. I must look like a fool."

"I can say this, if it does any good: From outside I can't see any shaking. It doesn't look like you're moving a muscle. It's probably a nervous reaction."

"Roy?" she asked. "Would you mind just holding me?"

He went around to the passenger's side and got in.

The strange fact was that when he first put his arms around her the experience seemed no more than the kind of superficial social embrace exchanged between members of opposite sexes (sometimes even man-to-man and performed by athletes and politicians) on meeting in public. But as it happened, he had never given Kristin such a hug. From the first, touching his best friend's wife in any way was covered by the same tacit taboo by which he and Sam never touched each other: These best friends, in twenty years of friendship, had never shaken hands.

Now his left arm was across her slender back, his hand cupping her shouldercap. His right hand was not yet in play. He did not know quite where to put it, for despite her request, Kristin at first did nothing to facilitate his compliance, maintaining her spine flush against the seat, bending forward only just enough for the insertion of his arm. He clasped rather than enclosed her, at the last inch of her narrow body.

The situation was altogether abstract until she finally leaned against him, her right arm against his left side. Slowly her head came into his neck.

"Thanks," she murmured. "It does help."

She was apparently more at ease than he. His prior experience of women went for naught. For an unthinking instant he wished he could compare notes with Sam, something he had never really done in the case of others, never having shared another with his best friend. Roy anyway was discreet about his liaisons. He had never had a taste for sexual gloating. . . . But then the moment at hand was not in the least sexual, nor was, seen from the corner of his eye, her sleek, styled hair and her fragrance, not nearly so erotic at close quarters as when it had been wafted from the interior of the parked car. She continued to be more idea than fact.

After a while he asked her if she felt better. "I ought to change that tire."

Several cars had passed them since his arm was around her. That sort of thing was always noticed. If they were recognized they would be compromised once again—as usual, unjustly.

"Hell with it." She spoke almost stridently, though her head remained on his shoulder.

"There ought to be a towrope in the Jeep, but there isn't. I'll call Towne Garage. Leave the key under the seat, and I'll run you home."

"Hell with it," she repeated, now lifting her head. But it was still too close for him to turn and look at her without a collision of faces.

"Well, I should do *something*." When he shrugged he was aware of her slight weight, still against his side but pressing now and not simply leaning. He had acquired her as, literally, a dependent. He could not leave the car without taking her into account. "Shouldn't I?"

She responded with a question of her own and, unlike his, with a point—insofar, that is, as he could rely on his hearing alone: What she asked was incredible to his faculty of reason.

"Do you want me?"

He did not, though briefly, when she had first entered the car in The Corral lot and again when she entwined her fingers with his, he thought he did. The question now made no sense when applied to what he felt for her. There was no romance in it. *Want* referred to that which he had often known, and frequently satisfied, with other women—too many of them, as he could only now admit, in his lifelong reluctance to see himself as mere lecher.

The fact was that he had never been, and perhaps did not know how to be, a lover.

His arm was still across her back, his hand on her far shoulder. He shook her slightly, in a be-a-good-fellow gesture, an effort to diminish the moment, saying, "Of course I do. Now I'd better call the garage."

"I've always wanted you," she said. "From the first time I ever saw you, as a kid. I guess that's why I asked about the car."

"You had contempt for me when you grew up."

"You don't have to admire those you want."

"Tell me about it!" That slipped out before Roy knew what he was saying. It was on the money but sounded awfully crude, so he lost his inhibition against candor. "I admire *you* tremendously. Just to be in your company means the world to me."

"We've spent hardly any time together."

"It has seemed like a lot to me. So to me anyway we already have a history." He reclaimed his arm and said gently, "Come on, now. I'll give you a lift."

She stayed in place. "Are you trying to get rid of me?"

"If you want to put it that way."

"You're being loyal to Sam."

"I'm also wondering what in the world I could do for a woman like you."

"Shouldn't I be the one to ask that?"

"But I suspect you won't. I should not have told you how I felt about you. What were you supposed to do with that information? It was selfish of me to leave you with such a burden."

"Do you think I'm acting now out of a sense of obligation?" She was seemingly more curious than angry.

"*I* certainly am."

"Well, *I'm* not. I've had enough of that."

He drew away, so that he had room to look at her for the first time since this moment of intimacy had begun. It had been years since he last sat in the passenger's seat of a motor vehicle, an incongruous place for any but coarse feelings. But by her very presence Kristin transformed it. "I think you can appreciate my position."

"Let me explain mine. I don't have a vast experience of men: I mean personal as opposed to professional. What I've always been focused on was my career. I didn't date much through school. I wasn't asked all that often, and when I did go out it was usually with the kind of guy with whom I had supposedly a good deal in common. We would talk finance all evening, then at the end he would start kissing me and feeling me up and want to go to bed. I finally tolerated this a few times so as to try to be normal. I wasn't a lesbian but I didn't care much for the company of such men, either, and I didn't know how I was ever going to meet any other kind. Worse, when I left school and went into the world, it was these kinds of men I was competing with. Well, eventually I met Sam. Did he ever tell you how?"

"He never has," said Roy, "and I didn't ask. I don't go out of my way to exchange information with him about women. Probably that's because he doesn't approve of mine—or maybe I should say that what he doesn't like are not my girlfriends but my relations with them. If I questioned him about you, he would have used it to preach to me."

"We turned him down for a loan," said Kristin. "As soon as he got the letter, he came to the bank. I was a loan officer then, out in the open, what we down there call the barnyard, and my main ambition at that time was simply to get promoted to a private office with a door. But when his huge figure loomed over my desk, I was happy to be where the guard could come to my rescue."

"I'm sure he was nice."

"'So, okay, keep your damned money,' he said, 'but have dinner with me. It might not be a very good meal, because as you should be the first to know, I couldn't afford one. But I'll keep my hands to myself and get you home early so your parents won't worry.'"

"That's old Sam."

"I didn't look that young and didn't want to. Furthermore I was insulted that he would think a line like that was attractive, but then I found myself feeling sorry for him. He has sad eyes even when he's laughing."

Roy remembered that he had earlier believed Kristin lacking in a sense of humor. By now he could refine it further to a particular incapacity for irony, of which Sam had a great supply that had remained undiminished by any success he had in life; he had of course assumed she would be amused by a caricature of bad-taste male-chauvinist flattery.

What Roy's own approach might have been could not be considered. He would not have made one. A tall, flat-chested short-haired blonde with cool eyes had never been his type.

Kristin continued. "So I went out with him and had a good time. We ate junk food and played machine games. He has all sorts of interests as you know, and that can be entertaining even if you don't share them, at first maybe especially *if* you don't share them." She frowned. "And he didn't try to convince me how important he was. I liked that about him then, but now I don't know. . . ." She put her face into her hands and suddenly wept without a sound.

Roy had a man's dread of a woman's grief, though with him it was rather the sobs than the tears that so threatened the natural order of things. He had heard too many of his mother's when he was a child, but by nature she was a histrionic woman. That was not true of Kristin—unless it was a side of her he had not seen before.

"Let me take you home."

"I still haven't explained why I married him," she said doggedly, clenching her fist. "It all happened in such a hurry, I don't even know why, except it was fun." She glared at him with reddened eyes. "Isn't that pathetic? I meet a guy whose chief recommendation is he's not threatened by me, he's not competing with me, and I have to marry him before he gets away. And here's just how pitiful it turns out to be: It didn't take long after I married him to realize it was a simpleminded illusion of mine. I can't really blame him for that. I hoodwinked myself. He's the most extreme competitor I've ever had, except that he does it in a subtle way I was too naïve to recognize. If he was only trying to get my job! I could handle that."

Roy could take no decent satisfaction in profiting by Sam's failure, if indeed he was so doing. However, his contempt for his best friend could not but increase: It was only human. At the same time he felt guilty for enjoying the confidence of a disloyal wife.

With an effort he managed to say, "He's really proud of you."

Kristin did not acknowledge this assurance. "Roy." She seized the steering wheel and not his available left hand. "Roy." She turned her face from him to gaze through the windshield and ask wistfully, "Would you mind taking me to bed someplace?"

After dropping Kristin off at the Towne Garage, to which her car had been towed and where it was now parked, the flat repaired, Roy felt too lonely to go home. He returned the Jeep to the lot behind his business. The big doors to the realm of Paul and Diego were closed, the windows dark. After all, it was almost nine. Roy could have used their company this evening. Simply to hang out while they tuned an engine, to risk having an eardrum shattered or being asphyxiated from exhaust fumes, exchanging no conversation, would have been therapeutic.

He climbed the hill, which proved steeper than he remembered. Should a man in his supposed condition be already feeling the effects of age? He could hardly have been worn out by excessive physical love-making. His performance, insofar as it could be so called, had been too chagrining to reflect on. He dreaded meeting Kristin again, yet he was more in love with her than ever.

He let himself in to the darkened showroom and groped his way to the office, trying not to touch any fenders in the process. The office was also dark, Mrs. Forsythe having forgotten his standing instruction to leave on one small source of illumination against which the police, in their regular drive-bys, might see the silhouettes of intruders or take suspicious notice that it was out.

He turned on the old gooseneck, clamshell-shaded lamp atop his desk, one of the few material souvenirs of his mother's family. He had kept it because it had first been owned by his maternal grandfather, whose little ornamental-iron shop had failed during the Great Depression and who subsequently found a job as a janitor at twelve dollars a week. His son, Roy's uncle, whose medals Roy kept at home in a silver box he had made for the purpose, was one of the twelve thousand Americans killed in the taking of Okinawa, where a hundred and ten thousand Japanese died, many by their own hand, including their generals, who disemboweled themselves while being simultaneously beheaded by their aides.

So far as Roy knew, the only person on either side of his family to commit suicide was his own father, and that was not for honor but rather after a diagnosis of illness.

There was a tapping at the front door. He stood up and squinted out between the cars, trying to discern who it might be, but could not do so before his eyes adjusted in the transition from staring at a light oak desktop under a sixty-watt bulb. Meanwhile he had walked out far enough so that his gestures could be recognized.

By then he could see the uniform. He went to open the door. It was Officer Velikovsky.

"Hi, Mr. Courtright. I just noticed a different light was on."

"Thanks for doing a careful job as always. . . . I'm particularly glad to see you. I tried to pick up your wife today, but I wasn't man enough to pull it off."

Velikovsky assumed a wide grin. "She told me about the incident. I says, 'You missed the only opportunity you're gonna get at your age.' She says, 'I always miss the boat. Look who I married when I was young.' She's got a mouth on her."

"She's a good woman."

The officer shrugged, though he looked proud. "I'm not yet ready to recycle her."

From Velikovsky's omission of any reference to the large tip, Roy suspected his wife was keeping it all for herself. He was amused during the few moments it took to return to the office and his predicament.

He was finally guilty of what his best friend had unjustly charged him with earlier. Kristin agreed with Roy that, given the delicate state of Sam's health, it would be unthinkable to tell him now. In effect this meant never, for when could a once ailing heart be made permanently invulnerable to an attack on the amour propre? Roy agreed with her that Sam's greatest love was for himself and not his wife and, certainly, not a friend. And to someone of that character, what could be so mortifying as a conspiracy between that wife and that friend?

"Believe me, it would kill him," Roy had told her as they were dressing in the shabby motel room, with its off-white furniture of plastic-faced particle board. He had a remorseful aversion to looking closely at her silver body, of which he caught more accidental glimpses in the mirror-wall than straight on. He wished their coming together had remained awhile longer as an unattainable ideal.

Roy's sole material souvenir of his mother, who was still living though not seen by him in two decades, was a booklet bound in fake red leather with a hollow heart inscribed in gold on the cover, inside which in gilt lettering appeared the simple title *Love Poems*. It was the kind of thing found in stationery shops around Valentine's Day. The flyleaf was inscribed, in ball pen, *Ms. Joan Melinda Shaw*. She had probably been an early teenager at the time of purchase; perhaps she had given the book to herself. Years later his father had called her a tramp, but Roy knew she was rather a romantic—unless the two were one and the same. But neither applied to those who found what they were looking for, and he had now done so, for all the good it would do him. He could not kill his best friend just to be happy.

# 11

For the next two days Roy hid out, not emerging from the place he called home, except for a four-mile run early Monday morning. So great was his turmoil of spirit as to overrule his sense of responsibility, and he switched off all telephones and their accessories, making himself inaccessible via the airwaves to all other human beings. This included Robin, meaning that if she had relented and accepted his invitation to a family outing, unlikely but not without precedent, she could not have reached him.

He could not avoid Sam forever. He had an even greater aversion to Kristin though his feeling for her was now more intense than it had been, because he felt he had not met her expectations as a lover. How rotten it must have been for her if he had provided what was only an embarrassment. If so, she had risked so much for so little. That she had subsequently been kind, even sweet, signified no more than good manners.

As to Sam, no matter how often Roy told himself he had nothing but contempt for the man, he did not believe it. If only he could take the matter to—Sam. Not that Sam had ever understood or even been sympathetic to him. In view of Kristin's revelations, the bastard might well have been downright hostile. Yet that could not alter the fact that Sam was his best friend, a fact that had a long, unrewritable history. He and Sam had been stuck with each other for more than half their lives. Whether they had actually ever liked each other was probably irrelevant.

For example, Sam was the only person to whom Roy could have confessed spending much of his two-day reclusion in surfing the 120 channels reached by the satellite service without finding anything to which he could attach his interest for more than a moment, and not only because it was Sam who dogged him into signing on to it. Sam himself would squander whole mornings in that sort of pursuit, the difference being that Sam would be fascinated by most of the programs he encountered. The same was true when the Internet had come into being. Sam would log on and stay for an hour at a site that offered only video images of the traffic on the bridge, and come up with an investment idea.

Nevertheless, because Roy so dreaded facing the music, two days passed as quickly as hours, and there he was, Tuesday noontime, sitting across the room from the newly arrived Mrs. Forsythe, whose phone was in her hand.

"I can't keep this up, Roy. He kept calling Saturday afternoon. I could at least tell him the truth then: I *didn't* know where you were. But I *do* now, and I'm not going to lie."

With all his dread of the fall of the ax, Roy was taken by surprise when, Mrs. F. having pushed the button that put him on the line with Sam, his best friend's greeting was breezily affectionate.

"How ya doin', kid?"

"How about *you?*"

"I can't believe how great I feel. Believe it or not, just those few days on hospital food, I lost four pounds. And I've been home three days without putting them back, though over the weekend Kris prepared some fantastic things. We were hoping you would turn up. What became of you? You slipped under the radar. I been callin' for days."

"I had to go upstate to look at an Alfa, a middle-sixties Duetto, if that means anything to you."

"What'll you make on that?"

"Didn't end up buying it. Needed too much restoration, and the owner wouldn't lower his asking price." The best lies consist mostly of the truth. Roy had made that very trip the year before. What he wondered now is whether he had told Sam about it at the time.

"So that's your excuse for the last three days," said Sam. "I certainly hope you can get over here today. How about dinner? Kris vows to come home at a reasonable hour. I got to take it easy on food and drink, but there's no reason for you to hold back."

Roy had not truly considered the practical consequences of what he and Kristin had done on Saturday. What was he expected to do about such an invitation? That is, by the heavenly powers? Sam was of course pressuring him to accept it.

"I've got this guy coming from Baltimore. He's supposedly driving one of the rarest of the great classics, worth millions—"

"I thought he was due on Saturday," Sam broke in to say. "But I guess he didn't show if you drove upstate. Or was that Sunday or Monday?"

"Yeah," said Roy. He declined to explain further. Sam could go fuck himself.

"Say," Sam said brightly, "here's an idea. You'll sure want a test drive in that classic of his. Mind swinging past here? Stop in for a drink. Anyway, just run up the driveway and give me a look. I'd love to see what's worth that kind of money. What is it, an old Rolls?"

The request was selfishly obtuse as to the protocol of the vintage-car trade in which his best friend had long been engaged, but had Roy not become Kristin's lover he would simply have laughed off Sam's sudden interest in vintage cars as phoney. But Roy and Kristin *were* lovers—this was the first time, tempering his shame with a certain pride, that he had defined them as such—and he could never again trust his best friend with the truth.

"Sure, I'll bring him around."

"You're full of shit. You seem to have lost your sense of humor lately. In my financial condition, do you think I want to meet some asshole who has so much money he can't find a better use for it than buying old automobiles?"

Roy had no stomach for this. "You're right. I should have known better."

"You're not going to defend car collecting?" Sam asked derisively. "I can't get a rise out of you today. That trip upstate must have taken a lot outta you."

Roy's promise to Kristin this time was absolute: He would once for all reject Sam's plea for the loan, and in justice to everybody concerned, that had to be done face to face.

"I'll be over later."

"Cheer up," said Sam. "*You* can eat and drink as much as you want. I just have to watch." He hung up on this ambiguous statement.

"You're expecting Maxwell Leander today?" asked Mrs. Forsythe, her head at an angle. "He changed the appointment?"

"I guess I didn't mention it. He was here Saturday morning. I lied just now to Sam Grandy."

"*That* might be none of my business, but I do like to know when we're expecting a visitor."

"You'll be the first to know, Mrs. F., if one is due to arrive during your hours here. If somebody comes at another time, I may forget to tell you if he does not buy or sell a car."

She made no response to the rebuking explanation but continued to stare at him. At last she said, "I wonder if I should tell you this, Roy. I've decided to do so because I think you basically have a good heart, and you've been very nice to me, I have to admit." Her thin eyebrows arched. "But you do have a reputation. And there's that terrible thing that happened to poor Mrs. Holbrook, and some of the dirt might well have brushed off on you. You have to realize that . . ." She cleared her throat and softened her voice almost to a whisper. "You were recognized on Saturday, in a parked car on Milburn Road in broad daylight, with a woman in your arms."

"Who was the woman?"

Mrs. F. gasped. "You don't remember?"

For some perverse reason, he found temporary relief from his cares in this exchange. "I can't tell one from the other, Mrs. F. There's such a long list, and they're interchangeable."

Surprisingly, she was not provoked, at least not in the expected manner. Instead she produced a rare smile. "Now, Roy, you're kidding me. You're a rascal but you're not that sort of man. I know that sort, or *knew*: Bob Forsythe. I was dumb enough to marry him."

"The woman's car had just had a blowout, and I stopped to help. That experience can be terrifying to someone not an expert driver, and she was in hysterics. I calmed her down and called Harry Bates at the Towne Garage to come and tow the car in, and I gave her a lift home."

Mrs. F. displayed self-satisfaction. "I *knew*, in this case at least, there was a good reason, and I said as much to the person who told me."

"I'm curious," said Roy. "Who was that person?"

"Juliette, as it happened. Her friend recognized you."

"I've never met your daughter." He made a mock frown. "I think you've kept her away from me."

Mrs. Forsythe looked aside. "No, Roy, that is not true." Her eyes came back and fixed on him. "She does not care for the male sex. And no wonder, with a father like hers."

"How old is she now?"

"She's eighteen. None of us are as young as we once were."

"That's certainly true of me," said Roy. "It's time I settled down."

"You took the words out of my mouth." Mrs. F. again looked away, as was her habit when speaking on a subject that touched a nerve at least with herself.

"Despite your own unhappy experience, you still believe in marriage?"

"I try not to be too self-centered in looking at things," said she. "I'll bet you would make a fine father."

"Really?" He was inordinately pleased.

"You're very manly. I know, there's still some childishness in you, but that's natural enough. For a while there were people who wanted men to be more like women, but that doesn't make any sense." She blinked. "Incidentally, the opposite of manliness isn't being effeminate, and it isn't necessarily cowardice. It's disloyalty."

He had never before seen the moralist in Mrs. Forsythe. Perhaps it was rather that he had never given himself the opportunity to speak with her on matters of fundamental importance.

"You may be overestimating me," he told her, "but it's nice to hear." Loyalty could sometimes be only habitual, but he would not make that point aloud.

She was not yet done with the subject. "Give me a loyal coward over a disloyal hero."

"The disloyal hero is devoted to himself, whereas at least the loyal coward does not betray his community."

"You understand very well."

"What about women?"

"Women," said Mrs. F., "*are* the community."

Yet to whom to be loyal? It was a serious problem but not a serious question. His love for Kristin had all but expunged his affection for Sam. But for the principle of friendship, he would not have given the matter a second thought. He had no feeling one way or the other for the husbands of the women with whom he had gone to bed. He felt neither triumph over them nor guilt. They played no part in his side of an affair, unless of course they acted as did Martin Holbrook in the parking lot of The Hedges. Until then, the man had been only a name.

He suddenly ached to be in touch with Kristin, with whom he had had no contact since delivering her to the foot of the Grandy driveway on Saturday evening. On parting they had not even made any arrangement to meet again. It did not occur to him at the time that she might have no intention of meeting him again, that he had served his purpose for that hour or so, that she did not reciprocate his love, but had rather been ruled by a temporary physical passion, the satisfaction of which on that single occasion would suffice forever.

She had never told him not to phone her at the bank. Nevertheless, doing so would violate the classic protocol of illicit liaisons. Roy was a traditionalist, not a rule-breaker; he would take another man's wife to bed but not flout the lesser conventions, just as he would drive a car far in excess of speed limits but always obey stop signs and use turn signals. However, unless he called Kristin at work she would be accessible only on the home phones of which Sam was again in command.

He could not afford to wait for her to call *him*, having convinced himself, all at once, that she would never do so.

After her tea was brewed, Mrs. Forsythe did not usually return to the lavatory until it was quitting time each day. He could certainly not phone Kristin in her presence.

"I'm going down to see if the guys have put the E-Type back together." To which assertion Mrs. F., eyes on monitor screen and fingers at keyboard, made a preoccupied nod.

He carried his cell phone to the lower level but at the bottom did not enter the garage, owing to the din of mechanics at work. At the moment the guys were in the farthest corner. A fire door between him and them muffled the noise of the compressed-air wrenches and ballpeen-hammer blows.

He asked the woman who answered the bank's telephone to connect him with Kristin Grandy.

"She's in a meeting. Can you give me your name and number? She'll call back soon as she can."

"I'm moving around. I better try again. When's a good time?"

"I couldn't say. She's awfully busy. Better pick a time when you're going to be in one place for a while, and let her return your call."

"I'll get back to you."

As Roy stepped into the office Mrs. Forsythe was saying, "Just a moment. Here he is now." She pointed toward the phone on his desk.

"Who *is* it?" he asked in annoyance. She knew he disliked taking business calls without preparation.

"You'll want to talk to *her*," said Mrs. F. "She's interested in that old Elvis of yours."

"The *Alvis*," he said, and not for the first time. He had almost given up correcting her defiant mispronunciation of the German sports car name as "Porsh," because, as she had pointed out, the same was used on television by every showbiz celebrity who owned one.

When he answered his desk phone, it was Kristin's voice that said, "Mr. Courtright?"

"Yes."

"Could I look at the car after six today?"

"By all means."

"Would that be convenient?"

"That will be fine."

"See you then."

"Thank you."

"That didn't take long," Mrs. Forsythe said. "Short and, I hope, sweet."

"She wants to take a test drive."

"Say when?"

"Maybe tomorrow."

"I really prefer specific appointments," said Mrs. F., wrinkling her nose. "But at least that woman phoned on business. You got another call during the few minutes you were downstairs. Somebody named Michelle. She didn't say anything about cars."

"I'm seeing her socially," said Roy. "She may be a bit young for me— she's just finishing college—but she's single. She's a very level-headed young woman. She might make a fine wife and mother, but I want to know her better."

Mrs. Forsythe was beaming at him. "I've never given up hope on you, Roy. Maybe you're finally on the right track. Now get back to your Michelle. She sounded awfully anxious."

He actually pretended to comply, dialing his home phone and listening to himself on the answering machine. "I'll catch her later," he told Mrs. F. "She was probably calling between classes."

Mrs. Forsythe went home at five, reminding him not to forget about Michelle, the idea of whom apparently pleased her.

"'Michelle, Ma Belle' has always been one of my favorite songs. I won't tell you how old I was when it first came out."

"You were in kindergarten."

Lingering in the doorway, she said, "If I were that young, you'd call me Margaret."

"I call you Mrs. Forsythe to show respect. I'll be glad to call you Margaret."

"I'd like that. Only not Maggie, please."

Suddenly she did seem younger. She was not an unattractive woman, with a trim figure and large brown eyes. She was probably no more than fifteen years older than he. But thinking in personal terms of a female employee was distasteful to him.

After her departure he locked the showroom door and turned off all the lights except the one in the office ceiling that burned all night. He decided to wait for Kristin in one of the cars, so that he was not likely to be seen, in a twilit interior, from the street.

The obvious choice was the Rolls-Royce Silver Wraith, with its generous back seat, the buttery-leather upholstery of which was so comfortable that he might have dozed off had he been waiting for anyone else. He had had many consecutive nights of normal sleep, which seemed a consequence of physical fitness, but had taken no rest from it lately. The sense of power that came with exercise was genuine but only muscle-deep, and relative to a given situation. That stronger men than he were extant did not bother him. He had never had reason to be an ardent competitor. In the few violent altercations in which he had participated, his purpose was to defend his friends, as in the case of Francine, not to score a victory or defeat an opponent.

Loving Kristin, he could not like Sam, but neither did he wish him ill. At the moment anyway, Roy had succeeded in not thinking, past that moment, of what was to come. He would not even anticipate becoming a better lover.

Eventually he saw Kristin as a silhouette against the light from the declining sun and hastened to the door to let her in.

She was uncharacteristically voluble, beginning to speak before he closed and locked the door. "It was all so sudden, Saturday. I didn't try to make sense of it. The weekend passed in a couple of hours, and there I was back at the bank, with a pile of work postponed or neglected because of Sam's illness, and I don't even remember saying goodbye to you. What kind of person would you think I was, but how and where could I get in touch with you to apologize? Because just saying 'I'm sorry' would be an insult. Anyhow, I'm not really sorry, but the whole situation is just a fantastic mess and gets worse the more it's thought about. I really do have a demanding job that I worked hard to get and I can't jeopardize it. Then there's Sam. He—"

Roy had meanwhile led her to the Rolls-Royce. She had continued to speak as he joined her in the back seat but fell silent when he cupped her left breast in his hand. It was small as an avocado but of an exquisite shape even when felt through several layers of clothing. He must have seen it on Saturday but had no precise memory of so doing.

Disrobing no further than was necessary, they merged, making real that which for him until now had remained all but imaginary, never more so than after their first embrace three days before. The transition from polite friends to intimate lovers now had a history of seventy-two hours. It was no longer a shocking outrage. What had been shattered was replaced by that which was united. Roy had never suspected that this kind of feeling was available to him, unlocking a door that he had not been aware was closed or even there. He became so much a part of her that their identities were indistinguishable. It was being, not doing, but the climax was a long moment of soaring nonexistence, succeeded gradually by a miraculous serenity on coming to rest in a new world.

"Look at what a mess we're in," said Kristin, from her crush of clothing. It was a kind of joyous boast.

Roy had rolled onto his back on the leather seat, in the rumpled jacket, shirt, and tie. He was not embarrassed that his trousers yawned open. Nor had Kristin pulled up her underwear.

"We are a sight," he said happily. He groped for and found a handkerchief, passing it on. "Let's never leave this car."

He had meant for her to use the handkerchief for her own purposes. Instead she did the most incredibly sweet thing ever done for him by any woman and tenderly dried him off.

By which gesture he was of course aroused again, and once more they joined and lost themselves in each other. . . . When finally they came back, weary and reluctant, to an awareness that a world of others might still exist, the showroom and the street beyond the big windows had disappeared in darkness. They needed no light to see each other. They were now naked, holding fast, the only life in the universe, her breath in his nostrils, her heart in his hand.

"I've never been in love before," he said. He was unable sufficiently to express his disbelief. *"Never!"* It was not enough. He kissed her in desperation.

She touched his cheek. "I know."

"It isn't what *he* thought or thinks. When he accused me, I hadn't even thought of you in that way."

"Did he give us the idea?"

"God," said Roy. "I hope not."

She clutched him with remarkable strength. She was slender and delicate but not fragile. She caressed him in a way more evaluative than erotic, running fine smooth fingers over his torso and the undulations of his far arm.

"What a body *you've* got."

He assumed from the emphasis that she was quoting him on hers, but he did not remember saying so. "One of the few things I've done in life is keep in shape. Until now, I could not have said why: It just seemed like I ought to, like frequenting women I didn't care about."

"You won't hear any complaints from me," Kristin said with a warm mouth against his neck. "However you learned what you do."

But it was not a technique. "I love you," he said. "I've never made love before." She continued to explore his body with sensitive fingertips. "Kristin?"

"I can't get any closer."

"Where do we go from here?"

Along her spine he could feel the vibration of the soft groan. "I *dread* going home, but I guess I have to."

"I don't mean now, today. What do we do from here on?"

She reclaimed her hand. They still were sprawled on the rear seat of the Silver Wraith, amid scattered clothing. He heard and felt rather than saw her get dressed. She said, "I can't even think about it at this minute. It's still too soon. It's been too quick. I didn't even know why I came here. I guess it was to try to understand. Now I'm more confused than ever."

"I'm clearer-headed than I've ever been," said Roy. "I want you."

"I believe you've just had me more than once," Kristin said, with a startling, airy laugh.

"I'm old-fashioned. I want to marry you."

"But I'm already married." As if to soften the blow, she leaned over and kissed him languorously.

"Yeah," said he when she had pulled free. "I can't forget that. I don't know what to do about old Sam."

"Nothing!" She was almost shrill. "The less he knows, the better."

"Just keep meeting on the sly?" he asked in disbelief. "That can't be right."

"I don't think we should go into what's right."

"If it was only about sex," said Roy. "But it isn't. I wouldn't have touched you if it were. This guy *is* my best friend. I couldn't stab him in the back."

"Haven't we already done that?"

"No! Love overrules all else. I don't mean Sam would agree with that, but *we* have to, you and me."

He finally exerted the effort necessary to put on his clothes, freeing the individual garments from the general tangle. He had done nothing close to this since he was a teenager. Love not only superseded morality; it transformed everything done in its interests, else he would have felt foolish after a roll in the backseat of a car. As it was, he felt like a hero. He would have liked to lift Kristin up and carry her in exultation among the high-performance machinery in his showroom, pausing to make love on the long, low red hood of the Lamborghini or against the cool lemon-yellow fiberglass of the Lotus Elite. . . . He was being more childish than heroic, and it did not matter.

Kristin brought him back to reason. "Do you have any idea what time it is? I can't see my watch in the dark."

"Mine's got a backlight." As usual it was the drugstore model derided by Sam. He felt for the appropriate button and depressed it with a thumbnail, suffusing the dial with a ghostly blue glow.

"It's after nine."

"Long after?"

"Almost nine-thirty, in fact."

She shrieked and hurled open the door on her side, illuminating them both for anyone outside to see that they were emerging from the backseat of a car in a darkened showroom.

There was no immediate way to tell if anyone did so. The sudden light had half-blinded Roy. It was momentarily worse when he had closed his door, returning to the blackout, in which they were now separated.

"Wait!" he called to her. "I'll come around and get you. I know this place by heart." His boast proved empty; he bumped against the coachwork of the Silver Wraith on the trip around, and when he got to where she was supposed to be, he could not find her, though he could see some by then. "Where are you?"

She was at the front door. "Is this locked?"

"Hold on just a minute!" He hastened there. He dared not touch her. The door was plate glass, and several pedestrians were on the far sidewalk, he now could see, but whether they were looking or had looked across he could not know. "There are people over there!"

"I'll have to take the chance. I can't wait any longer!"

She opened the door and stepped out, almost colliding with a man walking a small dog on an extra-long leash that permitted the animal to follow the curb while its master stayed adjacent to the show windows. The pair monopolized the sidewalk.

Roy was in no position even to bid her goodbye. The man grunted rudely at Kristin and glanced long enough at Roy to remember him, should the dog-walker prove to be one of Mrs. Forsythe's or Robin's—or Sam's—informants. God damn it to hell, as Mrs. Perkins, the housekeeper of his childhood, used to say. Mrs. Forsythe was in some ways a replacement for Mrs. Perkins.

There was no longer reason for concealment. Roy went back to the office and turned on the lights. The first thing he noticed was that blanket from the Grandy house, still in its folds atop the filing cabinet. Mrs. Forsythe had reminded him of its existence earlier in the day. Over on her desk the red-eyed answering machine was blinking. He was entangled in a complex of emotions, too exercised to eat dinner or just go home, and he could not trust his reflexes if he sought the most effective distraction, taking the Lamborghini to a highway on which he could drive 180 at night, with the lights off so as not to attract a cop. He had done things like that when younger.

He decided to listen to the messages, maybe learning that he would make a buck. The very first was promising.

"Mr. Courtright, Max Leander. I've changed my mind. I *will* make an offer on the Elite, if it's still in your possession. As with a woman, one might overlook unreliability for a beautiful body . . . which is probably why I'm spending my old age alone except for my cars! In any event, kindly supply me with your asking price. E-mail would be just fine." The old tenor left his numbers and addresses.

The next voice evoked now familiar feelings of guilt. "Roy? Michelle, Michelle Llewellyn, *if you still remember me.* Uh, you were going to call? I mean, I don't want to be pushy, but I got to know where I stand. That's fair, okay? I mean, do you really want to see more of me? Or were you just being polite? Also, I've *got that dress.* I need to take it back if I don't have any use for it. Just be honest. I'm a big girl."

The third voice from the machine was that of his best friend. "Where the hell are you? Your cell phone seems to be switched off, and if you're home you're not picking up. I'm calling there on the off chance that you might still be around. I'm worried sick. Kris is missing. A cleaning woman told me nobody's at the bank. It's . . . eight twenty-five now. She was supposed to be home especially early tonight. That's fifteen minutes from here. For that matter, where are *you*? You were supposed to come to dinner. . . . If she doesn't show up by eight-thirty I'm calling the police."

That was more than an hour ago, yet no cops had come to the showroom, which could mean either that Sam had never called them or that he had not named Roy as someone to look for as well—or that the lovers had been so occupied on the backseat of the Rolls-Royce as not to hear an officer's knock at the door.

Now what should be done? Kristin had left without telling him how she would handle the matter with her husband. Obviously Roy must stay altogether out of touch with Sam until he knew what to say. Nor could he reach Kristin till at least the following morning, at the bank.

According to the lighted red number on the machine, four calls had come in since Mrs. Forsythe had last answered the phone. To evade his major problem for at least another instant, Roy played back the fourth message.

Again he heard, though in another voice, "Where the hell *are* you?" This was his twin sister. "I've *really* got to talk to you, Roy, as soon as you can. This is crucial. Don't let me sit here forlorn." The poetic word must mean Robin was seriously upset, as opposed to her natural peevishness. "Call me whenever. I'm here alone. I won't be sleeping. I'm leaving this message on all your phones."

According to the robot timekeeper on his answering machine, she had made the call at 8:57. It was now almost ten. He went to his own desk and dialed Robin's number.

"Here's the situation," Robin began without returning his hello. "Ross forgot to use his business credit card and instead used the joint Visa Gold he's got with me. When I opened the bill I saw nine hundred and change for something called Leisure Island. I got their number and called them. It's an *escort service*, Roy. In other words, my husband last month paid almost a thousand dollars to whores. Why? Because they'll give him head when I won't? You're the authority on this subject, so tell me why."

Roy winced. Must she be so coarse? "Thanks, Robin. I needed that.

As it happens, I'm no authority on escort services. I've never used them. But what occurs to me immediately is that Ross entertains business clients sometimes, doesn't he? How do you know the escorts are not for his guests, customers, clients? A couple years ago a collector came from Iowa to look at a Ferrari Dino I had at the time. He asked me if I had a call girl's number. I didn't but said I'd ask around. He told me not to bother. Oh, he still bought the car."

"Screw you," Robin cried. "Don't try to con me out of my righteous indignation. I'm heartsick. I'll nail that motherfucker to the wall, even though he's the father of my children."

"What am I supposed to do?"

"Call Leisure Island and hire an escort. See what they charge. How many blowjobs for a thousand bucks? One? A hundred? A thousand?"

"Come on, Robin. I'm not going to do that."

"Then don't ever speak to me again." She hung up.

The conversation proved not as negative as it might have been. Robin would surely find a way to preserve her marriage, for it was her proudest accomplishment, and Roy had been furnished with a credible excuse as to why he could not be reached all evening by Sam.

Kristin would be home by now, but she never answered a call to the house except when Sam had been hospitalized. Even the bathroom was equipped with its own telephone.

"Sorry I never got back about dinner," Roy said quickly when his friend answered. "I was stuck with Robin." He was confident the very name would have its effect on Sam, and he was right.

"Oh."

"She's got a personal problem. I don't think it's devastating by any means, not a fatal illness or anything, but she's upset, and I'm her brother."

"Yeah. Sure."

"I don't know how much good I did, but you know Robin"—this was malicious—"as long as she can do the talking she feels better. Jesus. She didn't even give me anything to eat."

"Kris finally got home—I guess you don't know I thought she was missing." If Roy had been with Robin and not at any of the numbers at which Sam had called him, he could not have known. So he said nothing now. Sam went on. "I panic easily nowadays. She was just doing some food shopping."

"Well, hell, with what you've gone through . . ."

"Anyway, she's made pasta primavera—I'm supposed to avoid most red meat. We're just ready to sit down. You're welcome to join us."

"Thanks, but Robin wore me out," said Roy. "I'm going to bed after a hard day." The ending phrase too was malicious but not consciously so; it emerged on its own. Normally he would have signed off with an acknowledgment of Kristin's presence, something as antiseptic as "Give her my regards." But he now made only a simple goodbye.

He lowered his forehead against his clenched fists on the desktop but was allowed to keep it there only a moment before hearing the sharp raps at the front door.

Recognizing Officer Velikovsky while en route, he waved and smiled and opened the door. "Yeah, it's me again, working late."

"Can I step inside for a minute?"

"Come back to the office and I'll make espresso." Roy ushered him in from the sidewalk.

"I can't be out of the car that long," said the officer, looking around the showroom. "Are we alone now, Mr. Courtright?"

"Sure."

"This won't go any further, you can count on me." Velikovsky continued to glance about with his prominent nose. He raised his eyebrows and spoke almost in an undertone. "A call came in from your friend Mr. Grandy. He reported his wife was missing. Now, we don't consider anybody missing till they been gone for twenty-four hours unless it's a child of course or there's some evidence of foul play. So the dispatcher tried to calm him down but he got real abusive. Now, the dispatcher is a black woman and she's got a chip on her shoulder anyway, and I guess they got in a shouting match. The upshot was she wanted me to go out there and summons him for racist remarks. I get along with her all right and can probably talk her out of that, we're both Catholics and I worked with her husband for a while, he's now a state trooper—anyway, I figured the biggest part of the whole problem would be solved if Mrs. Grandy turned up soon." He took a breath and looked about again. "He never mentioned you by name, but I thought by chance you might be able to shed some light on the matter, on account of the description he gave of his wife was pretty close to the person my wife told me you was having lunch with yesterday at The Corral."

Roy maintained his polite smile.

"So I stopped outside, hour, hour-and-a-half ago, and it was all dark in here, but when my eyes got used to the dark, I thought I could just barely make out a person's head moving in the back of one of the cars. Maybe I just imagined it, but I thought I ought to mention it to you. I couldn't even swear it was a person, let alone recognize them, but I thought I should let you know. It might help. So far as anybody else is concerned, I didn't see anything. Have a good night, Mr. Courtright."

"You caught me," said Roy. "I sometimes sneak into the backseat of the Rolls-Royce and catch a nap. Oh, I just spoke to Mr. Grandy. His wife came home okay, some time ago. He's embarrassed he got so worried, but he's been sick lately, in the hospital. Bad heart. Tell the dispatcher he apologizes."

"I remember that," said the officer. "You was out at his house, a week back. I hope he'll be in good health."

# 12

I oughtn't talk to you at all," Michelle said in her slightly flutier tone
of indignation. "I know—I called *you*. But still . . ."

Roy had telephoned the Llewellyn number at nine-thirty A.M.,
expecting to leave a message with her mother, to the effect that he
would be out of town for a few days. It was a potentially foolish lie, easily exposed by accident, but as good as he could do with a mind as
uneasy as his after a restless night.

"I told you my friend's in bad shape."

"That's very well—I don't mean that he's sick, I mean you could just
of called me sometime. If you don't want to see me, just say so, that's all
I mean."

Roy was incapable of telling any female person that he had no interest in her, for it would not have been true. That he was now in love with
Kristin had no bearing on his friendship with Michelle, which existed
on another level of being.

"I do want to see you," said he, and as if that were not already too
much involvement for a man in his position, he heard himself add,
"I miss you."

"That should be easy to handle. We live in the same town. Well, your business is here. I don't know where you live."

"Parts unknown," he said, using the jokey generic address with which professional wrestlers were sometimes introduced, back when as teenagers he and Sam used to watch the simulated mayhem of Gorilla Monsoon, Captain Lou Albano, and Chief Jay Strongbow. "What," he asked Michelle, "are you doing out of class at this hour?"

Instead of answering his question, she said, "I'm home alone. My mom and dad are at work. I'm supposed to do the laundry, but I'm still in bed. What are you doing?"

"I'm at work, too. I've got a business to run."

She asked, "Are there actually a lot of people around here who buy fabulous cars early in the morning?"

"Hardly any."

"You're your own boss, Roy. You've got that girl there to look after the place. You can do anything you want."

"Mrs. Forsythe is about fifty," Roy said. "She'd be flattered."

"She has a very young voice. If she's really that old, I guess you're not involved with her. I thought that was why you were avoiding me. Look, we could do something today if you want. I can see out the window it's perfect weather."

He listened to himself in disbelief. "It's nice enough for a picnic, don't you think? I guess Mount Seneca Park is still open. I'll grab some food and a bottle of champagne and pick you up in—how much time do you need?"

"Just enough to shower and brush my teeth. I can't believe you're actually doing this."

*Neither can I*, he said to himself. But maybe he could get some breathing room thereby. His spirit stayed in turmoil when he was alone. Spending a carefree hour or two with this amiable college girl might soothe his soul and distract him from the matter of the Grandys.

He left a note for Mrs. Forsythe, using her given name for the first time since being asked to do so.

Margaret—

I'm picnicking with Michelle. Be back right after lunch.
Lie to anyone who wants to get hold of me before then.

   R.B.

The third sentence was for her amusement. Margaret was not without a sense of irony—as in fact Kristin seemed to be.

Michelle screwed up her small nose. "That's cheese, right?" She pointed
at the chunk of Pont l'Evêque.

Roy tried to anticipate her objection to it. "It's not so smelly."

She picked it up and sniffed. "That's what *you* say." She put it back
on the blue-and-white checked tablecloth and returned her fingers to
her nose. "Now my hand stinks!"

"You like the pâté, though?"

"What I really like is the champagne." She thrust the empty flute
toward the silver bucket from which the neck of the bottle protruded.

He poured her a refill. "Ham? More bread?"

"That's actually pro-zoot, isn't it?"

"What?"

"That's what this Italian guy I know says his dad always calls it."

"Oh, *prosciutto*. This is actually Westphalian ham. But it looks like
prosciutto."

"Uh-huh."

They were sitting on cushions at the grounded tablecloth laden with
an array of cold foodstuffs, a selection made by Roy from a local "gourmet" shop's offerings and, as he was not familiar with Michelle's tastes,
as diverse as could be asked: salads, spreads, smoked fish, five different
kinds of olives, three of roast meats, and more.

But thus far, on her second refill of Clicquot, she had only nibbled on a fragment of baguette, spread with duck pâté an eighth-inch thick.

"I hope you're going to eat enough to stay sober," Roy told her. "I don't want to take a young woman home drunk."

She mock-scowled at him. "Whose home? Yours? Oh, say yes, please. I'm dying to see where a person like you lives."

Roy had been delighted to locate this little blufftop hideaway again. He had not visited it in fifteen years. The level, smooth patch of glacial rock, always dry, offered a forward view of the lake but was screened on the other sides by thick vegetation. You had to know about it to find it. Apparently few people had done so in all those years, for there was no litter, vintage or current, and no graffiti on the rock, scrawled or carved.

"If you look real hard," he said, pointing south-by-southeast, "past that cell-phone tower, you might be able to see the roof of your house."

She squinted but soon shook her head. "That's miles."

"I should have brought binoculars. But you can see across the lake, right beyond where that canoe is, there's—"

"Kayak," said Michelle. "But they're more fun on the river, where you've got a current."

"You're a kayaker?"

"Sure am."

She was dressed as she had been on the only other occasion he had seen her, in jeans and a loose gray sweatshirt. Her face was bright with the internal illumination of youth. She wore no makeup whatever, except perhaps a little, perhaps not, at the eyes, which were a compromise between oval and almond. Her cheeks were rosy.

"You have lovely Asian eyes."

"My one grandma was Japanese." She was pleased to make the identification. "The big boobs come from the European side, mostly Italian, though 'Llewellyn' is Welsh."

The glossy black hair was no doubt also of Far Eastern origin. Michelle was attractive by any international standard. Hers was obviously an unfettered spirit.

"I'll bet the college guys like you."

She started a smile that never developed. "They're all full of themselves, or maybe I'm just in the wrong zone."

It occurred to Roy that her depths might not be as carefree as her surface, but then he remembered from his own youth, as well as the years since, that nobody's ever are. He wondered whether there was a corollary merriment at the heart of the conspicuously melancholy.

"Well," said he, "you've got a lot of time to come to terms with things. What are you majoring in?"

She showed him a broad-browed look of histrionic candor. "Can you handle this? I dropped out, end of last term. I mean, I just didn't go back."

"Any special reason?"

"Yeah, I'm a fuckup."

"What does that mean?"

She writhed on the seat of her pants and crossed her legs the other way. "This stone is hard on the butt."

"I should have brought thicker pillows," said Roy. "Sorry about that."

"No problem." She patted the back of the hand he had splayed on the rock for support as he reached for the open container of olives.

"You were saying?"

"Oh, yeah. Tell you the truth, Roy, I didn't know what I was doing in college, so why keep going there like a robot?" She swallowed what was left in her glass and was extending it to him for a refill when a yellow jacket buzzed her on its way to a landing amid the cold meats. Michelle shrieked and dropped the flute, which hit the rock on the edge of its flanged base and bounced high. "Well, look at that, willya? 'How is that possible?' You know that commercial for Qwest, 'Ride the Light'? Whatever that means."

"It's plastic," said Roy. "Could I interest you in a kalamata?" He offered her one, expecting by now that she would refuse it, but she seized the olive, popped it into her mouth, and performed a hidden depitting technique with only her teeth and tongue. His new expectation was that she would spit the stone over the edge of the rock, into the valley below, something he might well have done himself even at his current age, but again he was wrong. She used one of the paper napkins from the supply he had provided, carefully compressing it into a ball and keeping it in her palm.

"Want another?"

"Not me."

He retrieved the plastic vessel and filled it with contents not quite as sparkling as earlier. He still had not finished his own first fluteful. He did not want to feel the effects of alcohol while Michelle was in his charge, especially if she was drinking so much.

"Don't you think you should eat something more?"

She leered at him. "Are you afraid you might lose control and take advantage of me if I get wasted?"

"What I'm afraid of is what *you* might do."

She took this as a joke, which it was not quite, and enjoyed it immensely, chortling with a display of small, perfect teeth. "As well you might, my man. 'Warning: Do not use this medication when operating heavy machinery.'" She had waited till now to hurl the balled paper napkin, with its gnawed olive pit, over the precipice, ten feet away.

"Here," said Roy, cracking a piece off the baguette. "Eat some bread, anyway."

"I can't tolerate solid food till noon on weekdays."

"It's one-twenty."

Michelle groaned. "Oh, all right." She accepted the chunk of bread with her left hand while raising the champagne in the right and emptying the contents down her throat in one foaming flood, which amazingly enough did not spill over. She swallowed heroically, then lowered the glass and brought the bread slowly toward her mouth. "Excuse me," she said softly and slumped forward, head against her chest.

Roy spoke to her and shook her shoulder, but she was out. He put a finger under her small nostrils and felt that warm breath continued to emerge. He was relieved not to have to feel for her heart and have her suddenly wake up. She had the potential to be trouble.

After he had picked her up and carried her to the Jeep, he established even more reason to estimate her troublemaking potential as high. A wallet had worked most of its way out of the back pocket of her jeans. Before reseating it firmly against a firm buttock, Roy had opened it and found what he was looking for. Her driver's license indicated that Michelle Llewellyn would not be twenty until eleven months had passed.

She awakened when he had put the wallet back, twisted to face him and asked, grinning, "Are you stealing my money or just feeling my ass?"

He was not amused. "I've had enough of your bullshit, Michelle. You're not of legal drinking age."

"Look, I'm eating!" She had all this while continued to clutch the chunk of bread and now jammed it into her mouth and chewed vigorously.

Roy went back to the picnic site, roughly gathered up the food, and dumped it into the big basket from which it had been taken. He shook out onto the rock the foaming remainder of the champagne, which looked like less than half a glass, and added the empty bottle to the basket. He collected the cushions.

He drove her home with utter silence on his part, but a good deal of chatter on hers. She was not as drunk as she had first pretended but more so than she now wanted to admit, especially when he pulled up at the curb in front of her house, a comfortable-looking two-story dwelling-place on a street of many, erected rather too close together because the lots seemed undersized.

"Can't you come in?" she asked blearily. "Nobody's home. *I'm* not going to call the cops."

"The neighbors will. Can't you be serious, Michelle? You act like you're twelve, not nineteen. You're a pretty girl, and you have a lot of charm. If I were your age, you wouldn't be able to get rid of me. But right now, I want you to leave the car and walk, without staggering, to your door. Think you can manage that? I mean it."

"Oh, shit, yes." She took a deep breath and straightened her back. "I had a very nice time. Thank you. But you *still* haven't made good on your promise to let me drive a Rolls-Royce. When will I see you again?"

He pointed a stark finger at her house. "*Goodbye*, Michelle."

Her bouncy stride looked like that of an altogether sober young person.

He really did regret not having kept his promise, but it would be impossible for him now to profane the Silver Wraith by sharing it with anyone but Kristin.


"Well," a beaming Margaret Forsythe said when Roy reached the office, "that was quite a lengthy picnic. Do I assume correctly that all is going well?"

"You haven't ever seen Michelle, have you?"

"I haven't had the pleasure."

"She's a beautiful girl," said Roy. "She's also very young. I may have more in common with mature women."

"Oh?" Margaret frowned slightly as if in polite dismay, but she did not seem offended by the sentiment.

Seated at his desk, Roy was struck with a guilty awareness that he had not acted responsibly in the case of Michelle. Instead of just getting rid of her, he should, as a grown man, have shown some concern for her lack of direction, which was not unlike what his own had been at that age. Nor had he been a social success then, either. He had thought of the girls of his day much as she did of the boys of hers. Sam's friendship had been a lifesaver. Michelle needed at least one friend, preferably of her own sex, so that the friendship would not be compromised by other emotions, and more or less her own age, because nothing was more essential at such a time than a sense that one was not unique in the universe.

Margaret was speaking to him. "Excuse me?"

"Mr. Alt called."

"I'm sorry. I was thinking of something."

"Seymour Alt," said Margaret, who Roy only now noticed had done something to her hair that gave her a lower and younger forehead.

Sy practiced a profession that usually provided only bad news, if you were with the defendant majority of the human race and not a plaintiff: Rarely you might be let off the hook, but you never won. Roy always dreaded a call from the lawyer, and that was too bad, for Sy was also a friend.

The signal rang and rang, but nobody at Alt's office picked up. "How long ago did you hear from Sy?"

Margaret consulted the monitor for her phone log. "Twelve oh-two. I just got here. It was his assistant, Celia. She just said to call him."

"I'm not even getting voice mail. I'll redial." He did so and after a moment said, "Same thing," and hung up. "Let me try his cell number. But if he's in court it won't be on."

Alt's cellular telephone was answered on the third ring. The male voice was not one that Roy recognized.

"Please do not call this number until further notice. I'm switching it off."

"Wait!" Roy cried. "Isn't this Mr. Alt's phone?"

"This is an attendant at Mercy Hospital. I don't yet know the name of the patient. The phone was ringing in the pocket of his suit."

"Hospital?"

"He was just brought in to the E.R. He was in a car accident. I can't say more now, sir. We're real busy." The man hung up, despite Roy's protests.

Margaret asked, "Mr. Alt's in the hospital? Another heart attack?"

Roy stood up. "He was involved in an accident, but I can't find out anything else at the moment. I better go see what happened, before his wife's notified. He may not have been hurt all that seriously. I think they rush everybody there as a matter of course. But Dorothea's an excitable person. She'll find it hard to handle if she just hears where he is. Maybe I can intercede."

Margaret gave him a warm smile. "Go to it, Roy. He's fortunate to have a friend like you. Most people hate lawyers, even their own. . . . I hope he's okay."

•   •   •

Mercy, the other area hospital, was at the far side of the county. The traffic on the direct route there was bottlenecked because of highway repair, and Roy decided against detouring on unfamiliar roads. Therefore it took him fifty minutes to reach his destination. On his arrival more time was squandered in arguments with hospital personnel as to his status. A mere friend and business associate could not gain access to a patient except during regular visiting hours—and not at all to one admitted for emergency care.

The conflict was abruptly resolved by someone's coming through a stainless-steel doorway and calling his name.

It was Dorothea Alt. She wore no special expression. She came to him and took his hand. "Sy's gone, Roy. He was hit by a car right in front of the courthouse. There were cops all over the place, but nobody got the fucking license number. Nobody." She acquired a crazed smile. "How could that ever be explained to Sy? Nobody to sue! Oh, Roy, Roy, Roy . . ." She collapsed against him, sobbing into his chest.

He drove Dorothea home in the Mercedes CLK55 convertible in which she had come to the hospital. It had been Sy's gift to her on their twenty-fifth wedding anniversary, the previous May. "Seventy something," Alt had told Roy. "But it's got sensors that instantly put up a roll-bar if they detect the car is starting to roll over. Dodie's a good enough driver, but she's reckless. Remember when she totaled her Beamer?"

The Alt driveway was filled with vehicles, and more were parked along the curb on both sides of the street. "Will you look at that," said Dorothea. "I only called my son a little over an hour ago. The gathering of the clans. I must look awful. I can't bear to see."

She was eight years younger than Sy's fifty-six and had been well maintained, but she was now a haggard elderly widow, with bruised eyes in a face that had fallen to what it was before cosmetic surgery.

"You're as beautiful as always," Roy said, double-parking so she would not have far to walk. He took her to the front door on his arm.

Amid the throng inside the house Roy saw the Alts' son and called to him. "Wilson!"

Wilson Alt, a lanky, fair haired, long-jawed young man who resembled his late father in no way, had just begun his final year at law school.

"Hi, Roy. I just happened to run down to get some clothes I forgot. A trooper lasered me at eighty-two. I told him I was late for my father's funeral! Who knew? He didn't buy it, incidentally." Wilson looked around and called out his sister's name.

Sybil Alt emerged from the crowd. She was twenty and unfortunately looked very much like her male parent and nothing like her mother. So far as Roy knew, she was still an undergraduate at the local community college; perhaps she had been a classmate of Michelle Llewellyn's.

"Thanks, Roy." Sybil took Dorothea off his arm and led her haltingly away. They were detained by sympathetic relatives and neighbors who wanted to express condolence.

"I can't take over yet," Wilson told Roy. "We'll have to hire another attorney for a while, and I worry about what he'll want. My father always kept it a one-man firm until I could join him. But now?"

"I'm really sorry about your dad," said Roy. "I've known him most of my life. He was more my friend than my lawyer, or maybe the older brother I never had. He looked out for me."

Wilson, taller than he, took Roy by the elbow. "Roy, I won't let you down. Just give me a little time to get my shit together."

Wilson had always been a kind of punk. His sister was a better person, but in addition to her deficiencies of feature, she did poorly in school.

"How about a drink?"

Roy declined and left the house, purposely avoiding the other people, a number of whom he would surely know. He parked Dorothea's Mercedes in the next block and returned to put the ignition key in the mailbox. Cell phone in hand, he was about to call Bob's Taxi when he remembered Sam.

"It's me, kid. Have you heard about Sy Alt?"

"Is he in some kind of trouble?"

"He was killed, for Christ's sake. Hit-and-run."

For a moment Sam was so quiet that Roy feared the cellular transmission had failed. "Sam?"

"I'm trying to deal with it. . . . My God. He's the last guy I would have . . . It's one thing after another."

"Listen. I'm coming over."

"Here?"

"I'm at Sy's house. I'm walking." Sam lived only a couple of miles away, and the adjoining neighborhoods, while subtly different—Sam's was probably more parvenu in its prevailing architecture than Alt's, though Sy was a self-made man—were consistently residential without much traffic. In a high-performance car Roy could have made the trip in less than two minutes, but afoot, though a vigorous walker, he consumed the better part of half an hour and found himself slightly winded as he strode up the Grandy driveway, where there were more dead leaves than last time, or perhaps it was only that he noticed them now as he had not when driving. The fall was on its inexorable way, and he was growing older. Given his regimen of exercise, the short hike, really a stroll, should have gone unnoticed. Maybe it was the very modesty of the physical demand that made it more taxing than it should have been.

Though on foot, he went around to the rear entrance as if arriving by car. His ring was answered by Maria, the Hispanic woman originally hired to clean twice a week but who, spoiled by Sam, had elevated her job to housekeeper-cum-maidservant. She still did light cleaning chores but if on the premises when a visitor arrived, might don a little apron and serve refreshments. For more ambitious procedures of maintenance, the windows, floor-cleaning and waxing, and even the vacuuming of the larger rooms and longer hallways, she brought female relatives and friends.

Maria's round tan face often displayed a sunburst smile that was probably intended to make up for her limited ability to communicate in English, but on seeing Roy now she looked solemn and did not respond to his greeting.

"Mr. Saym is not feeling gude." Having said which she exited by the door through which Roy had entered, probably to wait for her ride home. She carried a tote bag and was obviously finished for the day.

En route to the entertainment center where Sam could usually be found, Roy passed the entrance to the many-windowed sunroom and saw his friend's bulk in a chair that faced the outdoors. Sam appeared to be contemplating the sward of lawn, still bright green through the iridescence of sprinkler spray, and beyond, the sweep of driveway and the dark stand of trees that concealed most of the pool and all of the garage.

"The hike was longer than I thought." For a moment Roy believed Sam was not aware of his arrival, and he whistled at him and cried, "Hey."

"I've got too much property here," Sam said. "There's at least an acre I don't use. I ought to do something with it to make a buck."

Roy took one of the empty chairs near Sam's, like his, of varnished bamboo with flowered upholstery. He moved it to face his friend, back to the big window where it could have been too warm had the direct sunlight not been blocked by foliage.

"I have to look up the zoning," Sam went on. "Maybe I could get a variance. Who's going to replace Sy?"

"It was a hit-and-run," said Roy. "Nobody even got the number. Right in front of the courthouse, for God's sake. Cops all over." He still knew no more than what Dorothea had provided.

Sam looked at him now for the first time. "I don't know how much more I can take."

Roy remembered Sam's inordinate grief when Roy's father died and wondered whether his friend had been personally close to Seymour Alt. He could not recall Sam's being at Dorothea's big parties, nor did he play much golf despite owning a set of the most expensive clubs Callaway made.

"Sy seemed like too alert a guy not to see a car coming."

Sam continued to stare at him. "Sy did some work for the mob, didn't he?"

"I never heard that."

"Your dad told me once." Sam looked away at last.

"It's news to me. . . . This is going to be tough on Dorothea."

Sam looked back with a sneer. "Are you putting the moves on her already? Or have you been doing it all the while?" The sneer became a bitter smirk. "Though she's a little long in the tooth."

"You're going too far," said Roy. "Take it easy. Sy was just run down in the street a couple hours ago, and she's a widow. Of course I've never touched her."

Sam lowered and shook his heavy head. He had needed a haircut for weeks. He was also unshaven, now that he had been home awhile. "Shit. Sy Alt is dead. That's all I need."

Facing him, here in their house, Roy felt so guilty about Kristin that he could not protest directly against Sam's self-absorption. "Sy was a good father."

Sam's nostrils dilated as if at a bad odor. "Think Celia'll be at the funeral?"

The reference was to Sy's assistant of twenty years; she was also his mistress. "It would seem funny if she wasn't, working for him as long as she did." Sy was the most discreet of men. In two decades he had never been seen with Celia in any social venue. Roy and Sam for years had joked about this subject but only with each other. They had no hard evidence; they just knew that Sy and Celia had an intimate connection. You could tell by the way they spoke together on business matters, or anyway Sam could. He was the one who made the point to Roy, who had no gift for smelling out illicit liaisons despite his own proclivities, or perhaps because of them, his basic assumption being that he was unrepresentative: Most men, more fortunate than he had been, had permanent and exclusive attachments.

"If she does, Alt's wife can take her cue from that old French joke," said Sam, patting the bamboo chair arms with his large, flat, hairy hands. "You know."

Roy did not.

"Well, it's usually the lover and husband, but in this case it would be

Mrs. Alt, seeing Celia's tears, saying, 'Don't worry, my dear, I'll get married again.'" His laugh was short, loud, and ugly.

Roy nodded, not sharing the laughter. He was struggling against being overwhelmed by a conviction that Sam knew about himself and Kristin. "I guess I never felt it up to me to speculate on what kind of arrangement Sy and Dorothea had, if in fact they had one. I considered both of them friends."

"And friendship is sacred to you."

Now Roy did smile, more in courtesy than affection, in an effort to keep the proceedings polite rather than personal, though well aware that he could not succeed. "It certainly means a lot."

"That's how you can fuck my wife without regrets," said Sam, in the warm, soft voice of mockery.

"For God's sake," Roy said, "you're back to that. How many times do I have to tell you Kristin and I had a meal together when you were in the hospital. You know that. In fact, we ran into Sy and Dorothea in the restaurant. That's as intimate as we've ever been. Maybe it's your medication. It won't do your heart any good to get so worked up about nothing."

"Swear to me you haven't touched her." Sam leaned forward, hands tensed on the chair arms, as if he might leap at his friend, except that even after losing a pound or two during his hospital stay, he was still far too heavy to rise from a sitting position so easily.

Roy groaned. "Want me to get a Bible? Okay, if that's what will satisfy you, I'll swear."

Sam let his heavy eyelids fall. "You dirty bastard you." He opened his reddened eyes. "You stupid prick. *Kris admitted it*." He paused to let the information establish itself. "Get the hell out of my house."

Roy started to rise, then sat back down. He put his hand in the air. "Listen, kid—"

"Not a word," Sam said. "You're shit. Get out of my life."

Now that he could be honest, Roy no longer felt morally crippled. "No!" he cried. "Not until I speak my piece. I'm not going to try to justify myself in any way. You're right to be outraged. I deserve no consideration. But I want to say that this is not just an affair. I'm in love with her."

Sam's grin was ghastly. "You . . . are . . . in love . . . with her," he said, dragging it out. *"It's not an affair."*

"It's no excuse," said Roy. "I admit that. But it's true. I fell in love, I couldn't help it. I didn't have any designs on her. I wasn't even attracted to her. This is different from everything else. I've never felt this way about anybody."

Sam's large body was shaking in some awful caricature of mirth. "I can't get over how stupid you are. That you're a corrupt, lying, cheating, backstabbing cocksucker doesn't surprise me as much as how goddam dumb you are. I at least thought you were bright."

The abuse relieved Roy of some of his debilitating sense of guilt. He had admitted the grave offense and had to take what he had coming. But though it might seem so to the injured party, he had not thereby become less than human.

"All I can say is I regret behaving dishonorably toward you. I apologize for that. I'm not sorry to have fallen in love with Kristin."

"I've been saving the zinger," Sam said. "But suddenly I'm not getting the satisfaction I expected from the suspense." He looked at the floor and exhaled audibly. "I lied, and you fell for it. Kris didn't admit anything."

"This started as a *joke?*" Roy could have smashed a fist into his fat flabby mouth, but that impulse lasted for only an instant. His feelings were in contradiction. Once again he sank into guilt, now for the damage he had done to Kristin. That he had been unwitting did not diminish his role in the destruction of her marriage. It was uniquely his accomplishment.

Wordlessly he rose to his feet. Not looking at Sam, he left the house and his best friendship.

# 13

Roy crunched along the gravel driveway and had almost reached its junction with the road when the tan Toyota turned in. Its approach had been blocked by the shrubbery and, were the car not crawling, he might have been struck. He jumped aside, and Kristin braked to a stop.

She put her head out the window. "Roy! Are you okay?"

He came to her window. "Kristin, I—"

"And I just heard about Seymour Alt being killed, my God. . . . Why are you walking?"

He explained and then began an attempt to introduce the crucial matter. "I came to tell Sam about Sy. We all go back a long way, you know. . . . And then I—"

"Get in," said Kristin. "I'll run you home."

It was probably the best thing to do. He hoped Sam was not watching, though that would have been unlikely.

She backed out, swinging the car to point in the right direction. The world had changed since the last time he had been her passenger. That had been less than a week ago, at which time he could not have imagined they would ever be other than they were then, wife and husband's best friend, always a sensitive and often an uneasy alliance, unless perhaps the latter was gay.

"I never met him till the other night at the restaurant," Kristin said, "but what a shock to hear *this*."

"Sy Alt," said Roy, "was the last person likely to get hit by a car. He was seldom on foot except inside an office or courtroom, although he hated to drive. I guess it made sense that he had no interest in cars. When he came to my place, only once or twice in all the years he represented me, he would walk in and out without turning his head to look at the collection."

Roy continued to speak nervously about Sy, giving an impromptu eulogy of the man. By this means he cowardly delayed revealing what had become of his friendship with Sam, an unbearable subject to address, all the more so in view of Kristin's current mood, which aside from an appropriate gravity in listening to what he said about Alt, was seemingly happier than he had ever seen her. This was subtle, and could have been imagined, but she looked at him with evident affection and spoke in a new, intimate tone. It was as if she felt even closer to him in this routine act of providing a lift than when making love. She was comfortable with him, and in fact this made *him* less so than he already was.

"You didn't know Sy, but I did and more often than not thought him a pain in the neck even though he was acting in my own interest. I played golf with him though I'm not good at the game, and I was bored out of my skull by the other members of the foursomes he put together." He did not specify who these people were, for they often included bankers, at least once Kristin's predecessor at First United. "Anyway, he's gone now, and I'll miss him."

After Roy concluded his remarks Kristin drove for a decent interval in silence. They were nearing the place he called home when, smiling warmly, she said, "Roy, I've made a decision. I'm no good at being false. I feel creepy when I try to lie, and even worse if I'm caught at it." Turning into his driveway, she kept her eyes on where the car was going. "I don't know how you feel, though. You're as close to Sam as I am. What I want to do is tell him."

Roy nodded miserably but said nothing.

Kristin braked and turned off the ignition. She took his hand in hers. "I don't think I should do this without your permission."

"I honestly don't know what I'd answer under other circumstances," he lied. "But Sam already knows."

She let go of him and clasped her hands to her lowered head.

"He tricked me!" Roy cried.

Her incredulous face came up. "I don't understand."

"It was really a filthy trick. He told me you had confessed."

"You believed him?"

Roy had not anticipated how this would seem from her side, but still. . . . "What could I have done? Called him a liar? What kind of man would lie in that case?"

Kristin's lips were contorted. "Apparently you *don't* know him as well as I do."

"Just because you know somebody for years doesn't mean you know everything about him. But you ought to get some idea of his basic character. I'm saying 'him' here, because I mean a man. I doubt this applies to women, though I haven't known any for long enough to say, except of course my sister."

"Do you know why she broke up with Sam years ago?"

"I've always wondered. She would never tell me." Looking at Kristin, he saw rain begin to fall against the window beyond her.

"This is his version,"Kristin said, carefully enunciating her words. "She accused him of being your father's lover when he was a young teenager."

Roy spoke quickly. "Robin is probably capable of something like that. She was the one hardest hit by finding out my father was gay. I can't say I didn't care, but I never liked him anyway. I was crazy about my mother. I blamed him for her leaving, which no doubt was true, but in the end he acted more responsibly than she in looking after us. She didn't want custody. My dad did. When I look back, I think better of him than I did when he was alive."

"What about the accusation?"

It was as if he had forgotten it. "Oh, that was not true, not true at all! The last thing my father did was ever show us any hint of that, and Sam was like a member of the family. To make a pass at my best friend would have been out of the question. My father was very discreet about his private life. Throughout the years I never saw him with anyone who could conceivably have been a boyfriend, unless some of his business associates doubled as that, and they were as old or older than he. Not to mention that Sam has never shown any gay tendencies as long as I've known him." Roy snorted in derision. "He and I spent all our free time together in those days. When he would have had the opportunity to submit to my father's, uh, seduction I don't know—providing my father would have done that under any circumstances."

"Would he have done it in the case of a sixteen-year-old who *wasn't* your friend?"

The rain had increased in force, drumming on the roof and continuously washing the window he faced. "I don't think so. My father, believe it or not, was pretty straitlaced. He was a reactionary except maybe in being gay. I can't see him pursuing a minor, which is against the law, isn't it?"

"What if," Kristin asked, "Sam confirmed it?"

Roy hung his head. "No, no, that's not *right*. There's nothing right about it." He punched the dashboard. "He oughtn't say that sort of thing. That isn't a joke. He's in a crazy mood nowadays. I've never seen him like this. Maybe it's the medication. Trouble is, he was wrong when he first accused *us*, but then events proved him right."

"I don't think we can blame it on events," said she. "It was us—hell, it was *me*. I can't blame it on you." She held his face in her hands and kissed him on the lips but sweetly, not erotically. "I just wanted you."

"I wasn't an innocent bystander," said Roy, savoring the taste of her fragrant mouth. He seized her hands as she was withdrawing them. "God, how I adore you."

"I could never have guessed how affectionate you are." She gave him a melting smile and kept her eyes on his. "Oh, my," she said fervently. "Let's run inside!"

They dashed through an intense cloudburst, which seemed to be timed precisely for their inundation, as if a great vat of water had been emptied directly overhead. It was the kind of harmless catastrophe that, along with ruining one's clothes by means of mud or wind or playing with a pet, can be hilarious between lovers, and when Roy could not immediately locate his doorkey, they were further soaked by the even funnier gush from a lofty gargoyle poorly mounted for serious roof drainage.

"This is a great goofy kind of place for you to live," said Kristin, as they finally gained entrance to the stout door and dripped on the hexagonal tiles of the vestibule below the staircase. "I've forgotten what you told us about who built it."

She and Sam had been there just once. Roy always considered it as a novelty, especially his residence in it, and showed it as such. But he had not wanted to bore them and did not let them stay long. The three of them had soon adjourned to a restaurant. Those were the days when Kristin admittedly had had a low opinion of him. He was now somewhat disturbed that she would bring up an experience they had had that included Sam. And not only included him: Sam was the central figure in the trio, the only one who enjoyed the confidence of the other two.

"I'll tell you about the guy later," Roy said as they hustled up the stairs. "I don't have time now."

She had never been so beautiful as she was now, swathed in wet clothing, wet hair compressed against her perfect head, waterdrops still dripping from her eyelashes.

By the time they had reached the bedroom, both were naked except for those garments that could not be conveniently shed while holding one's own in what, on the final lap to the bed, became a sprint.

"I won!" Kristin cried as her knee was first to touch down, and then immediately added, as her entire body followed, rolled over, and lay supine, "You *let* me."

Roy was soon in the same position beside her. "Why do you say that?"

"I guess I don't want to compete with *you*." She rolled about, removing her remaining underwear.

"Gee, it's all right with me if you do," he said on a rising note. He wouldn't take that seriously.

She collided with him. He could feel the immanent strength in her long, lithe person, which however slender was not in the least fragile against his bulk.

He lost himself in an act of love that became a continuum, with no remembered beginning and no anticipation of an end. It seemed all of life, now and forever. Then, when it was finally done, it had been but a measureless moment.

Once again the sky had lost its light while they were joined together. Tonight was even darker because of the rain still hurling itself against the leaded, multipaned windows.

They had only just let each other go at last when Roy reclutched her desperately.

"Stay here. Don't go home."

"I'd love to," Kristin whispered. "How I'd love to. . . . But I can't. I just can't."

"But he *knows*. He must realize we're together right now."

She sat up abruptly. "That clock of yours—Oh, *nooo!*"

He glanced at the big red numerals of the liquid-crystal display: 9:47. That was certainly unbelievable, but provided even more support for his cause.

He reached to switch on the bedside lamp. Kristin had become even lovelier through the uses of love, with now mostly dried but more disheveled hair and skin very near the pellucidity of pearl.

"You said before that you wanted to tell him—when you didn't know he knew."

"Yes." She sank back on the pillow. "I had made up my mind." She put her hands across her eyes. "So when I heard he already knew, you can imagine how I felt."

"You can be proud of the nerve it took to reach your decision. You took the high ground. I didn't have the guts for it. *I* lied."

"You were protecting me."

"I could claim that if I hadn't caved," Roy said in self-contempt.

"But maybe it's better in the long run that he found out before you told him. He'll have had a little longer to come to terms with it, and you won't have to face the worst of his rage."

Kristin's voice assumed her everyday style, cool and crisp. "That didn't and doesn't worry me. He never gets angry with me. When he's displeased, he whines."

It made Roy uncomfortable to hear something like that, as it would have done to learn of an intimate physical disorder known only to a bedmate.

He shrugged. "Well . . ."

"What I dread is he'll believe this is something other than what it is."

Roy agreed. "But it's going to be a tough job to convince him of the truth. And I can't blame him. He's known me all my life. To him I've always been simply a lecher."

She caressed his face. "Roy, I hate to, but I'm really going to have to leave. It's ten o'clock. He'll still be waiting for his dinner. He'll be starving."

That her husband could not feed himself—a hunk of bread, a chunk of cheese—was outlandish. "How you handle this thing between us and him is your business," Roy said. "You can speak for me in every matter. I'd be more than willing to help in any way, but I think I'd only make it worse. I've done too much of that already."

Kristin sprang up with astonishing energy and began to collect her discarded clothes from the floor. "I'll tell you how I'm going to deal with it. I'm going home and make farfalle with grilled breast of chicken, dried tomatoes, artichoke hearts, kalamata olives, and nonfat half-and-half. I'm not going to say anything about you or why I'm late unless he asks."

"*If he asks?*" Roy was up on an elbow in bed, watching her movements, as graceful as a dancer's.

She bent, with an exquisite sweep of flank, to collect her skirt from the threshold. "He might well not ask. I doubt that he will." She stepped into the skirt and closed the zipper with a flourish. She still wore nothing above the waist.

Roy at last left the bed to join her in reclothing themselves. It was something to distract him from the matter at hand, which had become more ambiguous than ever. The first garments discarded, out in the room he used as a gym, were the last retrieved. As usual, in her business clothes—today a brown suit with a tan blouse—she was more formally attired than he in his jeans and corduroy jacket.

"Let me go there." Kristin pointed toward the bathroom.

When she emerged her face was fresh and her hair back to normal perfection, though neither would have needed much restoring. Her makeup had always seemed minimal, and not even the soaking rain had changed the character of the short-cut fair hair that when dry conformed to the elegant contours of her head.

Roy was sitting on the Bowflex.

"Sam is supposed to exercise," Kristin said. "But I can't see him using anything as intimidating as that. If only I could get him to jog a little."

Roy stood up. "He should have tried to cultivate a little self-reliance. You weren't his mother."

"He wants kids," said she. "So do I. But it's not yet the right time, though we can't wait forever."

However he might interpret that remark, he could make no sense of it. So he had no choice but to dismiss it. "The time for that's gone by so far as he's concerned. I never really wanted children before, didn't *not* want them, just didn't give the matter much thought. But now, with you, I want children very much, but *when* will be absolutely up to you. I won't have any requirements." He took her fingers. "I can't demand that you love me. I just ask you to let me adore you."

Kristin was still smiling sweetly, but with an undercurrent of discomfort. "Roy," she said, turning his hands so that hers, though so much smaller, were in at least symbolic control. "If we are ever to see each other again—I mean, intimately—we really have to come to terms with just what we are to each other." She peered keenly into his eyes. "We're friends, we're dear friends. We've had sex a couple of times, and it's been heavenly. I didn't know my body could feel the way you've made it feel. You've realized all my fantasies. Dear Roy." She caressed his face again, as she had on previous occasions, all of them memorable to him.

"It's been like a dream to me," he said, "in which everything is the act of love, getting rained on, running through this place, leaping into bed. It hasn't stopped yet. I'm still in a state of ecstasy, standing here with you in this nutty gym I made in the goofy place I live, if this could be called living. I want a real life with you."

"I'm married."

"Oh, I know—"

"I want to stay married, Roy. To Sam."

"You can't love him!"

"Why can't I?" She let him take his hands back.

"And make love that way with me?"

Kristin looked sober. "I won't go into our sex life, I mean Sam and me. I can't stand it when married women talk about that stuff."

"I don't want to know about it anyhow," Roy said hastily. "What I meant was the intensity of *our* lovemaking—you just said it was unique. How can you have that with someone and then live with someone else?"

"I don't know. Maybe I can't. It hasn't been happening for very long. I haven't had time to get adjusted. Maybe I won't be able to." She hung her head for an instant. "If I can't, we'll just have to stop seeing each other—in this way, I mean. We'll still be friends."

It was not she who was crazy, tempting as it was to believe that. But what validity did he have if, demented, he called himself mad?

"*Stop being lovers?*"

Kristin wailed, "I don't *want* to, Roy!"

He reached toward but did not touch her. "It's not the bed that's important to me."

Her eyes, gunmetal in the light that came from the several sources— floorlamps, overhead fixtures, sconces—dilated in amazement. "It is to me!"

In panic and chagrin, Roy surrendered to spite. "You can't possibly want to stay with that queer. Whatever my father did with or to him, he must have liked it because he mourns him to this day."

"Sam's your best friend."

"That's over now. You should have heard the way he talked to me. I hate his guts."

"Oh," said Kristin, "don't say that. You don't mean it."

"What in the world do you have in common with him? He's wasted all his inheritance. He lives off you, runs up big bills, buying expensive gadgets for his own amusement. God knows he's no gourmet. Does he appreciate your cooking? He's a glutton. And you don't want to say it, but it's pretty obvious he's not much good as a lover. As a banker, you know you would never grant a loan for any of his so-called business projects. You even begged me not to lend him any more money!"

"That was for both your sakes. Money is ruinous for Sam. He sees it only in terms of expenditure. He talks of investing, but he would rid himself of any investment that was profitable. He despises money. He would be miserable if he was stuck with too much to squander."

"What in the hell do you see in him?"

"*You've* been his friend all these years."

"I guess I'm just dumb," Roy said. "You told me he doesn't wish me well."

Kristin shrugged. "That's only envy. He needs us, Roy."

"I don't care whether he lives or dies."

"Oh," said she, coming to him, her arms at his waist and her cheek against his, "don't say that. You don't mean it."

He found her embrace suffocating and hypocritical. "You better get going. Rush home and make his low-fat supper."

This of course was said bitterly, but Kristin took it as literal. She stepped away. "I don't even dare see how late it is *now*." She gestured at him. "Let's not say all is lost. Let's have a little patience when it comes to *us*. Meanwhile, don't turn your back on Sam when he's in this delicate condition. I think we might be able to work something out that we can all live with." She opened and closed her eyes ritualistically. "I've never made any trouble about Maria."

"Your maid?"

"I suspect he's been having sex with her for years. She worked for him before we were married." Her smile was more tender than ever. "I'm awfully fond of you, Roy. I wouldn't want to give you up. You're a wonderful man."

She kissed him quickly on the lips, with a closed, cool mouth, and hurried to the staircase. The heeltaps of her descent on the oak treads seemed to continue to echo even after the closing of the front door, but that, like all else about her that related to him, was obviously an illusion.

# 14

Roy saw Kristin and Sam at the lavish nondenominational funeral that Dorothea Alt arranged for the late Sy, but only at a distance that both parties were careful to maintain. His own companion was Margaret Forsythe, who had hardly known Alt even as a voice, for when calling on his own Sy preferred to reach Roy directly on the cell phone. But given her importance to Incomparable Cars, Inc., she felt obliged to attend the ceremony. The black dress looked good on Margaret's figure, which was somewhat full but in the right places. She was not an unattractive woman. Roy himself had begun to look older than his years. They were not an incongruous couple. He sensed that such was her opinion as she clasped his arm on arrival and departure.

But though he was almost as sexually prescient as ever, he was now utterly indifferent to what had no bearing on his exclusive purpose, which for the first time was other than making the most of the good fortune that had made it possible for him as an adult to practice an enjoyable, relatively risk-free, and intentionally harmless way of life.

He had too often been in Kristin's situation in a love affair not, after an interval of anguish, to understand hers. The difference was that *he* had had no spousely equivalent of Sam to go home to, nobody to look after but himself. On his part there might be regrets to one degree or another—sometimes, as with poor Francine, a regret that the affair had ever started—but *his* heart had never been broken. There was more than one woman who doubted whether he had a heart. The question had now been answered.

Kristin left a cell-phone message on his home machine several days after he had last seen her. "Things have been hectic at the bank, and I've really had to do some work on Sam. I guess he was hurt more than I thought, but you would know more about a male thing like that. But I think he's coming around. After all, he's only got one best friend in the whole world. As for *us*, it's hard for me right now to find any time I can't reasonably account for. And speaking of accounts, all the branches are being audited. The whole system is about to be purchased by Downstate, and I couldn't be happier. I see much greater opportunity for someone like myself. First United has been marching in place for years. You're with Downstate, aren't you? . . . I've got to run now, Roy. Please forgive me. I'll be in touch as soon as I can. . . . You know, I think if you made some sort of overture to Sam—it wouldn't have to be much, maybe just call and ask how he's feeling—you wouldn't be rejected. . . . God, I miss you!"

A young attorney named Jefferson Alcott, who had done some work with Sy, had been brought in by the Alt family to handle the practice while they decided what to do for the long term. He was expected to tread water on the major matters but certainly had the capacity to change a will. It was easier for Roy to deal with a stranger like Alcott on this matter than it would have been with Sy, who would have given him an argument.

After exchanging handshakes with Alcott, Roy asked about Celia Phelps, Sy's longtime assistant and mistress. He knew the family would oppose her continuing in her job, but had not expected to find her gone so soon.

"She's with us on a contingency basis," said Alcott, a sinewy man with a shock of sandy hair and a rather darker mustache. His suit, shirt, and tie each displayed a slightly different shade of gray. "I've brought in my own people, but we're going to need Celia to help us navigate through the maze."

That arrangement would undoubtedly be complicated. Celia, a drab little person, a total contrast to Dorothea but perhaps more devoted to Sy's professional success and personal well-being, was not to be seen at the funeral, surely in deference to the wishes of the family, who would also no doubt legally fight any clause in Sy's will that left a penny to the woman he habitually referred to as "good old Ceil."

"You asked us to dig out your will," said Alcott, tapping the document in question as it lay before him. "It seems to be in order." To see a stranger behind Sy's desk was not that startling, for Roy had seldom found Alt there.

Roy produced a sheaf of paper from an inside pocket of his jacket. "I've prepared a list of additions, codicils, or whatever you call them. Sorry about the handwriting, but I can't type and didn't want to ask anyone else to do it. At least I think it's legible."

Alcott's mustache quivered in a smile. "Lawyers love handwritten documents! Or at least if one supports their case. They're hard to challenge." He accepted the two sheets, unfolded and quickly read through them, emitting murmurs of assent. "Uh, yes, the Holbrooks are minors? Yes . . . yes . . . 'Llewellyn' is four ells?" He made a mark with a silver pen. "Yes . . . yes." He raised his head and lowered his pen. "You want the Holbrooks to get their bequests when each reaches his or her majority?"

Roy gave him an account of the incident involving Francine and her husband. Alcott of course knew about the subsequent murder-suicide, a famous event throughout the region. "Both families were talking about suing me. I don't know how this stood at the time of Sy's death, but if you can't find it in the files, that's something Ceil might help you with. I guess if I weren't alive, they could still sue the estate?"

"Excuse me for asking, Mr. Courtright. You're a young and very healthy-looking man. I hope you haven't an illness."

Roy tried to be disarming. "I sell vintage high-performance cars, and

I like to test them at speed. I'm not a reckless driver, but accidents can happen. I tend to be superstitious, and these recent deaths of people I've been associated with have had an effect." He paused. "I want to make sure the Holbrook children get something in trust that the adults in those families can't intercept."

He and the attorney discussed this bequest further and then went again through the list of the others, verifying spellings, addresses, and sums. Alcott promised the amended document would be ready for signing and notarizing as early as Monday afternoon.

"Tomorrow."

Alcott was incredulous. "Tomorrow's Saturday. And we're just moving in, Mr. Courtright."

"Then you'll be here," said Roy. "I'm nervous. I don't want to wait the whole weekend. I was a damn good client of Sy Alt's."

"Oh, I'm aware of that, Mr. Courtright. I hope you'll stay on with us. I know your business and those beautiful cars: It's a credit to this community. I'll put a couple of people on this right away, and it should be ready tomorrow afternoon."

"Noon, please."

Roy's existing will was as simple as one could be: His material worth was to be divided equally between his twin sister and his best friend. Robin would have been infuriated had she known, but she had not, nor had Sam. The latter was kept in the dark because Roy did not want to tempt Sam to commit murder during one of his frequent financial crises. A private joke at the time, this consideration was now obsolete. Today Roy would have provided the cocked gun, had he believed Sam was man enough to fire it.

The new codicils reduced what the two principal beneficiaries would divide by less than a fifth. He would leave the building, which he owned outright, to Margaret Forsythe, to do with as she desired, with the condition that the mechanics Paul and Diego be permitted to occupy the downstairs garage as long as they wished and at a reasonable rent for the district and time, which of course however low would be more than the nothing they had paid to date.

But Roy was bequeathing to the guys his entire inventory of classic cars, to sell or endlessly dismantle and reassemble the engines and transmissions as they wished.

Except for the Holbrook children, the monetary awards were comparatively modest, but it was Roy's intent to make some acknowledgment of the kindness that some women had shown him in recent days, women he had not touched, on whom he had no designs. To Suzanne Akins he would leave more than enough to pay off the loan she had taken, on a nurse's income, to buy the BMW 530i she drove that night they slept chastely in the same bed. Michelle Llewellyn had a dinner coming, at an expensive restaurant, and a good dress; Roy's gift provided for a half-dozen of each, but the escort was up to her. Finally, he decided that the overtip he left for Daisy Velikovsky had still not been sufficient to cow her police-officer husband, so Roy left them together the estimated equivalent of a waitress' annual income.

In the larger scheme these things of course were of little moral significance, meager gestures to leave a good taste in the mouths of acquaintances.

When it came to intimates, his motive was vengeance. The large inheritance, that which Sam Grandy had always craved, would destroy his best friend.

Next morning Roy took a long and thorough workout, returning to the free weights on which he had begun in early adolescence. It could be scientifically proven that dead iron was not as effective in resisting, and therefore strengthening, the human musculature as was a high-tech machine, but he found curling dumbbells to be more satisfying to the spirit than the equivalent exercise on the Bowflex, as was going through the traditional barbell snatches, cleans-and-jerks, and bench presses, in some of which there was danger in working alone with poundages heavy enough to crush a foot, or windpipe, if dropped—which hazard indeed was why he had purchased the machine.

Gritting his teeth, he took one last look at his body in the door-back mirror. Of course it was no more satisfactory to him than as of two days earlier. No one is at his peak at thirty-five, no matter how assiduously he has cared for himself. . . . He had never taken this shit absolutely seriously except maybe when starting out at fifteen, and not at all during the past decade. Yet he had continued doing it. It was really the sole effort he had made in life, the only resistance he mounted to any challenge, and as such he could not have dispensed with it and retained any selfrespect. His physique at least was his own accomplishment. His father, who had furnished the means for Roy to represent a hobby as a business, played golf and in swimming trunks displayed a body like a bloated tube without the ghost of a muscle.

Nevertheless Roy could see only his own inadequacies, not how far he had come from the skinny adolescent but how far he remained from his ideal . . . which only now he recognized was his ideal because it was impossible of attainment. That it could never be realized was the point of any ideal in friendship, in love, in life. Had he learned this at an earlier time . . . he would probably have come to the same end. That he could accept this truth now suggested he had finally grown to a maturity of heart, but it was nothing to gloat about.

He breakfasted on the perishable foods in his home fridge, essentially the leftovers from the picnic with Michelle Llewellyn, then went to take his leave of Incomparable Cars before Margaret Forsythe arrived, parking the Jeep at the curb in front rather than in the lot below where he might be distracted by the master mechanics.

Inside the showroom he made a last survey of the machinery the guys would inherit and, while he was at it, ran the duster over the coachwork of all five automobiles. He had always done well by his cars, spending more in restorations than he made in profit over the decade, but they deserved such care. He had never sold one that could not be driven, that would not perform as it had when new. Though none was human, each had been made by human beings and thereby acquired at least a kind of soul. What observant driver had not noticed that his engine always ran more smoothly after the body was washed?

He had first supposed, in a moral lapse, that he would do what he had to do in one of the classics, perhaps that which had the greatest monetary value, the 1969 Lamborghini Espada. Blasting out of life at

200 mph, or however great a speed he could develop on a straightaway unoccupied by other vehicles for those few moments, would provide the ultimate thrill and also free him from the limitation imposed by fear back in the days when he had dabbled in racing sports cars but soon retired because of the risk entailed by seriously trying to win. Kill yourself to beat some other amateurs in restored Austin-Healeys?

It had made more sense to waste a dozen more years, bringing nothing but disappointment to all concerned. . . . But the Espada was also the car in his current collection of which he was least fond, finding the elongated rear of the body not quite satisfying to the eye. Lamborghinis always tended toward the exhibitionistic, demanding more from the beholder than they should. German cars, on the other hand, often modestly asked less, with the sublime exception of the gullwing 300SL. The great British marques, in their golden years, the Astons and Jaguars, the Morgans and earliest MGs, were perfection in form.

No classic automobile of whichever marque deserved to be helplessly destroyed in the intentional self-obliteration of a human being. If its driver failed to slow down for the fifty-degree corner on Oak Bluff Road, went through the frail barrier there, and rolled down the precipitous slope, a Jeep Grand Cherokee would never be missed, would in fact get the blame as an unsafe vehicle with too high a center of gravity, thus serving another of Roy's purposes: He did not wish to give the impression he had committed suicide, thereby furnishing Sam Grandy with further cause to despise him and Kristin still another opportunity for indifference. *If you couldn't be maudlin at such a time, when could you?* was a question Roy asked himself with optional irony, the kind that alternates with the literal too rapidly to be distinguished from it.

There remained the matter of the moss-green blanket, still in a neat fold atop the filing cabinet. His assistant would never forgive him for not arranging for its disposition. With his cell phone he called the office answering machine, six feet away.

"Margaret, there's a Salvation Army drop box in the Grandway parking lot. On your way home tonight, would you mind putting the blanket in it? Thanks for everything."

• • •

Roy was en route to Alcott's office but trapped in a lunchtime traffic that was bottlenecked at the edge of the business district by an emergency excavation in the middle of the street, barricaded in black-striped yellow. He had restrained himself from discarding the cell phone because of just some eventuality like this.

He dialed the lawyer's number, to make sure someone licensed as a notary would stay on hand and not go out to lunch before his arrival. . . . The call was not going through. He looked at the display and saw SYSTEM BUSY—no surprise at this hour but infuriating to him in his urgent need. The big square end of the mover's truck just ahead of him blocked his view, but the traffic must be frozen for at least a solid block, judging by the distant sounds of the most insistent horns.

He was checking to see whether the redial system was programmed in when the phone rang.

"Roy?"

It was Kristin. He had not moved quickly enough to be spared one more meaningless exchange of all-passion-spent platitudes.

"I can barely hear you," he said truthfully, and then lied about the reason therefor: "The signal's very weak here." He did not of course ask, *Why are you bothering me at the eleventh hour?* "I'll have to get back to you."

"No, no!" she cried, and now was as audible as if she were sitting beside him. "*Sam is dying.* If you want to see him, get to County General right away."

He blurted something and dropped the telephone. He could move the Jeep in neither direction, but the far right lane was luckily between parking meters, so he used the vehicle's off-roading capacity to mount the curb. He drove along the sidewalk as fast as he could while giving pedestrians the opportunity to take evasive action. The outdoor tables of the coffee shop were in the next block, but he bumped down at the corner into the side street. He sped toward the hospital by whichever routes were least crowded. He felt best when he could keep rolling, even if temporarily obliged to travel in the wrong direction. To be locked in traffic again, with the company of only the devastating reflections evoked by fate's latest caprice, was unthinkable.

At the hospital Roy braked near the emergency entrance and left the Jeep in a forbidden zone, keys in the ignition and doors unlocked, so that it could be easily moved, impounded, or stolen. Inside the building, at a desperate speed and by a route he could not afterward have clearly traced, he eventually found, or happened upon, Kristin.

It was the first time he had ever seen her disheveled except in erotic passion. Though she was still seemingly impeccable in hair, eyes, attire, something basic had been as if subliminally altered. She was slightly out of focus; the change may well have been in him.

"Oh, my God, Roy." She embraced him frantically, as a savior, not a lover. "Oh, Roy."

He impatiently squeezed her for an instant, then broke away. "I better go to him. Where is he?"

Kristin seized him again and put her face against his chest. "He's dead, Roy. He died in the ambulance."

He wanted to cry out but of course did not do so. "I came as fast as I could."

They were in some bleak white-walled enclosure furnished with wooden benches. Roy sat down on one that was otherwise empty. Kristin joined him on its hard seat. People came and went; he saw only their shoes.

"We had that nasty fight last time. Well, it wasn't a fight on my part—"

"He never mentioned it, Roy." She took his arm in a comforting way. "He got over it. Sam was like that."

This was not what Roy wanted to hear. "How did it happen? Christ, he just got out of the hospital."

"Maria says she found him on the floor. I was out shopping for food."

"God damn it."

"Nothing any of us could have done," said Kristin, in her old cool style, but then began to sob.

Roy put his arms around her narrow trembling body, which felt so different when not in the act of love. "I really did love him," he said, speaking aloud but mostly for his own benefit, or detriment. "I never could have squared myself with him, and he was right to feel that way. He was a man of principle."

Though it had not been his conscious intention to do such—he had not been thinking of her—this statement distracted Kristin from her grief. She left his embrace to say, anxiously, "He was getting over it, Roy. Please believe me. I knew him in a way you did not, *could* not."

"Maybe it's just me, then," said Roy, as it was also he who had wanted to die and now been cheated out of the opportunity, one-upped by his best friend.

"I know I took a dim view of his way with money," Kristin said. "But I guess you couldn't have had his generosity of heart without a certain foolishness in practical matters."

For the first time he saw how naïve she was, if she believed that Sam was incapable of resentment; it had in fact been his ruling emotion. But had it not been she who had given Roy the information on which he based this judgment? He had loved Sam all the same. Until recently he had found it impossible even to disappoint his friend, let alone dishonor him.

Kristin continued. "He was the only person I could count on to take me as I am."

"Yes."

"He let me be the one with ambition," said she. "He just cheered me on. That takes an unusual man." She clutched Roy again. "I don't think I could get through this without you."

"I'm not going anywhere." He was at her disposal from now on, but there could be no more sex, ever—not that she would necessarily expect any, but he had to establish the rules for himself.

A pair of black trousers stopped near them and remained. Roy looked up to see a round white collar surmounted by a sorrowful pink face.

The priest asked, "Are you the young couple who lost your child?"

"No, Father."

"I'm sorry to have disturbed you. But you've had a loss?"

"A close friend," said Roy. "Thank you for asking."

"God bless you both."

When the clergyman had gone, Kristin said in wonder, "You're always so nice to everybody. Sam wasn't, you know. He wouldn't put up with people he felt were wasting his time."

"Maybe he had some kind of premonition he wouldn't live long."

She thought about that for a moment and then began to weep again.

"Let's go," Roy said. "There's nothing we can do here."

He took her out to the parking lot. Unexpectedly, the Jeep was where he had left it, unlocked door, keys in the ignition. He had half-hoped it would be irretrievably gone. Now that he had been denied the grand gesture, he would have endured inconveniences and discomforts as forms of atonement. He could never have envisioned that his penance would be paid as counselor to Kristin.

She repeated her earlier sentiment. "I couldn't handle this without you." He was driving now and could not look at her. "I mean it," she said. "I've never been through anything like this before. I can't ask my parents for help. It would be a confession of failure. They've never seen me except as winning."

"Count on me," Roy said. "I'll take care of everything."

"Wouldn't you know," she asked rhetorically, "it would be when Maria was there again that he had the fatal attack?"

"They usually happen in the morning, don't they?" Roy braked for a red light. Now, when there was no need for hurry, the traffic of course was thin.

"What I wonder is if they were in bed at the time." She hastily threw up her hands. "Not that I'm being critical of the poor guy. If so, he was in good hands. She did better than I could have. Her mother died that way; so did her older brother. . . . I've got to do something about Maria now. For all I know, she might hold me responsible."

"I'll talk with her, but I'm sure she knows you loved him. I'll take care of it," said Roy. "I'll take care of everything."

"Dear Roy, you're a treasure." She touched his hand. The light turned green and he had to drive. "Sam adored you," Kristin said, "and so do I."

So while escaping Roy's revenge, Sam had gotten his own at last. But in so doing, he had also given Roy a use. That's what best friends are for.

# ABOUT THE AUTHOR

*Best Friends* is THOMAS BERGER's twenty-second novel. His previous novels include *Regiment of Women*, *Neighbors*, and *The Feud*, which was nominated for a Pulitzer Prize. His *Little Big Man* is known throughout the world.

# It's My State!

# Puerto Rico

## The Island of Enchantment

Ruth Bjorklund and Richard Hantula

Cavendish
Square

New York

Published in 2016 by Cavendish Square Publishing, LLC
243 5th Avenue, Suite 136, New York, NY 10016

Third Edition

Website: cavendishsq.com

This publication represents the opinions and views of the author based on his or her personal experience, knowledge, and research. The information in this book serves as a general guide only. The author and publisher have used their best efforts in preparing this book and disclaim liability rising directly or indirectly from the use and application of this book.

CPSIA Compliance Information: Batch #WS15CSQ

All websites were available and accurate when this book was sent to press.

Library of Congress Cataloging-in-Publication Data

Bjorklund, Ruth.
Puerto Rico / Ruth Bjorklund and Richard Hantula.
pages cm. — (It's my state)
Includes bibliographical references and index.
ISBN 978-1-62713-216-9 (hardcover) ISBN 978-1-62713-218-3 (ebook)
1. Puerto Rico—Juvenile literature. I. Hantula, Richard. II. Title.

F1958.3.B56 2015
972.95—dc23

2015003854

Editorial Director: David McNamara
Editor: Fletcher Doyle
Copy Editor: Rebecca Rohan
Art Director: Jeffrey Talbot
Designer: Stephanie Flecha
Senior Production Manager: Jennifer Ryder-Talbot
Production Editor: Renni Johnson
Photo Research: J8 Media

Printed in the United States of America

# PUERTO RICO ★ ★ ★

## CONTENTS

# A QUICK LOOK AT

## ★ Official Flower: Flor de Maga

The official flower of Puerto Rico is similar to the hibiscus except the *flor de maga* grows on a tree and not a bush. Found throughout the island's forests, the tree has shiny, heart-shaped leaves and brilliant pink or red flowers. The trunks are used to make musical instruments and furniture.

## ★ Official Bird: Reina Mora

The *reina mora*, or Puerto Rican spindalis, is a tanager. Males have a yellow throat, orange collar, and bright white and yellow-green stripes on their back. Females are a dullish olive. The male sings high notes while flying through treetops while the female sings a whispery song when she rests in dense underbrush.

## ★ Official Tree: Ceiba

The ceiba tree is tall and grows quickly. It has small, peach flowers that later form long pods. When the pods ripen and fall, puffy, violet balls of fiber cling to the branches. Its seeds are used in making cooking oil and soap. The Taíno people carved canoes from this tree.

# PUERTO RICO
## POPULATION: 3,725,789

### ★ Coquí

The **coquí** (pronounced ko-KEE) is a tiny tree frog that lives in Puerto Rican forests. Many Puerto Ricans proudly say, "*Soy de aquí como el coquí*" ("I am from here like the coquí"). From dusk to dawn, male coquís chirp noisily. Some forests ring out with as many as ten thousand chirping coquís per acre (0.4 hectare).

### ★ Parrotfish

The parrotfish resembles a parrot's beak with a rainbow of bright colors. They live in **coral reefs** and can change their colors as well as their gender. At night, to hide from predators, the parrot fish wraps itself in a cocoon made of mucus that it has secreted from an organ in its head.

### ★ Common Mongoose

Sugarcane growers imported the mongoose from Southeast Asia in 1887 to kill rats in their fields. The mongoose ranges in length from 10 to 25 inches (25 to 63 centimeters) and feeds on rats, frogs, insects, snakes, birds, and fruit. Once a help to farmers, the mongoose with its enormous appetite is now considered an **invasive species**.

La Mina Falls cascades into a pool
in the El Yunque rainforest.

# The Island of Enchantment

Nineteenth-century Puerto Rican poet José Gautier Benítez called his homeland *un jardín encantado*, which means "an enchanted garden." In his day, Puerto Rico was a peaceful, tropical island bursting with exotic trees, flowers, fruits, birds, and fish. Today, much has changed. The island now bustles with modern activities. Yet, as gardens bloom, seas sparkle, and rain forests glisten, Puerto Ricans continue to call their home an "island of enchantment."

## Peaks, Valleys, and the Sea

Puerto Rico is actually a group of islands—a main island, called Puerto Rico, and several smaller islands, including Vieques, Culebra, Mona, and Caja de Muertos. The total land area is 3,424 square miles (8,868 square kilometers). The main island is almost rectangular in shape. It measures about 111 miles (179 kilometers) east to west and 36 miles (58 km) north to south.

The islands of Puerto Rico lie more than 1,000 miles (1,609 km) southeast of Miami, Florida, 500 miles (805 km) north of Venezuela in South America, and 70 miles (113 km) east of the Dominican Republic, from which they are separated by a stretch of sea called the Mona Passage. Surrounded by the Caribbean Sea, Puerto Rico is the easternmost

# PUERTO RICO
## MUNICIPIO MAP

Puerto Rico is not divided into counties. Instead, it is composed of seventy-eight *municipios*, or municipalities.

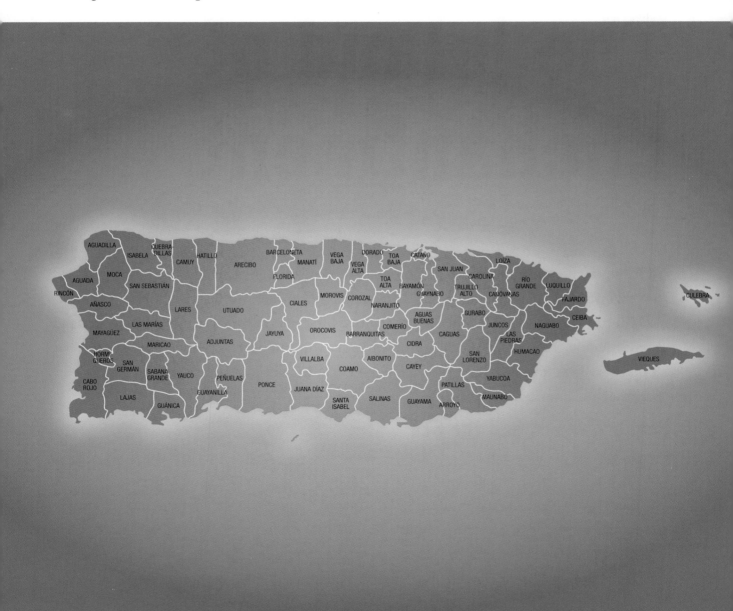

# PUERTO RICO
## POPULATION BY MUNICIPIO

| Municipio | Population | Municipio | Population | Municipio | Population |
|---|---|---|---|---|---|
| Adjuntas Municipio | 19,483 | Florida Municipio | 12,680 | Orocovis Municipio | 23,423 |
| Aguada Municipio | 41,959 | Guánica Municipio | 19,427 | Patillas Municipio | 19,277 |
| Aguadilla Municipio | 60,949 | Guayama Municipio | 45,362 | Peñuelas Municipio | 24,282 |
| Aguas Buenas Municipio | 28,659 | Guayanilla Municipio | 21,581 | Ponce Municipio | 166,327 |
| Aibonito Municipio | 25,900 | Guaynabo Municipio | 97,924 | Quebradillas Municipio | 28,129 |
| Añasco Municipio | 29,261 | Gurabo Municipio | 45,369 | Rincón Municipio | 15,200 |
| Arecibo Municipio | 96,440 | Hatillo Municipio | 41,953 | Sabana Grande Municipio | 25,265 |
| Arroyo Municipio | 19,575 | Hormigueros Municipio | 17,250 | Salinas Municipio | 31,078 |
| Barceloneta Municipio | 24,816 | Humacao Municipio | 58,466 | San Germán Municipio | 35,527 |
| Barranquitas Municipio | 30,318 | Isabela Municipio | 45,631 | Santa Isabel Municipio | 23,274 |
| Bayamón Municipio | 208,116 | Jayuya Municipio | 16,642 | San Juan Municipio | 395,326 |
| Cabo Rojo Municipio | 50,917 | Juana Díaz Municipio | 50,747 | San Lorenzo Municipio | 41,058 |
| Caguas Municipio | 142,893 | Juncos Municipio | 40,290 | San Sebastián Municipio | 42,430 |
| Camuy Municipio | 35,159 | Lajas Municipio | 25,753 | Toa Alta Municipio | 74,066 |
| Canóvanas Municipio | 47,648 | Lares Municipio | 30,753 | Toa Baja Municipio | 89,609 |
| Carolina Municipio | 176,762 | Las Marías Municipio | 9,881 | Trujillo Alto Municipio | 74,842 |
| Cataño Municipio | 28,140 | Las Piedras Municipio | 38,675 | Utuado Municipio | 33,149 |
| Cayey Municipio | 48,119 | Loíza Municipio | 30,060 | Vega Alta Municipio | 39,951 |
| Ceiba Municipio | 13,631 | Luquillo Municipio | 20,068 | Vega Baja Municipio | 59,662 |
| Ciales Municipio | 18,782 | Manatí Municipio | 44,113 | Vieques Municipio | 9,301 |
| Cidra Municipio | 43,480 | Maricao Municipio | 6,276 | Villalba Municipio | 26,073 |
| Coamo Municipio | 40,512 | Maunabo Municipio | 12,225 | Yabucoa Municipio | 37,941 |
| Comerío Municipio | 20,778 | Mayagüez Municipio | 89,080 | Yauco Municipio | 42,043 |
| Corozal Municipio | 37,142 | Moca Municipio | 40,109 | | |
| Culebra Municipio | 1,818 | Morovis Municipio | 32,610 | | |
| Dorado Municipio | 38,165 | Naguabo Municipio | 26,720 | | |
| Fajardo Municipio | 36,993 | Naranjito Municipio | 30,402 | | |

*Source: US Bureau of the Census, 2010*

The tallest peaks in the Cordillera Central are found in the western half of Puerto Rico.

island in an island chain called the Greater Antilles. Off shore lies the Puerto Rican trench, the deepest section of the Atlantic Ocean, at more than 5 miles (8 km) deep.

Puerto Rico is relatively small, just a bit larger than Rhode Island and Delaware combined, but it has a wide and colorful variety of plants and animals. There are many types of terrain—from ocean beaches to mountains—and a range of weather patterns.

## The Main Island

The main island is divided east to west across its center by high mountains called the Cordillera Central. The highest peak, Cerro de Punta, rises 4,390 feet (1,338 meters). More than fifty rivers flow from the mountains toward the sea, crossing green and fertile valleys.

### Puerto Rico Borders

| North: | Atlantic Ocean |
| --- | --- |
| South: | Caribbean Sea |
| East: | Atlantic Ocean |
| West: | Caribbean Sea |

On the northeastern part of the island, rises a mountain range called the Sierra de Luquillo. One of its highest peaks is called El Yunque. This same name, El Yunque, is also given to Puerto Rico's only national forest.

The island's northwestern landscape is quite different from the northeast. Much of the area is made up of limestone. Over time rivers, wind, and rainfall have eroded the limestone into dramatic caverns, caves, trenches, and towering cone-shaped hills. This type of geographic area is known as **karst**. Many of the rivers in the region flow underground. One of them, Río Camuy, is the third-largest underground river in the world.

# Water Environments

Many important plant and animal habitats are found along the soft sand beaches that encircle the island. Palm trees, pineapple plants, citrus trees, and other tropical plants are abundant on the coastal plains. Lagoons, which are ponds of **brackish** water (meaning a combination of salt and fresh water), lie separated from the sea by reefs or sandbars. Lagoons teem with young fish and other marine life and are a gathering place for waterfowl and sea birds. Mangrove swamps are found near many lagoons. Mangroves are trees that grow in tidal lowlands. Their roots twist downward into the water from their upper branches. When the tide rushes in, seawater floods the swamp, and when the tide flows out, the tangle of roots trap mud and debris, eventually forming land. Mangroves are an important coastal habitat. They provide a nutrient-rich environment for many plants and animals and protect the shoreline from damaging winds and floods.

Off the south and west shorelines lie many coral reefs. Corals are tiny animals related to jellyfish. They build a shell around themselves and attach themselves to each other to form colonies, or reefs. Corals come in a variety of colors, shapes, and sizes. Growing less than a quarter inch (6 millimeters) per year, the colonies of corals off the coast of Puerto Rico took thousands of years to form. Corals need wave action or currents to bring food toward them because they do not move. Instead, they grab passing food with tentacles. Sea grasses and algae attach themselves to the reef, as do sea sponges, anemones, starfish, and sea urchins.

Coral reefs provide protection for coastal areas by reducing erosion of the shoreline caused by waves. They also provide a healthy and safe habitat for numerous fish species. Small fish avoid their predators by hiding among sea grasses and the craggy nooks in the coral. The offspring of larger fish feed in the coral until they mature and go out to sea.

A coral habitat needs warm, clear, shallow water to survive. In many places around Puerto Rico, the fragile coral reefs are damaged when people walk on them or anchor their boats on them. Water pollution also threatens the reefs. In 2014, the US government named four Puerto Rican corals to the national threatened species list.

# Fresh Water

There are numerous rivers on the islands. The longest is the Rio de la Plata, which flows south to north for 60 miles (97 km) before entering the Atlantic Ocean. The second-longest

The underground Rio Camuy has carved out hundreds of caves.

river is the Rio de Loiza. It begins 3,500 feet (1,073 m) above sea level and also flows south to north. The Rio Grande de Arecibo, with its headwaters high in the mountains, flows north to the ocean through a gorge that is 650 feet (200 m) deep and 2,600 to 3,900 feet (800 to 1,200 m) wide. The Rio Camuy runs underground and has one of the largest cave systems in the Western Hemisphere. There are numerous lakes throughout Puerto Rico, which are found along coastal lowlands as well as high in the rainforests.

## Other Islands

Of the outer islands, Vieques is the largest and most populated. It is green and hilly with sandy beaches. Culebra and Mona islands are both are quite dry, featuring rocks, cliffs, and cacti. While there are forests and grasslands on Culebra, there is no fresh water. Because there are no rivers carrying silt and emptying into the sea, the water surrounding Culebra is astonishingly clear. Together with tiny neighboring islands, Culebra is the site of the Culebra National Wildlife Refuge, home to more than fifty thousand seabirds. The entire island of Mona is a wildlife refuge, which protects many iguanas, including the threatened Mona iguana, a giant and aggressive rock iguana. Sea turtles, such as the **endangered** hawksbill sea turtle, nest on the beaches. In winter, humpback whales inhabit the surrounding waters.

# Climate

Puerto Rico has a climate known as tropical marine, or semitropical. The tropics are the regions of the earth lying nearest to the equator. While most of the tropical areas are very hot, Puerto Rico is cooler because of nearly constant ocean breezes. Near the equator, the sun shines almost directly overhead year round, giving Puerto Rico the same amount of daylight in summer and winter, as well as the same amount of daylight and darkness each day. Year-round, the temperature barely changes, ranging on average from 74 degrees Fahrenheit (23 degrees Celsius) in winter months to 81°F (27°C) in the summer.

Puerto Rico's weather patterns greatly influence the landscape. May through October are the rainy months, during which time the average temperatures are a few degrees warmer. November through April are the drier, slightly cooler months.

Like many islands, the main island has a windier, stormier side, called the windward side. The calmer, protected side is called the leeward side. The north side of the island is the windward side. Storm clouds, carried along by steady winds from the Atlantic, push against the mountains, and heavy rains often fall. Rainfall in parts of El Yunque National Forest, for example, can reach more than 250 inches (630 cm) a year. El Yunque National Forest is the only tropical rainforest in the United States. It teems with lush plants such as giant ferns, orchids, mahogany trees, and bamboo.

Warm temperatures and blue skies make Puerto Rico's beaches popular year-round.

**El Yunque National Forest**

**Isla Mona**

**La Parguera**

## 1. El Yunque National Forest

El Yunque covers 28,000 acres (11,330 hectares) of lush tropical rainforest in the Sierra de Luquillo Mountains, where more than 1,200 species of trees and plants thrive. It is also home to the rare Puerto Rican parrot and sixty other species of birds.

## 2. Isla Mona

Fifty miles from Puerto Rico lies the rugged island of Mona. Rocky cliffs line the shore, and nearly 14,000 acres (5,666 ha) are covered in cactus or scrub brush. There are many rare plant and animal species, challenging hiking trails, and exceptional scuba diving.

## 3. La Parguera

La Parguera is a small village by a **phosphorescent** bay. Puerto Rico is the only place where **bioluminescence** appears each night. Nearby are mangrove swamps, and offshore, a giant wall of coral drops more than 1,500 feet (450 m).

## 4. Maricao

The municipio of Maricao lies high in the mountains amid streams, gorges, and steep valleys. It is often shrouded in fog and clouds. Nearby is Puerto Rico's largest state forest, Bosque Estatal de Maricao. More than eighty-five bird species live there.

## 5. Observatorio de Arecibo

Locals call the Arecibo Observatory "El Radar." The largest single dish radio telescope in the world, its reflective surface covers 20 acres (8 ha). It listens for extraterrestrial intelligence, pulsars, quasars, and distant planets.

# PUERTO RICO

## 6. Parque de las Cavernas del Rio Camuy

The underground park surrounding the Camuy River covers almost 10 miles (16 km). The river flows through limestone karst and has created caverns with ceilings as high as 170 feet (50 m) that are home to thousands of bats.

## 7. La Puerta de San Juan

The Puerta de San Juan (San Juan's door) is a seventeenth-century tunnel leading from the harbor into the old city. In times past, the massive wooden doors were shut each night to protect the city from invaders.

## 8. Refugio Nacional Cabo Rojo

At the southernmost part of Puerto Rico is the Cabo Rojo National Wildlife Refuge, where red limestone cliffs rise sharply from salt flats along the shore. The Los Morillos lighthouse is perched on a cliff nearby and looks out over a manatee habitat.

## 9. Rincón

Located on the west side of Puerto Rico, Rincón has some of the best surfing waters in the world. Nearby is the restored Punta Higuero lighthouse, which overlooks Mona Passage, where humpback whales often migrate.

## 10. Vieques Island

The former US Navy test site is a picturesque, undeveloped island of white sand beaches, tropical plants, caves, rolling hills, and turquoise water. Wild horses run free, and people visit to enjoy snorkeling, kayaking, hiking, swimming, and beach combing.

Arecibo Observatory

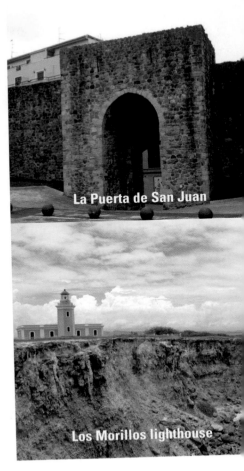

La Puerta de San Juan

Los Morillos lighthouse

Deadly Hurricane Georges hit Puerto Rico with winds up to 115 miles per hour (185 kmh) in 1998.

Quite opposite from the rainy windward side of the island is the dry, leeward side. There, covering 9,900 acres (4,006 hectares) on the southwest coast of Puerto Rico, lies the Guánica State Forest. It is the driest tropical forest in the world and home to more than one hundred species of birds, many types of cactus, and plants and animals not found elsewhere on the island. Annual rainfall in the more populated coastal areas averages 60 inches (150 cm) or more in the north and below 35 to 40 inches (90 to 100 cm) in the south.

Although Puerto Rico has a warm and agreeable climate, the weather can turn harsh during the hurricane season. According to the US National Weather Service, hurricane season lasts from June 1 to November 30. Hurricanes are intense tropical storms that produce heavy rains and wind speeds of at least 74 miles per hour (119 kilometers per hour). Hurricanes do not strike Puerto Rico every year. But when they occur, they are destructive. In 2011, Hurricane Irene produced widespread flooding and left more than one million people without electric power. In 2012, Hurricane Sandy pelted Puerto Rico with heavy winds and rains, flooding many parts of the island and destroying homes, businesses, and power lines. The island was declared a disaster area by the US government.

## Island Creatures

Few mammals are native to Puerto Rico. Because Puerto Rico is an island, mammals could not migrate there overland. Native mammal species arrived by flying or swimming, such as the bat and marine mammals—manatees, whales, and dolphins. Most mammals found wild on the islands, such as pigs, goats, horses, rats, deer, and monkeys, were introduced, sometimes accidentally, by humans. In 1877, farmers were distressed that rats, which arrived as stowaways from ships, were destroying their crops. To combat the rats, they imported Southeast Asian mongooses, which are small weasel-like creatures that eat rats. At first, the farmers were happy to see the rat population decline, but before long the mongooses became a nuisance, eating birds, reptiles, and amphibians.

Many reptiles and amphibians can be found in Puerto Rico. There are several types of snakes, though only one is poisonous, the Puerto Rican racer. Lizards, such as anoles and geckos, lurk everywhere—in forests and cities, and on beaches. They range in size from

### Into the Deep

Scuba diving scientists recently discovered a vast, deep-water coral reef off the coast of Puerto Rico. Marine life in shallow coral reefs along the coastline has been declining due to pollution, but in the deep water, many fish, such as grouper, snapper, and reef sharks, are thriving.

Four types of sea turtles found in the waters off Puerto Rico are endangered.

the tiny Monito gecko, a mere 1.5 inches (3.8 cm), to the Mona ground iguana, which can grow to more than 4 feet (1.2 m) from head to tail. Both are considered endangered, or at risk of dying out. Also endangered are four types of sea turtles: hawksbill, leatherback, loggerhead, and green. These creatures have been hunted for their meat, eggs, and shells. Sea turtles live most of their lives in the open sea. They come ashore only to lay their eggs in the sand. Finally, well over a dozen types of frogs live in Puerto Rico. The one most Puerto Ricans are familiar with is the coquí, a tiny, brownish frog that sings its loud, distinctive song throughout the night.

## Out to Sea

Marine life is abundant in the waters around Puerto Rico. Some areas of the ocean are very deep, while others are shallow and contain coral reefs. In the coral reefs around Puerto Rico, there are octopuses, lobsters, conchs, angelfish, parrot fish, puffer fish, damselfish, squid, shrimp, snapper, crab, and seahorses. Larger fish, such as blue marlin, tuna, and mahi-mahi, live in the deep water but venture close to the edges of the reefs to hunt smaller reef fish. Offshore, whales and dolphins swim. Mosquito Bay on Vieques and two other bays in Puerto Rico are known for tiny organisms called dinoflagellates. At night, these creatures emit an eerie light, called bioluminescence, causing the water in the bay to glow.

## Into the Air

Insects and spiders thrive in Puerto Rico. There are dozens of species, or types, of spiders, many of which are harmless. But some carry strong venom, including the black widow spider, the tarantula, and a wolf spider that can eat small frogs and lizards. There are also more than five thousand species of insects. Common types include mosquitoes, flies, termites, grasshoppers, dragonflies, beetles, and butterflies.

Many of Puerto Rico's 350 species of birds feast on the plentiful insects. The Guánica State Forest is host to many types of birds. They include migratory birds such as egrets, herons, ibises, and todies, and native birds such as the Puerto Rican lizard cuckoo and the Puerto Rican nightjar. Along the coast, seabirds gather. They include grebes, tropicbirds, pelicans, terns, boobies, bitterns, ducks, plovers, laughing gulls, and frigate birds. In the forests live hummingbirds, falcons, hawks, screech owls, tanagers, canaries, parakeets, mockingbirds, and doves.

Puerto Rico's most treasured natural region is El Yunque National Forest. It features one of the most diverse environments in the world. Its 28,000 acres (11,300 ha) contain 240 types of trees, 150 types of ferns, and fifty varieties of orchids. The forest is home to many rare animals, including the native Puerto Rican parrot. Environmentalists and concerned citizens are working to preserve this remarkable rain forest. They do not want to see it developed—turned into cropland or pasture for grazing animals. Vieques National Wildlife Refuge is another treasured resource. The refuge is home to numerous plants and animals, including wild horses and endangered species such as the brown pelican and the manatee. Many habitats are found, including beaches, forests, lagoons, mangroves, and coral reefs. Once the site of a US Navy bombing range, Vieques has otherwise been undisturbed by human development.

**Guánica State Forest is a haven for bird-watchers. This woman is walking in a field of melon cactus.**

**Barracuda**

**Flamboyant Tree**

**Ghost-Faced Bat**

## 1. Barracuda

The barracuda is a long, slender fish with a large mouth, flat head, and razor teeth. They are gray or brown with a white belly, and feed on fish along coastal reefs. They attack at speeds up to 40 miles per hour (64 kmh).

## 2. Brown Pelican

These large seabirds have long bills and a deep pouch in their throat, in which they capture and store baitfish. At dusk, pelicans fly in formation back to their nesting grounds. Brown pelicans are endangered.

## 3. Flamboyant Tree

The nonnative flamboyant tree, also called the flame tree, is very popular. Its colorful flowers and bright green leaves make a striking sight. The town of Peñuelas on the south coast is known as "The Valley of the Flamboyant Trees."

## 4. Ghost-Faced Bat

Bats are the most common mammals in Puerto Rico. The ghost-faced bat is small and reddish-brown, with unusual folds of skin across its face. It hunts at sunset and feeds on insects. During the day, the bat hangs upside down inside dark caves.

## 5. Higo Chumbo

The higo chumbo is a species of cactus found on three offshore islands, including Mona Island. It has prickly stems and large, greenish-white flowers. The fruit, also known as prickly pear, is delicious. Today, the cactus is considered threatened.

## 6. Leatherback Sea Turtle

Some leatherback sea turtles grow to 1,100 pounds (500 kg). They live at sea and come ashore to bury their eggs in the sand. They nest four to seven times a year, each time laying about eighty eggs. Only one in a thousand baby sea turtles survives.

## 7. Mangrove

Mangrove trees grow in salty wetlands along coastlines. They breathe oxygen through their roots. Their extensive root system gives shelter to small fish, shellfish, and crocodiles, and protects against storm erosion.

## 8. Puerto Rican Boa

Puerto Rican boas, some as long as 7 feet (2.1 m), are the island's largest snakes. They squeeze and suffocate birds, lizards, rodents, and bats for food. They wrap themselves around tree branches near cave openings to await bats at night.

## 9. Puerto Rican Lizard Cuckoo

The Puerto Rican lizard cuckoo lives only in the island's forests, woodlands, and plantation fields. The cuckoos are colorful with long tails and curved bills. They feed mainly on lizards and can imitate many sounds.

## 10. Puerto Rican Parrot

There are fewer than fifty Puerto Rican parrots in the wild, making this creature, with its large head and brilliant green and blue feathers, one of the rarest on Earth. Environmentalists are raising parrots for release.

Leatherback Sea Turtle

Mangrove

Puerto Rican Parrot

Work on Castillo San Felipe
del Morro began in 1539.

# From the Beginning

Over many centuries, people from all over the world have come ashore on the beaches of Puerto Rico. Most historians agree that the first people who migrated to the islands of the Caribbean, including present-day Puerto Rico, came from northern South America, in particular modern-day Venezuela.

Civilizations have existed in Puerto Rico for roughly four thousand years. While two or three native groups migrated in waves up until 700 CE, the last migrants before the arrival of Europeans were named the Taíno. By the time the Europeans arrived on the shores of Puerto Rico, the Taíno culture had risen to dominate all the former native cultures.

In 1505, a Spanish priest named Ramón Pané was one of the first Europeans to live in Puerto Rico. He kept a journal that described the islands and the people. He wrote that the Taíno people had built wide, straight roads and "artfully made" homes and other structures. He was impressed with their elaborate religious rituals. He described decorative pottery and baskets, well-carved furniture, tools, and dugout canoes carved from ceiba trees. He noted that they were successful farmers who grew crops, such as yucca (cassava), maize (corn), beans, squash, sweet potatoes, and peppers. They also grew cotton and used the fibers to weave cloth as well as fishing nets and sleeping hammocks.

The priest wrote that the Taíno tended orchards of fine oranges and lemons, and fields of pineapples. Besides fishing, the Taíno also hunted birds, iguanas, and sea turtles.

The Spanish priests were quick to note that many of the native Taíno religious beliefs had similarities to Christian beliefs, including a belief in one all-powerful and invisible god. The people also worshipped the mother of their god, just as some Christians honor the mother of Jesus. Each family prayed to a small, carved, stone or wood idol that held a place of honor in their home. Once Christianity had spread, the Taíno began the practice of carving small wooden statues representing Christian saints, called *santos*. Santos are still prized.

## Spanish Rule

In 1493, the Italian-born sea captain Christopher Columbus sailed from Spain to colonize lands in the New World, which he had visited on a voyage the year before. It was on this second voyage in 1493 that Columbus and seventeen Spanish ships first arrived on the island of Borinquen. At the time, an estimated fifty thousand Taíno were living there.

**Juan Ponce de León was the first Spanish governor of Puerto Rico.**

To the Taíno people, Columbus and his men, with their light skin, elaborate garments, and beards appeared unlike anyone they had ever seen. They greeted the newcomers with friendliness and awe. At the time of his first visit, Columbus had come looking for fresh water and provisions for his ships and crew. The Taíno provided the Spanish with gifts of food and other items. Columbus, however, was not interested in making friends. He was looking for land and wealth for Spain. During his brief stay, he gave the island a Spanish name, San Juan Bautista (Saint John the Baptist, a Christian saint). Over time, the name became shortened to simply San Juan.

Sixteen years later, in 1509, the Spanish explorer and soldier Juan Ponce de León was named the first governor of the island of San Juan Bautista. His duty was to continue

Spanish settlers spread the Catholic faith by building many churches in Puerto Rico. Porta Coeli was originally built in San Germán in 1609.

settlement of the island, maintain control over the natives, and extract wealth for Spain. In 1508, Ponce de León founded a settlement called Caparra close to the northern coast. The town was soon moved to a nearby site on a bay that provided a fine harbor. The new location was named Puerto Rico (Spanish for "rich port"). A few years later, the town became known as San Juan, and the island came to be called Puerto Rico.

King Ferdinand of Spain, now in control of Puerto Rico, had the island divided into large parcels, which he gave to Spanish landowners. Although both Columbus and de León reported that the Taíno people spoke softly and were the "friendliest people in the world," the Spaniards nonetheless forced their will upon them. The native Taíno were so convinced that the Spaniards were as powerful as gods that they did whatever the Spanish people ordered. They worked on Spanish farms, constructed buildings, and mined and processed gold. After a decade of abuse, a new Taíno *cacique*, or tribal chief, came to power. He defied the Spanish and led Taíno warriors into battles. In some instances, the Taíno were victors because they caught the Spanish by surprise. But ultimately the Spaniards, with their superior weapons, put down the revolt. A number of rebels fled to the mountains while others escaped by canoe to neighboring islands.

# The Native People

The first people to live in what is now Puerto Rico were nomads—people who travel from place to place, searching for new food sources and better living conditions. On Vieques, archeologists discovered a human skeleton that they have dated back to at least 2000 BCE. It was likely that the first people hunted and gathered fruits, berries, and plants. By 400 BCE, another group, the Igneri, arrived from the Orinoco River region in what is now Venezuela. These people made pottery and farmed manioc (yucca or cassava), a major part of the natives' diet.

The Taíno people arrived around 1200 CE, also from present day Venezuela. They were fishers, farmers, and hunters. They made clay pottery, wove baskets, and carved wood, including dugout canoes. They built orderly communities, with wood homes and wide streets. Chiefs (called caciques), healers, and spiritual leaders, led the people.

In 1508, Spanish explorer Juan Ponce de León arrived to set up a colony with the intention of mining for gold. The Taíno cacique greeted de León with warmth, believing in a prophecy that foretold special "clothed people" would live among them. But the Spanish soldiers forced the Taíno people to work in mines and on farms and Spanish priests sought to convert the native people to Christianity. When the first cacique died, his nephew resisted the Spanish invaders and the two groups clashed in many battles. The Taíno people were peaceful and were no match for Spanish weaponry.

The Taíno created petroglyphs, which are drawings or carvings on rock.

Additionally, the Taíno suffered from many, often deadly, diseases brought by the Spanish because they had no immunity against European diseases. On the day that de León arrived, there were tens of thousands of Taíno people living in Puerto Rico. In just a decade, due to maltreatment, war, and disease, fewer than four thousand of them remained.

Some Taíno people fled the colonizers by escaping to the mountains where they carried on their traditions. Others escaped in canoes. The US government does not recognize the Taíno tribe officially. In a national census in 1778, thousands of Taíno people were counted, but in 1800, the category of Taíno descent was deleted.

## Spotlight on the Taíno

The Taíno were people who belonged to a larger tribe called the Arawak who migrated by canoe throughout the Caribbean islands. The Taíno people named the island of Puerto Rico "Borinquen," meaning "great land of the valiant and noble lord."

**Distribution:** It is believed that there are no people of full Taíno descent living in Puerto Rico. However, it is estimated 40 to 60 percent of Puerto Ricans today are related to the Taíno people, as many Spanish colonists married Taíno women.

**Homes:** The Taíno lived in small villages, in which they built round homes constructed of bamboo and woven palm fronds. They slept in woven net hamacas (where the word "hammock" comes from). Their homes circled a ceremonial plaza. At one end of the plaza lived the cacique.

**Food:** The Taíno people hunted small animals, fished from canoes, farmed, and gathered roots, berries, and other fruits.

**Art:** The Taíno people were known for clay pottery, woodcarving, and basket weaving. They also made jewelry such as gold earrings, nose rings, and necklaces. Men and women also painted decorations on their bodies.

**Sport:** The Taíno played a ceremonial game that resembled soccer. Ten to thirty players kicked a rubber ball around the central plaza, while dancers performed and musicians played drums, maracas, and *guiros* (an ancient instrument carved from a hollow gourd).

The Spanish influence can still be seen in the colorful buildings of Old San Juan.

After the revolt, the Taíno gradually disappeared from the coastal lowlands. Over the years, many of them died from diseases caught from the Europeans. Since the Taíno had never been exposed to the diseases, they had no natural immunity to protect them against becoming sick. In just a few decades, the Taíno people's way of life was destroyed.

## Slave Trade

By 1570, the gold ran out in Puerto Rico. But the Spaniards had found other ways to create wealth. Puerto Rico and neighboring islands had the ideal climate to grow cotton, coffee, and sugarcane. Sugar had become extremely popular in Europe. To take advantage of easy profits, the Spanish colonizers established large farming operations, called plantations. They planted sugarcane, refined it, and exported the refined sugar to Europe. It was grueling work. The Spanish had exhausted the Taíno people and too few were left to tend crops, harvest, and process the sugar. In 1513, the Spanish government authorized Puerto Rico to participate in the slave trade. European merchants traded guns and luxury items to West African chiefs who in turn enslaved fellow Africans and traded them to the Europeans. The Africans were brought to the Caribbean to work on the plantations, and their free labor vastly improved profits on plantations.

San Juan became a valuable shipping port and a place of power from which Spain could manage its interests in the New World. Spanish engineers, relying on slave labor, built forts in and around San Juan for protection against Spain's enemies. Work on a large fort at the entrance to San Juan Bay began in 1539. It was called San Felipe del Morro, honoring Spain's King Felipe II. Commonly known as El Morro, it is now one of several fortifications belonging to the San Juan National Historic Site.

Piracy and warfare among the European powers that occupied the Caribbean islands were common. The English and the Dutch attacked Puerto Rico several times. Usually, Spain was successful in defending its colony. But in 1598, the English took over El Morro and occupied Puerto Rico for several months before an outbreak of disease forced them to leave. Later, in 1625, the Dutch attacked San Juan and burned it. Pirates, beginning with an attack in 1528 by French corsairs on the southwestern town of San Germán, also caused destruction.

## Black History

During the colonial plantation era, many free black people living in Spain, known as "ladinos," came to Puerto Rico to work as servants. The population of black people increased rapidly once slave traders brought enslaved Africans to Puerto Rico. Most of the Africans belonged to the Yoruba and Ashanti tribes.

## Falling Importance

By the late sixteenth century, Puerto Rico was losing its importance as a trading port for Spain. Many ships took more direct routes to Latin American territories such as Mexico. Also, the Spanish government would not allow the Puerto Rican people to trade with any other country. As a result, fewer ships entered Puerto Rican harbors, and the colony's economy suffered. Spain focused on Puerto Rico's military importance. The government spent money to improve and maintain fortifications on the island, which it saw as key to protecting its rich territories elsewhere in Latin America.

Meanwhile, Puerto Rican planters and small farmers, called *jíbaros*, began planting crops for themselves, not just sugarcane or other crops for Spain. They grew fruits, vegetables, coffee, and tobacco to sell for profit. Despite Spain's restrictions, farmers, businesspeople, and even some government officials began to trade openly with other countries, often with the help of pirates. This illegal trade activity, called smuggling, became widespread. Because of it, the Puerto Rican economy improved.

When the American colonies fought for independence from Great Britain in the American Revolution (1775–1783), Britain barred American trading ships from entering any of the ports in its Caribbean colonies. But Puerto Rico belonged to Spain, so the

# Making a Guiro

The guiro is a rhythm instrument usually made from a dried gourd and played throughout the Caribbean and South America. The Taíno people brought the guiro to Puerto Rico. The instrument continues to be heard in Puerto Rican folk music today.

## What You Need

An empty plastic water bottle with ridges

Permanent markers in any color or colors

A handful of any or all of the following:

    Beads

    Shells

    Pebbles

    Dried Beans

    Unpopped popcorn

    Glitter

An unsharpened pencil or wooden chopstick

## What to Do

- Remove the wrapper from the bottle
- Decorate the bottle with markers
- Fill the bottle/guiro with your selection of beads, shells, etc., leaving room for the objects to rattle
- Screw the cap back on tightly
- Slide the chopstick or pencil across the ridges and shake the guiro to enjoy the sounds of Puerto Rican music.

City Hall in Arecibo, built in 1866, housed captives following *El Grito de Lares*.

Americans could come to port in San Juan Harbor. They brought enslaved Africans and food, which they traded for Puerto Rican coffee, tobacco, and molasses. Puerto Rico also provided shelter for American ships fleeing from the British.

By the nineteenth century, many Puerto Ricans referred to themselves as ***criollos***. This term once described people of Spanish descent born in Puerto Rico. But it had also come to mean people who were a mixture of the island's cultures—Spanish, African, and Taíno. In the 1860s, tensions grew between the criollos and the Spaniards who still controlled the government, most commercial activities, and the military. On September 23, 1868, several hundred people, ranging from enslaved workers to well-off individuals, gathered in the agricultural town of Lares. Armed with machetes and a small number of guns, they declared Puerto Rico an independent republic. The uprising was quickly crushed, but some Puerto Ricans continued to want independence. The uprising is now remembered in Puerto Rican history as *El Grito de Lares* ("The Shout of Lares").

In response to the demands of many Puerto Rican criollos, the government made reforms, including banning slavery in 1873. But criollos continued to demand more rights. In 1897, Spain agreed to allow Puerto Rico limited autonomy, or self-rule. The island's new government began operation in February of the following year.

## The United States Takes Over

In April 1898, war broke out between the United States and Spain. US troops invaded the southern shore of Puerto Rico's main island on July 25. Less than three weeks later, a ceasefire was declared and Spain agreed to give up its claim to Puerto Rico. A US military governor took control of Puerto Rico on October 18. A peace treaty officially ending the Spanish-American War was signed on December 10 in Paris, France. It awarded Puerto Rico to the United States.

A civil government replaced the military government in Puerto Rico on May 1, 1900. Headed largely by Americans, it had a governor, an executive council, and a Supreme Court—

US troops march through Ponce during the Spanish-American War in 1898.

all appointed by the US president. The executive council served as the upper house of the legislature. The legislature also had a house of delegates with thirty-five members, elected by local people. Any laws it passed had to be approved by the US Congress. Puerto Rico was allowed an elected representative—called the resident commissioner—in Washington, DC, but the commissioner, although permitted to speak in Congress, could not vote. Many Puerto Ricans resented this arrangement. It felt like a return to colonial rule with yet another foreign government controlling the country.

To protest the presence of the United States on the island, the legislature refused to pass any laws in 1909. Then, on March 2, 1917, President Woodrow Wilson signed the Jones Act. This law made Puerto Rico a US territory and gave Puerto Ricans the right to US citizenship. It also gave Puerto Ricans some limited personal and

Luis Muñoz Rivera helped write the Jones Act when he served as resident commissioner in Washington, DC.

civil rights. These included the right to elect the members of both houses of their legislature, which now consisted of a Senate with nineteen members and a House of Representatives with thirty-nine. One month later, the United States entered World War I, during which more than eighteen thousand Puerto Ricans were drafted into and served in the US armed forces.

The United States built roads, bridges, schools, dams, and hospitals in Puerto Rico, but some US actions angered many Puerto Ricans. For example, US officials replaced the Puerto Rican peso with the US dollar as the island's

## Governor's Mansion

La Fortaleza in San Juan is the oldest executive mansion in the New World. Begun in 1533, the fort's huge circular tower and massive stone walls took seven years to build. It was attacked twice, by the British in 1598 and the Dutch in 1625. From 1640 on, Puerto Rico's governor has resided at the fort.

### 1. San Juan: population 381,931

San Juan is the capital of Puerto Rico and also the oldest European-founded city under US control. Once a thriving port city guarded by El Morro, a sixteenth-century fort, San Juan is now known more for tourism than for shipping.

### 2. Bayamón: population 185,996

Bayamón lies near a large agricultural area. It was the site of the first sugar mill built on the main island. The Braulio Castillo Theater, the Francisco Oller Museum, and the José Celso Barbosa Monument are located there.

**Bayamón**

### 3. Carolina: population 157,832

Carolina is the industrial center of Puerto Rico. The island's only international airport, Luiz Muñoz Marín International Airport, is located there. Carolina is known as *La Tierra de Gigantes*, "The Land of the Giants," in honor of Don Filipe Birriel, who was the tallest person in Puerto Rico's history at a reported seven feet eleven inches tall.

### 4. Ponce: population 132,502

Ponce was founded in 1692 by Juan Ponce de León's son, Loiza. It features many historic colonial buildings. Today, Ponce is an important trading center and one of the busiest shipping ports in the Caribbean.

**Ponce**

### 5. Caguas: population 82,243

Caguas was founded in 1775 and named after a local Taíno chief. Its many industries today include diamond cutting and the manufacture of leather, glass, and plastic goods, electronic parts, and clothing.

### 6. Guaynabo: population 75,443

Located on the north coast, Guaynabo is Puerto Rico's first settlement, once called Caparra, and was founded in 1508 by Juan Ponce de León. The remains of the explorer's house can be visited here.

### 7. Mayagüez: population 70,463

At the center of Mayagüez is a plaza dedicated to Christopher Columbus. Today, this city on the western end of the island is home to two major universities and the island's only zoo.

### 8. Trujillo Alto: population 48,437

Located in the north central part of the island, Trujillo Alto is a fast-growing suburb of San Juan. Lake Carraízo, Puerto Rico's largest lake, is nearby.

### 9. Arecibo: population 44,191

Arecibo was the third Spanish settlement on the island and was named after a local Taíno chief. It is the site of the world's largest radio telescope. The city hall, built in 1866, was used to house rebels of El Grito de Lares.

### 10. Fajardo: population 33,286

Fajardo is in one of the most beautiful areas on the island. The site of a nature preserve, Fajardo's beaches and forest habitats are home to many rare plants and animals. The largest marina in the Caribbean, Puerto del Rey, provides access for sailors to many islands.

Mayagüez

Arecibo

Workers received little pay for their efforts in the sugarcane fields in the 1930s and early 1940s.

currency. Also, in the first decades of the twentieth century, they tried to make English the main language in schools, although most Puerto Ricans spoke Spanish.

During the first part of the twentieth century, the sugar industry dominated the Puerto Rican economy. But there were problems. Many Puerto Ricans were poor and made a difficult living on small scraps of land. Sugarcane plantation owners, other business leaders, and politicians from the United States held such control over the land that people used the phrase "King Sugar" to describe the wealth and power of the controlling landowners. Most of the farmland was devoted to growing the profitable sugarcane, which left little land for the Puerto Rican people to grow their own crops.

In the late 1920s, Puerto Rico suffered many hardships. Ferocious hurricanes in 1928 and 1932 hurt growers of sugarcane and other major crops. Puerto Rico was hit hard by the Great Depression, a severe economic downturn that affected the United States and many other countries in the 1930s. Poor people struggled to feed and house themselves. Even wealthy people struggled.

## Line of Defense

The fort overlooking San Juan Bay, named El Morro, is believed to be the oldest Spanish fort in the New World. Its walls are 140 feet high [42 m] and 15 feet [4.5 m] thick. It took more than two hundred years to finish. El Morro was used to defend the city of San Juan from attacks by the British, the Dutch, and the United States during the Spanish-American War [1898].

## Taking a Stand

The political career of Luis Muñoz Marín started in the 1930s. A Puerto Rican writer who had studied in the United States, he was the son of Luis Muñoz Rivera, a poet and journalist who had advocated autonomy under Spanish rule and had served as resident commissioner from 1911 to 1916. Luis Muñoz Marín, then a supporter of independence, was elected to the Puerto Rican Senate in 1932. In 1938, he helped found the Popular Democratic Party, which sought to improve the lives of the jíbaros and other poor Puerto Ricans. It adopted "Bread, Land, and Liberty" as its slogan. It gained a majority in the Puerto Rican legislature in the 1940 election, and Muñoz Marín became president of the Senate. The party went on to keep control of the legislature for twenty-eight years.

The United States entered World War II in 1941. More than fifty-three thousand Puerto Rican men and women served in the US military during the war, which lasted until 1945. Puerto Rico became a key military post for the United States, which established army, navy, and air force bases on the main island and on the smaller islands Culebra and Vieques. The bases provided employment opportunities for Puerto Ricans and helped to attract new industries.

## Commonwealth

After the war, Puerto Rico began to gain more control over its own affairs. It received its first native-born governor, Jesús T. Piñero, appointed by President Harry Truman in 1946. The following year, the United States passed a law allowing Puerto Rico to elect its own governor. In 1947, Puerto Rico held its first election for governor. Luis Muñoz Marín won, and took office in 1948. He pushed for change in the relationship between Puerto Rico and the United States. The US Congress agreed to change Puerto Rico's status to a "free associated state," or **commonwealth**, with a constitution to be drawn up by the Puerto Ricans. While Muñoz Marín and his followers favored developing such a relationship with the United States, Puerto Ricans supporting nationalism wanted full independence.

US President Harry Truman rides in a motorcade in Aguas Buenas with Governor Jesús Piñero of Puerto Rico in February 1948.

In 1950, some turned to violence, attacking several towns and even attempting to kill Muñoz Marín and President Truman. The process of forming a commonwealth continued, however, and in 1952, the new constitution won approval from the US Congress and Puerto Rican voters.

Under its new status, Puerto Rico remained subject to the authority of the US president and Congress. However, Puerto Ricans now enjoyed a greater degree of self-rule. They could vote for their own government officials. They remained citizens of the United States, and they continued to use US currency. They did not have to pay federal income taxes, and they could not vote for the US president. As before, they had a representative in Congress—a resident commissioner, belonging to the House of Representatives—but he or she could not vote on legislation.

In addition to his political program, Muñoz Marín pushed for reforms to improve the Puerto Rican economy. Agriculture, long the mainstay of the economy, was shrinking. Muñoz Marín's plan, called Operation Bootstrap, began to take shape before his election as governor. The plan used tax breaks and inexpensive rents for buildings to attract manufacturing and other industries to Puerto Rico. The goal of providing good new jobs for Puerto Ricans was accomplished. By the 1960s, more than nine hundred plants had been established in Puerto Rico, representing such industries as **pharmaceutical** (drug) and textile manufacturing. The tourism industry also grew.

Overall, living standards in Puerto Rico were rising. Many local families were earning more money, making it possible for their children to attend colleges and universities. Most people seemed satisfied with the progress. In later years, however, businesses began moving to other countries where labor was cheaper and taxes were lower. Some of those that remained cut jobs. Unemployment would have skyrocketed if not for the fact that some Puerto Ricans moved to the US mainland to find work. They were continuing a migration that began in a small way after the United States took over Puerto Rico. During World War I and World War II, Puerto Ricans who moved or were brought to the mainland served as a valuable source of labor for US industry. An especially large

**Many cruise ships can dock in the harbor at San Juan.**

> "Puerto Rico is on the sea frontier between North and South America and the cultural and language frontier of both great civilizations of the Americas. This little island has always felt that it had a job to do in bringing about understanding and goodwill."
> —Santiago Iglesias, former Resident Commissioner to Congress

migration occurred in the years after World War II, helped by the growth of air travel. Between 1950 and 1970, for example, an estimated 25 to 35 percent of the Puerto Rican population moved to the mainland.

## The Status Question

Puerto Ricans have been debating one major political issue for a long time. Do they want Puerto Rico to be a US state, to remain a commonwealth, or to become an independent country?

In 1967, 1991, 1993, 1998, and 2012, voters attempted to resolve this issue. But the issue is complicated. Each of the three main political parties in Puerto Rico has a different point of view. The New Progressive Party says that Puerto Rico should become the fifty-first state. Supporters of statehood want their votes to count on matters affecting the United States. If Puerto Rico were to become the fifty-first state, then citizens would be able to vote for the president, two US senators, and members of the US House of Representatives with full voting rights. Also, with statehood, Puerto Rico would receive additional funds from the federal government.

On the other hand, the Puerto Rican Independence Party says that Puerto Rico has been no more than a colony and should now become an independent nation. Followers of the party believe that a new constitution, one that Puerto Ricans write independently of the United States, would better protect their Hispanic language and culture.

The Popular Democratic Party wants to continue commonwealth status. Commonwealth supporters believe that the tax benefits (they don't pay federal income taxes), protection of the US military, citizenship rights, and access to trade with US trading partners are the reasons Puerto Ricans are, on average, wealthier and better educated than most of their Caribbean neighbors.

In the 1967 election, a majority—60 percent—voted to keep the status of commonwealth, 39 percent were for statehood, and only about 1 percent wanted independence. But the results of later elections were not so clear. In 1991, Puerto Ricans were asked whether they wanted to approve a constitutional amendment that would,

The question of Puerto Rico's relationship with the United States remains open to debate.

among other things, assert the right to freely decide between the three choices. "No" received 53 percent of the votes. In 1993, 48.6 percent voted for commonwealth status, 46.3 percent for statehood, and 4.4 percent for independence.

The governor in 1998, from the pro-statehood New Progressive Party, presented voters with a ballot that had five choices: statehood, "territorial" commonwealth, "free association" (roughly midway between commonwealth and independence), independence, and "none of the above." Statehood received 46.5 percent, and independence 2.5 percent. Free association was the choice of 0.3 percent and commonwealth was chosen by 0.1 percent. The biggest vote share, 50.3 percent, went to "none of the above."

In 2012, with the New Progressive Party once again in control of the governor's office, Governor Luis Fortuño and the legislative assembly scheduled a new vote on the status question. Although for the first time a slim majority of Puerto Ricans voted in favor of statehood, voters also elected a new governor, Alejandro García Padilla of the pro-commonwealth Popular Democratic Party. In 2014, the US government promised to provide Puerto Rico money to educate voters on the pros and cons of the issue of statehood. President Obama stated, "The results were clear. The people of Puerto Rico want the issue of status resolved."

## The Road Ahead

There are mixed opinions about the outlook for Puerto Rico's future. Because of the loss of businesses and industries in recent years, along with pollution problems caused by factories and military bases (now mostly closed), some experts believe the future looks poor. Despite migration to the US mainland, many of its people do not have jobs. Puerto Rico suffered during the global economic recession that began in late 2007. While the US average unemployment rate in 2014 was 5.8 percent, the figure for Puerto Rico was 14 percent.

Many Puerto Ricans believe that there is new hope for the island. Sugarcane plantations are no longer a way of life. Farmers have mainly turned to other crops, such as coffee and other tropical foods, and to dairy and livestock farming. And tourism, a major source of income, is helped by the fact US citizens don't need a passport to escape the cold by vacationing in Puerto Rico.

# 10 KEY DATES IN ISLAND HISTORY

**1. 1200 CE**

The Taíno people arrive by canoe from what is present-day Venezuela and establish themselves as the dominant culture in Puerto Rico.

**2. November 19, 1493**

Christopher Columbus and seventeen ships land on the main island during his second voyage to the Americas.

**3. 1513**

Spain officially allows Spanish colonists to bring African men and women to Puerto Rico to work as enslaved laborers. Slavery isn't abolished until March 22, 1873.

**4. September 23, 1868**

Six hundred Puerto Ricans revolt against the Spanish, near the town of Lares. The revolt is called El Grito de Lares, or The Cry of Lares.

**5. April 11, 1899**

The Treaty of Paris officially ends the Spanish-American War. Puerto Rico is ceded to the United States by Spain, along with Guam and the Philippines.

**6. March 2, 1917**

President Woodrow Wilson signed the Jones Act into law, establishing US citizenship for Puerto Ricans.

**7. November 2, 1947**

Luis Muñoz Marín wins the election to become the first governor of Puerto Rico.

**8. March 3, 1952**

Puerto Rico holds a constitutional convention and ratifies a constitution establishing a republican form of government for the "Estado Libre Asociado de Puerto Rico," (the Associated Free State of Puerto Rico).

**9. May 1, 2003**

The US Navy closes its military practice and bomb-training range on the island of Vieques.

**10. January 2014**

Mosquito Bay, a popular tourist attraction on Vieques and the site of an important bioluminescent bay, goes mysteriously dark. Park rangers close the area to most tourism and scientists look for a cause.

Colorful masks mark the San Sebastian
Street Festival on Calle de San Sebastian.

# The People

The commonwealth of Puerto Rico is about the same size as the state of Connecticut. The main island is densely populated and has about one thousand people living in each square mile (2.6 sq km), making it more crowded than any state except New Jersey. Approximately 3.7 million people live on the islands of Puerto Rico. Another 4.6 million people of Puerto Rican origin or descent live on the US mainland. People of Puerto Rican origin or descent who live in New York City call themselves Nuyoricans. In 2010, they numbered more than 720,000, or almost 9 percent of the city's population. That total was nearly twice as large as the population of San Juan.

Among the most famous people of Puerto Rican descent living in the United States is Supreme Court Justice Sonya Sotomayor. Her parents, Juan and Celina, were both born in Puerto Rico, but she was born in the South Bronx neighborhood of New York City. She is the first Latina appointed to the Supreme Court.

Other states with large Puerto Rican populations are Florida, New Jersey, Pennsylvania, and Massachusetts. But no matter where they live, or where they were born, Puerto Ricans are proud of their culture and proud of the rich traditions of their island. As actress Rosie Perez noted, "You may not be born in Puerto Rico, but Puerto Rican is definitely born in you."

## Criollo Culture

Puerto Rican society is diverse. Many Puerto Ricans are descendants of the native Taíno people, Africans, and Spaniards. This ancestry is often described in Spanish as *criollo*.

Many other groups have contributed to Puerto Rican diversity, including French, Italian, and German immigrants, along with Irish and Scottish farmers, Chinese workers, and Haitian and

Many ethnic groups contributed to the lively culture of Puerto Rico.

Dominican refugees. Over the years, Puerto Ricans have blended many cultures to create one special culture that shapes all parts of life: language, religion, art, music, dance, food, celebrations, recreation, and more.

## Language and Religion

Because it ruled the island for four hundred years, Spain has had the strongest influence on Puerto Rico. Both Spanish and English are official languages, but more Puerto Ricans speak Spanish than English. Spanish is the language used in public schools, and English is taught as a second language. Only about 25 percent of the people speak, write, and read English fluently. However, the everyday Spanish spoken by most Puerto Ricans is often influenced by English words.

The Spaniards also introduced Catholicism to Puerto Rico. Today, 85 percent of its people worship as Roman Catholics. Others are of Protestant or Jewish faith. However, many people follow a religion known as Santería, a blend of African, Taíno, and Catholic spiritual beliefs and practices.

## The Arts

Through the centuries, Puerto Rico's culture has inspired local artists to create remarkable paintings (including murals), craft items, and sculptures. The earliest well-known Puerto Rican artist was an eighteenth-century painter named José Campeche, the son of a freed slave and an immigrant from the Canary Islands (off the northwest coast of Africa). Campeche painted religious scenes and portraits, like the European artists of his time.

The Puerto Rican government commissioned sculptor Tomás Batista to create a monument to Puerto Rican workers and farmers. It is titled the *Monumento al Jíbaro Puertorriqueño* (Monument to the Puerto Rican Countryman). He is also renowned for his work in restoring colonial buildings and artwork as well as sculpting in wood and gold.

Many craft traditions have roots in the cultures of Puerto Ricans' ancestors. Skills for these crafts have been passed from one generation to the next. Since the sixteenth century, whole families of artisans have carved wooden statues called santos. In Latin America, santos are figures typically showing Catholic saints. African and Taíno craftspeople in Puerto Rico carved statues of their gods. The artisans of each Puerto Rican culture influenced one another, creating this unique art form.

A distinctively Puerto Rican tradition is the masked *vejigante* character seen at many festivals. Vejigantes represent evil spirits from an old Spanish legend. Puerto Ricans created this character by combining the idea of evil spirits with African mask-making skills and the Spanish tradition of wearing costumes in carnival celebrations. The masks have brightly painted horns, snouts, and devilish expressions.

The masked *vejigante* is a combination of European and African influences.

A type of lace called *mundillo* is another Puerto Rican handmade item. Only artisans in Spain and Puerto Rico know how to make it. The traditional center of mundillo is the town of Moca, which has a museum devoted to this five hundred-year-old craft. Nearby Isabela holds a weaving festival each spring that celebrates mundillo.

## Literature

Puerto Rican history is filled with the names of poets, journalists, playwrights, and authors. Luis Lloréns Torres was a poet and journalist who wrote about *criollismo*, which described Puerto Rico's unique blended society and culture. Luis Palés Matos, a black Puerto Rican, became known as the creator of a style of poetry called Afro-Antillano, which brought African words and rhythms to Spanish-

Roberto Clemente

Judith Ortiz Cofer

## 1. Roberto Clemente

Roberto Clemente was named the National League's Most Valuable Player in 1966 and the World Series MVP in 1971, and was the first Latin American inducted into the National Baseball Hall of Fame. He died in a plane crash while on a humanitarian mission.

## 2. Judith Ortiz Cofer

Judith Ortiz Cofer is a Puerto Rican-American author of books, short stories, and poetry. Her book, *An Island Like You: Stories of the Barrio*, was named one of the best young adult books of the year by the American Library Association.

## 3. Manuel Fernández Juncos

Manuel Fernández Juncos wrote for several newspapers and promoted ideas such as free education for children. In 1898, he was elected Secretary of State. After the Spanish-American War, his poem "La Borinqueña," was chosen as Puerto Rico's official anthem.

## 4. Ricky Martin

Enrique Martin Morales, known as Ricky Martin, has starred on Broadway and has had numerous hit songs, such as "Livin' La Vida Loca." Martin has received six Grammy Awards.

## 5. Rita Moreno

Rita Moreno, born in 1931 in Humacao, began acting at an early age. She was the first Latina to win an Academy Award for Best Supporting Actress for her role in *West Side Story* and the first of a very few people ever to have been awarded an Emmy, Oscar, Tony, and Grammy.

Ricky Martin

## 6. Antonia Novello

Antonia Novello of Fajardo received her medical degree from the University of Puerto Rico. In 1990, President George H. W. Bush appointed her the US Surgeon General. She was the first woman and the first Hispanic to hold that post.

## 7. Francisco Oller

Born in 1833, Francisco Manuel Oller y Cestero studied art in Europe but returned to Puerto Rico to teach and to paint. An impressionist, Oller painted Puerto Rico's natural beauty as well as depicted the island's social problems.

## 8. Lola Rodríguez de Tió

Lola Rodríguez de Tió was born in San Germán in 1843. She championed women's rights, **abolition** of slavery, and independence for Puerto Rico with her political poetry. Many schools, public buildings, and streets are named in her honor.

## 9. Esmeralda Santiago

Esmeralda Santiago was born in Santurce in 1941. After attending Harvard University, she wrote for the *New York Times, Boston Globe,* and *Sports Illustrated.* Her second book, *Almost a Woman*, received the Alex Award from the American Library Association.

## 10. Edwin Torres

Edwin Torres was born in 1931 to Puerto Rican parents and grew up in a poor New York neighborhood. He served on the New York Supreme Court. He has written many novels, some of which have become movies, such as *Carlito's Way* and *After Hours.*

Lola Rodríguez de Tió

Esmeralda Santiago

Edwin Torres

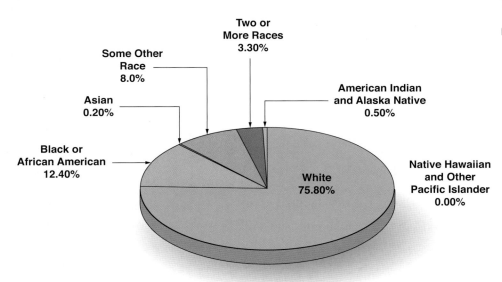

**Total Population
3,725,789**

**Hispanic or Latino (of any race):**

• **3,688,455 people (99.00%)**

**Note:** The pie chart shows the racial breakdown of the state's population based on the categories used by the U.S. Bureau of the Census. The Census Bureau reports information for Hispanics or Latinos separately, since they may be of any race. Percentages in the pie chart may not add to 100 because of rounding.

Source: US Bureau of the Census, 2010 Census

**Two or More Races
3.30%**

**Some Other Race
8.0%**

**Asian
0.20%**

**Black or African American
12.40%**

**American Indian and Alaska Native
0.50%**

**White
75.80%**

**Native Hawaiian and Other Pacific Islander
0.00%**

language poetry. María Bibiana Benítez Constanza was an important poet and the first Puerto Rican woman to write a play, a theater production based on the Dutch invading El Morro. Quiara Alegría Hudes is a novelist and playwright who won the 2012 Pulitzer Prize for drama for her play, *Water by the Spoonful*, and was nominated for a Tony award for her work on the Broadway musical *In the Heights*. José Rivera is a writer and an Oscar-nominated playwright who wrote the screenplay for the movie *The Motorcycle Diaries*, the story of the life of the revolutionary Che Guevera.

## Music and Dance

Music is another favorite art form in Puerto Rico. "Everything that happens in Puerto Rico is accompanied by music," says one Puerto Rican. Puerto Rican musical styles are a blend of Taíno, African, and Spanish rhythms and instruments. The Taíno danced to story-songs in ceremonial dances called *areytos*. They played instruments such as maracas, which are dried gourds filled with beans that rattle when shaken, and guiros, which are notched gourds that are scraped with a stick. Africans brought drums to Puerto Rico, and the Spanish brought guitars.

Puerto Ricans combined all of these influences to create unique musical sounds and dances such as *lamentos*, which are sad ballads, *danzas*, which are like ballroom dances with a Caribbean beat, and the *bomba* and *plena*, which are dances with African roots. In the bomba, drummers and dancers challenge each other. The plena is usually performed with drums and tambourines, along with a guitar, a guiro and/or maracas.

Modern music in Puerto Rico also includes the lively and rhythmic merengue, salsa, reggaeton, and Latin pop and jazz. Many Puerto Rican musicians have become famous around the world. Examples include the native Puerto Ricans José Feliciano and Ricky Martin, along with the New York–born Tito Puente, Marc Anthony, and Jennifer Lopez.

Classical music in Puerto Rico owes much to the great cello player Pablo Casals. Born in Spain to a Puerto Rican mother, he spent most of his final years in Puerto Rico, where he died in 1973. The world-renowned Casals Festival, held in San Juan every year, was founded by him in 1956. He established the Puerto Rico Symphony Orchestra in 1958 and the Conservatory of Music of Puerto Rico in 1959.

The bomba originated in Puerto Rico in the seventeenth century.

# Festivities

Festivals and celebrations are frequent in Puerto Rico. They vary in custom, but they typically feature music, dance, costumes, crafts, parades, and traditional foods. Many types of festivals celebrate harvests of crops such as sugarcane, flowers, coffee beans, and pineapples. Major music festivals include the Casals Festival, the Puerto Rico JazzFest, and the National Bomba and Plena Fiesta. Political, religious, and ethnic festivals are held throughout the year. Puerto Ricans, being citizens of the United States, honor all US federal holidays, as well as their own national holidays. Some of these national holidays are Abolition of Slavery Day (March 22), the birthday of Luis Muñoz Rivera (third Monday in July), Puerto Rican Constitution Day (July 25), and Discovery of Puerto Rico Day (November 19).

Each of the seventy-eight municipios, or municipalities, holds a festival honoring the town's patron saint. *Fiestas patronales*, as they are called, commonly begin with a church service on a Friday, two to twelve days before the saint's official holiday. After the religious events end, everyone leaves the church and goes into the town plaza. Then, for as long as two weeks, musicians play day and night. Food vendors, farmers, and artisans line the plaza, and people dance, shop, and join in parades. Some of the largest and most popular of the saints' festivals are Festival of Saint James (Fiesta de Santiago Apóstol) and Festival of Saint John the Baptist (Fiesta de San Juan Bautista). Other important religious celebrations are Easter week (Semana Santa, or Holy Week) and the Christmas season (Las Navidades). During these holidays, many city dwellers go back to the countryside, where their extended families gather to celebrate.

## Food and Fun

While typical US foods can be found in its markets and restaurants, Puerto Rico also has its own style of cooking. Food is a major part of every celebration. Farmers' markets,

Fresh fruits are plentiful in Puerto Rican markets.

outdoor food stalls, and open-air cafés all send their tempting aromas into the streets. Fresh fruits such as pineapples, mangoes, coconuts, papayas, and avocados are plentiful.

The word "barbecue" comes from the Taíno language. For hundreds of years, Puerto Ricans have barbecued meats such as chicken and pork on outdoor grills. Rice and pigeon peas (similar to sweet peas) are included in a meal almost every day in most households. Plantains are another favorite food. They look similar to bananas, but plantains taste more like sweet potatoes. Cooks prepare plantains by frying, boiling, or sometimes mashing them. Cooks use a variety of sauces to flavor many meats and vegetables. One example is *sofrito*, which is made from peppers, onions, garlic, tomatoes, and spices.

## Sports

Puerto Rico's mild climate is good for many outdoor activities. Puerto Ricans enjoy boating, fishing, swimming, surfing, hiking, tennis, and golf year-round. In plazas everywhere, people can be seen seated at tables in the shade, playing dominoes or chess. Other athletic passions are baseball and boxing. Puerto Ricans learned about boxing from the US military.

Surfing is a year-round sport in Puerto Rico.

The first official bout is said to have taken place in 1899. Since then, the sport caught on. A number of Puerto Ricans became world champions, beginning with Sixto Escobar in the 1930s. Champions in recent years include Edwin Rosario, Héctor Camacho, Félix Trinidad, and Miguel Cotto. The Taíno enjoyed ball games centuries ago, and today Puerto Ricans play baseball year-round. Many major league players from the United States play winter baseball in Puerto Rico. Also, hundreds of talented major league players have come from Puerto Rico or are of Puerto Rican ancestry. Among those born in Puerto Rico are Roberto Clemente, Orlando Cepeda, Juan González, Javy López, Roberto Alomar, Bernie Williams, José Cruz, Carlos Delgado, Jorge Posada, Iván Rodríguez, and Carlos Beltrán.

## City and Countryside

During Operation Bootstrap, people began leaving their homes in the countryside to move to jobs in the cities. The cities grew and spread into neighboring towns, creating suburbs made up of rows of apartments and houses. People were concerned that urban areas of Puerto Rico were becoming overcrowded. However, since 2010, many of the larger cities have been losing population.

Although today only a small percentage of the Puerto Rican population lives in the countryside, people remain loyal to the small towns and villages of their birth. During major holidays, families return to these places. Many mountain villages look the same as they did a century or more ago. Throughout the countryside, town plazas are lively centers of action. During summer's heat, many Puerto Ricans escape to the mountains. Whether from the city or countryside, Puerto Ricans love their land. They treasure its rich culture and are proud of its unique place in the world.

### 1. Aibonito Flower Festival

For more than a week starting in late June, the mountain town of Aibonito comes alive with Puerto Rico's biggest festival devoted to plants and flowers. Thousands visit to buy flowers and enjoy crafts, music, dance, and traditional foods.

### 2. Calle San Sebastián Festival

San Juan's Calle San Sebastián, or Saint Sebastian Street, is the center of one of Puerto Rico's biggest festivals. It honors Saint Sebastian, whose feast day is January 20. The event features music, dancing, performers, food, a parade, and arts and crafts.

### 3. Carnaval de Ponce

The city of Ponce, on the south coast, is famous for its colorful Carnival, or Mardi Gras. It occurs the week before the start of Lent, a forty-day period of fasting before Easter. The Carnival features a parade, vejigantes, and music, dancing, and food.

### 4. Feria Dulce Sueño

In March, the streets of Guayama fill up for the Dulce Sueño festival, featuring Paso Fino horses, a breed imported by Columbus. During the two-day event, festivalgoers enjoy horse races and shows.

### 5. Festival del Juey

In June, the beach town of Guánica comes alive with crabs. The Festival del Juey (crab festival) features Puerto Rican foods made from crabs. There is also a crab costume parade and a crab race.

Aibonito Flower Festival

Carnaval de Ponce -

# PUERTO RICO ★ ★ ★

### 6. Festival Nacional Indigena Jayuya

In one of the highest mountain areas in Puerto Rico lies Jayuya, a traditional home to the Taíno people. In November, the town celebrates its Taíno culture for ten days. The highlight is a Taíno costume competition.

### 7. Fiesta de Santiago Apóstol

Several towns honor the July 25 feast day of Santiago Apóstol (Saint James), but the most famous celebration happens over three days in Loíza. People pay homage with parades, music, dance, food, and vejigantes.

### 8. Hatillo Masks Festival

Hatillo's mask festival on December 28 reenacts the Massacre of the Innocents, which was meant to kill the baby Jesus. Besides masked and costumed "soldiers" running through the streets, there is dancing, music and traditional foods.

**Hatillo Masks Festival**

### 9. San Juan Bautista Day

The day for San Juan Bautista (Saint John the Baptist), June 24, is celebrated all over Puerto Rico with food, music, and fun—beginning at midnight, when people jump into the ocean backward, a tradition meant to renew good luck in the year ahead.

### 10. Three Kings Day

Three Kings Day, January 6, marks the end of the Christmas season, or Las Navidades. On the night before, children put shoeboxes filled with grass under their beds. The kings fill the boxes with gifts after their camels eat the grass.

**Three Kings Day**

The Puerto Rico Capitol stands not far from Old San Juan.

# How the Government Works

P uerto Rico underwent centuries of changing rules and governments before it became a commonwealth of the United States in 1952. Perhaps that status will change again. Meanwhile, people in Puerto Rico live under three levels of government: local, commonwealth, and federal.

## Levels of Government

Residents of states in the United States commonly live under more than one level of local government, such as city and county. Puerto Rico, however, has only one level.

The commonwealth is divided into seventy-eight municipios. Each municipio elects a mayor and an assembly for a four-year term of office (there is no limit on the number of terms an official can serve). A municipio with many residents, equivalent to a big city, typically has a larger assembly than a less populated municipio, which might be compared to a town or village on the US mainland.

The second level of government in Puerto Rico is the commonwealth government. In March 1952, the people were asked to approve a constitution that had been drawn up by their representatives subject to approval by Congress.

The governor's residence, a former fort named La Fortaleza, overlooks San Juan Harbor.

More than 80 percent of the people voted in favor of the document, and Congress approved it a few months later. Many of the provisions found in the constitution are similar to those found in the state and federal constitutions. For example, there is a bill of rights, and there are three branches of government—the executive branch, the legislative (law-making) branch, and the judicial branch (the courts). In the commonwealth, the executive branch is headed by a governor, who is elected by the voters. The governor appoints judges and other executive officeholders. Citizens also elect the members of the law-making body, known as the legislative assembly. It consists of two chambers: a Senate and a House of Representatives.

Puerto Rico belongs to the federal court system of the United States and is under the jurisdiction of the US First Circuit Court of Appeals. Puerto Ricans are US citizens and are free to come and go to the mainland of the United States without having to get a visa, or special permission, which is often required when a person travels abroad.

# Branches of Government

## Executive

The governor is the powerful head of the executive branch. The governor appoints all judges and all department heads, subject to approval by the Senate. He or she signs bills into law and can also refuse to sign bills. This refusal is called a veto. The governor is elected to a four-year term, and there are no term limits.

## Legislative

The legislative assembly is made up of twenty-seven senators and fifty-one members of the House of Representatives. A proposal to reduce the number of legislators has appeared on the ballot, but as of 2014, it has not been approved by voters. Most members of the legislative assembly represent a particular area, or district. For the Senate, Puerto Rico is divided into eight districts, each of which elects two senators. For the House of Representatives, Puerto Rico is divided into forty districts, with each electing one representative. In addition, eleven senators and eleven members of the House of Representatives are elected "at large"—that is, they represent Puerto Rico as a whole.

All members of the assembly are elected to four-year terms, with no limit on the number of terms they can serve. If voters elect members from one political party to hold more than two-thirds of the seats in either the house or the senate, then seats are added to that chamber and assigned to members of the minority parties on an at-large basis.

## Judicial

The judicial branch is a system of courts made up of the Supreme Court, the court of appeals, and the court of first instance. The governor appoints all judges, with approval of the Senate. The highest court, the Supreme Court, is made up of nine justices, who serve until the age of seventy. The Supreme Court hears appeals of decisions made by lower courts and decides whether laws are in accordance with the commonwealth's constitution. It also oversees the court system. The court of appeals, whose judges serve sixteen-year terms, hears challenges to rulings made in lower courts. Judges in the court of first instance are appointed to twelve-year terms. This court is divided into two sections: superior court and municipal court. Superior courts hear the major civil and criminal trial cases. Municipal courts make decisions on small claims and lesser crimes.

# Commonwealth Compared to a State

Puerto Rico is self-governing. It controls its own internal policies, such as public education, public health, and environmental laws. The United States controls all other policies—as it does for individual states—such as foreign and interstate trade, foreign relations, customs and immigration, currency, maritime laws, military service, military bases, army, navy and air force, declarations of war, constitutionality of laws, treaties, radio, television, and other forms of communications, agriculture, mining and minerals, highways, and the postal system.

**Puerto Ricans are citizens of the United States, and many of them have served in the army. These soldiers are training in 1942.**

When living in Puerto Rico, Puerto Ricans do not pay US federal income tax. However, they do pay federal Social Security tax. They can collect Social Security benefits and some other types of income payments from the US government. (Social Security benefits help people who are retired or unable to work.) Puerto Ricans can enlist in the military of the United States and are included in the military draft, when it is in effect. One of the most contentious issues at the time that the United States took over Puerto Rico was that while Puerto Rican citizens could not vote for president, they were nonetheless drafted into the military to serve in World War I.

Puerto Rican voters can participate in the presidential primary elections of the two major political parties in the United States, the Democrats and the Republicans. But they cannot vote in the main presidential election. They do elect one representative to a four-year term to the US House of Representatives. However, that representative—the resident commissioner—is not allowed to vote on legislation.

## How a Bill Becomes a Law

Like the United States and most of its fifty state governments, Puerto Rico has two chambers in its legislative assembly: a Senate and a House of Representatives. Each of these chambers is sometimes referred to as a house. The chief duty of their members, also called legislators, is to create laws. A legislator in either of the two houses can introduce a proposed law, which is called a bill. One exception, however, is that all tax-related laws must begin in the House of Representatives. When a legislator has an idea for a bill, the bill must be printed and given to a committee to decide whether or not to officially propose the bill.

Each committee within a house focuses on a particular topic, such as education, agriculture, natural resources, health, transportation, or taxes. During committee meetings, members discuss the bill and listen to people who have come to express their views. If a committee approves a bill, it is presented to all the members of the house. The other legislators debate the bill and may suggest changes, or amendments. The bill is then put to a vote within the house where it was created. If the bill receives a majority of the votes, it is sent to the other house. When the bill is received in the other house, it goes through much the same process of committee discussion and voting. If the second

house wants to amend the bill, the two houses must come to an agreement on the final wording for the bill to be sent on to the governor for his or her consideration.

The history of Puerto Rico is told in paintings on the inside of the capitol's dome.

If the bill does pass in both houses, it is presented to the governor. The governor can sign the bill, making it law. Or the governor can refuse to sign the bill and return it to the house where it began, sending along with the bill his or her objections or suggestions for changes. This action is called a veto. If the bill is vetoed, it will still become law if the two houses decide to reconsider it and two-thirds of the members of each house then vote in favor of it.

When the governor wants to veto a bill, he or she usually must return it to the legislature within ten days. Otherwise, the bill will become law without the governor's signature. If the legislature is no longer in session, however, the governor does not have to return a bill in order to veto it.

# POLITICAL ★ FIGURES
## FROM PUERTO RICO

### ★ José Luis Alberto Muñoz Marín: Governor, 1949-1965

Luis Muñoz Marín led the Popular Democratic Party, and was elected to the Puerto Rican Senate in 1932. In 1948, he took office as the first elected governor of Puerto Rico. As governor, Marin achieved many reforms. In 1963, he was awarded the US Presidential Medal of Freedom.

### ★ Sila Calderón: Governor, 2001-2005

In 1996, Sila Calderón was elected mayor of San Juan. In 2001, she became the first woman to be elected governor of the Commonwealth of Puerto Rico. She was widely praised for her achievements, including overseeing the withdrawal of the US Navy bombing range from Vieques Island.

### ★ Aida Alvarez: US Cabinet, 1997-2001

Aida Alvarez attended public school in Puerto Rico and Radcliffe College in Massachusetts. She worked as a journalist, then went into banking. When President Clinton appointed her the administrator of the Small Business Administration she became the first Hispanic woman, and first Puerto Rican, to hold a US Cabinet post.

# PUERTO RICO

## YOU CAN MAKE A DIFFERENCE

### ★ Contacting Legislators

To search for Puerto Rico's legislators, visit this Spanish-language website:

**www.oslpr.org/new**

Select the tab *Legislatura*, then from the drop-down menu, select either *Camara des Representantes* or *Senadores*. Click on each legislator for contact information.

To search for recent legislation, select the tab *Leyes*.

If you would like to search for legislators in English, visit this website:

**openstates.org/pr/legislators**

### ★ The Gag Law

Ley 53 (Law 53) became commonly known as the Ley de La Mordaza (Gag Law). The law was passed by the Puerto Rican legislature in 1948, which at the time was controlled by the Popular Democratic Party (PPD, short for Partido Popular Democrático). The PPD supported being a free-associated state of the United States. The gag law was meant to squelch the rise of the Puerto Rican Nationalist Party, which wanted Puerto Rican independence, and to intimidate any of the party's supporters. Law 53 made it illegal to sing a patriotic tune, display a Puerto Rican flag, to speak or write of independence, meet with anyone, or hold any assembly, in favor of Puerto Rican independence, or to fight for the liberation of Puerto Rico.

Following the passage of the law, there were many demonstrations that turned bloody, and dozens of citizens, police, and soldiers were killed, injured, or imprisoned. For nearly a decade in the 1950s, Nationalists revolted. The Gag Law wasn't repealed until 1957. It was repealed on the basis that it was unconstitutional; freedom of speech is protected by the First Amendment of the United States Constitution.

**Supporters of independence were rounded up on November 4, 1950.**

Resorts, beautiful scenery, and glorious beaches bring many tourists to Puerto Rico.

# Making a Living

For many centuries, the people of Puerto Rico supported themselves by hunting, fishing, and growing crops. When the Spanish colonists took over, they planted only moneymaking crops. Today, the islands' economy is far more diverse.

## Agriculture

Over time, agriculture production in Puerto Rico has undergone many changes. As one citizen recounts, "Puerto Rico grows the finest coffee in the world. All the houses of kings once ordered coffee from the island growers." At the height of Puerto Rico's success as a coffee exporter at the end of the nineteenth century, a couple of severe hurricanes destroyed the big plantations. It took years for the farms to recover. By the time they did, the United States had begun buying coffee from Brazil. Coffee production is once again a part of Puerto Rico's economy, but not in the quantities it once was.

The United States continued to import huge quantities of sugarcane until the 1940s, after which sugarcane production dropped. Only a few plantations remain today, as a result of competition from sugar-beet farming in the United States.

Currently, only about eleven thousand Puerto Ricans are working in farming. The government believes that Puerto Rico relies too heavily on the United States for food. For

Coffee plants, started in pots, produce one of Puerto Rico's most valuable crops.

example, Puerto Ricans grow only a small percentage of the rice they consume. Most is imported from the United States and other countries. Attempts are being made to develop more, and larger, farms. A government program gives annual bonuses to farmers and persons who store or transport food for local markets.

Puerto Rican farmers, especially in the western region, grow fruits and native root vegetables. The mainstay of Puerto Rican agriculture—the chief source of income—is dairy and livestock farming, which includes the production of milk, eggs, and meat from cows and chickens. The most valuable crops are plantains, coffee, and ornamental plants. The chief agricultural product Puerto Rico exports is rum. Other food exports include spices, soft drink syrup, and a range of products processed by Goya Foods, one of the largest Hispanic food companies in the world.

## Natural Resources

Puerto Rico is a small island group with limited natural resources. Many of its forests have been cut to make way for plantations and housing. Today, there are efforts to replant some of the tropical forests.

Fishing was once a typical way to earn a living, but it is no longer a reliable source of income. Commercial fishers catch tuna and grouper as well as lobsters, shrimp, crabs, and conchs. Fish farming is carried out on a small scale, mainly involving the raising of tilapia, shrimp, and ornamental fish.

Valuable metals such as gold, copper, iron, and silver were once mined in Puerto Rico, but the mines have closed. Today, the chief minerals mined are sand, gravel, lime, clay, and stone—used to build houses, roads, and bridges.

Salt was mined by the Taíno people as far back as 700 CE in the area around Cabo Rojo. The seawater there is particularly salty. For centuries, large pits near the shore have been used to collect seawater. As the tide comes in, the water sinks into the pits. The sun evaporates the water, leaving behind the salt. The Spanish quickly saw the value of these salt flats and took them over. Many battles between neighboring villages have been fought over the salt flats.

# Transportation

"It used to take half a day to get to Mayagüez. Now, there are highways everywhere, and it takes twenty minutes," comments a man from San Germán.

In the past two decades, roads and highways have been extensively improved. There are nearly 17,000 miles (27,359 km) of roads and more than 2.4 million cars. Streets are often packed with the despised *tapones*, or traffic jams.

"Oh," says one shopkeeper, "you should see the cars thread their way through Old San Juan. They go one after the other all day and on into the night!" Today an efficient mass transportation system, called the Tren Urbano, or Urban Train, relieves some of the congestion. The line was the first rapid transit system in the Caribbean.

While cars, buses, and the Tren Urbano move people around Puerto Rico, airplanes and boats move people to and from the commonwealth. San Juan has a large international

The Tren Urbano was the first rapid transit system in the Caribbean.

# ★ 10 KEY INDUSTRIES ★

**Agriculture**

**Fishing**

### 1. Agriculture

Coffee is Puerto Rico's most valuable crop. It has a fine aroma and a medium bitter-sweetness prized by gourmet coffee drinkers. Other crops include sugarcane, mangoes, pineapples and other fruit, and rice. Sugarcane is now seasonal and wages remain low.

### 2. Dairy and Livestock

Dairy products, such as milk, butter, cheese, and eggs, are the largest agricultural products as well as pork, poultry, and beef cattle. The dairy industry accounts for about one-quarter of the income that comes from the islands' farms.

### 3. Fishing

Commercial fishing is a smaller part of the economy than it once was. Fishers catch tuna as well as shellfish. They also raise freshwater fish such as bass and catfish. More important than commercial fishing is sport fishing. Tourists charter boats to try to catch a big marlin or swordfish.

### 4. Food Processing

Many Puerto Ricans have jobs in food processing, such as preparing and packaging spices, soft drink syrup, and canned and packaged beans, peas, sauces, and rice.

### 5. Government

After the service industry, the government is the next largest employer in Puerto Rico. More than 250,000 people, or about 20 percent of the workforce, hold jobs in government such as mayors, council members, public health and education workers, park rangers, administrators, and others.

## 6. Manufacturing

The primary products are chemicals, metal products and machinery, clothing and textiles, pharmaceuticals and medical equipment, and computer and electronics equipment. A small furniture industry uses local bamboo and hardwoods.

## 7. Minerals and Mining

Almost all of Puerto Rico's mineral production contributes to the construction industry, such as cement, sand, gravel, and stone. Other minerals mined include clay, graphite, lime, and salt.

## 8. Rum

Puerto Rico is known as the "Rum Capital of the World." The making, bottling, selling, and shipping of rum contributes to more than four thousand jobs and more than $400 million in income.

## 9. Services

Most of the population, about 75 percent, works in the service industry. People who work in banking, business, education, health, insurance, real estate, and publishing are all considered service workers. This sector brings in about half of the money earned in the commonwealth.

## 10. Tourism

Sunshine, historical buildings, and white sand beaches attract 3.5 million tourists each year; and spending by visitors exceeds $1.4 billion annually. There are excellent hotels and restaurants, and visitors also come for the golfing, tennis, boating, hiking, and snorkeling.

Manufacturing

Tourism

# Making Budin

Budin, or Puerto Rican bread pudding, is a traditional dessert enjoyed during holidays, but is also a delicious treat year-round.

## What You Need

2 12 oz. (710 mL) cans evaporated milk

1 cup (237 mL) raisins

1 stick (118 mL) butter, melted

1 tsp (5 mL) vanilla extract

1 tsp (5 mL) salt

1 cup (237 mL) sugar

2 eggs

1 can (355 mL) coconut milk

1 (0.9 l) quart regular milk

1½ loaves bread (preferably stale bread)

1 tbsp (14.7 mL) ground cinnamon

Mixing bowl and spoon

9 x 12 inch (23 x 30.5 cm) or circular baking pan

## What to Do

- Preheat oven to 350 degrees Fahrenheit (180°C)
- Tear the bread into small pieces, place in bowl
- Add cinnamon and stir
- Add evaporated milk, eggs, vanilla, salt, butter, coconut milk, and mix well
- Add regular milk and sugar, and mix
- Add raisins and mix
- Grease the pan with a small amount of butter or cooking spray.
- Pour mixture into baking pan.
- Bake for one hour.
- Let cool, cut, and enjoy!

airport, named after Luis Muñoz Marín. There also are at least ten smaller public airports in Puerto Rico. Planes and ferries serve the islands of Culebra and Vieques. San Juan and Ponce are among the Caribbean's chief ports for container and cruise ships. San Juan is the biggest and busiest port for cruise ships in the Caribbean.

## Manufacturing

Almost 10 percent of the labor force in Puerto Rico is employed in manufacturing. In the late 1940s, people began leaving their fishing and farming jobs to go to the cities to work in the new factories launched by Operation Bootstrap. Many large corporations are there to this day, including General Electric, Hewlett-Packard, Johnson & Johnson, Goya, Pfizer, and Procter & Gamble. Puerto Rican factories make clothing, medicines, chemicals, electronics, and many other products.

Many medicines are made in Puerto Rico.

Over recent years, changing US tax laws made Puerto Rico less appealing as a place to do business. As a result, many companies reduced the number of employees they hired in Puerto Rico and moved factories to countries where taxes and labor were cheaper. Yet, Puerto Rico still has an educated workforce, so jobs involving chemical, medical, and high-technology products remain an important part of the economy. Some of the most commonly prescribed medicines in the United States are manufactured in Puerto Rico.

## Service Jobs

Most members of Puerto Rico's labor force are employed in service jobs. These jobs include all types of work not involved in making things. Service workers include hotel and restaurant employees, health care workers, lawyers, shopkeepers, and bankers. They also include people who work for the government, including public school teachers, police officers, and firefighters.

## Education

Puerto Rico has a long tradition of public education. The first program for preschool in the United States began in Puerto Rico. Puerto Rico's literacy rate is high, at 94 percent. Children receive a free and required education from ages five to eighteen. There are also many colleges and universities, such as Inter-American University of Puerto Rico, University of Puerto Rico, the Puerto Rico Music Conservatory, and the School of Tropical Medicine.

**Beautifully carved *santos* are still sought after.**

## Tourism

There are many service jobs in Puerto Rico's large tourism industry. Each year, roughly five million visitors come to Puerto Rico, three million of them from the United States. Although the tourists' money is welcome, some Puerto Ricans believe the many hotels, restaurants, and cruise ships add to crowding on the islands and strain resources.

However, one form of tourism that protects the environment while still providing jobs is **eco-tourism**. Eco-tourists are people who visit a place to study its natural areas. They stay in small inns or in people's houses and eat at local restaurants. Eco-tourists come to Puerto Rico to kayak in the lagoons, hike in the rain forest, bird-watch, spelunk in caves, snorkel over coral reefs, and study other natural features. The Puerto Rican eco-tourism industry is working with scientists, environmentalists, local businesspeople, government officials, and others to preserve and protect the commonwealth's tropical beauty. Possessing such a special place in the world, Puerto Ricans have a bounty that they are proud to share.

Artisans also benefit from the tourism industry as visitors buy the many fine native crafts of the island. Fine needlework such as lacemaking is a centuries-old skill among Puerto Rican women. Their crafts became popular in the United States when President Franklin Delano Roosevelt and his wife, Eleanor, and the wife of inventor Thomas Edison, purchased traditional Puerto Rican textiles. Since the sixteenth century, Puerto Rican artists have carved santos—wooden figures of Catholic saints—for display in people's homes. Today, art collectors, museums, galleries, and tourists seek out santos crafted by contemporary wood carvers.

## Going Forward

Puerto Rico suffered through the economic recession that began in 2007, as did the rest of the world. While Puerto Rico may be recovering more slowly than the United States, it is nonetheless striving to revive its economy, invest in new businesses, create new jobs, protect its environment, and improve the quality of life for its people. At a recent gathering, the president of the Puerto Rican Heritage Organization declared, "We're not going to let anything stop us."

# PUERTO RICO ★ ★ ★
## COMMONWEALTH MAP

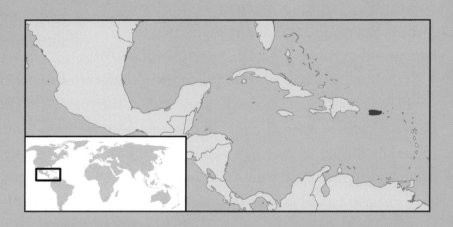

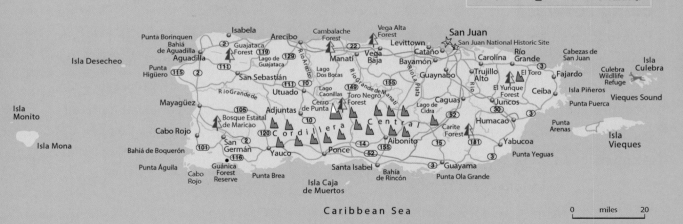

ATLANTIC OCEAN

**Legend:**
- Expressway
- Major Highway
- City or Town
- Capital
- Highest Point in Commonwealth
- Mountains
- Historic Site
- Forest
- Wildlife Refuge

Isla Desecheo

Punta Borinquen
Bahiá de Aguadilla
Aguadilla
Punta Higüero
(115)  (2)
(2)

Isabela
Guajataca Forest
(179)
Lago de Guajataca
(129)
San Sebastián
(111)  (10)
Rio Grande de
Utuado

Arecibo
Rio Arecibo
Lago Dos Bocas
Manatí
(22)

Cambalache Forest

Vega Baja
Vega Alta Forest
(155)

Levittown
Cataño
Bayamón
Guaynabo

San Juan
★ San Juan National Historic Site
Carolína
Río Grande
Trujillo Alto

Cabezas de San Juan
El Toro
Fajardo
Ceiba
Isla Piñeros
Punta Puerca

Culebra Wildlife Refuge
Isla Culebra

Vieques Sound

Isla Monito

Mayagüez
(105)
Adjuntas
(10)
(120)
Bosque Estatal de Maricao
Cabo Rojo
Bahiá de Boquerón
(101)
San Germán
(116)
(2)
Yauco

Lago Caonillas
Cerro de Punta
Toro Negro Forest
Cordillera
Ponce
(14)
(52)
Santa Isabel

Lago de Cidra
Central
Caguas
(149)
Rio Grande de Manatí
Rio La Plata
El Yunque Forest
Juncos
(30)
(3)
Humacao

Aibonito
(155)
(15)
Carite Forest
(52)
(181)
Yabucoa
Punta Yeguas

Punta Arenas
Isla Vieques

Isla Mona

Punta Águila
Cabo Rojo
Guánica Forest Reserve
Punta Brea

Isla Caja de Muertos

Bahiá de Rincón
Guayama
Punta Ola Grande
(3)

**Caribbean Sea**

0    miles    20

# PUERTO RICO

## ★ MAP SKILLS

1. Arecibo lies near which ocean?

2. Is Isla Culebra north or south of Isla Vieques?

3. What city is nearest to the Bahía de Rincón (Rincon Bay)?

4. What city lies west of Lago Caonillas?

5. What city lies southwest of El Yunque National Forest?

6. What highway runs between the cities of Rio Grande and Ceiba?

7. The Rio de la Plata empties into the Atlantic Ocean just west of what city?

8. Which forest is further south—Guajataca Forest or Carite Forest?

9. Which city is not on Highway 2—Aguadilla, Mayaguez, or San Sebastian?

10. What body of water surrounds Isla Caja de Muertos?

Isla Caja de Muertos

Rio de la Plata

1. Atlantic
2. North
3. Santa Isabel
4. Utuado
5. Juncos
6. Highway 3
7. Levittown
8. Carite
9. San Sebastian
10. Caribbean Sea

# Official Flag, Seal, and Anthem

Puerto Rico's flag was adopted in 1952. There are three red stripes and two white. On the left is a single white star resting in a blue triangle. The triangle represents the three branches of the government. The red stripes signify the blood that feeds the three branches of government. The white stripes represent citizens' rights. The star stands for the commonwealth.

Many of the images in the Puerto Rican seal come from the sixteenth century. A lamb represents peace and brotherhood. The letters F and I stand for King Ferdinand and Queen Isabella of Spain. Spanish symbols such as the Towers of Castile, the Lions of Léon, the crosses of Jerusalem, and various Spanish flags also appear. The motto *Joannes Est Nomen Ejus* is Latin for "John Is His Name." It refers to San Juan Bautista (Saint John), after whom Puerto Rico was originally named.

The official anthem of the Commonwealth of Puerto Rico is "La Borinqueña." Originally, it was a dance song, but poet Lola Rodríguez de Tió changed the music to a marching song. Lyrics also changed over the years. The poet Manuel Fernández Juncos wrote the lyrics used today. You can read the lyrics and hear the anthem at: **www.nationalanthems.info/pr.htm**

# Glossary

**abolition**      The act of doing away with something.

**bioluminescence**      Light that is emitted from living organisms.

**brackish**      A mixture of fresh and salt water.

**commonwealth**      A political region that is like a US state but pays no federal taxes and has only a representative in Congress who does not vote.

***cacique***      A native chief or local leader in a Spanish culture.

**coral reef**      A hard mass formed on the bottom of the sea by small sea organisms.

***coquí***      A small tree frog native to Puerto Rico.

***criollo***      A person born and usually raised in a Spanish-American country.

**eco-tourism**      The practice of visiting natural habitats without making an impact on the environment.

**endangered**      A species threatened by falling population with going out of existence.

**invasive species**      An organism (plant, animal, fungus, or bacterium) that is not native to an area and has negative effects on its economy, environment, or health.

**karst**      A rugged limestone landscape with pits, underground streams, and caverns.

**pharmaceutical**      Relating to the production and sale of drugs and medicines.

**phosphorescent**      Light coming from an object without combustion (fire) or heat. This light lasts longer than its source.

**santo**      A religious symbol, especially a wooden representation of a saint.

# More About Puerto Rico

## BOOKS

DaSilva-Gordon, Maria. *Puerto Rico: Past and Present*. New York: Rosen Publishing, 2011.

Foley, Erin. *Puerto Rico.* Festivals of the World. New York: Cavendish Square, 2011.

Stille, Darlene R. *Puerto Rico*. New York: Children's Press, 2015.

Trumbore, Cindy. *Parrots Over Puerto Rico*. New York: Lee & Low Books Inc., 2013.

## WEBSITES

**Puerto Rican Culture and History**

www.prboriken.com/culture.htm

**Welcome to Puerto Rico**

welcome.topuertorico.org

**Wildlife Refuges of Puerto Rico**

www.fws.gov/refuges/profiles/ByState.cfm?state=PR

**El Yunque National Forest**

www.elyunque.com/elyunque.htm

## ABOUT THE AUTHORS

**Ruth Bjorklund** lives on an island in Washington State. She has written more than forty books for young people and has especially enjoyed exploring the special islands of Puerto Rico.

**Richard Hantula** is a writer and editor who lives in New York City.

# Index

Page numbers in **boldface** are illustrations. Entries in **boldface** are glossary terms.

# Index